A DEATH OF PROMISE

A DEATH OF PROMISE

DAVID PENNY

RIVERTREE PRINT

The Thomas Berrington Prequels

A Death of Innocence

The Thomas Berrington Bundles

Purchase 3 full-length novels for less than the price of two.

Thomas Berrington Books 1-3

The Red Hill

Breaker of Bones

The Incubus

Thomas Berrington Books 4-6

The Incubus

The Inquisitor

The Fortunate Dead

Thomas Berrington Books 7-9

The Promise of Pain

The Message of Blood

A Tear for the Dead

Unit-13: WWII Paranormal Spy Thriller

An Imperfect Future

DECEMBER 1501

LUDLOW, ENGLAND

CHAPTER ONE

As Thomas Berrington ran across the outer bailey of Ludlow Castle, he realised how much he had forgotten of English winters. In particular its snow, ice and frost. For that is what this day had brought. Bad weather, as well as an appointment with bad-tempered gentlemen. Skidding on a patch of ice beyond the castle gatehouse, he was only saved from a fall by his son.

"Careful, Pa," said Will. "You might have knocked the brains from your head."

"If he had any," said Jorge Olmos, who followed behind, a thick coat wrapped around himself, an even thicker felt hat pulled down almost to his eyes. "If he had any brains he would not have become Justice of the Peace, and he would not have dragged us all to this land of ice."

Thomas recovered his balance and glanced back to check that Amal was still with them. She was, though the falling snow obscured his daughter's features as if he saw her through a lace screen. It was the thirteenth day of December in the Year of our Lord 1501 — if Thomas believed in the Lord. Not that his lack of faith made any difference to the date. Today was his first appearance at the Quarter Sessions, the first serious test of his authority, and he had already been warned to take care by better men than himself. Sir Richard Pole, for one, Chamberlain to Prince Arthur in Ludlow Castle. Gruffydd ap Rhys, Prince Arthur's Master of Horse, was another. Their advice had been contradictory, so of little use. One told him to follow the letter of the law and ignore his own feelings. The other to judge men, not matters. Which is why Thomas had asked Jorge to attend. He was a far better judge of men and women than he was.

Having both his son and daughter working alongside him also offered Thomas a sense of confidence, though on what basis he preferred not to shine too much light on, in case it was found wanting.

Will released his hold on Thomas's arm but kept a close watch on him in case he slipped again. Broad shouldered at eighteen, and a skilled fighter just like his grandfather, Will would provide the muscle if any were needed. Amal had already walked ahead towards the meeting house on the corner of Market Square and Mill Street. Short, lithe and beautiful. She might only be fourteen years of age, but Thomas relied on her a great deal. He knew today he would rely on her even more. To a casual observer, or even a not so casual one, Will and Amal would never be mistaken for brother and sister. Will was the son of a northern woman whose blonde hair and blue eyes he had inherited. Amal was the daughter of a Moorish wife Thomas had taken then lost in battle. Now, Thomas had returned to England from a Spain he no

2

longer recognised. Will and Amal were strangers in this strange land of the English Marches, but seemed to be making a better job of fitting in than their native father, who had been born not three leagues south of Ludlow.

Thomas fell into step beside Will, one hand out to grab him, in case he slipped again. The smooth leather soles of Thomas's boots offered little grip and his feet slid as much as trod the hard-packed snow.

The meeting house was already crowded by the time the trio arrived. At least half of those present turned to see who had entered, only to turn away seconds later. Few would recognise Thomas. By the end of the Sessions that state of affairs will have changed — whether for good or bad Thomas did not yet know. He was here to stand in judgement on a plenitude of cases, from trivial to significant, and knew he could not please everyone. He had been warned of such.

"These two might give you some trouble if they're both there," said Sir Richard Pole before Thomas had left Ludlow Castle, pointing to one entry on the list of submissions.

Thomas read it upside down. "Croft vs. Cornwell. Why?"

"The first is Sir Richard Croft. He has a manor house in a village of the same name. The other is Sir Thomas Cornwell, who has a larger manor house in Burford."

"The case seems a simple dispute over land."

"Those cases are always the worst, mark my words, and no dispute over land is simple, whether the plaintiff be lord or cottar. Croft and Cornwell are sworn enemies. One or other was no doubt involved in the trouble you had when Arthur was off marrying Catherine. Croft has Welsh connections but is the more sensible of the two. If pushed, I would say Cornwell might have been behind things. The man has an inability to turn aside from a fight, whether big or small. He once assaulted a man for what he claimed was a sideways look at his wife. Didn't let it lie there, either. He made sure the man was hounded from the area. So take care, Thomas. And know that by the time evening comes almost every man in the meeting house will hate you."

"Even those I might judge in favour of?"

"Even those, for they know the next time you may not do so."

"Am I to do nothing, then?"

"Do what best serves justice, but remember the status of some of those you deal with. It is not a thing you have shown much skill at in the past, but in these matters you will have to learn."

"Did Hugh Clement serve justice?" Thomas spoke of the previous occupant of his position, a man he had been involved in bringing down and, ultimately, his death.

"Clement served whoever would pay the most or offer a favour. It is no doubt one of the reasons Cornwell thinks so highly of himself." Sir Richard Pole clapped Thomas on the shoulder. "So take care today. Take that big son of yours. I reckon he should be enough to settle most people down."

Which is why Will, together with Jorge, were at his side as he entered the room. One to put fear into a man, the other to judge the truth of that man's words. Fires burned at opposite ends of the room and most of those

4

present had migrated towards one or the other. Late-comers would need heavier coats to stay warm.

As Thomas made his way to the long table at the head of the room heads turned again as they realised who he was. Thomas took the ornate chair set at the middle of the table and motioned for Amal to sit to his left. Jorge sat on his right, while Will stood close to the end of the table, so he could move fast if necessary.

Amal laid a leather-bound journal in front of herself and opened it to the last entry before pushing another towards her father. She arranged three sharpened pens and a small pot of black ink. She had prepared everything two days earlier, and the ink residue still marked the tips of her slim fingers. The oak gall she had used to make the ink had been sourced locally, for there was a surfeit to be gathered free in the woods. Iron vitriol would have had to be imported from Spain had Thomas not brought his own supply. Gum arabic he had also brought, but there was little left now and Amal would have to source more before too long.

Thomas watched those in the room, judging their positions and what purpose might have brought them here today. Some, he knew, had come for the free enter-tainment. Others likely had petitions to deal with. He had spent the night before sitting beside Amal in Ludlow Castle while they went through every one of the thirty items.

More men entered, some in fine clothing, others in rough-spun linen or felt. There were no chairs other than those at the table. No refreshment. No food.

When the bells of St Laurence's Church struck the

hour of ten, Thomas banged his hand on the table to draw everyone's attention. He stood, not knowing if he was meant to or not, but it felt right.

"My name is Sir Thomas Berrington, and I am the Justice of the Peace for Ludlow, Lemster, and all districts bordering them." He used his title despite believing himself unworthy. Thomas had a surfeit of titles and felt unease with every single one. "We have much work to get through this day, so I would ask you to state your cases as swiftly as you can, and I will attempt to rule just as swiftly."

"You are the foreigner," said someone Thomas could not see.

"I don't know where you heard that, but I was born in Lemster. Unless you consider that town foreign." He waited to see if there would be any argument, but none came.

Thomas re-took his seat and opened the thin journal in front of him. His eyesight was not as sharp as it had once been, and he squinted to make out the writing, grateful Amal had made it larger than her normally concise script.

Thomas read the words twice before calling two men forward. The matter, like many others that day, concerned a disputed patch of land. Thomas was confused why either would want it. The four acres adjoined the Teme south of Ludlow, the ground too poor and damp to grow much other than weeds. Perhaps the fishing was good. One man claimed tenancy, the other disputed it. One man had papers showing it had been left to him by his father, which he then set down on the table.

Thomas slid them across for Amal to read and make a note of. The other man also had papers which showed he paid rent to Sir Thomas Cornwell for tenancy.

Thomas passed those along as well before looking up.

"Do we have anyone present representing Sir Thomas Cornwell?" he asked.

A well-dressed man stepped forward. "I am Sir Thomas's steward, James Marshall, and I believe I can settle matters now if I may hand you some papers, Justice."

The spoken tone trod a fine line between disrespect and civility. Thomas was sure the man had walked that same line many times before. He waved a hand for him to approach. James Marshall was short but held himself like a tall man. He was well dressed, with a fine jacket slashed to reveal a crimson silk interior. His boots were of a kind in fashion half a century before, with long padded toes. Everything about him stank of privilege.

Thomas took the paper and scanned it. As he did so, exhaustion ran through him, because he knew this would be the manner of the day. Poor men's rights overridden by those of wealth. Cornwell's document could not be questioned. It was stamped with the seal of the Justice of the Peace of Bewdley district and evidenced that the land was in the ownership of Sir Thomas Cornwell. Thomas passed it to Amal so she could make a note of the details. As he did so he saw Marshall's eyes on his daughter. When Will shifted on his feet and placed a hand on the pommel of his sword Thomas knew his son had seen the look as well.

"Judgement against the plaintiff," Thomas said, waiting as Amal recorded his decision.

The morning proceeded in the same manner. Only twice did Thomas rule in favour of parties he considered deserved to win their case. The rest of the time politics and power ruled. When they did not, often enough it was because of idiocy. Many plaintiffs had agreed to contracts without having them read aloud, or chose to ignore what they said. One man lost his holding and would need to find another, but almost certainly not in this district.

When Thomas looked down at the next case his heart sank. Croft vs. Cornwell had arrived. He glanced up and saw Cornwell's steward had moved closer after spending most of the morning at the far end of the room conducting business.

"Do we have a representative for Sir Richard Croft?" Thomas asked, looking around the room. He expected another substitute, but a man he had not noticed earlier stepped closer.

"I am Croft. I am here to represent myself, unlike that coward Cornwell."

The man was of above medium height and less well dressed than Cornwell's representative, though he held himself with a surety that marked him as a man of station.

"I suspect this matter may take a little time," Thomas said. "Can I suggest we break for an hour and reconvene after we have eaten and quenched our thirsts?"

Croft agreed with a nod.

James Marshall did not. "Can this matter not be settled with a simple decision, Justice? The case is plain to see. Or have you not read the papers?"

"I have read the papers, and it is my opinion the matter may not be as simple as you state. We will break for an hour. Return when St Laurence's bell strikes one." Thomas stood and pushed his way through the crowd, which was making for one or other of the doors. It made progress slow. When a hand closed around Thomas's arm he turned, half-expecting James Marshall to be making another plea for swiftness. Instead, he found himself face to face with Sir Richard Croft.

"I can hear no argument here," Thomas said.

"I am not here to argue my case. I leave such machinations to the other party. I only wanted to welcome you to the district, Thomas Berrington. Rumour has it you will make a better Justice than the last tenant of the position. Not that such would be hard to do."

Thomas expected some additional words, perhaps a reference to the judgement he would make later. Instead, Croft turned away and pushed through the crowd.

Outside, the snow had stopped but the sky remained grey. The clouds that seemed to touch the spire of St Laurence's Church promised more bad weather before long. Thomas and the others entered their rooms, set hard against the outer walls of Ludlow Castle. The rooms had been assigned to him while his own house was being rebuilt. He suspected even after the work was complete he might spend much of his time in these accommodations. Amal had grown ever closer to Princess Catherine since both came to the town, and they had been close even before leaving Spain. Prince Arthur had also taken a liking to Will, fascinated to hear his tales of battles fought, some at an age even younger than the Prince himself. Everyone, of course, liked Jorge. Even Thomas sometimes, despite the man's ability to annoy him.

Thomas headed for the stone staircase leading to the rooms on the upper floor.

"Belia will have prepared food for us," said Jorge.

"I will join you soon. I want to wash before I eat."

"Don't take long then, or it will all be gone." Jorge accompanied Will to the large room they used as a common space.

Amal accompanied him, concern on her face. "Are you all right, Pa?"

"I'm fine, my sweet. I need to wash the stink of making judgements from my hands, that is all." He touched his daughter's dark hair. "Go see Belia and the others. I will only be a moment."

When she left, Thomas continued to the upper level. He wanted to wash, but he also needed a moment of solitude to gather his thoughts. The case he needed to rule on when he returned was not trivial. It involved two men, both powerful in the district. Both had been sheriff in the past and no doubt would be re-appointed in the future. Both were close to Prince Arthur and King Henry. Thomas was unsure whether either would accept the judgement of a man they no doubt looked down on.

Thomas was half way to the table, where a bowl of water sat, when he stopped dead at the sight of an object resting on it.

It was a severed hand. Not one recently removed from its owner; these bones had lain in the ground for some time. A year at least, if not more. All flesh had dropped from them to leave only yellowed bones, which were arrayed so the index finger extended to point at whoever entered the door.

CHAPTER TWO

Everyone was in the main room when Thomas entered. Jorge stood beside Belia, his hand on her shoulder. He held a warm roll in the other and had a look of contentment on his face.

"Who entered our rooms today?" The sharpness in Thomas's voice caused Belia to turn and frown.

"Catherine came to see if Amal wanted to walk beside the river, then the Prince wanted to talk to Will. Both had forgotten you would be at the Quarter Session. And the man who lights the fires, of course, and the cook who came to ask me about spices. Nobody else. Why?"

"Somebody left an object in my room."

"What manner of object? A gift?"

Thomas offered a tight smile. "Perhaps, but if so it is a strange gift. A full set of hand bones are laid on the table where I wash."

Amal rose to her feet and left the room.

"A hand or just the bones?" asked Jorge.

"Only the bones."

"Which hand?"

Thomas shook his head. "Does it matter?"

"It might." Jorge stared at him, and as he did so, Thomas knew he was correct. It might indeed matter.

"I don't know. I was too shocked to notice. I came here to find out who left them."

"It would not be Catherine or Arthur," said Belia. "And I doubt it was the cook. She only came in here, and stayed a half hour to discuss recipes. It seems Catherine is attempting to broaden her husband's tastes. That leaves the lad who laid the fires."

"Did you see him today? Talk to him?"

"Both, but not here. I was in the castle kitchen preparing our meal. He wanted to know which rooms needed to be seen to. I told him all four, and that I needed wood for the fire here. He seemed displeased but grunted he would see what he could do."

"Do you know him?"

"Not his name, but his face, yes. Though I believe he is new." She gave a smile. "I have the impression he believes tending fires is beneath him."

"Pa?" Amal entered the room with something concealed beneath her robe.

"I will send the children upstairs." Belia herded the three youngsters to the door and told them they could play a game in the rooms above. They each took their food with them.

Only when five of them remained did Amal remove the bones from beneath her robe and lay them on the table. Once she had arranged them, her fingers dextrous, her knowledge of anatomy as good as Thomas's, did it become clear the bones belonged to the right hand of someone. The same hand Philippa Gale had lost when she attempted to fire a flintlock pistol at Thomas's daughter. To believe the bones a coincidence was too much of a stretch for any of them.

"Why?" asked Jorge. "If it is her, what manner of message is she trying to send?"

Will leaned over the bones and moved a few around. When he stepped away Amal put them back in place.

"These are from a man's hand," she said. "A woman's would be smaller and slimmer."

"Philippa was tall for a woman," Thomas said.

"But slim. Her fingers were long and very fine. These are the bones of a labourer or farmer. Look, here." Amal touched the index finger. "This was broken and healed, but the injury is clear." She looked up at her father. "How long would it take a body to break down?"

"It depends whether they were buried and what manner of soil they lay in."

"The body must have been buried deep or animals would have scattered the bones," said Will.

"The burial could be more recent. If someone placed a hand in a vat of hot water long enough the flesh could simply be picked off."

"Can you tell from looking at the bones, Pa?" asked Amal.

"Possibly. It would take time, which is something I have little of. People are waiting for us." Thomas glanced at the bones. "Put them back in my room. We can examine them this evening. I need to find out who this person is who tends the fires." Thomas ran a hand through his too-long hair that had streaks of grey these days. "I could do without the Session this afternoon. I suspect this next matter will be hard." He looked at Jorge. "I want you to judge both men and offer me your counsel."

"Of course, but I can already tell you that Sir Richard Croft is a man I would trust. The other, Cornwell's steward, is only doing his job. It is his master you need me to judge, not the servant."

"Cornwell is not here. Do the best you can."

"And the bones?" asked Jorge.

"I can't do anything about them now."

"Do you think it's her?"

"Of course it's her. I hoped she might have learned her lesson after what happened, but it appears she continues to hold a hatred of me."

Thomas turned away and pulled on his coat. Outside, snow was falling again, muffling sound. It had already obscured the footprints they had made on their way to the castle.

Yes, Thomas thought, *it has to be Philippa Gale.* Pip, as he had called her when they lay naked together. Pip who betrayed him and almost betrayed the entire country. Pip who pretended love where none existed. Pip who had tried to kill Thomas and his daughter.

He had captured her but she escaped. She could easily bend men to her will, just as she had bent Thomas.

He lifted his head and looked ahead. A few men stood outside the merchant house, but the others had likely gone inside. Snow swirled around the chimneys at either end of the roof. Dark smoke showed where someone had recently fed the fires. Just as someone had fed the fires in Thomas's room.

When he entered the building, Sir Richard Croft and James Marshall stood near the front. Amal, Jorge and Will took their places, and the proceedings continued. As Thomas sat, he was still trying to decide on what judgement to make, his mind filled with confusion, and awareness that his decisions had consequences.

"What am I meant to do?" Thomas asked. "Rule in favour of a bully?"

Gruffydd ap Rhys shook his head. "I thought Richard spoke to you about him this morning. Did he not remind you how important Sir Thomas Cornwell is?"

"He told me Sir Richard Croft is also an important man. Both have been sheriff of either Shropshire or Herefordshire. Apart from which, Cornwell clearly encroached on Croft's land. What annoyed me most was his fencing off of common land, preventing cotters from grazing the few animals they possess. Allow him to get away with it and he'll be asking payment for pannage in the woods next."

"He already tried that before when Hugh Clement was Justice. Clement allowed it and Sir Richard had to intervene, using the authority of the Prince to put a stop to it. Cornwell is relentless in pursuit of his own ends, but King Henry seems to find him useful, so he thinks he can get away with whatever he likes." Gruffydd scratched at his head, pinched something out and looked at it before snapping it between his nails. "You know you will pay for what you did today. Cornwell does not forget nor forgive."

Thomas had come in search of Lady Margaret Pole but found Gruffydd instead. Perhaps it was best he had, and not Lady Margaret's husband, Sir Richard. He would have taken an even harsher view of Thomas's ruling. Although perhaps not if he'd already had words with Cornwell.

"At least it's done now for a three month," said Gruffydd. "Keep your head down. Try not to annoy more men of influence, and you might make a good Justice after all."

After all? Thomas thought. "Am I not meant to be a good Justice now?"

"You have not been raised to the post, Tom. When you were Duke of Granada you must have had the same manner of decisions to deal with."

"I did the same as today — ruled in the name of justice."

"Did that go down well in Spain?"

"Not always."

Gruffydd smiled. "Damn, but I like you. I worry about you as well. Perhaps making you Justice of the Peace was not such a clever move ... or maybe it was the cleverest move the King has ever made. An honest Justice. It will be interesting to see how that goes." Gruffydd clapped Thomas on the shoulder and he tried not to flinch. "Now, how is the building work coming at this house of yours? When do you move in?"

"Do you want me out of the castle, Gruff?"

"Not at all. I rather like your presence, not to mention that son and daughter of yours. As for the Spaniard, he amuses everyone and enchants the ladies. Even Lady Margaret has taken a shine to him and she never takes to strangers. His wife is very fine, is she not? And his children are all sweet."

"When in the company of important men. Less so with their own family."

"As it should be."

"The year will turn before all the building work is complete," Thomas said. "I extended the plans so we all have a place of our own. A workshop for Belia and another for me. The old house forming one side is now habitable."

"I hear Princess Catherine went to Belia for some kind of female problem. I hoped she might be with child by now and have no need of such remedies. Belia is gaining a reputation as a healer, just like you, but don't tell John Argentine I said that. He still considers you an interloper."

"Amal attends to Catherine these days, as I am sure you know. She insists on it. If it was seemly I would attend her myself, but know how such would be viewed."

"You're not usually much of one for protocol."

"I would say the same about you, Gruff." Thomas received a punch to the arm in confirmation.

"Aye, perhaps you speak true. I hear you had some little trouble today. Nothing serious, I hope?"

"It is why I am in search of Lady Margaret. Someone left an entire set of hand bones in my room."

Gruffydd stared at Thomas. "That I did not hear. A hand, you say?"

Thomas nodded.

"Is it something to do with that woman?"

"If you mean Philippa Gale, then yes, I believe it may be, but what manner of connection she has to it I don't yet know. But I intend to find out. Hence my search for Lady Margaret."

"I don't expect she will know either, Tom."

"Someone left those bones in my room. The only person who has access without raising suspicion is a new member of the castle staff. He came to make up the fires. Lady Margaret is in charge of the household. I hoped she might tell me who he is and where to find him."

"She will be in the chapel. Princess Catherine likes to pray before eating and Maggie usually accompanies her. They have become firm friends. Catherine's English is improving day by day. I think she owes much of that to your children."

"Catherine is a bright girl and a fast learner."

"I'd be happier if she was a little less clever and a little more fruitful. What this country needs is a clear line of succession. The sooner Catherine has a son in her belly the better we will all sleep at night."

"I hear they are doing all the right things for such to happen. They are both young, so a son will come soon enough."

"I hope you're right."

Thomas perched on a stone bench set at the north end of the Great Hall, where three wide arches offered a view into the large room, sixty feet long by thirty across. The table at the far end was set in expectation of the arrival of

Prince Arthur and his new wife. A fire burned beyond it but none of the warmth reached Thomas. He wrapped his cloak more tightly around himself and wished he had brought his tagelmust, but it would have been inappropriate for the Sessions.

Servants came and went, bringing wine, ale and warm bread, but Thomas's mind was not on them. He was thinking of the bones, and a woman.

Recollection of her brought the image of another. One he had loved as a youth before leaving England. It surprised him when he returned to discover Bel Brickenden had not forgotten him. Oh, she had moved on, married, had children. But that long-ago spark ... might it still remain? He could not tell, but believed he wanted it to. He had grown closer to Bel since his return. A question he did not yet have an answer to was did she want them to grow closer still? Perhaps...

The other was more problematic. Almost certainly she was behind the leaving of the hand bones. He had shared her bed, but never loved her. And she had not loved him. Her heart had belonged to Peter Gifforde. Which of them was the more evil Thomas could not tell. Only that Peter was now dead, and Philippa Gale blamed him for his death, even though he did not strike the fatal blow. Her hatred simmered until she tried to kill Thomas's daughter, Amal. An attack that had resulted in the loss of Philippa's own right hand. Hence, he believed, the bones. They were a message, but not one he altogether understood. Only that she wanted him to receive it.

The thought of her scared him, because he had caused the death not just of her lover but also her father.

Now, she had returned for vengeance.

Footsteps on the wooden floor made Thomas turn. He was surprised to see Prince Arthur approach, who in turn seemed surprised to see Thomas crouching on the cold stone perch.

"What are you doing here, Thomas? Waiting for scraps from my kitchen?"

The Prince's manner had softened since his marriage and Thomas believed much of that was Catherine's doing. That the two were deeply in love was clear from every glance and touch they offered each other. Love was not expected in a royal marriage butThomas was relieved to see it in theirs. Catherine of Aragon had grown from a babe-in-arms to a confident young woman in his presence, and there were times he felt almost as much a father to her as King Fernando.

"I need a quick word with Lady Margaret. Gruffydd tells me she and Catherine are praying in the chapel."

"She is a more devout Christian than me. Is the faith stronger in Spain than England, Thomas?"

"I think not, Your Grace, but they have spent centuries expelling those they consider unchristian from their lands. I believe it has hardened their faith into something more akin to steel than gold."

"Then it pleases me that our countries are now joined." Arthur looked at one of the stone seats but decided against sitting, which made Thomas rise to show respect.

"If they do not appear soon I will leave you to enjoy your meal in peace, Your Grace. I am sure my own is going cold as we speak."

"Eat with us. Catherine will be pleased, and I will ask

Lady Margaret to send for your children. Catherine tells me they are as close to her as her own brother and sisters."

"They have known her most of their lives. Catherine is the youngest of Queen Isabel's offspring and spent more time with my children than her own siblings. Some of her sisters went to their own marriages, as did her brother, Prince Juan, who is deceased these three years."

"That makes a boy more important to both England and Spain, does it not? Are all the sisters married?"

"They are, Your Grace. Those that still live."

"Pity. It would be good if Harry also married a Spanish princess. It would tie the knot between our countries all the tighter. He might even become King of Spain one day."

"I am not sure Spain is ready for your younger brother just yet, Your Grace."

Arthur offered a laugh. "No, perhaps you are right. Ah, here come my wife and Lady Margaret. You must eat with us."

Thomas wanted to find out more about the man who set his fires from Lady Margaret, but knew he could not refuse the Prince.

"I will send for Amal and Will both if your invitation still stands, Your Grace."

"Of course it does."

Catherine slowed and kissed Thomas on both cheeks, for which he had to bend his knees. From habit, he ran his gaze across her until satisfied she was healthy.

Thomas remained beside Lady Margaret Pole as the

newly married couple made their way to the table, where cooks were laying out pots and plates of food.

"I need to ask you something, Lady Margaret, if I may?"

"Will it take long? I have matters to attend to, as well you know. A castle does not run itself."

"This will take no time. What is the name of the lad who lays fires in our rooms?"

"John Miller, newly appointed these two months." Her sharp eyes searched Thomas's face. "Has he done something I should know about?"

"That I have yet to work out. When I do you will be the first to know."

"He is a good worker, but has ideas above his station which are not welcome in a servant."

Thomas wondered if the same might also refer to him.

When Lady Margaret turned away, he asked her, "Could a message be sent to my children? Prince Arthur wishes their attendance here."

Lady Margaret stopped abruptly and turned back. Once more, Thomas was sure she was thinking of those with ideas above their station in life.

"I will have someone sent to ask. Now I must go."

Thomas waited until the sound of her footsteps faded, then turned and walked across the echoing room to join Catherine and Arthur, where additional places and chairs were already being set.

CHAPTER THREE

When Thomas returned to their rooms, he found Jorge and Belia sitting in the room they all used as a place to gather and eat. There was no kitchen in the guest accommodation, set against the wall of the outer bailey, so Belia went to the castle kitchen to cook their food. She told Thomas the staff made her feel unwelcome at first but had since offered a grudging acceptance. Now, a few of the girls even asked her how to use spices to prepare meals for Catherine — though Prince Arthur was less keen on them.

Thomas pulled a wooden chair close to the fire, sat and stretched his legs out.

"Are Will and Amal still with the Prince and Princess?" asked Jorge.

"They are, and may be for a while yet, though Arthur looked ready for his bed when I left. It is one reason why I did so. That and my wish to talk with Lady Margaret again, but she had already gone to hers, so I will have to wait until morning. Which might be for the best, because I also need to sleep."

"None of us are as young as we were," said Jorge. "Though I find I need less sleep these days."

"But you are unlike most men."

Jorge smiled. "For which I am grateful every single day."

"As am I." Belia's face showed no expression, but Thomas believed she might have been making a small joke. Thomas loved both these people as much as he did his own family. Then he corrected the thought. Jorge and Belia were his family too.

Thomas thought of rising and going to his bed, but the room was warm and the fire freshly fed. It made little difference if he fell asleep here or in the chill of his quarters. The thought of his room reminded him of what he had found there earlier in the day, and his sense of contentment faded. He rose, kissed Belia on the cheek, touched Jorge's shoulder and made for the door.

"I assume you want to ask Lady Margaret Pole about the man who makes up your fire," said Belia. "Which he has not done this evening, so your room will be like ice."

Thomas stopped and turned back. "She gave me a name, but I need to talk to others to find out what he is like. And then to the man himself."

"John Miller," said Jorge. "I asked in the kitchen when I helped Belia fetch the food. Though I hear of late he has been telling everyone to call him John Chambers. Everyone laughs at him behind his back, believing he is trying to elevate himself."

"Which is what Lady Margaret also told me. Did you find anything else out?"

"He's a good-looking lad of nineteen years and keen on the ladies. He doesn't make a nuisance of himself, but can be overattentive. His family has a mill close to Ludford bridge, one of near a dozen mills in the town, but with an excellent reputation. I believe your sister buys her flour there, so I went to see Agnes to ask her about them. She told me they are hard-working, honest, and well-liked."

"Did this judgement include John Miller?"

"She knew him but said, like everyone else, he sought better things for himself. The way she told it, he has been employed by several families of note locally but never stayed with any long. Perhaps now he is employed by the man who will be the next King of England he will be content."

"People like that are never content," Thomas said. "Their ambition burns bright and makes them want more, even when they have all they might need."

"Says a man who never turns away from any problem or threat. Though I have to admit, I would never accuse you of ambition."

"I thank you. Does this John Miller have rooms within the castle?"

"He's not elevated that high yet, so no. He lives in Ludlow somewhere, though nobody I spoke to knew exactly where. Do you have duties tomorrow, Thomas?"

"Not yet, but who knows? Amal will make a record of today's proceedings and write to each who brought cases, confirming to them my decisions, but I trust her to do that without supervision."

"Which she would not welcome in any case. You are fortunate in your children."

"As are you."

"You are right. As am I. But yours are…" Jorge had to search for the words. "My children are beautiful, kind, sweet, and happy. But their contentment means they lack ambition."

"As do you. It's no bad thing to live a contented life. I often think I would have preferred such for myself. I found it once, only for it to be snatched away."

"You have a restless soul." Belia had watched the conversation without comment until that point. "Which is no bad thing. There are times the world needs restless men. Men who will not back down from trouble. Men who exact retribution on those who deserve it. Will is the same. Amal is like you as well but in a different way. One is the brawn, the other the brain." She smiled. "My children have a little of you in them, of course, but we raised them differently so they are more like us."

"I'm glad you raised them to be happier, for I would not wish my life on them, nor anyone else."

"And yet here you are, still alive, though I often wonder how that can be the case. You are Duke of Granada and work alongside the Prince of Wales and Princess Catherine of Aragon. Tomorrow, you and Jorge will find this John Miller and discover why he left those bones. Though I expect we all know the answer."

"Do we? I know what the obvious answer is, but I

expect Philippa Gale is dead, or far from Ludlow by now. There is nothing to bring her back here."

"Except for you, Thomas." Belia rose and came to him. She embraced him, then went to Jorge and did the same, except this time the embrace was returned. "She blames you for all the ills that changed her life. If she is behind the leaving of those bones then you will seek her out and punish her. It is what you do."

"I don't want to punish her."

"Perhaps that is what she wants you to do." Belia turned back to Jorge. "Now come, husband. Our bed awaits and the children are sound asleep." Belia touched Thomas's arm as she passed and Jorge grinned at him, though he did not allow Belia to see how pleased he was.

Thomas thought of his cold room and returned to the chair by the fire. He would doze until Will and Amal returned, then ask what they had learned. But when he woke a weak sunlight illuminated the room and he found himself in his own bed with no recollection of how he got there.

When he went downstairs, he found Amal and Belia sitting at the table eating bread, cheese and some remnant of last night's meal.

"Where's Jorge? We are meant to be finding this John Miller."

"He is still in bed," said Belia. "Go kick him out. I tried, but it never works when I do it. I suspect you can kick harder than me."

"Not this morning. I fell asleep in the chair and woke in my bed with no idea how I got there."

"Will carried you up," said Amal. "You looked so

27

uncomfortable when we came in. I tried to wake you but you were like a dead man, so Will put you to bed before going to his own."

"Where is he now?"

"Arthur sent for him."

"Are they truly friends?" Thomas asked.

"I believe so. Arthur is in awe of Will's strength and skill, and we both know how Catherine feels about him, though she is a married woman now and deeply in love with her husband."

"Did you see them offering each other morsels of food at the table last night?"

"I tried not to look, Pa. I am too young for such sights"

Thomas laughed. "You are only three years younger than Catherine, and two younger than Arthur."

"But those two years make a difference at my age, don't they?"

"You are asking the wrong man."

"No, I don't think I am. One day you will have to accept I am growing up. One day you will have to accept I will leave your household and set up my own."

"Then let it be many years in the future."

Amal shook her head, her long, dark hair half covering her face. "I will always be your daughter, Pa. I will always love you. But I will also find someone else to love." She smiled. "I hope so, anyway."

"You will, my sweet."

"It might have to be someone special for you to accept them."

"I will try for your sake. I am sure you will never choose someone I don't approve of."

Amal smiled again and popped a slice of duck into her mouth.

"So, are we going to find this man or not?" asked Jorge as he entered the room, already fully dressed and with his boots on. "What is the weather like outside? Snowing again or not?"

"It was snowing when we came back last night but has stopped now," said Amal. "It is cold though."

Which sparked a thought in Thomas. "Did you take my tagelmust to wash?"

Amal laughed. "As if I would dare. Why?"

"I was going to wrap it around myself today but couldn't find it."

"It probably fell behind something. I will look for it while you are out."

"Come on then, Thomas," said Jorge. "Don't stand there talking when we have business in hand."

Thomas shook his head. He kissed Amal and Belia, then followed Jorge into the outer bailey. Fresh snow stretched to the drawbridge which offered entrance to the inner bailey of Ludlow Castle. A line of footsteps led from the gatehouse, showing where servants from the town had entered.

Outside the walls, despite the cold Market Square was busy with traders and those purchasing their wares. Thomas glanced towards his sister's bakery and waved to her daughters, who were standing at the small hatch. They waved back.

"Agnes has dutiful daughters," said Jorge.

"She does. Do you know where this John Miller lives?"

"I don't, but I know where his family is, so we should start there. It is this way."

Thomas followed Jorge into Mill Street. As they descended the icy slope down to Mill Gate, they had to hold on to each other to stop from sliding wildly towards the river. There were two mills operating along the riverbank at the foot of the road, but one was clearly better maintained than the other, so Thomas made his way there first. A great waterwheel creaked and groaned as it was turned by the river. It reminded him of the waterwheels in the mighty Guadalquivir in Sevilla, which Queen Isabel ordered silenced at night so she could sleep undisturbed. These wheels were all distant enough from the castle to allow them to operate day and night if they wished.

Two strapping youths were loading sacks of flour onto a small handcart. Thomas asked if they were brothers to John Miller.

"Aye, we are," said one. "But he doesn't live here anymore. Who is asking?" The youth looked Thomas up and down but seemed to find nothing threatening. When he glanced at Jorge he offered a nod, as if to an acquaintance. Thomas was used to the reaction and knew it meant nothing more than Jorge being Jorge. Even on first acquaintance people always treated him like an old friend.

"I am Thomas Berrington, Justice of the Peace." Thomas thought it worth adding his position but, by the look on their faces, it seemed he might have made a mistake.

"What has our John gone and done now? A girl again, is it?"

"I know nothing of your brother and girls. I merely

30

want to question him about some work he did at the castle."

"I heard he works at the castle now, but he still doesn't visit his family, even if he walks past our door most days. Thinks he's too good for us now. But I tell you, he and half the town eat bread made with our flour."

"Good flour it is too," Thomas said. "My sister uses it in her bakery."

"Who is your sister?"

"Agnes Baxter."

"Aye, she does, and works wonders with it. Are you her brother that went away?"

Thomas wondered if the whole of Ludlow knew about him. He suspected they might. Most of them seemed to visit Agnes's bakery, and people were always eager for any gossip about a new face.

"I am. If John doesn't live here, do you know where he lodges?"

"More than lodges, sir." The youth shook his head. "Though he must spend all he earns to live in a cottage all to himself." He offered a wink. "I expect it makes for easier assignations."

"Your brother likes girls then, does he?" asked Jorge.

"Much as I suspect you do."

"Only the one these days, for I am growing excessively old."

"You don't look old, if I may say so," said the youth. He glanced at Thomas, who he was clearly comparing Jorge to.

"I have led a blessed life. Can you show me where this cottage is?"

"I could, but I have these sacks to deliver, and then more work to do."

Thomas rummaged in a pocket and pulled out a coin without bothering to check its value. Only as he held it out did he realise it was far more than he intended to offer. The youth must have seen his mistake and took the coin before he could change his mind.

"His cottage lies in a row of a dozen behind St Giles Church on the Ludford road. You'll need to follow the track to the bridge so you can cross the river. If you see John, tell him to come to see us now and again."

"If I see him I will. My thanks."

"My thanks to you, sir. Good day to you both."

Once they were out of earshot Jorge said, "How much did you give him? I saw your face and I saw his. He was trying hard not to grin in case you took the coin back."

"More than I meant, I admit, but it is of no matter. Enough for him to rent a house for himself for a month if he wants."

Jorge shook his head. "You should take more care of your wealth. Half of it is mine, remember."

"And that half will last you ten lifetimes, so take no heed of my occasional extravagance."

"I wonder what it would be like to live ten lifetimes?" said Jorge. "Imagine how the world might change over that time. How many beautiful women I could seduce."

"I assume Belia would like to live ten lifetimes as well, which might clip your wings."

"Belia understands me."

Thomas smiled as they climbed an icy slope to the wooden bridge leading to Ludford. For all of Jorge's talk,

Thomas had never known him to be unfaithful to Belia. When he was a eunuch in the palace of Alhambra in Granada it had been a different matter. Jorge had taken full advantage of his position, fortunate it had been Thomas himself who had unmanned him by taking only those two nuggets that might set seed inside a woman — a danger no Sultan could countenance. Thomas thought back to the day he had cut him; Jorge had been a boy of barely thirteen years when captured by the Moors. Thomas's suggestion he would make a fine eunuch, remarking "look at how pretty he is", had saved Jorge's life. It had amused the Sultan to have the task done.

Now, thirty-five years had passed and somehow they remained friends. More than friends. Thomas thought the fact only showed how strange the world truly was.

He was drawn back to the present when Jorge nudged him.

"Do you think it is one of those?"

Thomas looked up at a row of cottages, their walls made of dark beams and plaster. The tiny windows would allow little light inside. There were twelve doors, the two end cottages slightly larger than those between. Smoke spiralled from five of the chimneys. The narrow track they followed ended at a stand of sad-looking trees, their branches denuded of leaves. To the right lay a small church with a square tower, its roof coated in a thick layer of snow that hinted at no heating inside. Beyond the church, the roadway led south towards Ludford.

They had found where John Miller lived. Thomas knew he was close to finding out why the bones had been left in his room, and perhaps their meaning.

CHAPTER FOUR

"I hope he's at home," said Jorge. "I take it you checked whether he turned up for work at the castle this morning?"

Thomas stared at him. "I assumed you had."

"You saw me come straight from my bed." Jorge smiled. "At least your daughter still has her wits about her. She went to ask and told me he has not been seen since yesterday, when he left around seven last night."

Thomas cursed. "If I had made time to look for him when the Session ended, I would have caught him."

"If it is catching he needs. Perhaps he is sick and one of those smoking chimneys is his."

Thomas looked along the row of twelve cottages. Each was small, one room on the ground floor and another above. A privy would stand at the back and possibly a small garden. Or there might be one privy for the entire row and no gardens. Even with those limitations, the properties were beyond the means of a fire maker, even if he did work in Ludlow Castle.

"In that case, we had better knock on doors," Thomas said. "His will not be the first of these houses."

"Why not?"

"Those at both ends are larger and have only one neighbour. Therefore, their rent will be higher. Whatever John Miller earns making fires, I am surprised he can afford even the smaller one."

Jorge strode to the nearest door and rapped on it hard.

Nothing happened.

Thomas glanced up at the roof and saw no smoke rising from the chimney shared with the next cottage. He passed Jorge to knock on the third door, which opened almost at once to reveal a woman wearing a voluminous coat and hood, a rush basket crooked under her arm.

"What do you want?" Her voice was sharp. "I'm going to Ludlow to get something for my supper. If it's money you want come back when my husband returns. He deals with all that."

"It is not money, goodwife. I am looking for John Miller. I understand he rents one of these cottages."

"John Chambers he calls himself these days, in the hope the title will make people believe he serves the Prince himself. I have known him since he was a lad, always with ideas above his station, that boy. What do you want with him?" She narrowed her eyes. "You are not somebody's husband, are you?"

"Not anymore, no."

"Well then, that is good, I suppose. Grand ideas and an eye for a pretty lady, John has, and not so concerned if they be married or not. He made a try for me but I put him right."

Looking at the woman, who had to be over forty, each of those years showing hard, Thomas wondered if John Miller's eyesight might be in question.

"Can you tell me which cottage is his?"

"The seventh. Seventh son, seventh door." She cackled at her own wit, then closed the door behind her and pushed past Thomas. He watched her stride away towards Ludford Bridge.

"Can you remember all of that?" asked Jorge.

"I will try, despite my obvious great age and waning abilities. Come on."

Thomas rapped on the seventh cottage door, glancing at Jorge when the sound came oddly. When he pushed at the door it caught on a stone tile and opened.

"John?" Thomas called out. "John Miller?"

"Perhaps he only responds if you call him by his new name," said Jorge.

"What would you do if a stranger entered your house and called out any name?"

"I would find you and ask you to defend me, of course."

As Thomas took a few paces inside he found his earlier judgement correct. The ground floor consisted of a single room with a narrow window beside the main door, a second window next to a door at the rear. A table took up a good portion of the floor, two chairs drawn up under it. A stone sink stood beneath the window at the far end. A narrow staircase led up from beyond the fireplace.

"John!" Thomas called out again, but the house sounded, and looked, empty. Not abandoned, but there was nobody home. Small touches and objects showed someone lived here. A pewter goblet on the table. A knife lying as if it had been tossed down.

"You should check upstairs," said Jorge, "in case he is lying in bed with his throat cut. Such things happen when you come looking for people."

"Only five or six times in the past, but I will go. I would not wish for you to suffer any shock."

Thomas climbed the staircase, which moved precariously beneath his weight. There was no door at the top and he entered a room matching that below. This one held a large bed, a rack where clothes hung, and a narrow table set with a copper bowl and jug. A small, square table beside the bed held a candle and the means of lighting it. A second fireplace was set four feet from the end of the bed. Kindling and fresh logs lay in the grate, with more in a basket to one side. The domesticity of the room came as a surprise.

"Is there a dead body up there?" called Jorge.

"There is not. Are you coming up?"

"Do I need to?"

Thomas looked around. "No, I don't suppose you do. Find out if anyone else is at home in the other cottages. Ask if they saw John Miller today or yesterday."

"Are you sure you can manage without me?"

"I will attempt to do my best."

"That's what I'm worried about. I will do as you ask so as not to make you sulk."

"Sulk?" Thomas said to himself as he surveyed the room.

He went to the bed and drew back the covers with care, so as not to disturb any trace beneath them. An indentation on the thin pillow to one side showed where a head had rested. A second pillow, equally thin, might have shown a second depression, but if so it was less clear. Thomas leaned over and studied the rough flannel sheet covering a horsehair mattress. It was not particularly clean. Thomas lit the candle and held it so the light fell across the bed. He nodded. Yes, two people had lain there. Not last night, possibly not the night before, but within the week. Stains gave evidence of what they had been up to, and Thomas grimaced at having to bear witness to it.

He pulled the covers up and smoothed them down as best he could, not sure if he cared whether John Miller knew someone had been here or not. The man was not important, only what he knew. Thomas needed to know who had told him to leave the bones, even though he suspected it would come as no surprise. He wanted to find out the when, where and why. The most important of which was the why.

Thomas descended the stairs and conducted a cursory examination of the ground floor. He went out through the back door to find a small patch of garden where a few turnips and cabbages poked up through a covering of snow. There was no privy, but beyond the garden a well-trodden path ran along the entire row. Two wooden huts sat, one at each end. It made Thomas realise how fortunate he had been in his life. His latter life, at least. Until the age of thirteen he had lived in poverty, even though his father had been an important man in the district. Important enough to cross the sea to Castillon in France in the company of John Talbot, Earl of Shrewsbury, where both lost their lives on a muddy, blood-soaked battlefield.

Thomas had been cut adrift, left to wander without purpose until he found one.

He went through the house and out to find Jorge talking with a short woman of indeterminate age, dressed all in black. She glanced at Thomas as he approached, her gaze only reluctantly leaving Jorge, who had conjured his usual charm.

"It is all right, my sweet," said Jorge. "He is not as dangerous as he looks. This is Thomas Berrington, Justice of the Peace for the district."

Her expression brightened, and Thomas feared she wanted to raise some matter.

"Has she seen anything?"

"Ask her, not me."

Thomas shook his head. Sometimes Jorge could be frustrating.

"I am looking for John Miller," Thomas said to the woman. "Have you seen him today?"

"Not today, no. What has he done? Something serious, I hope." It was clear she would welcome some snippet of gossip to pass around town the next time she crossed Ludford Bridge.

"Not as far as I know. I merely have one or two questions for him about what he did yesterday."

"Forget to make up your fire, did he? Wouldn't surprise me. He told me the work is beneath him, but at least it is for the Prince of Wales now. Thinks he is going up in the world."

"Perhaps he is. So, have you seen him today?"

The woman shook her head — a sharp movement. "Did not see him today, did not see him since Sunday when he came to church." She inclined her head to the stone building beyond the narrow track. Graves dotted the surrounding ground, but there was no outer wall or fence. It was just one more small church, like a hundred others dotting the locality.

"He kept to himself?" Thomas asked.

"Oh, I wouldn't say that. John likes the ladies, see, and the ladies seem to like John. Few weeks pass when I can't hear them at it through the wall." Her expression did not show whether she approved of such behaviour.

"And recently?"

"Three nights since, on Friday. I remember because I had trout which my son caught from the Teme for my supper. They were at it half the night, so I expect they ate something more substantial."

"But you did not see John Miller?"

"No. Only the woman. Better than his usual conquests. She was dressed like a lady. Very tall. Beautiful. Though she had an odd way of holding her arm down by her side so you could not see it clearly."

"Which arm?"

The woman put one arm down, then the other, before lifting her right hand. "This one."

"You are sure?"

"I am, because she waved to me with the other and smiled. John was a lucky man that night."

"Yes, he was."

"Do you know this lady?" she asked.

"I believe I might. How long did the woman stay with John?"

"Only the one night. They made enough noise to wake

40

the dead in the churchyard, so I remember it well. I saw her leave Saturday at noon. Only saw her back, but it could be no one else. She was as tall as a man."

"Did you see John that day?"

"I told you, I saw him at church on Sunday, same as always, but not..." Her voice trailed off. She glanced at Jorge, perhaps seeking some comfort in him. He smiled at her and reached for her hand.

A flush came to her cheeks as she returned the smile.

Thomas waited, trusting Jorge.

"When did you see him again, my sweet? You can tell me."

"I forget," she said.

"We all forget things. Even Thomas here, though he will never admit to it."

The woman was captured by Jorge and her gaze did not stray.

"It was last night. Late last night. I was already in bed but woke. I needed to ... well, I had forgotten something outside and went to fetch it. When I returned, I glanced through my window at the front and saw a man walk across the road towards the church. There was a little piece of moon, and the snow seemed to make everything lighter, like it does. He stopped when he reached the buttress and glanced back, as if checking for anyone watching, but he did not see me because I had snuffed my candle by then. I saw then it was John."

"Do you know what time this was?" Thomas asked.

"I would not have, had the sound of St Laurence's bell not rung off midnight. You can hear it from here on a still night, and last night was still. Snow can do that, can't it?"

"Yes, it can. Did you see anyone else?"

A shake of her head. "No, only John. He must have been going to the church, because if he was going into town he would take the track to the bridge. And if his destination was Ludford he would have followed our track and taken the footpath through the woods."

"Even late at night?"

"I admit it would not be easy, but he did not go that way, did he? He went to the church."

"My thanks, goodwife." Thomas turned away and crossed the lane. He stopped on the far side and stared at the ground ahead. It was snow-covered. More had fallen overnight, but it had not been as heavy as the previous two days, so he was hoping to see if any sign showed of someone crossing the churchyard.

"Are you all right?"

Thomas glanced at Jorge, then back to the cottages. The woman had gone inside and the scene was peaceful.

"I'm looking for tracks."

"But it snowed."

"Not hard. Look." Thomas pointed at low depressions in the snow cover. "That might be where he crossed to the church."

"Except we already know he did, so it tells us nothing. And there are fresh animal tracks. Do they tell you anything?"

"Only that a large fox and two small boar crossed since the snow stopped falling just before dawn. No doubt returning to their lairs. I am looking to see if anyone else might have followed him, but all I see are the animal tracks."

"Sometimes you surprise me with what you know."

Thomas looked at Jorge. "Only sometimes?"

Jorge smiled.

Thomas stepped across what might or might not be the remnant of John Miller's footsteps. He glanced at the headstones on either side, curious whether John had come this way on purpose, but they were only headstones. Most had nothing to show who they belonged to. This was a small, no doubt poor church in an out-of-the-way place. There would be no mausoleums lying within. He was surprised there was a service every Sunday, but most likely only the one. Men of God were thick on the ground in these parts. One would likely have intoned the service in Latin that few of the flock would have understood.

As he reached the buttress where the goodwife told him she had last seen John Miller, a thought occurred to Thomas.

"We forgot to ask something. That woman saw Miller come this way, but we should have asked if he returned."

"Do you want me to knock on her door again?"

"If you would. She was no doubt in her bed again by then, but she might have heard something. I will look inside the church."

Thomas went on alone, making his way around the wider north side. There was a stout door at the western end, but when he tried the latch it swung open on well-greased hinges. The interior of the church was even colder than outside, and Thomas wrapped his coat more closely about himself. He missed the comfort and warmth of his tagelmust.

Despite its modest size, the church was ornate with

iconography, the windows rich with stained glass. Small it might be, but money had been spent here. Not that the Church was short of money, power, or influence — all of which it would want to demonstrate. Thomas imagined the space with a hundred candles lit and the voice of the priest intoning the mass, and a brief shiver passed through him. Once, as a boy, he had believed in all of this. Now, as the years accumulated, and he grew more aware that fewer lay ahead than behind, the trappings of religion cast its subtle net towards him. Not that it had caught him yet. He knew Amal visited both the chapel within the castle and St Laurence's Church with Catherine. She claimed it brought her a sense of peace, even if she failed to understand the reason.

Thomas started when Jorge's voice interrupted his reverie. "She saw nothing, but did hear someone enter the cottage. They moved around for some time afterwards, moving things, banging about, but at what time it was she couldn't say. Are you all right, Thomas? You had a strange look on your face when I came in. Are you sickening?"

"Only for answers."

"We have some of those, don't we? Just not the ones we are looking for. No sign of the man in here, then?"

"I haven't looked yet. I was … thinking."

Jorge tapped his head with a finger. "You know that is bad for you, and the cleverer a man, the worse it is for him. And, much as it pains me to admit it, you are clever."

Thomas considered the day was growing stranger and stranger, but he had a man to find. John Miller was clearly not in the church, but there might be some sign he had been here, or at least a sign of what he might have come for. The most logical explanation was John used the church as a meeting place and, whoever he met, both had fled.

Did that imply some manner of guilt? Thomas suspected it did.

All the same, he knew he had to conduct a search.

"You start at the nave. I will do the other end. Call me if you find anything."

"The building is full of things," said Jorge. "Am I meant to be looking for anything in particular?"

"A body."

Jorge pulled a face, but went to where a font and platform lay at the eastern end of the small interior. Thomas turned to the other end, where he found a small door, which gave access to a space where the priest would don his robes and gather himself for his performance. There was nothing of interest there. Thomas came out and walked the pews, some with hassocks of cloth stuffed with hay. He had covered half the distance when Jorge called out.

"Thomas, I think I have found him." Jorge's face was pale, and he stood hard back against the side wall of the nave.

Thomas walked fast and jumped up, ignoring the steps. Behind the altar, he found the body of a man. The age was right for John Miller, but Thomas had never seen him. For a moment he thought of fetching the woman from the cottage, then changed his mind.

"Can you find your way back to the mill beyond the bridge?"

"Of course. I can see it from outside."

"Then fetch one of John Miller's family to tell me if this is him or not."

"What about the—"

"Would you want her to witness this? Go to the Millers. Go now."

Once Jorge had left, Thomas looked down at the body, then knelt. Not to pray for the man's eternal soul but to examine how he had died. It did not take long, nor require anyone with Thomas's experience to discover the cause of death. As soon as he turned the body over, he saw where a slim blade had entered John Miller's back and pierced his heart. There was little blood because he had died instantly.

Thomas sat on his heels and looked around, not expecting to find the murder weapon, and in that he was correct. He looked at John Miller. Not as tall as Thomas, but tall for these parts. Whoever had killed him had got close. Too close for someone he didn't know or trust.

Close enough for a lover, perhaps? Thomas already had an idea who that lover was. If he was right, it made the leaving of the bones even more significant. If he was right, it was a matter that would have to be dealt with. Permanently.

CHAPTER FIVE

Thomas turned full circle, his eyes scanning the narrow tables laden with gold and silver crucifixes, cups and candlesticks. Nothing appeared missing. Without moving, he examined the floor, not wanting to disturb any evidence that might lie there. He saw nothing. Only the body of a man, his eyes wide open, an expression of shock on his face.

As well it might be.

Had John Miller come here to meet Philippa Gale? Thomas believed he had. Had she given him the bones and instructed him to leave them in plain view where Thomas would find them, knowing he would glean their meaning and know what their promise was? Or their threat? Almost certainly.

Thomas knew Philippa used her beauty to further her own ambitions. She had done so with Thomas, seducing him even though she loved another man. She blamed Thomas for the death of that man, Peter Gifforde, even if he had not struck the fatal blow himself.

Thomas went to his knees. He pushed the body on its side so he could check beneath, but saw nothing there, other than the expected stain of blood. Next, he checked the few pockets. None in the man's hose, but two in his jacket, which was dark blue with a slashed yellow lining. An incongruous garment for a servant, one more suited to a gentleman. Had John Miller worn it to impress the woman he considered his lover? Whatever the reason, there was nothing in either of the pockets.

As Thomas rolled the body over, the church door slammed open and a stocky man barged in, Jorge following behind.

"What are you doing?" he demanded.

Thomas rose. "You are?"

"I am John Miller the elder, and have been dragged from my work by this fop."

Jorge merely raised a shoulder to show the unfairness of the world.

Thomas took a step to one side. "I may have bad news for you, sir. How is your constitution?"

"I am strong as an ox, not that it is any business of yours."

"I believe it may be. Beneath me is the body of a young man I believe to be your son, also named John Miller, and I would like you to confirm that to me."

The man stayed where he was, but his eyes widened.

"Dead, you say?"

Thomas nodded.

"What makes you think it's John?"

"His neighbour saw him come to the church late last night. His age matches your son, as does his description, but I could not ask her to make an identification so I sent my companion to fetch you." Thomas waited. He could not force the man to identify the body, but if he could not he would have to find someone who could. One of the other castle servants would suffice, but it would mean carrying the body there. He regretted not bringing Will. The weight of the body would be no trouble to him.

The man took a step closer, then stopped. "I told him no good would come of going to the castle. No good at all. He should have stayed with the rest of us. Is milling flour not an honoured profession, sir?"

"Yes, I believe it is." Thomas took another step back, and the man did as he hoped and started forward again.

John Miller the elder ascended the four shallow steps and walked through the chancel arch. He stopped again when he caught sight of splayed legs, but made himself come on.

"Is this your son?" Thomas asked.

The man gave no sign, said nothing, and Thomas gave him time to become accustomed to what he saw. Minutes passed, but still everyone stood unmoving. Finally, the man offered a sharp nod.

"Aye, that's our John. What has the harecop got himself mixed up in now?"

"I was hoping you could help me with that. Are you aware of any women your son might have associated with recently?"

The man grunted a sound that might, under other circumstances, have been a laugh. "Who has the fool not tupped? I worry he'll get one with child and have to marry her. And some are the kind of girls a man with ambition

49

would not want to marry." The man raised his eyes to meet Thomas's. "Who are you, sir, and how is this your business?"

"I am Thomas Berrington and I am—"

"You're the new Justice. Word is you're odd, but they say you're honest. Can't remember the last time we had an honest Justice in Ludlow. Are you going to find out who killed my boy?"

"If I can."

"Is there anything you need from me?"

"I would like to know more about John. Why he left your house, and where he went. People he knew. I want to know as much about him as I can."

"Then there's no point talking to me. You need our Grace. She's the only one of us John kept in touch with."

"She lives at the mill?"

"She does, sir. Grace is a good girl. If anyone knows what our John has been up to, it will be her." He glanced down at the body of his son. "Can I take him home?"

"Will you make the arrangements?" Thomas asked.

"It is my job to do so, sir, so yes. I will go now and fetch a cart to carry him home. His mother will want to see him."

"I will make him as presentable as I can," Thomas said. "Then will wait and come back with you so I can talk to your daughter."

"She went up to Agnes Baxter's with a delivery of flour. She is friends with her daughters. They are of the same age and interests. I sometimes think Grace would rather be a baker than a miller, but we live the life we are given." He looked down at his son again. "Most of us. And

50

if this is the result of ambition, it tells me all a man needs to know of it."

John Miller the elder turned and strode from the church.

"I like him," said Jorge.

"So do I. He is both brave and honest."

"Do you need me, or should I go back to the castle and tell them what happened?"

"Stay. I want to talk with Miller's neighbour again and find out more about what she heard last night. You said someone returned to his house?"

"That is what she told me."

"Well, it can't have been him, can it? Not unless the dead can walk."

Jorge scowled and shook his head. He disliked it when Thomas talked of such things.

"And I almost forgot, there is this." Thomas went to one knee and uncurled the fingers of John Miller's fist. They resisted, telling him something about when he had died, but he believed he already knew that. John Miller had come here to meet Philippa Gale, perhaps believing they were about to run away together. She would have killed him almost at once.

Thomas worked the scrap of blue linen out and stood. He held it out, but Jorge took a step backwards.

"Do you recognise it?" Thomas asked.

"Am I meant to?"

"Look closer."

"I don't want to."

"Then I will tell you what it is. A scrap torn from my tagelmust, which he must have stolen from my room at

51

the same time he left the bones. I can think of no reason a lad who dresses as he does would want it. I suspect he was told to steal it, which is why I couldn't find it this morning."

"Why would Philippa want it? I assume it was she who asked him to take it."

"That is my belief And she wants it because it's mine, and identifies me. Have you ever seen anyone else in England wearing a tagelmust?"

"There was that man in London, when we visited. Do you remember?"

"Anyone other than a Moor?"

Jorge shook his head. "But why is it in his hand? Did he snatch out and tear it loose from whoever killed him?"

"We both know who killed him. Philippa Gale. And if that is the case, yes, I suspect in his death throes he clutched at it and tore this scrap loose. Which means she was wearing it."

"You are obsessed with that woman. She has gone and would be a fool to return."

"Then she is a fool. You heard the neighbour. Miller was visited by a tall woman, well dressed and beautiful. How many women do you know that match that description?"

Jorge smiled. "More than people who wear a tagelmust."

"Perhaps you are right. But it makes sense, doesn't it?"

"I am sure to you it does, but you will have to convince me. You may also have to convince Sir Richard Pole and Gruffydd ap Rhys. Not to mention Prince Arthur. He takes a keen interest in what is happening in the district."

"As well he should if he is to be a good leader. Which I think he will be." Thomas turned away from the body. "Come on, let's go ask the neighbour some more questions."

"Do you want me to woo her again?"

"Of course. I only seem to frighten people."

"I could try teaching you how not to do that, but you may be too set in your ways by now. Apart from which, I don't even know how I do it. It seems to flow out of me, as if I am casting some kind of spell."

"You never use it on me, do you?"

Jorge laughed as they left the church. "Why would I even try? I know you are immune to my charms. But I taught a little of it to Belia. I know you enjoyed lying with her."

"I did it as a favour to you and her, so you could have the children you so wanted."

"I didn't ask you that but whether the favour was also enjoyable."

"You know it was. Your wife is both beautiful and skilled."

"As I am well aware."

Thomas crossed the narrow track and rapped on the cottage door next to John Miller's. When it opened, Jorge conjured his very best smile and reached for the woman's hand.

Thomas thought he might have to step in and catch her before she swooned, but it seemed Jorge was completely in control of his power as he began to ask questions.

"You did well," Thomas said.

"Was that a compliment?" asked Jorge.

"It was the truth."

"I will take it as a compliment all the same."

They were approaching Ludford Bridge, the water of the Teme iron-grey beneath its wooden struts, the snow-shrouded town rearing up beyond. Almost every single chimney curled smoke into the air. The day was half gone but the sky was so heavy with cloud there was little sign it had even started. There would be more snow before nightfall and yet more in the coming days. A steady north wind blew a relentless promise. Summer seemed a long time gone and spring a long time yet to come.

"We should call and speak with John Miller's sister," Thomas said.

"Not now," said Jorge. "Best to leave it until tomorrow. The family will have enough on their minds today. Let them mourn their son and brother. Tomorrow is soon enough. Besides, you already know who killed him."

"Do I?" The boards of Ludford Bridge sounded under Thomas's boots. His good boots, with heavy soles to keep out the cold from the ground.

"You said yourself Philippa is behind it."

"But did she kill him?" Even as he spoke the words Thomas wondered why he did so. She had been seen with Miller. She had lain with him in his bed. And, Thomas was sure, she had enticed him out to the church on some pretext and thrust a dagger through his heart.

"We should talk to the servants in the castle and find out what they know about the lad," said Jorge.

"I will also have to tell Sir Richard and Gruffydd about what happened. They may assign the murder to the local coroner and then it will be out of my hands."

"Is that what you want?"

"It would make life simpler. I still have matters to attend to after the Quarter Session, and there is our house to consider. Would you like to live apart from my household in a place of your own?"

"Are you throwing me out after all these years?"

"Not at all. I meant on the land I own. There is more than enough space. The men have already started on my workshop, and I know how I can extend the existing site to make it into a Moorish house, with an enclosed courtyard and room for everyone. Belia could carry out her trade, and you would not have the rest of us under your feet."

"You are trying to get rid of me." Jorge trudged on up the slope, his expression for once sombre. "I like us all living together."

"So do I, and our doors will never be locked. I enjoy having Belia cook our meals."

"She has been teaching Amal. Was that your plan all along, for your daughter to cook for you once I am exiled?"

Thomas shook his head at Jorge's stubbornness. "I will ask the masons to make my house three or four times the size. We can all have our own space beneath the same roof."

"Can they do that?"

"I don't know, but I expect so. Is that what you want?"

Jorge smiled. "You are already building a workshop for Belia, so I suppose it would make sense for us all to be together."

"Is there anything else you would like that I have forgotten?"

"Perhaps a room for bathing, like the one in your house in Granada."

"Already planned," Thomas said.

"With hot water? In England?"

"Yes, with hot water. And steam if you want it."

Jorge stopped beyond Mill Gate and turned to Thomas. He said nothing, but drew him into an embrace. When Thomas tried to push him away, they both slipped on the ice and landed in a heap, laughing.

"You are fortunate I didn't try to kiss you," said Jorge.

They helped each other to their feet and carried on.

"Do you think John Miller's neighbour was telling the truth?" asked Jorge. "Or did she dream what she told us?"

"It would be a strange kind of dream. Or rather, not strange enough for a dream. Someone returned to the cottage in the small hours and it could not have been John Miller."

"Are you sure? We don't know when he died."

"There are signs. The inside of the church was ice cold and would have slowed the onset of stiffening, but I accounted for that. He died between midnight and two in the morning. Closer to midnight."

"So she killed him almost as soon as they met?" said Jorge.

"If it was her. There is not enough evidence yet to be sure."

"Except you know it was. She must have gone back to the cottage after she killed him. Why?"

"The neighbour said she stayed there in the days before. I think she wanted to make sure nothing remained that would point to her. She searched the entire house, which would not have taken long, but made no effort to be silent. Perhaps she didn't realise how thin the walls were."

"Or didn't care."

"That is a possibility."

They came out into Market Square, their breath pluming white around their heads.

"I need to get warm." Jorge turned left towards the castle entrance.

"So do I, but I can do that just as well at Agnes's bakery. She will know the Millers, and I want her to tell me about them. John in particular."

"Do you need me?"

"Not for this. See if Will is around and tell him I may need him later today. We have to go to the land in Burway and change my instructions to the masons. Will has been supervising for me so he needs to be there."

Thomas watched Jorge walk towards the castle. Heads turned to follow him as they had always done, but perhaps not as often as they used to. Age had eroded all of them.

Thomas pushed the thought aside as too maudlin and crossed Market Square, offering a wave to the two girls serving at the hatch, which was still busy. It would be worth asking them about John Miller. Both were pretty. Both of an age to interest Miller. There were questions Thomas needed answers to and Jilly and Rose might be able to help. They would have known John Miller. How well? Did he give them the same attention he had given to other women? Was it the kind of attention that might get a lad killed?

CHAPTER SIX

"The Millers are an excellent family," said Agnes. She and Thomas stood in the dry warmth of her bakery where open ovens sat empty, their work complete for the day. Arrayed on two shelves, rows of clay pots held the yeast for tomorrow's loaves, the scent of it flavouring the air.

"And John Miller?" Thomas sat back against one of the heavy oak tables dusted with flour.

"John was a good enough lad until a few years ago, then he did as other young men have done in the district. He found ambition." Agnes smiled. "Or more likely grew bored with a small town where every face you see is familiar. Most leave and go somewhere bigger. Gloster, Bristol, Oxford. The braver ones venture as far as London. Some, like you, travel even further."

"Leaving Lemster was not my choice, sister."

"I was too young to know, only that I had my own family one day and then my aunt's the next." She reached out and grasped Thomas's hand. "I don't blame you, Tom.

You were a lot younger than John Miller and his like. You had no choice."

"I could have returned sooner."

"I don't blame you," said Agnes again.

"Tell me more about John Miller."

"There is not much to tell. He was a good lad until he turned fifteen, then that tide rose in him like it does in some men. He went from position to position. Some I know about, others not. He always seemed to do well at first, but soon enough he was ready to move on again. There was always something better waiting for him just beyond the horizon. You need to talk to his family if you want to know more, or the names of those he worked for. His sister Grace was closest to him."

"His father told me the same. I intend to speak with her tomorrow. Today, the family must mourn their son and arrange his burial."

"He will be put in the ground at St Giles Church. It is the closest to their mill and all the family lie there. The ground surface will be frozen though, so the digging will be hard."

Thomas wondered if that was a reason John Miller lived close to the small church, because it maintained a connection to his family home. What Thomas failed to understand was why the lad had been killed there when he had a bed in his cottage. On what pretext had Philippa drawn him to the church? Some wicked promise of sin? He would not put such depravity beyond her. To lie with a man in God's house might appeal to her. To kill him possibly even more.

"His father told me Grace was close to your girls."

"It is true enough. They used to play together when they were younger, and often enough it is Grace who brings our flour. Good flour it is, too. I have enough to last me until Friday. I hope they mill again before then." Agnes put a hand to her mouth, her eyes wide. "Listen to me, Tom, thinking of myself while that poor boy lies dead."

"Life has to go on, sister." Thomas hated the triteness of his words, true though they were. "Would you mind if I spoke with Jilly and Rose?"

"Not as long as you get their names right."

Thomas smiled. "I have been watching them and can tell the two apart now. Rose has a smaller nose, but not by much. Jilly is an inch shorter, despite being a year older. Am I right?"

"You are right, Tom. I used to tell them to dress differently, for one to cut her hair shorter, so as not to confuse the customers, but I think they like to do so. They are good girls, though. Just as you have good children."

"I have reminded Will they are blood relatives," Thomas said.

Agnes waved the comment aside. "As I have also told them. I can't blame their doe-eyes. He's a handsome lad, and any girl, any woman, would welcome his protection. But I trust them all, as I know you do."

"Will is a man now, albeit not at his majority yet, but I believe he is more mature than men ten or twenty years his senior. As for Amal ... sometimes I think she is more mature than me."

"You have raised both your children well." Agnes

touched his arm again. "When you have spoken with the girls, I will give you sweet pastries to take with you."

"I will pay."

"No, you will not. You saved this town, Tom, and more than me are grateful to you."

"And I know others who would be pleased to see the back of me."

"There are always those. Now talk to my daughters, for they will have sold all our wares by now. But can I ask a favour if you do?"

"Anything, sister."

"Take them with you to your rooms in the castle. They have never been beyond the outer wall and are sore curious about what it is like. I suspect they have images of gold, silver and jewels, but they will be impressed all the same, I am sure."

"My rooms are hard against the outer wall, albeit within it."

"It is still the castle."

Which is why Thomas, accompanied by Rose and Jilly Baxter, passed through the outer gate and turned towards the accommodation wing for senior staff and honoured guests. Thomas was unsure which he was regarded as.

Before they could enter his rooms a voice called out, and Thomas halted. When he saw who it was, he cursed under his breath.

"Go inside without me and ask for Jorge. Tell him what you know of John Miller. The truth, remember. I need to hear only the truth, good or bad."

"Go inside on our own?"

"Or return to your own house." Thomas knew he

sounded harsher than he meant, but the man who had called him was almost on them. He pushed the girls and reluctantly they made their way towards the entrance. Thomas turned and steered Sir Richard Pole back in the direction of the inner bailey.

"I would say those girls are a little young for you, Thomas."

"My sister's daughters, Sir Richard. There has been a death in the town."

"There is always death in a town this size, and winter is hard upon us, which only makes it worse. If you are involved, I take it you consider the death suspicious?"

"I do."

"Then you can tell it to me and Gruffydd somewhere warmer than the bailey. We also need to talk about what went on at your Quarter Session."

Thomas accompanied Sir Richard Pole without comment, wondering how much trouble he might be in. John Miller the elder had already commented on the unusual state of affairs for the district to have an honest Justice of the Peace. Thomas suspected the conversation to come might follow similar lines, but with more probing. As they entered the main buildings Sir Richard led them to the Solar, where Gruffydd ap Rhys waited.

"Thomas tells me there has been a death," said Sir Richard.

"The dead man is John Miller, and he made up the fires in the castle," said Thomas. "He made up the fire in my accommodation as well. Whether he was meant to I don't know."

"I have seen the lad around," said Gruffydd. "Always

seemed a touch surly, as if he considered the job beneath him. Had an eye for the girls, I believe. What happened? Did he drown?"

"Drown?"

"Happens at this time of year. Boys go fishing, slip on ice and fall into the water. The cold kills them before they can climb out. Mind, most of the fools can't swim anyway. Was that it, Tom?"

"He was murdered."

"Damn it," said Sir Richard Pole. "Have you informed the coroner?"

"I have started to look into the matter myself."

"Not your job. You are Justice of the Peace. A constable will carry out any investigation under an order from the coroner. You have more serious matters to deal with, not least of which is Sir Thomas Cornwell. He does not take kindly to your ruling against him in the matter at the Quarter Session." Sir Richard looked at Gruffydd. "I told you there would be trouble appointing an honest Justice."

"You did," Gruffydd replied. "But Arthur likes Tom, and Arthur likes the idea of imposing justice on the Marches. He says the Marcher Lords have been a law unto themselves for too long. When he is King he wants the whole of England under his rule, not these pricked up Barons ruling the roost."

"Want what he likes; he has to deal with the pricked up Barons." Sir Richard wiped a hand across his face. "Ask a page to send for some ale and food, Gruff. We might be here some time."

"What am I to do about John Miller?" Thomas asked after Gruffydd had gone to the door. "Ignore his murder?"

"Are you sure it was murder?"

"I doubt he stabbed himself through the heart. Even if he had, where was the knife? He was in no state to hide it."

"Someone else took it?" Sir Richard waved a hand in dismissal at the idea. "I am sorry, Thomas. I trust your judgement in this, but are you the right person to investigate?"

"What investigation?"

Thomas turned to discover Prince Arthur had returned alongside Gruffydd. Thomas glanced at Sir Richard, seeking a sign of whether he should tell the Prince or not. Sir Richard looked away, distancing himself from any decision. So Thomas took it for him. The only one he could.

"A member of the castle staff has been killed, Your Grace."

A look of shock crossed the Prince's youthful face, but he recovered his usual composure quickly. "Do I know them?"

"A lad by the name of John Miller. He tends the fires, but perhaps not those in your rooms, Your Grace."

"Was he dark haired, handsome, and had an eye for a pretty face?"

"He was."

"Catherine said she did not trust him. I was going to dismiss the boy, but she told me not to. Who killed him?"

"That is what I don't yet know. But if the three of you agree, I would like to spend some time investigating." Thomas did not want to raise his suspicions of Philippa Gale. He knew Arthur liked her and, if it was up to him, he would pardon any crimes she had

65

committed. He had grown up with her as nurse and then tutor.

"Sir Richard tells me you have other matters to attend to. Sir Thomas Cornwell for one. I hear you ruled against him."

"I ruled in favour of the law, Your Grace. There was nothing personal in the matter."

Prince Arthur suppressed a smile. "I suspect that is why he is so incensed. Am I right, Richard? Cornwell does not appreciate an honest Justice of the Peace. He liked Hugh Clement well enough."

"As did everyone else who behaved like Cornwell," said Gruffydd. "If Tom holds his nerve, there may be some changes for the good around here."

"Can you meet your responsibilities and look into the death of this man, Thomas?"

"I believe so, Your Grace. My son and daughter are assisting me and take on much of the day-to-day work."

"I know you to be honest, but there are people out there who might regard you employing members of your own family as nepotism."

"Both my children are in a very small group of people I trust implicitly, Your Grace."

"I hope the three of us belong in that group."

"Of course." Thomas was not so sure about Sir Richard Pole, but the man served the Prince well, and was honest. But he preferred matters to run smoothly, even if that meant sometimes looking the other way from certain transgressions. Thomas disagreed with him about that. The Marcher Lords were not the threat to the crown they had once been, but still held too much power for comfort.

"In that case, look into the man's death. Report to Sir Richard and Gruff, who will inform me of anything I need to know. Now, if that is settled, I want to ask you about the January hunt. Will has already agreed to ride with me. How about you, Thomas? Can you draw a bow?"

"I'm not so sure these days, Your Grace. You would be better to ask Will to invite Usaden rather than me. *There* is a man who can draw a bow. Or a sword or knife."

"But he is a heathen."

Thomas bit down a retort and took a breath. "I am not entirely sure what he is, Your Grace, but if I was riding after deer or boar, I would want him beside me. And Princess Catherine is fond of him."

"So she tells me." Arthur shook his head. "It is time your son found himself a woman. I can suggest some ladies to him if he wishes. Girls of good standing in the district. Or even one of Catherine's ladies. There are enough of them to offer him a good choice."

"I thank you, Your Grace. Perhaps you can ask Catherine to pass on some names to Amal, who in turn can tell Will. It will come better from her."

"You may be right, but Will and I get on well enough. I like your son, Thomas. I like him a great deal, and would bestow some honour on him if he would accept."

"He is like me in that respect, Your Grace."

"But you have honours, Thomas. Duke of Granada, for one. Could you not refuse Queen Isabel?"

"I could refuse her nothing, Your Grace, but now my loyalty lies with you, your wife, and the King and Queen."

"Which is good to hear. Now, tell me what you intend to do about the death of this man." Prince Arthur sighed.

"I expect Lady Margaret will need to find us a new lad to tend the fires, and quick."

It was an hour before Thomas got away. He left Sir Richard, Gruffydd and Prince Arthur in the Solar discussing the best weapons to use in close combat. He crossed the inner bailey to the kitchen, where he expected to find Lady Margaret Pole arranging the menu for the Prince and his new bride. Advent meant red meat was not allowed, and other restrictions applied. Lady Margaret was fully aware of what Arthur and Catherine would expect, and her own meals would match theirs. Despite his lack of faith, Thomas followed the same strictures because it was easier to fit in.

Lady Margaret was in conversation with the head cook, and Thomas waited until they were finished. He noted some of the other workers glance at him with expressions of interest and wondered why, because after almost two months of living within the castle walls he was a familiar face.

The reason for their interest became apparent when one of the younger women approached, a local girl from her accent. "Sir?" She stood in front of Thomas. "Is it true John is dead?"

"If you mean John Miller, then yes, he is." Thomas had no time for softening the news. "Did you know him well?"

A flush touched her cheeks. Thomas judged her as having somewhere around seventeen years. "A few of us did, sir."

"Did you—" Thomas cut off the question he was about to ask. It was none of his business. Not yet. Later, perhaps, he would have to dig deeper, but for now the girl could hold her secrets close.

"Did I what, sir?" The knowing smile on her face gave him all the answer he needed. It also told him how simple a matter it would be for Philippa Gale to seduce John Miller. Just as she had drawn Thomas into her bed the day they arrived in Ludlow.

"Nothing." Thomas saw Lady Margaret had completed her instructions and he moved to intercept her, leaving the girl to return to her work. "Lady Margaret, if you have a moment, I would like a word."

"About the lad who was killed? Word spreads fast in a town the size of Ludlow, and kitchen staff hear the gossip first."

Thomas tried to interpret her expression but could not, and wished he had Jorge with him.

"It concerns John Miller, if that is what you mean."

"I have a little time. Come, we can talk in your rooms where we will not be overheard by everyone."

CHAPTER SEVEN

Thomas stood in the main room of the accommodation assigned to him — almost certainly by Lady Margaret Pole herself — and asked if she wanted any refreshments. There was no sign of Rose or Jilly, but the faint sound of voices reached him from another room.

"Ask me your questions, Thomas. I have little time and am sure I could find a better use for it."

Thomas bit back his first response.

"John Miller was murdered." He hesitated, then added some detail, wanting Lady Margaret to know the seriousness of the crime. "He was stabbed through the heart."

Her lips tightened in disgust.

He continued. "I understand he was employed at the castle for only a short time."

"Six weeks."

"Did you speak with him when the appointment was made?"

"For a fire maker? Of course not. Someone else did, but I know the details. What is it you want to know?"

"Was his work sound?"

"Again, I never witnessed his work, but the reports I received were that he felt his responsibilities beneath his talent."

"I heard he started calling himself Chambers."

"It was one of the reasons he was going to be dismissed if his attitude did not change."

"One of the reasons?" Thomas asked.

"The lad had a high opinion of himself and a lack of self control. I believe he even flirted with Princess Catherine."

"She told you this?"

"Of course not. I heard it from one of her Spanish ladies who was in attendance. I believe the lad made an approach to her as well." Lady Margaret sighed. "As he appears to have done to almost every single female within the walls of Ludlow Castle."

"Not all, I am sure," Thomas said. Lady Margaret was young and pretty, but carried a fearsome reputation. Enough to put a lad of eighteen years in his place. "He must have come recommended to be offered a place here." Thomas knew posts within the castle were held in high regard. The stipend was no more than could be earned outside its walls but status carried its own value.

"He was employed by both Sir Thomas Cornwell and Sir Richard Croft before coming here." Lady Margaret glanced away from Thomas, who turned to see Amal and Belia enter the room. Rose and Jilly hovered outside, expressions of awe on their faces. Everyone knew who Lady Margaret Pole was, and her position in Prince Arthur's household.

"I am sorry, I did not know you had company," said Belia. "Can I get you anything, Lady Margaret?"

"Nothing, thank you. Thomas has already offered. But I would have a word with you after we finish here, if I can."

"We will return to the other room then." Belia turned and went out with Amal. Rose and Jilly had already disappeared.

"You are fortunate in your friends and family, Thomas," said Lady Margaret.

"I am indeed. As are you, my lady. Did both households provide a good reference for Miller?"

"Excellent, which made his poor performance a surprise to everyone. Had he been more willing he may well have advanced to some position he felt more suited to his abilities. But when he could barely even make a fire correctly, questions were asked."

"Might his references have been forged?"

"I spoke with my husband and showed them to him, and he said they looked genuine enough. But all it takes is access to a seal and some wax. Do you intend to speak with the households of his previous employers?"

"I do."

"Except I hear you have made an enemy of Sir Thomas Cornwell. Sir Richard Croft is a different matter. You ruled in his favour, did you not?"

"I ruled in favour of the law."

"Which is also what I heard," said Lady Margaret. "You are a brave man. I would suggest you speak with Croft first. Not because you ruled for him, but because he too is an honest man. If you are fortunate, you will not need to speak to Cornwell and will be better for the lack of doing so. Now, do you have any more questions?"

"Only one. Do I have your permission to speak with the household staff?"

"Ask what you will, but do not make too much of this man's death. He was about to be dismissed. It is not as if he was one of us."

"But he is still dead, my lady."

Thomas kissed the back of her proffered hand and watched as Lady Margaret turned right out of the door, on her way to see Belia. He went to find Jorge.

"Where are we going?" Jorge rode beside Thomas on a gelding borrowed from the castle stables, while Thomas sat astride his own horse, Ferrant.

"To see John Miller's previous employer."

"Is it far? And will it snow again before we get there?"

Thomas smiled. "Can you not tell?"

"This is your land, not mine. The vagaries of its weather, of which there are far too many for my liking, are not something I wish to become familiar with. When can we return to Spain?"

"That I don't know. I promised Isabel I would watch over Catherine."

"You will be dead before her or her husband. How will you watch over her then?"

"I have a son and daughter who can take my place."

"Have you spoken to them of this obligation you put on them?"

"No. Do you think I should?"

"I expect not. Will would serve Catherine to his final breath. Amal the same. They are friends, all three of them. And you have not yet told me how far this place we go to is."

"We ride to Croft Manor. It is a little under three leagues."

"So it will take us some time. Will it be dark before we return?"

"Are you afraid of the dark now?"

"I am thinking there will be no moon because of the cloud."

"The cloud is going to clear later, and despite there only being a quarter moon, its light will shine bright on all this snow. We will find our way home."

As they rode, Thomas attempted to teach Jorge something of the phases of the moon, its rising and falling. Also, how to tell when the weather might change. But Jorge was uninterested. He claimed other people would tell him such things if ever he needed to know.

Croft Manor sat on a slope below a low crest. Woodland grew close behind, but in front the land fell away to the valley of the Lugg. Its proximity to Lemster brought Bel Brickenden to Thomas's mind, and he wondered if there would be time to visit her and her sons before returning to Ludlow. He pretended to himself it was Edmund he wanted to talk to about the work at Burway, but the real reason was Bel. Since returning to England and discovering Bel Brickenden still lived in the same house she and Thomas had fallen in love in, his mind had dwelled long on the situation. It would make sense to discuss his conflicted feelings about Bel with Jorge, but Thomas suspected the advice he got would be long, convoluted, and lost on him.

They were greeted by Sir Richard Croft's steward, who introduced himself as Charles Carter. He was a man four inches shorter than Thomas and around ten years younger, though those years sat more heavily on him. His belly was rotund and his cheeks florid. When he asked about their business, Thomas told him he would like to speak with Sir Richard Croft.

"Concerning what?" The man appeared to make an attempt to block their passage to the house.

"There has been a death in Ludlow, and the man killed was employed here before his present post. I am seeking information about him."

"Then you are better talking to me. Sir Richard never troubles himself with domestic matters. He trusts my judgement. What business is this death to you?"

The man's manner irritated Thomas, who had deliberately dressed in the clothes of a gentleman to avoid this exact situation. He had made sure Jorge did the same. Not that Jorge would not stand out whatever he wore. A steward was not meant to question a gentleman in the manner this one was doing.

"I am Thomas Berrington, Justice of the Peace for the district, and my interest is in who killed the man I speak of. If you can answer my questions all well and good, but while I am here it would be only fitting to see your master, who introduced himself to me at the Quarter Session two days since. Now, if you could arrange for

75

someone to attend to our mounts, we would like to go inside out of the cold."

Charles Carter's face showed several expressions in turn. Anger, which faded to irritation, which eventually became acceptance.

"Tie your horses to the rail. I will have a lad attend to them." The man turned away. Thomas glanced at Jorge, who raised a shoulder in some kind of judgement.

As they followed twenty paces behind, the sound of hoofbeats caused all three to slow. Thomas turned to find a rider approaching on a fine, black stallion. He veered towards them, as if curious, and dismounted. Sir Richard Croft held his reins out, waiting for Carter to take them, which he eventually did after trotting to close the distance.

"I have to thank you for ruling in my favour at the Quarter Session, Thomas Berrington," said Sir Richard. "Is Charles giving you a hard time? He likes to think he protects me, but there is little to amuse a man out here and visitors are always welcome. What brings you to Croft Manor?"

"A man died in Ludlow and I was told he used to work for you."

"Charles is your man if it is about staffing, but let us go inside to warm ourselves." He glanced at his steward. "I assume the fires are lit in the big hall?"

"They are, sir."

"Then bring some of the good wine. Or would you prefer ale? Or are you not partaking during Lent?" It was clear Sir Richard Croft was.

"Wine would be most welcome for both of us,"

Thomas said. "My companion is Jorge Olmos, Sir Richard."

"I saw you at the Sessions. You are the Spaniard. I have heard some tales about you." He smiled. "They say half the women in Ludlow have fallen under your spell."

"Only half? I must be losing my powers."

Sir Richard laughed and clapped Jorge on the shoulder. "Then it is fortunate my wife has gone to London or she might also fall under your spell. She dislikes the cold and spends half of winter at our house in town." An explanation was not required, but it seemed he wanted to make one.

A fire burned at either end of a large hall with tall windows that looked east towards the lower land and the river Lugge. Thomas searched the view, trying to find the smoke of Bel's son's brickworks and failing.

"I would tell you to ask me your questions, Thomas, but fear it would be a waste of time since Charles deals with all matters of domestic staff. Though I would welcome being allowed to stay when you question him."

"Of course, Sir Richard."

"I hear you were born in Lemster. Is that why you look on it with such earnestness?"

Thomas glanced at Sir Richard. "It holds little attraction for me these days. My home is in Burway now — or will be soon."

Sir Richard turned to Jorge. "And you, sir, where were you born?"

"I was born in Sevilla in Spain, then again beside the mighty Guadalquivir near Córdoba when Thomas made me what I am now."

"And what are you now?"

"A eunuch."

Sir Richard stared at Jorge, but his expression showed neither surprise nor distaste.

"Was it painful?"

Jorge almost smiled. "It was. But not as painful as it would have been if someone other than Thomas had performed the procedure. And he was kind with what he removed, so most who see me might take me for a whole man."

"That is interesting. You must have many tales you can tell. Some more bawdy than others, I expect."

"Both regarding my life in the harem of the Sultan of Granada and my life since. But we are not here to talk about me, Sir Richard. Thomas wishes to know more about John Miller."

"And as soon as Charles returns with the wine, you shall. Where is the man, damn it?" As he spoke the door opened and Charles Carter entered.

"My apologies, Sir Richard. The best bottles were difficult to find. I brought two." He set the bottles on a table, then turned to leave.

"Where are you going?"

"We need glasses, Sir Richard."

"Call for a girl to fetch them. These gentlemen have travelled from Ludlow with questions and it is you who can answer them."

The man went to the door and called out in a loud voice. When a young woman appeared, he gave instructions before returning. He stood with his hands folded in front of him, his expression closed.

"When did John Miller come to work for Sir Richard?" Thomas asked.

"I would need to consult my records for an exact date, but I believe it was in May of this year. I recall the hawthorn was coming into full bloom."

"And he tended the fires?"

"Among his other duties. You will have more fires to manage in Ludlow Castle, I expect."

"Yet you have two fine blazes burning in this room." Thomas glanced at Sir Richard Croft and back, curious how he was taking the conversation. He appeared to be interested, but not fascinated, which Thomas understood. The work of low level staff was hardly something the man would involve himself with.

"We have a new lad now, of course. His duties are the same as Miller's were. Attend the fires first thing and throughout the day. Between that duty he cleans boots and shoes, helps carry flour and food for the kitchens, and anything else requested of him."

"Did John Miller always do these extra duties willingly?"

"He—" Charles Carter broke off when a young woman returned, carrying a tray of fine goblets. "Put them beside the wine."

After woman left Carter started across the room and made to open a bottle.

Thomas followed. "He what?"

"He believed much of what he was asked to do was beneath him. He did not last long here."

"How long?"

"Six weeks, perhaps seven. Again, I would need to

consult my ledger, but certainly no more than nine or ten weeks."

"Did he dispute his sacking?"

"Far from it. He cursed both me and my master, as well as half the staff — though not the girls. He claimed he already had another place settled which would suit him better."

"Do you know if this was true or merely a boast?"

"I know he went to work for..." Charles glanced at his master before lowering his voice, "...for Sir Thomas Cornwell. He and Sir Richard are sworn enemies."

"I can hear what you are saying, Charles," said Sir Richard in amusement. "And I am sure Thomas knows well of my disputes with Cornwell. But until this point, I was not aware this lad went into his service. It would explain some of the information Cornwell has in his possession about my affairs."

Charles poured wine and handed the first goblet to Sir Richard, the second to Thomas. He almost neglected to hand one to Jorge, but he came and stood close until he also held one.

Thomas waited for Sir Richard to taste the wine first before following suit.

"This is fine indeed, Sir Richard," her said. "Our thanks."

"You are welcome, sir. More than welcome after the favour you did me."

"As I explained at the time, I only followed the law."

"Which is why I thank you. It has been some time since a Justice followed the law around here. Some of us welcome it, even if we may fall foul of your decisions now and then."

"I would like to question some of the other staff with your permission," Thomas said.

"I have no objection. What say you, Charles?"

"It is an unusual request, Sir Richard."

"Is it? Why?"

"Staffing is my responsibility. I do not see what extra information this man may glean from others."

"Is there any harm in him trying?" said Sir Richard. He turned to Jorge. "Do you need to accompany Thomas, or can we talk while he concludes his business without us? I am interested in hearing some of your tales of the harem."

"Thomas is usually capable of managing without me, Sir Richard," said Jorge. "And I hope you are a man with a broad mind."

Sir Richard barked a laugh and patted Jorge on the shoulder.

"I expect I have some tales I could tell in return, but not in front of my staff. Charles, take Thomas wherever he asks."

Charles took Thomas's barely tasted goblet of wine from his hand and placed it on the table before turning away. Thomas nodded thanks to Sir Richard and followed. He hoped Jorge would temper some of his tales, and that he would not include him in any of them. But he doubted it.

He caught up with Charles Carter, who walked fast, as if he wished to outpace Thomas.

"Did you deal with John Miller often?"

"Rarely. He was the most junior member of staff, so was responsible to others."

"Then I would like to start by speaking with whoever they are, and then some of the girls."

"They all know how to behave in this household, despite what that boy might claim."

"I have no doubt they do." They approached the kitchen, always the heart of any large house, and most of the smaller ones, where often enough it might be the only room. "Now, who did Miller report to?"

"That would be Anna Pryce, our head cook." The words came out slowly, as if they were being pulled from his mouth. "We are only a small staff while Lady Croft is in London. She takes many of her own attendants with her."

"Then I shall speak with Anna. I will not need you to be present. You can return to your own duties, of which I am sure there are many." Thomas made no effort soften his curtness. He did not like Charles Carter, and suspected the opinion was mutual.

CHAPTER EIGHT

Anna Pryce was a woman of surprising youth to be a head cook. Still in the early years of her second decade, she was pretty, with russet hair, and wore a plain dress dusted with flour from her work.

"Charles tells me I am to answer your questions, sir. Do you mind if I continue to work as I do so? Sir Richard does not like it when his supper is late, and tonight it is a pie which will take several hours if the chicken is to melt away as he likes it."

"Please continue. How long have you worked for Sir Richard?"

"Ten years now, sir. I came as a girl of fifteen years and want nothing else. Sir Richard is an excellent master."

Thomas noted she made no reference to Charles, whose instructions she was most likely to work under, and drew his own conclusions as to the reason for the omission.

"Are you married?" The question was irrelevant, but she seemed happy enough to answer.

"I am, sir, to Paul. He is the stable master, and a good man. We have three children and the master has given us a cottage to live in. It sits a quarter mile downslope and is fine indeed. We have two rooms downstairs and two upstairs. The children have a bedroom all their own." She smiled and placed a clay pot on the table. It already contained a baked pie crust ready to receive its filling. A whole chicken lay beyond, already plucked but not yet butchered.

"Do you remember a servant called John Miller?"

An expression passed across Anna's face, too brief for Thomas to interpret. He knew Jorge would have gleaned the meaning from it, but he was regaling Sir Richard with torrid tales of concubines, Sultans and eunuchs in the perfumed halls of Alhambra.

Thomas took a chance. "I take it you did not like him?"

"He was not a good man, sir. Far from it. And too full of himself. He objected to taking orders from a woman. Not that it stopped him trying to lift my skirts, and those of every other woman in the household."

"Other than Sir Richard's wife, I assume."

Anna only pursed her lips.

"He was a bold man indeed, was he not?" Thomas said.

"Bold, and with a head full of nonsense dreams. He had a good place here. Sir Richard is the best employer in the district. Charles has been in this household since he was orphaned and Sir Richard took him in. But I soon put John in his place. I told my Paul about what he did and they had words. They may even have fought, but Paul is far stronger than John." She reached past Thomas and drew the chicken towards herself before selecting a large knife and cutting off the head and legs. "Do you like chicken pie, sir?"

"I am fond of it, yes, but have not eaten chicken since the start of Lent."

Anna gave a laugh, back on safer ground. "Sir Richard attends church regularly, sir, but does not hold with starving himself or anyone who works under his roof. Are you pious?"

It was Thomas's turn to laugh. "Not in the least, but I live within Ludlow Castle and Prince Arthur is exceedingly pious, as is his new wife."

"I hear she is a beauty, sir. Is it true?"

"Indeed she is."

"Do you see her often?"

"I have known Princess Catherine since the day she was born."

"Are you from Spain as well? You do not sound it. Your speech is not local, but you speak our language well enough."

"Yes, I lived in Spain for a time." Thomas had no wish to regale Anna with his entire history. "Did any of the girls report John Miller to Charles?"

"Most did not want to. They hold a false sense of duty and honour among themselves. I did not tell Charles either, only my Paul. But Charles knew. How could he not? That boy had more wants in him than is seemly. We were all glad when he left. He cursed me when he walked out of here. Filthy curse words. He called me names no man should ever say to a woman, and told me things would be different in Burford. He said his new master was Sir Thomas Cornwell. It would be him, of course. He and Sir Richard do not see eye to eye."

"As I am already aware."

"The whole of the three counties know of their enmity, sir. I expect Sir Thomas Cornwell only appointed John to send a message to Sir Richard." Anna removed the breasts from the chicken with practised ease and sliced them into square chunks. "I need to fry these off. Come to the stove with me if you have more questions."

"Only a few." Thomas followed her to where a skillet was already heating above the flames. "Did John Miller ever mention any other women? Not from this house-hold, but someone outside of it?"

"Not to me, but then he rarely spoke to any female staff other than to make lewd suggestions. He thought himself above us all." She shook her head. "When what he really wanted was for us to be beneath him, if you take my meaning."

When Anna blushed at her own openness Thomas liked her even more, which is why he said, "John Miller will accost no more women. He is dead."

Anna glanced at him as she stirred the pieces of chicken. "Dead, sir? How did he die?"

"Murdered."

"No doubt he put his dirty hands on someone else's wife and paid the price. Good riddance is all I can say. He will not be missed here."

Thomas gave Anna's words consideration. Such had not occurred to him, but the scenario made sense. A beautiful woman had visited John Miller's cottage. He assumed it was Philippa Gale, but what if it had not been? What if it had been someone's wife, or daughter, or lover? Which meant a hundred new suspects.

"John did not stay long with Sir Thomas Cornwell either," said Thomas. "He was employed at Ludlow Castle when he died, and would not have been employed much longer had he lived."

"That sounds like John, up to his old tricks again." Anna poured stock over the browned chicken before adding carrots, swede and parsnip, and letting it simmer. "Twenty minutes and then I will cool it before putting it in the pie." She brushed hair from her face with the back of her hands. "Look at me, chattering away and never even asking your name. Are you someone important, sir? I expect you are if Sir Richard has let you ask your questions."

"I am Thomas Berrington, and not so important."

"But you are. I heard Sir Richard and Charles talk about you. You are the Justice of the Peace, and friend to Prince Arthur and his wife. They say you were a duke in Spain." Without thought, Anna offered a little curtsy. "And here I am going on about poor John Miller. Is there anything else you need to know? Or perhaps you would like to talk to some of the girls? They will tell you what John Miller was like."

"I think I have a good picture of what John Miller was like. Unless any of them know who might have killed him. I have to ride to Burford before dark."

Anna glanced at one of the small windows. "You will

not get there before dark, sir. Already the day is fading. The days are short at this time of year and will be for some time yet. You will need a lamp if you are to ride safe to Ludlow. I will ask Paul to find you one. Sir Richard has a surfeit of lamps. He does not like the dark either."

———————

"I liked him," said Jorge as they rode north. A dull light remained in the clouded sky but it was fading fast. Thomas carried an unlit lamp tied to the end of a stout shaft. Anna's husband, the stable master, had provided it. He would use a flint to spark the wick when they could no longer see the track ahead.

"I assume you are referring to Sir Richard Croft."

"Of course. And I liked the man who gave us the lantern. But I did not like that man Charles."

"Neither did I. Did you regale Sir Richard with tales of your rich and debauched life?"

"A little. He was curious about everything. I would take him as a man curious about many things. A little like yourself."

"We need to ride out again in the morning to speak with the household John Miller went to work for after leaving Croft Manor. You will come with me again?"

"Of course, but I may need a thicker jacket. Can you see where you are going, Thomas?"

"Almost. And I will try to find you something warmer to wear."

"Have you forgotten Edmund is coming to talk about our house in the morning?"

Thomas had. The arrangement had been made a week before, and it was too late to change it now. "Will and Amal can deal with it. They know what I want."

"No. You must do it. Yes, Will and Amal know, but a lot is in your own head. Edmund needs to know how you mean to use these small bricks you had him make, and then he needs to pass that on to the masons."

"Will knows as much about Moorish arches as I do."

"It is still your responsibility. I know you, happy to let Will decide until he does something you don't agree with. So you must meet with Edmund. We can ride to this other place afterwards, or even a day later. John Miller will be no more dead than he is now."

"Then his killer might escape."

"We know who his killer is."

"Do we? Anna said something that—"

"Who is Anna?"

"The cook at Croft Manor. You would like her. She is pretty and has a sweet nature. It was her husband who gifted us the lantern."

"Then I probably would. What did she tell you?"

"She suggested John Miller could have been killed by a jealous husband. The boy seemed driven to make a tilt at any girl or woman in his presence. Even Lady Croft. It's not a possibility I had considered. The bones of a hand. The neighbour's description of a tall, dark-haired woman. I assumed it was Philippa and that she killed him, but assumptions can make a fool of anyone."

"You can be hasty," said Jorge.

"I admit to impatience, but hasty…?"

"Be hasty and light the lamp, Thomas. I can't even see you."

St Laurence's bells struck the hour of seven as they crossed Ludford Bridge. The water wheel turned at the Millers, and Thomas expected John was lying in his grave by now. He recalled his father saying that if he wanted to know more about his son, to speak with his daughter Grace.

"Can you find your way to the castle from here?" Thomas passed the swaying lantern to Jorge.

"All I need to do is keep going uphill until there is no more up. I am hardly going to miss a castle, am I? What are you going to do?"

"Talk to Grace Miller. Her father said she knew John better than anyone."

"Then you might need me with you." Jorge handed the lantern back to Thomas.

When they reached the Miller's house a woman Thomas had not seen before opened the door to his knock. From her age, he assumed she was the matriarch of the house.

"Yes?" Her voice was abrupt but not unwelcoming.

"My name is Thomas Berrington, Justice of the Peace for the district. If possible, I would like to speak with your daughter Grace."

The woman turned and called into the house, "Grace, that man is here to talk to you. Come, girl."

A few moments passed before a slim girl of around seventeen years appeared. Her grey dress was dusted with flour, as was the air inside the house. The sound of the grinding stones could be heard from above.

The girl offered a brief curtsy as manners required. "Father said a man might call. Are you he?"

"It depends who he meant, but I believe I am. I would like to talk to you about your brother, John."

"He lies beneath the ground now in St Giles' church-yard. Father told me you live in the castle."

"For the moment, yes."

"I would like to see inside the castle. It would be better if you asked your questions there, otherwise everyone here will listen in and offer an opinion."

Thomas hid a smile. "I hope you have a warm coat in that case."

"Of course I do. Wait here."

Thomas and Jorge remained outside the door. The lantern swung in the wind and a few flakes of snow started to fall, auguring more.

"She knows her own mind, doesn't she?" said Jorge.

"Yes, she does. And clever to suggest we question her inside the castle walls, though I suspect she will be disappointed when we don't take her into the inner bailey."

"It will still be the castle."

Jorge took a step back when the girl came out wrapped in a heavy wool cloak, the hood pulled down so low her face was almost hidden.

"Will there be anything to eat?" she asked.

"I expect so, but it might be too spiced for your taste."

"I like many kinds of food. Come on then, or the snow will make the track slippery." She started off and Thomas and Jorge walked fast to catch her up, leading their horses by the reins.

She said to Thomas, "Father told me you are Agnes Baxter's brother. Is that true?"

"It is."

"Then I will answer your questions as honestly as I can. I loved my brother and would see his killer punished. The word I hear is you are the man to do it."

CHAPTER NINE

Belia and Amal were setting food out when the three of them arrived. The open fire filled the main room with scented warmth, and Belia's children filled the space with noise.

"Where is Will?" Thomas asked Amal, who slapped his hand aside when he leaned across her to taste the stew.

"Go wash before you put your fingers in our food, Pa. Will is across with Arthur and Catherine but says he will be home for supper." Amal glanced at the newcomer but did not ask who she was.

"This is Grace," Thomas said. "She is John Miller's sister and has come to answer some questions."

Amal turned from the fire and went to Grace. "I am sorry about your brother." She embraced the girl who, after a moment of shock, returned the embrace. When Amal stepped back Grace wiped tears from her eyes.

Thomas went to wash. When he returned, Grace and Amal had their heads together like old friends, and Will had returned.

"How was Catherine?"

"Very much in love. As is Arthur." Will grinned. "Fortunately, with each other."

Thomas noted Grace's eyes stray to his son — attention he could understand. Will had inherited his mother's beauty. In him it provided a handsome countenance, and gave him blond hair thicker than Helena's. Will had worn it long in Spain, but had cut it short for the journey to England and kept it that way since. It suited him short. His height and strength came from his grandfather, Olaf Torvaldsson, once the Sultan's general but of late a man with no role to play in Spain. Thomas saw little of himself in his son but knew others did.

"Have you made any progress, Pa?" asked Will, as he reached for a hunk of bread. "Ami introduced me to Grace. Is she here to help?"

"She has offered to. Do you want to sit in when we talk?"

Will looked at Grace. "Would you object if I did?"

Her cheeks flushed and her eyes could not meet his. "If you wish it, sir."

"I am no sir, Grace. Call me Will."

"If you ask it, si—Will."

Will smiled and offered a wink to Jorge, who was also an object of fascination for Grace, now he had changed from his travelling clothes into rich cotton and silks. He made Thomas feel dowdy, which he supposed he was. At least he had no one he wanted to impress.

Food was set on the table and conversation turned to the coming festivities once Lent ended. Grace asked if their Yule log was dried, and Thomas told her he had forgotten all about the tradition.

"You will struggle to find one now, in that case. The log must be set aside for months if it is to burn for all twelve days of Christmas. You can probably buy one if you know who to ask and have enough money. I will ask father, and come and tell you if he knows of one. Your son looks strong enough to carry a log on his own."

"I expect he is."

A half hour passed before the table was cleared and Thomas asked Grace to accompany him to another room. Will decided to remain behind, perhaps not wanting to offer the girl any distraction, but Amal came, together with paper, pen, and ink.

"Are you happy to answer questions about your brother?" Thomas asked.

"If it helps you find who killed him, I will answer whatever you ask."

Thomas thought for a moment, then started at the beginning. It was often enough the right place.

"When did John leave home?"

"That is easy. Half a year ago. It was a month before first harvest, a busy time for us."

"He didn't want to stay and be a miller like the rest of you?"

"John had ambitions. The rest of us are content enough to follow, like my father followed his father, and he his. It is what we do. We are millers. John was different, and..."

Thomas waited, but Grace appeared to have stopped what she had been about to say.

"And what, Grace?" Thomas tried to soften his tone but knew Jorge would be better at this kind of thing. He thought to send for him but did not want to break the mood so soon after starting. "You said you would be honest with me. Is there something he did?"

Grace shook her head. "No. John did nothing. It was what mother feared he might do. To us girls."

Now Thomas wished he had sent for Jorge. "John liked girls, didn't he? I have heard it from others, and now from you. But he would never have touched his sisters."

"No, he would not. I know he would not. But mother had other ideas."

"Why?"

"She would not tell us. Perhaps she had heard stories about him and feared what might happen. We all live on top of each other as it is. Mother and father have one small room, the rest of us share another." Grace avoided looking at Thomas, focusing instead on something behind him.

"He was ambitious, I hear," Thomas said.

"He was. He talked all the time of finding a position for himself in some grand house, or here in the castle." She offered a small smile. "And he did come here, only to have it snatched away from him."

"How did he find a place? Working in a large house is a much sought after occupation. Did John know someone who helped?" Thomas thought of Philippa, but the timing was wrong. She had been in London half a year ago. Prince Arthur had been in Ludlow, together with his entourage.

"My father knew someone in Croft, a man he dealt with. I believe mother was afraid of John. He had a temper, as well as ... needs. Sometimes they go together. Does your son have a temper?"

"Will? Not unless someone crosses him. Even then he never acts in anger, only to protect others."

"John was not like that. He could be cruel and he could be violent. He hit my father once, but father put him on the ground and John had to leave. We all knew he had to leave."

"Your father found him a post to get him away from you all?"

Grace nodded, her eyes meeting Thomas's now. "Yes, I think that was it."

"Your father also told me you continued to see John."

Another nod. "I made no secret of it. I did not want John to lose all connection to our family so I saw him now and again. When he went to Croft Manor we walked the woods behind, sometimes even as far as the cunning-woman's cottage. John told me he was sure he would soon have a better position than fire boy. He also said there was a girl there keen on him." Grace offered a sad smile. "That was always the way with John. Girls were keen on him, when in truth it was the other way around."

"Did he give a name?"

"No, and I did not ask."

"You said your father helped him get the position at Croft Manor."

"The baker in Croft was brother to the manor's stable manager, and he asked a favour. Whether he would have done so had he known what John was like is another matter."

"I met Paul Pryce when we visited the manor earlier today. It was where we were coming from when I called to see you. I liked the man, and his wife, who cooks for Sir Richard Croft."

"John told me he liked neither of them. He thought they looked down on him. Which is one reason he left."

"He told you he left of his own accord?"

"Because he did. For a better job. He went to work for Sir Thomas Cornwell at Burford Manor. A far more elevated personage, John said, though his own position was little better. He had more responsibility, but he still had to make up the fires. He said there were almost twice as many in Burford than at Croft."

"I expect John had little free time at either Croft or Burford, so how did you keep in touch?"

"I went to him when I could. On a Sunday afternoon, always in the hour after noon, so we knew when to meet. We had a place he would expect me. Sometimes he did not come, but most times he did. I gave him news of home, which he was always interested in, and he told me how he was getting on, and about those he worked for. He did not like Sir Thomas Cornwell but rarely saw him, so it did not matter."

"That must have meant a great deal of trouble for you. Croft is three leagues from Ludlow. Burford almost as far. It would take several hours to walk to either."

"Father let me take our horse."

"He knew you were going to see John?"

"He did. I think he felt bad about him leaving. Sometimes he asked if John wanted to come back home, but I told him he was doing well in his new positions. It was not the truth, even though John made out he was gaining promotion. I knew him well enough to recognise his little lies."

"And then he came to Ludlow?" Thomas said.

"Yes, not long since. In fact, I think only a week after the Prince arrived with his new bride." Grace smiled, her happiness transforming her from pretty to radiant. She would be a catch for some young man in Ludlow.

"I came to Ludlow in their company," Thomas said. Had Philippa Gale come across the lad and recognised his need? "The location would have made your meetings easier, would it not? Did John say how he came to his position at the castle? I imagine they are much sought after."

"He told me through a friend of his, a woman who was staying at Burford Manor, but he did not tell me her name and I never met her. John said she was a friend to the Prince and new many people in the castle."

"Do you think John and this woman might have been more than friends?"

Grace said nothing for a long while. She chewed at her bottom lip and her hands lay one on top of the other, moving slowly together.

"John claimed they were, but… if she was a friend to the Prince, why would she be close to John in … that way? Oh, he is handsome enough, but is too…" She shook her head, the words not coming to her.

"Too sure of himself?" said Amal for the first time

since coming into the room. Her pen had scratched away and Thomas saw she had filled two pages.

Grace glanced at her and nodded. "Yes. He always has been. It often seems to others he is over-confident, and it puts people off. It would have put this woman off if she was as elevated as he claimed."

"Unless she wanted to use him." Thomas knew he might be leading Grace to his own conclusion but said the words anyway to see how they lay.

"She was older, John said. Almost as old as our mother, so it is not likely she would want him for the usual reason, is it? I think he probably met her now and again while he was tending fires at Burford Manor and she offered a kind word or two. He would have spun imaginings from those few words, as he always did." Grace looked around the room. The fine furnishings, the solid walls decorated with paintings and hangings. "We are inside the castle now, are we not?"

"In the outer bailey, yes, but there is an inner sanctum where the Prince lives with his new wife."

"You told me you came here with them. Do you know her?"

"I do. Princess Catherine of Aragon. She is known to all my family."

"Will, too?"

Thomas suppressed a smile. "Yes, Will too."

"Did you ever see John? Would he not come here to tend your fires?"

The question interrupted Thomas's train of thought because it occurred to him that Grace Miller had spoken an important truth. If John Miller made up the fire here, why had he never seen him? When he looked up Grace was staring at him, with no idea of the thoughts that swirled in his head.

"No, I never met John. I would have liked to."

Grace shook her head. "No, you would not have. Nor your pretty daughter. She would have recognised him for what he is. Sometimes you cannot help but love your family, even when you know the truth of them."

Thomas agreed with Grace's sentiment. He had loved his mother but hated both his father and brother.

"You knew the truth about John?"

"Of course, and forgave him his transgressions, as I hope the girls he transgressed against also did." Grace straightened in her chair. "Have you finished with me now, sir?"

Thomas believed he had.

"It is late. I will ask Will to walk you home."

"Thank you, sir. I will feel safe with him."

Yes, Thomas thought, *I believe you will.* Whether Will would feel safe with Grace was another matter.

When she had gone, in the company of Will, Amal said, "Are you matchmaking, Pa?"

"No, only ensuring a young woman arrives safe to her door."

"She is a sweet girl."

Thomas rose to return to the main room, Amal at his side.

"She said something that made me wonder about John Miller. You, Will and Jorge were with me in the merchant house when he left those bones."

As he entered the main room Thomas asked Belia,

"Were you and the children here when John Miller came to make up the fires?"

"I would not have seen him because at that time I was in the castle kitchen preparing our midday meal," said Belia. "I took the children with me. They like the kitchen."

"For how long did he tend to our fires? You used to do it, didn't you?"

"I did, and was happy to do so, but he came … oh, ten days ago and told me he had been asked to include our fires in his work. I did not ask who told him to come, only grateful he intended to help." Belia glanced at her children. "Leila, you came back for something, didn't you? Did you see anyone when you did?"

"I saw John." Leila glanced at her mother. "He told me I could call him John. Is that all right, Mama?" When she received a nod her eyes sought out Thomas. "He asked where your room was, Uncle Thomas." Her voice was soft, as if she worried she had done something wrong. "He said he had a present for you. I told him he could leave it with me but he said it was too important and was for only you. I told him I would not look at it, but still he wanted to know where your room was. So I told him. Did you like your present, Uncle Thomas?"

"I did. You're a good girl."

Leila smiled and stacked the wooden blocks again.

"Did you see what he was carrying?"

She paused, one block grasped in her fist. "It was wrapped in some cloth, so no."

"Did you see him when he left?"

Leila nodded.

"Was he carrying anything then?"

"The same piece of cloth." Leila frowned as she realised what she had said. "Did you get your present, Uncle Thomas, or did he take it away again?"

"Oh, I got it, but I think he took something of mine with him when he went. You did well."

Leila offered another smile and placed the block on top of one of the fallen ones to start a new tower.

CHAPTER TEN

Two days passed before Thomas managed to find time to ride south to Burford across sheep-scattered slopes. Jorge rode beside him on the same horse he had used when they visited Croft Manor. He claimed it suited him because it was a handsome beast.

Thomas had questions for Sir Thomas Cornwell because Lady Margaret had told him of Philippa's movements earlier in the year. Thomas knew she had come to Ludlow in October in the company of Prince Arthur and himself. What he had not considered was whether she had been to the castle before. Lady Margaret confirmed that Philippa had been there earlier in the year. From late spring until the end of summer, in the company of Arthur.

"She spent most of her time at the castle, but some weeks she did not." Lady Margaret had told him as they stood amid the bustle of the kitchen.

"Where did she go?"

"Nobody thought to ask her. She may have told the

Prince — they have always been close — but most likely did not. There were times she would disappear for days at a time, sometimes longer. She was a presence when she was here, but had little to do with anyone other than the Prince. She tutored him in Spanish and the ways of regal ladies, in preparation for his marriage."

Thomas wondered where Philippa had gone when not in Ludlow. At Burford Manor? Was that where she met John Miller and hatched a plan? He was still examining his thoughts about those absences when Jorge broke his concentration.

"What was it Bel gave you when she came yesterday?"

Without thought Thomas put his hand to his throat. "It was nothing."

"It is something. I can see the thong around your neck. Are you embarrassed by it?"

Thomas reached beneath his shirt and drew out a plain cross. Bel had come with her sons when they delivered more bricks to Burway, and she bore a gift. When Jorge was satisfied he nodded, and Thomas slid the cross back against his chest.

"Why a cross, Thomas? You're not religious. Does she think she can convert you?"

"I may not believe in any God, but Bel does. Hence it has significance to her."

"Are you and she going to … you know…?"

Thomas smiled at Jorge's coyness. It was not like him. "Most likely not. Friends, I hope. Lovers is too much to ask for at our age."

"God's teeth, Thomas, you're old, not dead!" Jorge shook his head and changed the subject, much to

Thomas's relief. "Remind me why we are going to talk to this man? John Miller left those bones. He was a fool with women and wanted to better himself. We also know who killed him. Should we not be looking for Philippa Gale instead of talking to important men of the district?"

"John Miller's death is the key to where we might find her," Thomas said. "I told you what Lady Margaret told me about Philippa's time in Ludlow, and her absences. I am sure she killed the lad. I thought she might have had someone else do it, but now I believe she stabbed him herself. She wouldn't trust the act to anyone else. We are going to Burford Manor to find out what they know of John Miller and whether they also know of Philippa. He had to have met her somewhere, and one of his employer's houses makes sense. He would have precious little time to meet her anywhere else."

"Unless she went after him."

"Why would she do that?"

"Because he had a new post at Ludlow Castle, which is also where you live. She can't enter it herself, so she needed someone who could come and go without suspicion."

"John didn't get his post until after I came to Ludlow, and Philippa was close to me then. I think I would have noticed if she had been charming him. Besides, Grace told me a woman helped John get his post. That had to be Philippa, so she knew him before he worked at the castle. Why she asked him to leave me bones instead of slipping a knife between my ribs, or slipping poison into my drink, is a mystery."

"John Miller might have been an idiot, but he wasn't

stupid enough to do that. He knew — and Philippa would know — he couldn't do so without getting caught. The bones are an invitation. She expects you to do exactly what you are. To come after her. And when you do she will be waiting."

"I assume in that case she will have men around her."

"That would make sense. But it won't stop you, will it?"

"This matter must end before she hurts someone close to me. She may have men, but she wanted to kill John Miller by her own hand. He knew too much and had to be silenced. He had one job to do and one job only. To leave the bones so I would know Philippa was coming for me. After that he had no use to her so she killed him."

"Why the church and not his cottage?" asked Jorge.

"You no doubt remember what his sister said. The man was lascivious to an unnatural degree. It is why he was chosen by Philippa, because she could twist him to her will, though I suspect he believed the choosing was his to make. Men such as that might welcome an assignation in a church. It would carry a level of transgression which might enhance the lovemaking."

"I am, as you know, an expert in matters of love, but I cannot see the attraction of a freezing stone church when he had a perfectly serviceable bed in his cottage. Did Philippa ever suggest you and she…?"

"Not once, for which I am grateful. The church must have been her idea. She wanted John Miller doing what she asked. Wanted him out of his cottage."

"Except it was hardly far from his cottage."

"Agreed, but if someone had gone there to seek him,

they would have found his body. There would be no service in the church for several days, which gave Philippa time to get away. The time delay would also muddy the waters as to when he was killed. His corpse would not begin to—"

Jorge held a hand up. "Please, no details. How far off are we from this place now?"

Thomas glanced around to see where they were. Ahead, the land fell away towards the Teme, which wound its way through a shallow valley. They had crossed Bleathwood Common, following the twisting Ledwyche brook which marked the boundary between Shropshire and Herefordshire. The boundaries twisted and turned as much as the brook, all three counties intruding into each other. Likewise, the land undulated, with snow lying deep in the hollows. None had fallen overnight, and the day was bright with a near-cloudless sky. Thomas took it as a good omen.

"A half hour if we urge our mounts to more effort."

"As long as you don't want mine to gallop."

"I am aware that your falling off would only delay us all the more, so no, a gentle canter will take us there soon enough."

"Do you think this Thomas Cornwell will allow us to question him?"

"It would surprise me if he does. He's not the same manner of man as Richard Croft, but at the manor I gleaned more information from his staff than the man himself. Men of their calibre don't converse, or even notice, people like John Miller. But it's possible Cornwell will not allow even his staff to speak with us. He won't have forgiven me for the ruling at the Quarter Session."

"Perhaps he won't be home, so unable to stop us."

"His case was brought only four days ago, so he will be there. He has another property in Derbyshire and spends half the year there, but he will be at Burford Manor today."

Which, when they arrived, Thomas discovered was correct, but were informed the man would not see them — though he doubted Cornwell even knew of their presence. They approached the house from the north, following the banks of the Ledwyche to the point where it lost its individuality in the larger waters of the Teme. A stone wall surrounded much of the land around the substantial house, and a small cottage was set beside the unguarded entrance. Smoke rose from the chimney, but Thomas saw no one as they passed. Halfway to the manor house, which was more substantial than the one at Croft, a rider came out to meet them. Thomas recognised James Marshall, Cornwell's steward.

"Have you come to tell my master you have changed your ruling?" he asked, as he came level with them. All three stopped, horses facing each other, their breath and that of their riders white in the cold air.

"I have not."

"I did not expect you had, but I doubt I need to tell you Sir Thomas intends to appeal to a higher jurisdiction. He is not a man to let such a ruling stand against him."

"He can try, but I won't be bullied into changing my mind."

"You do not strike me as a man who would. So if you

have not come to pander to my master's wishes, why are you here?"

Thomas heard something in the man's tone. A lack of respect for his employer that he made little attempt to hide. It offered hope they might find out what they came for. Confirmation of John Miller's true nature, perhaps, but that was unlikely to change however many people he asked. Perhaps some confirmation that Philippa Gale was involved.

"A lad who worked here not long since has died."

"Lads do. They fight. Take risks. Fall sick. It happens."

"This lad had a knife thrust into him."

"I hope you do not think anyone here did it."

"I have a good idea who did it but I can't find her. I hoped someone here might have information on her whereabouts."

"Her? A woman did the killing?" James Marshall shook his head. "Look at us, standing out here in the cold. Come to the house, we can talk just as well there and it is warmer. But first, tell me the name of this lad, though I think I already have an idea who it is."

"John Miller."

James Marshall nodded. "As I thought. There are several here will be glad he has received just punishment for his actions." He turned his horse and started towards the house. When Thomas fell in on one side Marshall asked, "When did he die?"

"The night of the Quarter Session, an hour or two after midnight."

"You can tell that closely?"

"I can." Thomas offered no other explanation.

"I was drinking in Ludlow that night and did not return until late, but it was before midnight. There are people here who will vouch for me."

"I don't suspect you." It surprised Thomas that James Marshall thought he might. He wondered if there had been bad blood between him and John Miller. From what Marshall said, there had been bad blood between Miller and several others here. Women, he suspected, or the husbands or lovers of women.

They reached a wide yard with a stable block beyond. James Marshall dismounted as a young lad ran out to take the reins of his horse.

"Look after these other two." He turned away, knowing the boy would do as asked.

Jorge leaned close. "Marshall doesn't appear to like his master much."

"I agree, but I'm surprised at him making it so obvious."

"I think he was pleased when you said you would not be cowed by him."

"A man doesn't have to like his master, only to serve him."

"I like you," said Jorge.

"Now, if only you could learn how to serve me as well."

Jorge smiled. "I believe I do, in my own way."

They entered a wing running from the main house and emerged directly into a wide kitchen. A woman of middle age was ordering two younger ones to peel, chop and marinate.

"This way." James Marshall led them through to another room which looked as if it was where he worked from. There was a desk, a bookcase, shelves and all the tools of administration a man might need.

"Sit, unless you prefer to stand." He took a seat behind the desk and Thomas pulled one up to face him.

"If I ask you questions, how likely am I to receive honest answers?"

"I was told you do not sweeten your words," said Marshall. "Good. I will answer as honestly as I can until you ask me something I am unwilling to answer. But I will tell you if you do, so you know my boundaries."

"How long have you been in Sir Thomas Cornwell's employ?"

"Eleven years now."

"You must have been young when you started."

"I had sixteen years. Sir Thomas was my first employer and will no doubt be my last. He is..." James Marshall seemed to think for a moment before starting again. "Sir Thomas can be a troublesome man, both to his neighbours and those who work for him. He demands much of his staff, but also allows me a deal of freedom to deal with matters as I see fit."

"And if what you do doesn't meet with his expectations?"

"It has happened, but he knows we occasionally differ in our methods. I am content in my post."

"Tell me about John Miller. What was his work like? When did he come to you? When did he leave? Although I believe I already have that information. And why did he leave? That I don't know."

James Marshall took some time to consider how to

answer. When he did, Thomas believed he spoke the truth.

"He came at the start of August, with good references. As matters turned out I suspect he wrote them himself, or more likely had them written. He came hoping for a job as footman at least, but we set him to tending the fires because that is what he had done before. As for his work, I rarely witnessed it, but from what I heard he did it well enough. There are many fires to tend here, though I expect there are more at Ludlow Castle." James Marshall broke off for a moment to stare into space before continuing. "His work was sound, and I believe in time he might well have gained promotion to footman, or even butler. It came as a shock when he asked to be let go."

"I assume you could have refused his request?"

"It was in our right to do so, but it is not good practice to keep staff on if they have no wish to stay. It makes for discontent. And a fire boy is easy enough to replace."

"You said he was comfortable in his post. If so, why did he want to leave? Did he not know that if he was patient promotion would be offered?"

"It was made clear when he came. Do a good job and you will be rewarded. Many of the staff have been with Sir Thomas for a long time. Some are getting too old to do the work they are assigned. We are always looking for good men and women to replace them."

"What happens to those who are dismissed?"

"No one is dismissed. They are all taken care of. Sir Thomas can be a hard taskmaster, but he has built cottages both here and in Derbyshire. Anyone who can no longer fulfil their duties, if they have worked well, is offered one of the cottages. They may live the rest of their days there. I expect one day the same will happen for me."

"Not for some years yet," said Jorge.

John Marshall smiled. "I trust not, but who knows?"

"I am curious about John Miller's change of mind," Thomas said. "Was it sudden? Was he discontent?"

"I am the wrong man to ask. As I told you, I rarely saw the lad. Even when I did it was only as he came into a room to tend a fire or passing in a corridor. I took no notice of him."

"Who is the right man to ask? Who was close to him?"

"Not a man, a woman," said James Marshall. "Stay here and I will fetch her." He rose and left the room, all business now.

"What do you think of him?" Thomas asked Jorge once they were alone.

"He is a trusting man to leave us here. There are papers on his desk, papers on the shelves, and journals no doubt recording deals made, offered and struck."

"He will know the position of everything in this room and note if it has been disturbed. But yes, he is trusting. I wanted to know what you think of him as a man."

"Honest. Dedicated. I would not wish to cross him."

"Yes, I think he could account for himself in a fight. I am confused regarding his master, though. Sir Thomas Cornwell has a reputation as a hard man who looks only to his own advantage. This tale about the cottages doesn't sit with that image."

"Perhaps the reputation you have heard comes from those who have crossed him."

"As have I now, by not ruling in his favour."

"James Marshall doesn't seem to blame you for that," said Jorge.

"No, he—" Thomas broke off when he heard footsteps.

James Marshall entered with a woman aged around thirty, dressed in clothes that were plain but well made. She was buxom, with florid cheeks and a wild cascade of red-brown hair. Her sharp hazel eyes took them both in before settling on Jorge as the more pleasant view. Thomas could not blame her.

"This is Jean Chambers. She takes care of the staff attending the rooms, particularly those of the master. She had more dealings with Miller than I did." He turned to the woman. "Answer their questions honestly, Jean. You can use this room or your own. I have matters to attend to."

When he had gone, Jean Chambers looked around, before moving to sit at the chair vacated by James Marshall.

"James tells me to be honest with you, sirs. He says one of you is Justice of the Peace." Her eyes remained on Jorge, so Thomas knew he would have to disappoint her.

"That would be me. My name is Thomas Berrington, and my companion is Jorge Olmos. He is a man of Spain."

"I thought he had a look about him. Ask away then, sirs, for I too have work waiting."

"Tell me about John Miller."

"Everything? Where do I start? He was a good, hard worker. Never complained. He only had one vice and that was a pretty woman. Some of my girls said he made inappropriate comments, and occasionally touched them in places he should not, though I never saw that side of him."

"Yet you are a woman of great beauty," said Jorge, which reddened Jean Chambers' cheeks even more.

"I was also his senior employer."

"Did this touching ever go any further?" Thomas asked.

"No, he was easily chastised. He was not as handsome as your friend, but he was a good-looking lad. He was finding his place in the world and, I suspect, struggling with some parts of it."

"If he was a good worker, and enjoyed that work, why did he leave?"

"He became discontent after that woman came here."

"What woman?"

"Philippa Gale. She was a friend to Sir Thomas and his wife both. They knew her from when he stayed in his property in London."

Her response did not come as a surprise to Thomas, but he took a moment to compose himself before continuing. Jean Chambers had confirmed all his suspicions, and an excitement rose through him.

"When did she come to this house?"

Jean Chambers looked up at the ceiling. "She came towards the end of summer, just after John started here. Then again in November time." She continued to examine the ceiling. "Yes, I remember. She came on a Friday before the start of Lent."

Thomas considered the timeframe. In summer he was in northern France and had not met Philippa. Ten days before Pentecost he had been in London tracking down Philippa's father, Galib Uziel. Tracking down and causing the death of the man. A week before that, Philippa Gale had escaped her capture in Ludlow Castle and fled. She had not come directly to this house, but it was not long after.

"Did she stay in the main house?"

"Sir Thomas has a cottage beside the gate that he offers to special guests. It is a fine cottage but lies empty most of the time. He asked me to set fresh bedding, towels, and bowls for his guest before she arrived, so he had been expecting her."

Something in Jean Chambers' words hinted at more than was being said. He glanced at Jorge and saw he had noted it too, but he set it aside for now.

"Was Pip the reason for John Miller's discontent, do you think?"

She raised an eyebrow. "You call her Pip. Do you know her, sir?"

"Oh yes, I know her. Was she?"

"John would have made her fire up in the mornings, fed it during the day and last thing at night, to keep it in for the next day. I know because he complained about the long walk there and back. Said it made him late for his other duties."

"Would that be the reason he left? He didn't like the extra work?"

Jean Chambers shook her head, but her lips were pressed together, as if she was trying to hold words inside.

"How long did Philippa Gale stay in the cottage?" Thomas asked.

"Oh, she is still there, sir. She has her feet under the table now and has no intention of moving out."

"She is still at the cottage?"

"Is that not what I said?"

Thomas rose to his feet. "Jorge, finish up here. I have something I have to do."

Thomas strode back through the house, only making a wrong turn once. He ran across to the stable, but the stable lad had removed the saddle from Ferrant. Thomas turned and ran along the track towards the gate he and Jorge had come through not an hour since. It was a half mile, and Thomas's lungs burned before he reached the cottage.

He tried the door but it was locked. Cupping his hands to the glass, he peered in but saw no one. A fire burned in the grate, which meant John Miller had a replacement.

Thomas walked around the cottage. At the back it was less well tended, and brambles grew close to the wall where he found another, smaller door. When he tried this one, it opened at his touch. It stuck when he pushed, and he had to put his shoulder against it. It squealed in protest but opened enough to give him entry. He found himself in a small kitchen, which looked unused. It told him Philippa Gale either had meals brought here or ate in the big house.

He went through to the room at the front, which was warmed by the fire, though the logs had almost burned down to a glowing pile of ash. More logs sat in a wicker basket to one side, ready to feed the fire. Thomas went to one of the two windows and looked out but saw nothing of interest. He was about to turn away when he noticed the glass of the window was new. When he touched the flaunching it gave a little. He wondered who had broken the old glass, and whether there had been an argument in this room.

There was no staircase, no upper floor, but a door led into a bedroom. When Thomas entered it he recognised a familiar scent. Philippa Gale had slept here, and recently. The bed was neatly made, but no doubt a chambermaid would have done that. Thomas could not recall Philippa ever making a bed, only unmaking one.

A rail set behind a curtain held clothes. Long, dark dresses and men's hose, which Thomas knew Philippa occasionally wore because they made riding like a man easier.

A shelf was laid with undergarments, stockings, towels and cloths.

There was nothing else, nowhere to hide anything. The bedroom was only a little larger than some of the monk's cells in Wigmore Abbey and Lemster Priory, but a little more comfortable.

Thomas unbolted the door at the front and went out. After a moment, he turned and went inside again. He took some of the logs and set them on the ashes. Smoke rose from their edges and he knew they would soon catch, telling Thomas it was good, well-seasoned wood. He wondered if John Miller had cut it and laid it aside somewhere to dry. As he stared into the flames he let his mind go still and tried to imagine what might have happened in these few rooms.

He suspected John Miller had done more than make fires and tend them. Had Philippa come to Cornwell's house to seek someone out to do her will? If so, John Miller would have been a perfect choice. Or was it nothing more than coincidence? Thomas thought not. Burford Manor was too close to Ludlow for coincidence. Philippa had come here seeking vengeance and a tool to help her gain it.

The question Thomas did not know the answer to was what Sir Thomas Cornwell's involvement might be. He hoped Jorge had learned something in his absence. It was the reason he had left him with Jean Chambers. Jorge would tease every secret from her and leave her unsettled for days.

CHAPTER ELEVEN

"Where is Hereford?" It was the first time Jorge had spoken since they left Burford Manor. Now they followed the road west which would bring them to the main road that ran south to north along the border lands.

"It's a small city eight leagues south of Ludlow. Why?"

"That is where Philippa Gale went two days ago."

"Presumably not until after she killed John Miller."

"Do you think she might still be there?"

"It's possible, though the cottage fire was burning, as if she was expected back. I assume you heard this from Jean Chambers?"

"Do you consider it strange John Miller wanted to change his name to Chambers? Was that Jean Chambers influence, do you think?"

"It is a common name in great houses. It indicates someone with a position, who attends to the management of the rooms. I suspect he may have got the idea from Jean Chambers, but there is no connection."

"She knows everything that goes on in that house. I liked her, and I think she liked me in return."

"All women like you." A thought crossed Thomas's mind and he twisted in his saddle to look at Jorge. "You didn't leave her too unsettled, I hope."

"Of course not. But I left her with the impression I was mightily tempted by her female charms. Of which she has many."

"I noticed. What else did you learn?"

"That John Miller was well enough liked but too much like a puppy, always underfoot, always touching, always wanting to please."

"What else?" Thomas asked. "I know she held something back when she was talking to me."

"John Miller did more than make up the fire in Philippa Gale's cottage. He stayed there several nights, just before he asked to be released."

"She seduced him?"

"You know how persuasive she can be, and I think Miller would have required little persuasion. He was a boy on the cusp of becoming a man, and the sap rises strong in such lads. Even so, he was unlikely to have followed through on his advances without encouragement. Philippa could have wound him round her little finger."

"Of her left hand," Thomas said.

"Of course," said Jorge. "So, when do we ride to Hereford? I assume that is what you want to do?"

Thomas looked at the sky, judging how much daylight remained.

"We could turn south now. We are two leagues closer

to Hereford from here than if we start from Ludlow."

"They are expecting us back today. Will they not worry something has happened to us? And do you not want Will or Usaden with you?"

"I think between the two of us we can take care of a one-handed woman."

Jorge smiled. "You are harder hearted than you used to be, do you know that?"

"I must be getting grumpy in my old age. So, do we turn south or return to Ludlow?"

"I know you want to ride to Ludlow," said Jorge. "But better if we set out in the morning, three or four of us."

"I'd prefer to pursue her now, while she's still close. Do you think you can find your way back on your own?"

"I expect so, but why would I want to?"

"I'm going south. You don't need to come with me, and I will make better time on my own. Tell Will if I am not back by tomorrow evening to bring Usaden with him. I will meet them outside the cathedral in Hereford. It's too big to miss. With good fortune, I will have captured Philippa by then."

"I can't let you go on your own," said Jorge.

"Are you unable to find your way back to Ludlow?"

"I know the way. Once over that hill ahead I will be able to see it. Even I can manage that. But I worry about you, Thomas."

"Don't. Ride to the castle and pass on my message. I go south."

Thomas turned his horse and encouraged it into a canter, then into a gallop. He knew Jorge would want to follow, but could not keep up with him as he flew across the ground. If Philippa Gale was in Hereford he wanted to find her before she tried to flee again.

After a while, Thomas slowed and looked back. There was no sign of Jorge, so he continued on, wondering if he had done the right thing. Wondering what plan Philippa might be hatching next and whether he could stop it.

Descending from the low slopes below the hamlet of Lyde, Thomas watched as the houses clustered around St Ethelbert's Cathedral and the castle dissolved into the settling dark. The winding ribbon of the Wye melted into the fields beyond. He hoped Jorge had returned safely. Amal might wonder where her father had gone, but Will would trust Thomas to look after himself. At least he hoped he would. He had no wish to bring them any concerns.

Full dark fell and one by one, lights sparked into life, outlining the city. Thomas passed Black Friar's Monastery, then through Widmarsh Gate into the city itself. He found a stable and left Ferrant in the care of a lad there before walking into the centre of the city, wondering where to start — with something to eat and drink, and perhaps a few questions. Philippa Gale was not someone who would pass unnoticed.

Thomas asked a passer-by for a good place to eat and was directed to the Catherine Wheel. He was unsure of the welcome it might provide, given its name. He had never seen the gruesome torture device known as a Catherine Wheel in use but knew its purpose well enough. Tie or nail a criminal or traitor to its spokes and spin him until blood seeped from his limbs, his eyes, every orifice. To his relief the inn was welcoming, with a roaring fire of apple logs scenting the air and a pleasant buzz of conversation. The accents were different to Ludlow or Lemster, but not so much to make understanding difficult.

Thomas took a seat at the end of a long table where half a dozen men ate stew from trenchers. When a girl asked what he wanted, he merely pointed and said he would have the same. The trenchers must have been waiting ready because she was back in a moment to place one in front of him, together with a flagon of cider. He had heard the reputation of Hereford cider when he was a boy and sipped it with care. It was sweeter than ale, less fearsome than he had been led to believe.

"Are you passing through, sir?" asked one man.

Hereford was a small city and most faces would be familiar. This made Thomas hopeful he might hear some word of Philippa.

"I am looking for a friend."

"And who would that be? Between us here, I am sure we can tell you where most folks live, both within the walls and without. All except the monks and the sheriff in his castle, but I expect you would go there if that was who you sought."

"A woman. Tall, dark haired and beautiful."

The man laughed. "Well if you find her, bring her back so we can all see this vision. We've not seen such a thing in many a month here in Hereford. Does this angel have a name?"

"Philippa Gale, or she sometimes goes by the name of Gala Uziel."

"Why two names, sir? Is she some manner of royalty?"

"Far from it. The tale is long, and I am unsure I know all of it myself. I owe her money, that is all, and heard she had come to Hereford."

"If she is a lady she will not be staying at the Catherine Wheel. It may have the best food in town but it has no rooms. You would be better trying the Wilton."

"And where will I find that?"

"Head for the cathedral, then follow Castle Street. Turn left when you can go no further and you come to St Owen's. You will find the Wilton Inn hard by St Owen's Gate. You cannot get lost, but if you do, ask anyone you pass and they will put you right."

"My thanks."

"You're not from these parts, are you?"

"Lemster." Thomas took a swallow of cider, changing his mind about its strength.

"Don't sound like you're from Lemster either, sir, if you don't mind me saying."

"I don't mind at all. I have lived in Spain these past forty-five years, but I was born and bred in Lemster."

"I have family live close by. What is your name, sir?"

"Berrington. Thomas Berrington."

The man stared into space a moment before draining his tankard and holding it aloft for one of the serving girls to see. "Aye, I know the name, but I thought all the Berringtons were long dead. That's what my cousin told me. Said she used to know a Tom Berrington but it was a long time ago."

Thomas tried to judge the man's age, but he could be anything from thirty to eighty. If he worked in the fields, he would look older than his years.

"Who is your cousin?" Thomas asked. "If she knew me, perhaps I will remember her."

"Lizzie," said the man. "Lizzie Martin as was. She is Lizzie Dawbney now."

"Yes, I knew Lizzie Martin. She was a friend to Bel Brickenden."

The man laughed. He reached out for his fresh flagon of cider and Thomas motioned for the serving girl to lean close, which she did with only a little reluctance. "I will pay for whatever my friend has had," he said. "Add it to my bill if you would."

"I know Bel Brickenden," said the man when the girl left. "She was the prettiest girl in Herefordshire when she was a young'un. She's still not far off being the same for all her sixty years."

"Sixty-two," Thomas said.

The man's eyes tracked Thomas's face. "Maybe I do know you. I visited Lizzie often enough. Her mother and mine were right close. I carried a torch for Bel at one time, but she told me she already had a man and was going to marry him. Might that be you?"

"What age were you?" Thomas asked.

"Sixteen, I s'pose. And now I have sixty-three years. Where those years went is a mystery, but I expect they are to you too, sir."

"I'm afraid I recall most of them. I have visited many lands and fought many battles. My life would have been different had I stayed and married Bel."

"So it was you she was sweet on?"

"It was, and I on her."

"You should have stayed. That brickworks is a fine business."

"I don't believe I was cut out to make bricks," Thomas said. "But I thought much of Bel after my father died."

"You should have come back for her. She married John Stanley and seemed happy enough with her lot. Though she never married again after he died, and most thought she would. She had enough offers. I might even have set myself at her again if my wife would have let me." The man chuckled at his own wit.

Thomas laughed. "I would say you have led a life of contentment. Tell me, which of the Dawbneys did Lizzie marry?"

"Symon, of course. He set his sights on her and wouldn't take no for an answer. It took a while, but Lizzie weakened in the end. I think her life has been less contented than mine, but Symon is an important man in Lemster these days. They have a fine house close to the Kenwater."

Thomas drained his flagon, then turned it upside down so the serving girl would not refill it.

"I thank you for your time, sir, and your information. Perhaps our paths will cross again. Do you still visit Lemster?"

"Not for some time now. For all that Lizzie is a cousin, our mothers are dead now and there seems not so much call for it. And I admit I find Symon Dawbney a hard man to like."

"Yes, he is."

"You knew him, then?"

"I did. We had several arguments and more than a few fights. He—" Thomas cut himself off. This man did not need to know what had happened. An accusation of murder. A trial interrupted when pestilence came to Lemster. It surprised him that Lizzie Martin had married Symon, because he and two other boys had attacked her one night. They might have done more than frighten her if Bel had not chased them off.

"He didn't like me, nor I him," Thomas said, for want of telling the truth.

He rose and went to the goodwife, paid for the meals of the men at the table and left more so they could drink all night if they wished. Then he went out into the dark streets to find his way to the Wilton.

He wished he had asked the man his name, and almost returned. He might have, but believed he was close on the trail of Philippa Gale and wanted nothing to distract him. The brief history of Lizzie and Bel had pleased Thomas, reminding him of what he had lost by travelling to France, and he wondered why he had not returned. He had intended to. He believed after the battle at Castillon he was indeed returning, only to discover weeks later he had been going south instead of north.

Thomas had told the man the truth. His life would have been different had he returned. He would be a different man.

He dismissed what might have been flights of fancy, nothing more. Now, he was what he was, and had vengeance on his mind.

CHAPTER TWELVE

The Wilton Inn was less busy than the Catherine Wheel. Whether that was because the food was more expensive and came served on plates rather than trenchers, or there was wine on offer as well as ale and cider, Thomas did not know. It had a more refined air to it, and the men sitting at the tables were better dressed.

The landlord watched Thomas approach, his face not particularly welcoming. A slight frown troubled his brow as if something puzzled him. Life, perhaps.

"I need a bed for the night," Thomas said.

"Then you have come to the right place. I have one left in a room of six, or two in a room of ten."

"You have no rooms for single use?"

"Not here, sir."

"Is there anywhere in Hereford I could find such?" Thomas was not concerned at sharing a room, or even a bed. He had done it often enough in the past, but he did not think Philippa would be so keen. Particularly as the room's other occupants would all be men.

The landlord laughed. "In Hereford, sir? I wish you good fortune in searching that out."

"I'll take the bed in the room of six, then."

"Do you have a horse?"

"I do, but it is already stabled."

"Food? Drink?"

"What is the wine like?"

The landlord frowned at the question. "It is wine, sir. I don't drink it. Do you want a bottle?"

"Ale." Thomas put money on the table for both room and ale, then looked around.

"Are you here on business, sir?" The landlord placed a pot of ale on the narrow trestle table, his mood more welcoming for the payment.

"Looking for a friend. I was told she might be staying here."

The landlord shook his head. "The only women who stay here are strumpets. I do have a room they use with the one bed in it, but none stay long."

Thomas took his ale and, after surveying the room, went to a table with two empty places. He nodded a silent question that asked if he could join those already there, and one man nodded back. No words were needed. Not yet.

The questions soon came, and they were the same ones Thomas had heard in every other alehouse, tavern or inn that he visited.

"I haven't seen you in here before, sir. Be you a stranger to Hereford?"

"I am." Thomas thought it easier than explaining he had been here twice before, but that had been forty-nine years ago. Which would still have made him a stranger, he supposed.

"You be here on business or passing through?"

Such questions were not unusual, particularly in these parts. Hereford, Lemster and Ludlow were small places, even if Hereford possessed a cathedral. Its inhabitants would want to know the business of strangers, and Thomas was content enough to make use of their curiosity.

"Neither. I am here to meet a friend. She told me she would be staying at the Wilton, but the landlord tells me there are no women here at the moment."

"The Wilton ain't much of a place for a woman to stay. Not unless they want to earn a penny or two lying on their backs."

"He also told me there are no other places she might stay, so I suspect my journey is wasted."

"Come far, have you?"

"Ludlow."

"A fair way, then. Never been there, but I heard of it. Is it right the King's lad lives there with a foreign woman?"

"His wife, Catherine of Aragon."

"Is this Aragon place foreign?"

"It is." Thomas took a swallow of his ale. It had a sharp taste underlying the hops but he was relieved it was weaker than the cider that still sang in his blood. "Are the beds here clean? I have taken one upstairs."

"Don't know about that, sir. I have a house of my own. Well, I say my own. It belongs to my master, but he's not so bad as masters go. I've had worse. Are you a rich man or not?"

Thomas smiled at the man's impudence, but once again it was not unexpected.

"Not," he said, for safety's sake. The man and his companions, who sat listening as their spokesman peeled the layers from the stranger, seemed harmless enough, but it was always wise not to offer anyone temptation. "I am a physician."

"A puller of teeth?"

"I do more, on occasion."

"Don't trust healers myself. No insult meant, sir. You seem a sound enough person, but a man should put his trust in the old remedies."

"No insult taken." Thomas drained his ale and held his pot up for a refill. "I expect I will be on my way back to Ludlow at first light." He shook his head. "My friend has obviously not come here. Or come and gone again."

"Tis a long way to come for nothing," said the man. "This friend of yours — a woman, you say?"

"Yes. Perhaps you have seen her. She is tall for a woman, with black hair. Pretty enough to be noticed."

"Aye … she was here. Came four nights since asking for a room all to herself." The man laughed. "She was sent packing with her airs and graces. A room to herself? Where did she think she was, London or Gloster?"

"Philippa is a woman of fine sensibilities."

"Is that her name? Philippa?"

"Philippa Gale, but sometimes she goes by Gala Uziel. She is foreign, too."

The man shook his head, making it clear he did not altogether approve of foreign. No doubt he had lived his entire life within a few miles of the inn they sat in, and would die within those few miles after living a contented life. There were times Thomas wondered if he might have settled for such an existence, but knew it was not in his nature.

"I saw a woman who matches your description, sir," said the man across from Thomas. "I don't recall her giving a name. She sat with three other gentlemen, over there." He pointed to a smaller table set close to the fire. "She left with them, so would not have been staying here."

"What did the men look like?" Thomas asked.

"Men. Nothing more, nothing less."

"You said gentlemen. Is that what you thought they were?"

"Well, sitting with a fine woman such as she was I believe they must have been."

"Did you know any of them?"

The man thought for a moment before shaking his head. "No, strangers all. To me, anyway." He looked around at his companions. "Were they known to any of you?"

There came a round of head-shakes and grunts, and Thomas knew he was no further forward. Philippa had been here but not stayed at the inn. He knew it was a gamble she would still be here and it had not paid off. Tomorrow he would start again. Someone, somewhere, must know of her.

"I thank you for your time, sirs. May I buy you more ale?"

"Ale is always welcome, sir."

Thomas drained his flagon and rose, swaying a little, surprised at how drunk he had become. He weaved his way to the landlord and left four pennies, before asking directions to his bed. The stairs presented more of an obstacle than he expected and he had to pause twice to catch his breath and shake the dizziness from his head. When he reached the room three of the beds were occupied, three empty. Thomas took the one at the far end of the room, barely enough space between it and its neighbour to allow his legs to pass. His head spun as he lay down and sleep came instantly amid sounds of lust filtering through the thin wall.

When Thomas woke, he tried to sit up but could not. He attempted to raise an arm but could not do that either. As he came to his senses, he felt coarse rope binding him. He blinked, searching the darkness for some assailant, but the dark was solid. He lay still, listening. The sound of men snoring. Someone passed wind loudly. Then, like a flash of lightning, a lamp was lit and hung above his face.

"Aye, that's him. Get him up."

Two others came past the lamp holder and dragged Thomas from the bed.

"Hey, what are you doing?" One of the other sleepers had been woken by the light and noise.

"There's nothing happening here, friend. If you know what's good for you go back to sleep and mention nothing you might have seen. Understand me?"

No reply came, which was answer enough.

The two men were none too gentle as they dragged Thomas down the narrow stairs. They took him by his feet, tied them then pulled so his head banged against each step. At the bottom Thomas saw the landlord watching, his face expressionless, and knew the man had betrayed him. More than likely he had slipped something into his ale, which would account for his state when he fell into the bed. The men lifted Thomas, one on either side, and dragged him, his feet sliding.

As they came out into St Owen Street, Thomas saw a slim figure standing on the far side. The man with the lantern went to her and a brief conversation took place before he returned. Philippa Gale turned away and disappeared into the darkness almost at once.

"She says to put him in the river and make sure he's weighted down."

"A knife would be simpler and just as final," said one of the others.

"I agree, but it has to be the river. She was clear on that. She wants him drowned."

"She might do, but how will she know? I say stick him first, then throw him over the bridge."

"We do it her way. Unless you want to tell her you chose not to?" The man stared at his companion until he shook his head. "No, I thought not."

"What do we weigh him down with?"

"We passed a butcher's shop in the next street. I wager he has lead weights there for his scales. One of you go, see if you can break in. Bring as many as you can carry."

The two men stared at each other.

"Well?" asked the man in charge, then shook his head. He nodded at the man on the left. "You do it, and do it now. There are two hours of dark yet, but early risers will be out and about in half that time. Meet us at King's Ditch, then we toss him from the bridge. The water is deep there."

Thomas felt one of the men release him. As soon as only one pair of hands grasped him he threw himself forward at the lantern carrier. He crashed his skull into the man's nose and the lantern fell to the cobbles. Burning oil spread and both men cursed and drew back. Thomas started to hobble along the alley, but had no chance of outrunning them. He had gone only ten yards when both gripped him again. One of them cracked him hard on the back of the skull and his senses fled once more.

When they came back, Thomas found himself on cold, hard ground. The faintest of light spread across the sky in the east, allowing him to see the third man had returned. He had brought weights meant for a scale, each heavy with a curved handle above it. The men were tying them with ropes to Thomas's legs, his waist, around his neck. So heavy did they make him that when the time came to raise him they failed.

"Take some off him," said the man Thomas believed was their leader. "He'll sink just as fast with half."

The two men did not bother to untie the leather straps, but simply cut through them. When the three tried again, they managed to get Thomas to his feet. The stone wall of the bridge was only a foot away.

Two of the men raised his legs while the third held him beneath the arms. Between them, they lay him across the top of the wall. Thomas tried to throw himself back away from the river but they were ready for the move.

They inched him towards the drop to the river. As they did so Thomas accepted the inevitable. He breathed fast, filling his lungs over and over with air.

"He's scared now, ain't he? She said he'd fight, but he

can't tied like a hog. On my count now, lads. One, two, three!"

Thomas fell.

He hit the water and sank. The weights saw to that. The river was deep beneath the bridge but the current slow, unlike the last time he had plummeted to what he thought was certain death.

Thomas sank to a gravel bottom. With his eyes open, he could make out a faint glimmer from the surface. He tried to look beyond it to the men but could not see them. He wondered if they were watching the river or had already fled.

The air he had filled his lungs with was running out.

Thomas twisted his arm, pain lancing through him. He extended his fingers but could not reach the hilt of the knife tucked into his belt. The men had been fools not to search him for a weapon, but perhaps not such fools if Thomas could not release it.

He stretched again, the pain almost unbearable. His fingertips found the hilt and he drew it free, only for it to slip from his grasp and fall away. If he could speak Thomas would have cursed. Instead, he tried to roll over, his fingers searching the gravel. In less than a minute his body would grow still, his mind dark.

He found the knife again. Lost it a second time. Found it once more, and this time had it in a firm grip. He bent double and used the blade on the ties at his feet first. As soon as they were free he crouched in the water, then launched himself upwards, kicking his legs as he went. His head burst through the surface and he took a great breath, just in time as the weights still strapped to him drew him back down. But he had bought himself a little time. Enough, he hoped.

He cut the ties at his waist, relieved when they parted beneath the blade's sharpness. Those at his ankles came next, and then he repeated the same manoeuvre before rising for another breath. He freed his left arm as he sank once more, but the right was more difficult and he lost the knife. Instead of searching for it, Thomas walked across the gravel, hoping he was going in the right direction. One more thrust to the surface and he sank again, but slower this time, almost free but not quite. He bumped against something, but it was only a submerged tree and not the river bank. Thomas surfaced, sank, drifted, then he found gravel beneath his feet and his head emerged above the surface. The current pushed against him, but he forced his way to where a shingle bank allowed him to climb from the river. With freezing fingers, he worked loose the remaining ties and left them where they were, still attached to the weights.

To his right lay a wharf, beyond it a blacksmith's shop where the owner was feeding fires with charcoal. Thomas staggered there and begged to be allowed to sit for a while to dry his clothes.

"Too much to drink last night, lad?" said the smith, despite being less than half Thomas's age.

"That's sure to be, my friend. I thank you." Thomas felt in a pocket for a coin, but the smith waved it away.

"You be welcome. We've all been there one time or another, though I admit I never ended up in the Wye." He narrowed his eyes. "You be a stranger to me."

"I'm from Ludlow," Thomas said, recalling the same

confession not long since. He wondered who had given his presence away. He already knew why he had been taken. Philippa had stood across the alley when he was dragged out. It was she who ordered him drowned. No doubt in punishment for the drowning of her father, which she clearly blamed him for.

Thomas suspected she may remain in Hereford, assuming now he was dead and no longer a threat. It might offer him a chance. What to do with Philippa when he captured her was another matter, and one he had no answer for. There would be the three men to take care of as well, but he was less concerned about them now his wits had returned.

Thomas pushed wet hair from his eyes, the heat of the smith's brazier already drying his clothes. He rubbed at his neck where the rope had bitten into him, and as he did so realised something was missing. The pewter cross Bel had gifted him was no longer there. He must have cut through it as he sawed at his bindings. She had set it around his neck only two days since, and now he had lost it. It felt like a judgement on his stupidity.

Before his clothes had fully dried, he thanked the smith and made his way towards the bridge and back into Hereford. There were people to question. Not least the landlord of the Wilton.

CHAPTER THIRTEEN

It was dark by the time Thomas retrieved Ferrant from the stables and rode north out of Hereford. The heavy cloud that accompanied his journey south had cleared and cold stars sparked the black sky. As he passed Holmer, a narrow moon rose on his right to light the track ahead. It was an hour before he approached Lemster and knew the longest part of his journey was over. Instead of skirting the town he turned Ferrant towards the centre.

His body ached from being tied and his belly ached with hunger. He needed to gather his thoughts before returning home to tell of his failure. He wondered if he should have been more patient and taken Jorge with him. Thomas had questioned and probed, but the only information he had gleaned was from the landlord of the Wilton, who admitted some small guilt as soon as Thomas lifted him off his feet and slammed him against the wall of his taproom.

Philippa had indeed stayed at his establishment. She

had described Thomas to him and given him something to put in this particular man's drink if he came asking after her. Why the poison had not been strong enough to kill, Thomas did not know. He suspected the drowning of him held some significance for her. Thomas had considered hurting the landlord, but in the end had simply dropped him to the stone slabs. He had been about to turn away when the landlord offered one final piece of information, as if to make atonement for his actions.

He had been out early buying bread when he saw Philippa leave the city through St Owen's Gate, a little before dawn. She was accompanied by three men, and Thomas guessed they must be the ones who tried to drown him. The only small comfort to him was that she now believed him dead. Which meant she would not expect him when he pursued her. He needed a plan, but there was no haste. Haste had got him into trouble already. He wanted to let time pass, allow Philippa's confidence to grow. If she had left to the east, he suspected she would be returning to London, and he knew where she might live there. The address of her house had been recorded in the papers Amal had scoured through after the death of Peter Gifforde.

As he passed Castle Fields, Thomas decided to break his journey. He needed food, ale — though less than the night before — and the chance to gather his thoughts. He tied Ferrant to a post in the market square and stood patting the horse's flank as he stared across at The Star. Both the square and tavern carried memories for him. Most of them bad. But The Star served good food and fresh ale, and Thomas was too tired to ride farther without both inside him. He even considered taking a bed for the night and riding the remaining distance in the morning, but decided to wait and see how he felt after he had eaten. With a last pat on Ferrant's back, he crossed the square and entered the tavern.

It was busy, and he could see no empty chair so pushed his way through to where the landlord served ale from a low trestle table. A new landlord since his father used to drink here, of course, and most of the younger men crowding the space would not have been born when Thomas left Lemster.

He sipped at his ale and asked what there was to eat.

"Mutton pottage with turnips and parsnip. Do you want some?"

"As soon as a chair comes free. I prefer not to eat standing up."

"I can find you a stool from the back, and I am sure someone will make a space if you ask."

Thomas scanned the room, looking for a table where such space might be found. He had searched half the room without luck when he saw three familiar faces. Bel's sons, Edward, James, and Michael were at a table with two other men.

"I will sit over there." Thomas pointed to the table before winding his way through the throng. He wondered if there had been a market that day or if The Star was always this busy. It had been a popular drinking place when he was young and seemed to have remained so.

"Well met, Tom!" Edward rose and offered his arm to

be gripped, as did James and Michael. "What brings you to Lemster? Are you looking for Ma?"

"I'm on my way back from Hereford and need something to eat and drink."

The men sat and Thomas perched on the stool brought over by the landlord. It creaked beneath him and felt none too stable. A pot of ale was set in front of him, together with an empty trencher.

"Pottage is on the way," said the landlord.

"What happened to your face, Tom?"

"Ran into a little trouble in Hereford."

"It's not usually a rough town, but it seems you can find trouble where others can't. Ma says even when she knew you it was the same."

Thomas could not disagree. He leaned to one side as a young girl brought a steaming pot and ladled pottage on to his trencher. As he did so, the stool creaked even more and almost tipped him to the flagstones.

"Harry, didn't you say you were going home to that wife of yours?" Edward spoke to a man at the table, who looked close to falling asleep.

The man offered a nod and stood without a word. Thomas took the vacated seat with gratitude.

"Harry married a new wife half his age last year," said Michael. "I think he might have bitten off more than he can chew. He stays in The Star until he thinks she's asleep, but still complains at her attentions. She's right handsome, too. Few would complain about sharing her bed."

"What age is Harry?" Thomas asked.

"He has forty years and a few more," said Edward. "His wife less than twenty."

"I was married to a woman less than half my age at one time."

Thomas received a wink from Michael and the other two grinned.

"It's strange to think you might have been our Pa," said James. "That is right, isn't it?"

"It was a possibility once, yes. But you would not be who you are if I had married your mother. We might have had no children, or a dozen. There is no rhyme or reason to it, but yes, I suspect we would have had children. I have fathered at least eight I know of and likely more."

"Fine children, too," said Edward. "The two you brought back with you. What are the others like?"

"Some died, some became strangers." It would take too long to explain how Jorge's children were also his, so Thomas made a show of eating his pottage, which was good. There was wild garlic to flavour it and the mutton was soft with a rich flavour.

"Where are you staying tonight, Tom?"

"I may ride on to Ludlow. Less than an hour will see me home. If not, I will see if there is a bed here."

"You can stay with one of us, or try your luck with Ma." James offered another wink.

"I thought you all lived with her," Thomas said.

"Not for a few years now. We have families of our own, children of our own. There wouldn't be enough room at the brickworks. We work there but return to our own cottages at the end of the day."

"Does Bel live alone, then?"

"Ever since Pa died."

145

"Is the house not too big for her? And is it safe? It's set a way off from Lemster."

"Nobody would ever mess with Ma," said Edward. "They'd answer to us and half the town if they did, and everyone knows it. And the house is not so big. One room downstairs, two upstairs."

"And the one above the barn."

"You know about that, do you?" said James. "It's used to store hay now, as was always intended. We have another cartload of those small bricks ready for the masons if they want them."

"I will make sure they want them. I was hoping we might be able to move into the new house for the Christmas Feast, but it looks unlikely now."

"Two of the sides are finished, aren't they?" said Edward. "At least they looked finished to me the last time I visited."

"I suppose they are, yes. I hadn't considered moving in without it all being finished, but you are right, there would be room. No furniture, but space enough."

"We can find you furniture, Tom, and there is plenty in Ludlow if you have the funds. Your sister can help with that, I'm sure."

"There's no time now. It's only four days until the twenty-fifth. For the change of month, perhaps."

"No, we will come with you tomorrow and arrange it. We can bring the bricks and a few chairs. Ma will have surplus and we can get you moved in. I expect that son of yours can carry a bed all on his own."

"Yes, he probably can. Thank you, all of you."

Edward looked past Thomas as the door opened to let in a blast of chill air.

"Here comes trouble. Keep your back turned, Tom. Arthur Wodall's never slow to curse your name, even after all these years. I can't believe you and his father used to be friends."

"Not friends." Thomas wanted to turn and look at the man but did as Edward suggested. When he and Philippa had met Arthur Wodall at Thomas's old house on Eaton Hill, he did not know the man's name, nor did he spark any recognition.

"Hard to think your father and his were the same age," said Edward, uttering the same thought that had occurred to Thomas.

"I take it this Arthur is his son." Thomas found it difficult to believe because the man looked older than he did. "Does his father still live?"

"Died ten years back. Cursed your name every chance he got. Seemed he would never let it go."

"He believed I killed his son, so you can't blame him for that."

"Did you?" Edward raised a hand in apology. "Sorry, Tom, I should never have asked. Ma said you didn't, despite what others believed."

"They hold their hatred close in Lemster, don't they?" It did not surprise Thomas. His memories of that time told him the truth of it.

"Watch out, Tom, he's seen you."

Thomas turned, then rose. He half expected some kind of attack, but when he saw the man he knew that would never happen.

"What are you doing here, Berrington? You ain't welcome in Lemster."

"He's welcome at my table any time, Arthur." Edward rose to his feet, as did his brothers.

"I have a request to make of you," Thomas said. "For old friendship's sake."

Arthur Wodall scowled. "You were never a friend to the Wodalls. Enemies more like. Whatever it is, my answer is no."

"You haven't heard me out yet."

"Go on then, ask away so I can say no to your face."

"I want permission to move the bodies of my ancestors from behind the old house. They deserve to be buried on land I own, not there."

Arthur Wodall grinned, white spittle at the corners of his mouth. "Do I need to say the words?"

"You do, so others can witness them."

"I refuse you permission. That land is mine now and you will keep off it, or I'll see you in the next Quarter Session for trespass."

Thomas smiled. "That might prove interesting. Have you not heard who the new Justice of the Peace is?"

"Some arsehole, same as all the others I expect."

"You might be right," said Edward, "but this arsehole goes by the name of Thomas Berrington."

Thomas watched the emotions play across Arthur Wodall's face before the man reached a conclusion.

"It would still be trespass, no doubt about it." He poked a finger against Thomas's chest. "You stay off my land, hear me? Put one foot on it and there'll be consequences, Justice of the Peace or not. There are laws in this country, and land is a big part of them." Another poke and then Arthur Wodall turned away.

"You should have punched him," said Edward.

"It would have changed nothing, and you're right, he looks ten years older than me." The realisation made Thomas feel better. He had thought himself old, but looking at Arthur Wodall made him feel ten years younger. He was still healthy, still strong, despite not being strong enough to fight off the three men the night before.

Thomas realised he had barely thought of his near drowning for several hours, and wondered if he had faced danger so often it meant less to him than other men. He could have died, yes ... but had not.

"So what are you going to do, Tom?" asked Edward. "Stay with one of us, take your chance with Ma, or ride to Ludlow?"

"There was a good moon when I arrived. It will guide me the rest of the way home."

"I won't tell Ma you were drinking in The Star, then. She will only ask why you didn't visit, and I have no answer for that. No doubt you have your reasons. I only hope they are good ones."

Thomas went to the landlord and settled the bill for them all. When he returned to the table the others were pulling on coats and gathering their things.

Edmund said, "We can afford to pay our own way, you know. You do that all the time, and it makes some men feel beholden, and some of us don't welcome that."

"I'm sorry. I..." Thomas hesitated, as he wondered how far he could trust these three. He had already learned he could trust them, but could he with what he had been about to say — that he was likely the richest man in the area?

"Too late to apologise now. Remember it next time, Tom." Edmund slapped him on the shoulder. "No harm done."

"Is it too late to add something to the plans for the house?"

"For the finished parts, it is, but not the rest."

"Then we will talk tomorrow. You said you were coming to Burway?"

"I did. Tell me in the morning, then."

Outside, the moon Thomas expected to have risen higher had disappeared behind thick clouds that scudded in from the east. There was a smell in the air that augured snow and it surprised him that he still recognised it. A sharpness and softness mixed together. Snow within the hour, almost certainly.

Edward had smelled it too. "Changing your mind about the offer of a bed, Tom?"

"Maybe, yes."

"My place is closest. You will need your mount though if you want to visit Ma."

"I will come with you if your offer still stands. My horse is on the far side of the square. Let me get him and we can walk together."

Thomas found Ferrant standing with his head down as if asleep, but it came up quickly enough at the sound of his footsteps. Thomas wondered if the horse recognised them. When he reached for the reins, Ferrant reared away with a snort and Thomas pulled him back. A moment later, something heavy crashed into the back of his head and he went to his knees. His first thought, if thought he could call it beneath the ringing in his ears, was that his life had degenerated into an uncalled-for series of attacks on his person. Less than a day had passed since men tried to drown him in Hereford, and now someone was picking a fight in Lemster. Thomas wondered what great sins he had committed to deserve such.

A second blow came, this one aimed less well so it landed against his shoulder. Thomas rolled away. When he looked back he saw five men. Arthur Wodall stood at the fore, breathing hard, a stout length of wood in his hands. As Thomas came to his feet, Arthur attacked again. It was what Thomas expected, and he was ready for it this time. He deflected the blow with his forearm. He still took a hard knock, but not as bad as if the staff had cracked into his skull as Arthur clearly intended.

"Help me, lads, he's a sneaky bastard," said Arthur.

Two of the men came closer. The other two held back. Thomas suspected they already knew how the fight would play out. Or perhaps they were waiting to come in as reinforcements.

One man held a staff, longer than Arthur Wodall's — not as thick, but it could still cause damage. As he whipped it in a savage blow Thomas ducked, deflected the follow through and gripped the staff hard. With a jerk it was his. Thomas flicked it around and snapped it out at its previous owner, to catch him above the ear. The blow was meant to surprise him, not cause harm. The pain was enough to drive the man back. Thomas flicked the staff at another man who went backwards so fast, he stumbled and fell. Which left only Arthur Wodall and Thomas facing each other.

"This reminds me of a time I fought your brother, Raulf, many years ago."

"I heard about that on my father's knee. I also heard you cheated, just like you're doing now."

"Am I meant to lie down and take a kicking, or worse — is that the way of it?" Thomas flicked the staff at Arthur. He didn't intend to hit him, but the man took two paces back.

"You're not welcome in Lemster anymore, Berrington. You go away and then come back full of airs and graces. Living in Ludlow Castle. Justice of the Peace. You'll be the fucking sheriff before the new year."

"What is this all about, Arthur?" Thomas set the tip of the staff on the ground, using it to support himself so his adversary would not see how tired he was. Ferrant bumped against his back and he patted the horse's belly to settle it. "I don't want to fight you. I don't even want to think about you, but I have to take my family's bones, from behind my old house."

"You'll be waiting a long time before that happens. I intend to have the lease transferred to my sister, so that even after I'm dead it will be Wodall land."

"I didn't know you had another sister." Thomas had once been promised to Susan Wodall, until she believed he had killed her brother.

"It's not as if we're friends, is it?"

Thomas sighed and shook his head. "Go home, Arthur, just as I intend to."

Movement on the far side of the square caught his

attention, and for a moment he thought Arthur's companions had sent for reinforcement. As had happened when Thomas was thirteen years old and took his first bad beating. Instead, Edward, James and Michael started across.

"What's going on, Tom? We were waiting for you. Thought you might have ridden off to Ludlow without saying goodbye." Edward reached the group of men. He patted one on the shoulder, then stood next to Arthur Wodall.

"Nothing's going on. Arthur and I were having a conversation, is all." Thomas tossed the staff to its owner and mounted Ferrant. He bullied the horse through the group, forcing Arthur Wodall to step aside. Thomas half expected another blow, but the presence of Bel's sons had cowed the man.

"I thank you for the offer of a bed, Edward, but I will sleep better in my own. I will see you in the morning, yes?"

"We leave at first light. And you can show me these changes you want, eh?"

"I will."

Thomas raised a hand and encouraged Ferrant into a walk. He did not look back, even though he wanted to.

The first heavy flakes of snow started to fall as he left Lemster, but at least fresh snow would reflect what little light filtered through the cloud cover to help him find his way. Ferrant carried him without need of guidance, letting Thomas's mind work on how he could dig up the old graves in secret and move the bones to his land at Burway. The old Berrington house and land was Priory owned, so it was possible he could ask Prior Bernard if anything could be done.

The thought raised another, because moving the graves implied permanence. A home. A place where Thomas's bones might one day eventually lie, and he wasn't sure he was ready to accept the truth of that yet.

CHAPTER FOURTEEN

It was early when Will, Amal and Jorge accompanied Thomas through Linney Gate to descend towards the shallow plain bordering the Teme. Kin had joined them and ran ahead, not as young or swift as he used to be, but more than fast enough to catch his own dinner if a rabbit or hare was fool enough to show its ears. The long hair along the dog's strong back legs was almost entirely grey. It made him look as if he wore a short skirt. His long tail curled high, also tipped with white. Thomas had no idea how old Kin truly was, because he had inherited him from a youth who had died at the hands of an evil man that Thomas had in turn taken the life of. Now, Kin lived most of the time with Usaden, who had found himself a woman in Ludlow. But whenever Thomas called on them Kin was, as ever, ready to run with him. Occasionally, Thomas thought about finding another dog, but had not done so. Perhaps after the house was finished and they moved in would be the right time.

"So Philippa was in Hereford at the same time as you?" asked Will.

"She was."

"And she sent men to kill you? Jorge told you not to go on your own but you went anyway, telling no one."

"I told Jorge, and I'm still alive."

"Fool's luck," said Will. "I wanted to come after you, but Jorge told me not to. He said your stubborn streak is getting worse."

Amal walked on Thomas's other side, but knew better than to offer her own counsel.

"I have never known you to take Jorge's advice before," said Thomas to his son.

"He talks more sense than you these days, Pa. Do you know what happened to her?"

"Philippa? She was seen leaving the city on the road east. No doubt running back to her hideout in London. Except we know where it is, don't we, Ami?"

"I do. Can you remember the address, Pa?"

"No, but that's why I have you to do it for me."

Amal smiled and said nothing.

They reached the bottom of the slope and set off across the fields. The fast-flowing river ran to one side. The bulk of Ludlow Castle lay behind. It took only a quarter hour before they all heard the hammer of metal on stone and the house Thomas was having built appeared. It was perched on a knot of higher ground to protect it against the frequent winter floods, from which the surrounding low-lying meadows benefited. As they approached, a voice hailed them from behind. Thomas turned to see Edward and James walking beside a cart being pulled by two donkeys. Their mother Bel sat on the pile of bricks, her skirt pulled up to show her ankles. They looked, Thomas thought, as slim and fine as the last time he had seen them, many years before.

He stopped to wait for them, but Will and Amal walked back to embrace the men, and Bel leaned down for a kiss from each. Edward said something to Will, who turned to look at Thomas, shaking his head. Thomas knew what the conversation concerned. His failure to take care of himself. Again.

"I brought you a Yule log," said Bel, once they reached him. "It's along the side of these bricks. I'll get it once they are unloaded. Do you want the log here or up at the castle?"

"Here. I want to try moving into the finished part of the house for the Christmas Feast." Thomas looked in at the log, then reached across to lift out a brick. He turned it in his hand, examining it.

"Will it pass muster?" asked Edward.

Thomas nodded. "It's exactly what I want. They will do well. My thanks."

Edward grinned. "No, our thanks. You're paying enough for them."

Thomas offered his hands and Bel let him lift her down. She was as light as a feather. She walked beside him as they made their way to where a dozen masons worked on the third side of the house.

"Is this all your idea, Tom?" She looked around with curiosity.

"I stole most of it from the houses in Spain. From one in particular. A palace perched atop a red hill that in

Arabic they call *al-Hamra*. This is far more modest, but if someone who knew that palace saw my house they would know where the idea came from."

Bel took his hand. "Show me inside the parts that are finished."

Thomas glanced back to see Will helping to unload the cart. The masons continued working. Inside the almost completed wing, one man applied lime plaster to a wall. Another pointed gaps in the mortar of a stone chimney. A third hammered nails into a set of stair risers. To Thomas it looked unfinished, but he had been promised they could move in within three days. The roof was watertight. A well had been dug and doors would be hung at the last moment.

The room was large, spanning thirty feet from front to back. Each of the windows facing the courtyard had curved arches at the top. Narrow windows were set in the outer wall, designed as a defensive measure. Thomas recalled the masons cursing when he told them exactly what he wanted. Small Moorish bricks lined the arches. Others had been used in the wide hearth. Thick sandstone slabs made up the floor. They would be cold in winter if Thomas had not had stone pipes laid behind the fireplaces, to heat water that would run through them. The same arrangement would be used in the bathing chambers, both here and in each of the four wings when complete. It was a house like no other in England, and Thomas knew there might never be another. It was what he had wanted, and standing in the room he felt a tension leave him he had not until that moment been aware of. Only with its passing did he recognise he had carried it ever since leaving Granada more than half a year before. He had a place to call home once again.

"I like this room," said Bel. "Will you show me the rest?"

He did. Three other rooms on the ground floor, one a kitchen, the second an office for Amal, the third a bathhouse. A carpenter stood aside as Thomas led Bel up the almost completed stairs. Above lay four rooms and an enclosed privy with another bath installed.

"Which is your room, Tom?"

"I haven't picked one yet. I will take the second biggest, I expect. At least until the rest is finished and Jorge and Belia have their own place."

"Show me the biggest room," she said.

He went wrong the first time and had to come back out and follow the hallway to the room at the end. It, like the one below, ran the depth of the house but was less wide.

"You need furniture. A bed. Chairs. Tables and shelves." She laughed. "You need everything, Tom."

"Agnes is asking for me. She says she knows of a house where furniture is being sold and it will do until something can be made. I'm not much for comfort, so it will suit me fine."

Bel smiled. "And Jorge? He strikes me as a man much suited to comfort."

"He is, which is why this will be his and Belia's room at first. Then mine later."

Bel walked to a window, those on the upper floor larger, facing out and already glazed with thick panes.

They offered a view along the valley of the Teme, the bulk of Cefn Hirfynydd rising to the north.

"I heard you had some trouble in town last night." Bel continued to look through the window.

Thomas walked over to stand beside her. The top of her head did not even reach his shoulder, which had not been the case when he first knew her. She had been almost as tall as him then.

"I asked Arthur Wodall for permission to move the graves behind my old house. He refused."

"He would. Even after all these years the Wodalls still haven't forgiven you." Bel laughed and shook her head. "His father's friends are still in Lemster, still the same as ever. Symon Dawbney might be an important man now but he has not changed either. He's a bully, as he always has been."

"I heard he married Lizzie Martin. You two were close once. Are you still?"

"Symon won't allow us to be. He's turned her against me." Bel shrugged. "I have other friends now, including one who has returned from a long way off." Her hand found his and she turned to him. "Did you not like the gift I gave you, Tom?" She reached up and tapped his throat where the pewter cross should hang.

"I..." Thomas stared into her brown eyes. What he saw there was not anger but disappointment. He seemed to have a knack for disappointing people but wished he had not disappointed Bel. "I was attacked in Hereford. Men tried to drown me in the Wye. I must have cut through the leather thong when I was saving myself. Your gift lies at the bottom of the river, lost. I'm sorry, Bel. I am truly sorry."

She smiled. "I will make you another."

"You made it?"

Another smile. "Do you not think me capable?"

"You were always the most resourceful girl I ever knew. Of course I think you capable. But how?"

"It's easy enough. I could probably show you how if you wanted to learn. Sand, a mould, a fire of charcoal, which my sons have plenty of, and the metal cut into shards and melted."

"Yes, teach me and I will make one for you in return."

"As long as you don't think it makes us a couple. I have given up on men." Still her hand remained in his. Its small warmth was a comfort and, perhaps, a promise not present in her words. If he wanted it. Which he was not sure he did. Thomas knew he had hurt too many women over the years. He had hurt Bel when he left and failed to return. He could not do that to her again.

"I remember you told me that when we met again after all those years. As I have given up on women." Thomas was pleased to see her smile before she cut the expression short.

He stared at her pretty face and wondered if he should kiss her. He was about to when heavy footsteps sounded on the stairs.

"Pa, are you up here?"

Thomas released Bel's hand and went into the corridor. Will stood at the top of the stairs.

"What is it?"

"Prior Bernard sent a message. I expect he wants to see

you about some matter or other. Your time isn't your own anymore. Should I fetch horses, and perhaps Usaden?"

"What does this message say?"

"I don't know, Ami has it. Well, should I fetch horses and Usaden?"

"I'll go alone, but you can bring Ferrant if you would. I will be safe enough. No doubt it will be some legal matter or other he needs to discuss with me."

Once Will had gone, Bel came to stand beside Thomas.

"Can I ride with you, Tom?"

"Of course. I'll call down to Will and ask him to bring another horse."

Bel laughed. "I'm only small. I can ride behind you."

When Thomas went outside Amal held the note out to him. "I didn't read it, Pa."

"You could have, you know."

"It's addressed to you. Show it to me after, but you must be the first to read it."

Thomas broke the seal and unfolded the small sheet of paper. He recognised Prior Bernard's neat hand. The note was brief and said barely anything, but the words were enough to send a shock through him.

A man is dead. Come directly to the Priory and ask for me. Do not go into town. We must talk.

Thomas handed the note to Amal, who read it.

"Is this not a matter for someone other than you, Pa?"

"If Bernard sent for me he must think it my business."

Thomas returned to Bel, who was waiting patiently at the doorway of the house.

"There has been a death in Lemster. Bernard asked me

to go to him. You may be better off staying here with your boys and return with them."

"Do you not want me riding with you, Tom?"

"I do, but I'm thinking of your safety."

"Nobody in Lemster will do me harm. I want to ride with you. Is this matter urgent?"

"I assume it is. Why?"

"I was going to suggest we go by my house, but it will be quicker to ride direct to the Priory. I can walk from there."

Thomas turned at the sound of hooves and saw Will riding Ferrant. He must have run to the town to return so fast, but did not seem out of breath.

A sense of urgency filled Thomas. He had a mind to try again to persuade Bel to stay here, but knew it would take too long. He had no wish to make her think he was abandoning her. There had been a moment in the room upstairs when it felt as if some spark of what they had once shared might remain. If so, he felt a need to nurture it into a flame, if he could.

So long as that flame did not burn them both.

CHAPTER FIFTEEN

Approaching the walls of Lemster, Thomas saw a brown-robed figure turn away from the Ludlow gate and run towards the Priory.

"It looks as if the Prior wants to know as soon as you get here," said Bel. Her arms were around his waist, as they had been throughout the journey, her slight body a welcome pressure against his back.

As Ferrant neared the Priory gate Prior Bernard stepped out. He looked at Thomas, then Bel.

"You are both welcome, but you, Bel, might prefer not to see what I have to show Thomas."

"I will walk to Edward's house and see my grandchildren. Tom can find me there when he is finished." She leaned around to kiss his cheek, then slid from behind him.

Both men watched her walk away until she turned a corner and was lost from sight.

"She is a good woman," said Prior Bernard.

"She is. Now, where is this body? I assume that is what you want me to see?"

"It is, but I also need to talk to you."

They walked faster than was usual for the monks within the Priory, which told Thomas something of the urgency.

"Do you know who the dead man is?"

"I do. So will you as soon as you see him. Which is why I asked you to come directly to me. I expect Bel will have already heard the name by the time she reaches her son's house. Bad news spreads fast." Prior Bernard entered a wide corridor before turning into a small room.

When Thomas followed, he experienced a shock of recognition both at the surroundings and the man lying on the slab, covered to the neck in a sheet. Arthur Wodall.

"This the same room you brought Raulf Wodall all those years ago."

"Where else other than the infirmary would we bring a body? The room faces north, and even in summer it remains cool. In winter, the temperature rarely rises high enough to melt ice." Prior Bernard pointed to a shelf where blocks of ice were stacked. "Those are here so we can use them to keep food edible for longer in the kitchen."

Thomas turned his attention away from the ice. It was not the reason he was here, but they had given him an idea he could utilise in his own house. The ability to stop putrefaction would be useful, for himself, Belia and Amal.

"Do you want my opinion on how Wodall died?"

"You will see how he died if you uncover him. I recall how you studied the body of his brother all those years ago and now, having studied in Moorish infirmaries, I expect your observational skills will be even better." Prior Bernard stepped back.

Thomas pulled down the linen sheet covering Arthur Wodall's body to reveal a wound in his throat. He glanced at the Prior. "Where are his clothes?"

"Burned. They were covered in blood."

"Pity. They might have told us something."

"I examined them before they went on the flames. He had coin in his pocket, which will be handed to his sister, and a short knife at his belt, which was not drawn. Nothing else."

"If his knife was still sheathed he must have known his attacker and trusted them."

"Or someone caught him by surprise," said Prior Bernard.

"If I had approached he would have drawn his weapon."

Thomas leaned over the pale body of the man he had fought only the night before. The same man he had argued with in front of everyone in The Star tavern. He thought he knew what Bernard wanted to talk to him about. At least a constable had not been awaiting his arrival. Not that one or more might not yet come.

Instead of starting on the wound to the man's neck, Thomas began with the feet and worked his way upwards. He touched the cold thigh, the hip, the chest.

"These bruises were on him when he was brought here?"

"They were."

"I assume you heard he fought with me?"

"I did." Prior Bernard's expression showed nothing.

"The bruises on his shoulder and back I gave him, but there is a lump on the back of his skull I didn't put there. What time was he discovered?"

"A little after four this morning. He was found in the street by a baker woman who came out of her shop to cool down before taking the first bread from her oven. She came at once to the Priory."

"Why here?"

"Where else? Lemster has two constables, but both are old men and she knew I could do what was needed."

"Does his family know yet?"

Prior Bernard nodded. "I sent someone to tell his sister."

"He told me he had a sister, but Susan Wodall is dead. She died in London, according to Peter Gifforde. Or did he lie about that as well?"

"No, he did not. I refer to Alice Wodall. She was born a year after you left Lemster."

"Does she also hate my name?"

"Her father had little to do with her, so no, she doesn't. I don't suppose she even knows who you are, or what you were accused of. Like his son, Arthur Wodall did not respect women or believe them capable of carrying the hatred a man can. Alice is fortunate he believed the way he did. She is married and has a good life. If you met her you would know who she is because she looks like her older sister, who I believe you were once promised to."

"You know I was. Until Raulf died. That changed everything. Changed my entire life. But I ought to be

167

grateful for it because my life has been richer for leaving Lemster."

Prior Bernard smiled. "I expect it has. You were always too clever to stay here. If you had not been dragged off to war, then something else would have taken you away."

"Perhaps Alice will be more receptive to my request to move the graves from behind my old home."

"There is no need to ask her. The deed which Arthur took on the property and land reverts to the Priory on his death. Alice will not want it, and it is unlikely she would be assigned it even if she asked, which I do not expect her to do."

"Who will it go to, then? I hope someone who will grant my request."

"I can make it yours if you wish."

Thomas shook his head. "I already have land, but I would like to move my family from there."

"Then I will hold it for now, and you can ask me for permission, which I will grant. Only when you have moved the bones will I allocate the land to someone else. I expect either Croft or Cornwell will want it, if only to stop the other having it."

"Do they not already own more land than they need?"

Prior Bernard laughed. "You might have grown up, Tom, but sometimes you are still the innocent boy I knew. Men like them never have enough land, and Cornwell's property already comes to the boundary of what was once yours. I believe he wants everything east of the Lugge. He would take everything to the west of it as well if he could, but most of it is Croft's and he will give nothing up. I hear you ruled against Cornwell in the Quarter Session. How did he take that?"

"As you would expect." Thomas turned back to the body. "You must have sent for me around the time Arthur Wodall was brought here."

"I sent a brother, one who can ride a horse without falling off. It is surprising how many never acquired the skill. You need to know that half the town believes you killed Arthur. There were many who saw you fight him in the market square. Is that why you pointed out the bruises? Is that why you carry your own bruises?"

"We argued, but Arthur did most of his fighting with a length of wood. The bruises you see on my face came from an earlier altercation in Hereford."

Prior Bernard shook his head, but his expression was benign. "As I recall, you were always getting into trouble as a lad. It seems to me nothing much has changed. What happened? Not in Hereford, but between you and Arthur?"

"He came at me with his friends as I was preparing to leave town. I admit to putting two of the friends down, younger men, but I wouldn't hit an old man unless he was about to kill me."

"Arthur is fourteen years younger than you, Tom."

"Then he must have lived a far harder life, though how that is possible is a mystery to me."

"I know you have killed men," said Prior Bernard.

"You were a soldier. I never was, but yes, I have fought. And yes, I have killed men. But only when they tried to kill me. Or when..." Thomas sighed and pushed hair back from his face. "Or when they tried to hurt those I love."

He turned back to the body to examine the gash in its throat. It was clear the strike would have killed Arthur Wodall instantly, and there would have been a great deal of blood. He leaned closer and drew the wound open before looking up at the Prior.

"Do you see this the way I do?"

"That depends on the way you see it, Tom."

"The gash is shallow but done with skill. The main blood vessels are cut clean through. The blade must have been sharp, and whoever wielded it knew what they were doing."

"I agree."

"This isn't the same way John Miller died."

"Was that the lad killed in Ludlow? I heard about it, and that you are involved in tracking down the culprit, but it seems a stretch to believe both were killed by the same person. That is what you are suggesting isn't it, Tom?"

"I don't know."

"Arthur was not a likeable man, but he managed to live this long without anyone trying to kill him. Why now?"

"Because someone saw us fighting. Arthur wasn't killed because he angered someone. He was killed because his death makes it look as if I did it."

"You sound irrational now, Tom, and that is not like you. What makes you think the two deaths are related?"

Thomas sighed, pushed fingers back through his hair. "Perhaps I am making too much of it. I have a friend who tells me I do that too often. Even my daughter and son tell it to me these days."

"Then it is probably true. You were always hasty as a

lad, and it sounds as if the man has not changed so much. But suppose I humour you — tell me who you think killed both men and why."

"Philippa Gale."

"The woman you were involved with last year? Tall, dark haired, beautiful?"

"And evil."

"She would have to be to do this, but I did not sense that in her, though we met only briefly, I admit. Besides, I am a poor judge of a woman's mind. I expect you have some theory why she might be killing people. Other than you once disappointed her in love."

"She is doing it because I killed her father." When Prior Bernard's eyes widened, Thomas waved a hand as if it was a matter of little importance, which was not the truth. So he told the Prior the truth. About Galib Uziel, who was Philippa's father and head of the bonemen in London. How Thomas had fought him in an attic room of a house on London Bridge. How they had both fallen into the raging waters of the Thames.

"Except I survived and he did not," Thomas said. "And now his daughter seeks vengeance against me." He shook his head, scarce able to believe what he was saying. Laid out in plain words it sounded like the jabbering of a crazed man. Except he knew he was right.

Looking into Prior Bernard's calm eyes he saw that the man did not believe him. So be it. He did not need to be believed.

"I am finished here, Bernard, unless you tell me there is something I have missed."

"You missed nothing. Have you worked out when he died?"

"It would be ... you said he left The Star after midnight and was found at four? So between those hours."

"Any idiot can work that out," said Prior Bernard, "and you are not an idiot."

"It's cold in here, so rigor will take longer to set in." Thomas lifted one of Arthur's arms. When he released it, the limb fell only slowly back to the table. "And it was cold outside, too. So not long after he left the tavern. I would say very close to that time. Which would make sense. Did no one see or hear anything?"

"People saw you fight. I asked about nothing else, knowing what most in town think. I assumed you would ask the questions when you arrived, but you may need a chaperone. It will go better if I am with you."

"What did he do after I left town?"

"He returned to The Star and downed more ale than is good for a man. You can still smell it on him. After that—" Prior Bernard shrugged, "—somebody killed him."

Thomas nodded. "What time did he leave?"

"Past midnight, according to the goodwife. Plenty of time for you to leave your horse and creep back into town, people say."

"Why would I want to kill him?"

"Arthur was not a likeable man. There are plenty in Lemster who will be glad he is dead, but you and his family share a past he has never forgotten. It does a man no good to hold such a grudge all this time."

"That happened years ago. I bear him no ill will, for all

his family bears it me. I am not who I was back then, and he is not his father."

"But his father raised him with a hatred for the name Berrington," said Prior Bernard. "And there will be people in Lemster happy to believe you carry the same hatred for the Wodalls. Enough hatred to kill him."

CHAPTER SIXTEEN

As he walked through Lemster beside Prior Bernard, Thomas grew aware of people watching them and knew the words spoken to him were true. Not many expressions were welcoming, but Thomas believed nothing would happen as long as the Prior was with him. They crossed the market square and took a narrow alley heading south.

"Is this the way he would have taken to go home?" Thomas asked.

"His house lies north of town, so no, it is not."

"Why this way, then?"

"Short of being able to revive the dead we have nobody to ask. There is a woman who lives a short way from here who will pleasure a man for a groat, so he might have been going there. Rumour is he visited her often enough."

"Was he married?"

Prior Bernard shook his head. "Never has been."

"Isn't that unusual in these parts? Arthur Wodall

looked rough enough that I understand why nobody would want him, but he can't always have looked that way. His brother Raulf wasn't handsome, but good looking enough to get a wife if he had lived."

"I don't know why Arthur Wodall never married, Tom, only that he didn't. We are here. This is where he was found."

They approached the far end of the alley which led into a street only a little wider. A dirt track ran between houses built on both sides.

"This is the exact spot?" Thomas asked.

"That is what I was told."

Thomas looked around, relieved there was nobody in sight. He paced the ground, staring down at it. He kicked at the dirt, which was damp with snowmelt.

"He might have been found here but he wasn't killed here," he said. "There would have been a great deal of blood and it would have sprayed some distance. Short of someone digging up the soil and replacing it, there would be some sign if he died here. I would expect blood on some of the walls. There would have been blood on whoever killed him too, even if they stood behind him. He was found on his back, I take it?"

"On his front."

"Definitely not killed here, then." Thomas walked a little way back along the alley before going to one knee. The ground here was also dirt, a little drier than in the street. He reached out and ran a finger along a shallow ridge on the surface.

"What have you got, Tom?"

"It might be something else, but it might be where a

boot heel dragged across the ground." Thomas rose and walked on slowly. He pointed. "And here, and … yes, here as well. But still no blood." He thought of the body he had examined. "Did you notice soil on Arthur's heels?"

Prior Bernard shook his head. "I am sorry, Tom, I did not even look. In this weather everyone has mud on their boots."

"Arthur Wodall was not a light man. Too heavy for most men to carry, even over a shoulder." Thomas looked around before nodding. "At least two men brought him here. They held him, one under the arms, the other by his legs. But he was too heavy, and they had carried him some distance. The man holding his legs dropped them here, here and here, where the marks are. Why they chose this spot, I don't know. It might not even be where they intended to leave him. Perhaps someone disturbed them so they dumped him and ran."

"Which means I would have heard of it sooner than I did," said Prior Bernard.

"In that case, they probably grew tired of their burden and simply left him. This alley is quiet enough and would have been even quieter at that time of night. I wonder where they meant to take him? What lies at the end of the street the alley leads to?"

"One way leads turns back to the market square, with other roads going off west and north. One of them leads out past Bel Brickenden's house, but do not get any ideas she is involved."

"I would never do that."

"Are you and she together again now, Tom?"

"We are not. What lies to the south?"

"The street meets Castle Fields, where a track leads to the lime works. Beyond there, as you know, lies the road to Hereford. Does Bel not want you?"

"I haven't asked, but I'm not much of a catch these days. Do you think they might have been taking the body to the lime works? Drop it in the pit there and within a month or less the lime would have dissolved most of it, bones as well."

"Which would mean, if you are right, they intended it never to be found. Why would they do that? Kill a man then hide him?"

"To throw suspicion on someone else. Someone like me. I told you I was attacked in Hereford. I was informed my attackers left the city to the east, so I assumed they were riding to London with their mistress. But what if they turned back and only wanted people to think that was where they were going? I made no effort to hide myself when I spent the day in Hereford asking questions. If they returned, they would no doubt see me and know they had failed to kill me. If so, they might well have followed me to Lemster to finish the job. But then they saw me and Arthur fighting and realised they could throw suspicion for his death on me."

"Why would they bother?"

"If Arthur simply went missing then there is no time-frame for when he disappeared. It is easier to cast the blame on me than if he is found this morning, the day after we fought. If nobody knows the time of his death it makes it harder for me to prove I was elsewhere."

"You have a most convoluted mind, Tom," said Prior Bernard. "Why would they do that? It seems to me you are building a web with no substance. I have already told you, Arthur Wodall was not a popular man. What if someone took the opportunity of your argument to kill him, hoping everyone would believe it was you who did it? For your theory to hold water it would be better that Arthur was found at once, I would say."

"Did he have enemies?"

"He did, but whether the enmity was strong enough to want to kill him I don't know. It takes a certain kind of man to steal another's life, as you know. Not everyone is strong enough for it."

"Then I am no further forward." Thomas walked to the end of the alley and out into the street before turning right and hammering on the first door he came to.

"What are you doing?" Prior Bernard came to stand at his side.

"I want to question the people who live here. They may have heard something. Perhaps this is where his killers meant to leave him." Thomas hammered on the door again, but it seemed nobody was home. He moved to the next house, with the same result. He tried the doors on the other side of the alley, but whoever lived along the road was at work or refusing to open their door, even to the Prior.

In the distance a bell tolled.

"Is that the bell for Sext?" Thomas asked. "Shouldn't you be making your way back to the Priory?"

"It is and I should be, but I cannot leave you out here alone."

"I can take care of myself."

"I know you can, but what if you end up killing another man?"

Thomas stared at the Prior. "Do you believe I killed Arthur Wodall?"

"My apologies, Tom. It was a turn of phrase, nothing more. But you already confessed to me you have killed many men. That is what I meant."

"Where does Edward Brickenden live?"

"On the road west, a quarter mile beyond the town walls. Why?"

"Walk with me to the gate then you can return to your prayers. I will be safe enough to find the house on my own. Bel said she would be there and I want to talk with her before I ride north. I will ask her to come with me to fetch my horse, and take her home. I will be safe if she is with me."

"Probably safer than you are with me," said Prior Bernard. "And she is less likely to accuse you of any crime."

Thomas smiled. "I never thought you meant it, Bernard."

Thomas parted from Prior Bernard at the Welsh Gate. The road ahead ran straight for a mile. Cursneh Hill rose to a small peak to the north. West, the bulk of the Welsh mountains dwarfed it.

Cursneh Hill, where everything had started. Where Raulf Wodall had been murdered by Walter Gifforde. Except Thomas was the only person who knew that.

He passed a cottage on his right, but knew by its air of dilapidation it did not belong to Edward. A little farther on lay another cottage set a hundred paces from the road. The frontage was unusual, made of brick, unlike most of the houses in the district. A woman was hanging washing on the bushes lining the track to the door. Thomas assumed this was Edward's wife, aware he did not know her name. Aware also he did not know enough about Bel's children, their families, their own children. Thomas wondered if he wanted to know. Knowing implied a sense of permanence. Of place. Implied this may be where he would spend the rest of his days, and perhaps that might not be so bad. It was colder than Spain, did not have the sense of grandeur that land and its cities possessed, but it had been his home at one time and could be again.

The woman glanced up as Thomas approached.

"You must be Tom." She smiled, the expression transforming her. "Ma is inside with Ed. She is expecting you. I will come in once I finish hanging the washing."

"Let me help." Thomas took half the sheets, shirts, hoses and dresses from the basket sitting on the snow and began to lay them across the hedge. Being taller, he could reach places she could not.

Edward's wife said nothing, made no protest that he should not be doing women's work, and between them they finished the task in half the time.

"You have the advantage of me," Thomas said. "You know my name, but I don't know yours."

Again, she offered the smile. "I am Maggie." She gave a little curtsy. "It is a pleasure to meet you, Tom Berrington.

Do important men hang their own washing out in this far off place you come from?"

"They have been known to. And it dries far faster there than here. Spain is both hot and dry, at least where I lived in the south."

Maggie looked around. "Not like here, then."

"No, not like here."

Inside, Bel sat at a table with a girl of little more than two years on her lap. She was bouncing her up and down to make her laugh. Two other older children sat on low stools close to the fire where a pot hung on a hook. Edward stood next to it with a wooden spoon in his hand, as if he intended to stir it, but he handed it quickly enough to his wife.

"You have a fine house here," Thomas said.

He reached for the girl on Bel's knee and she allowed him to take her. Thomas held her up so he could look into her face, and the girl stared back at him with wide eyes and a stern expression that made him smile. "What is your name, little one?" He waited, as if expecting her to speak.

"The young'un is Joan," said Maggie. "Named after her great grandmother."

"I knew Bel's mother. She was a good woman. As this one will be one day." He rocked the child from side to side and she offered a sudden bright smile, just as beautiful as her mother's.

"The other girl is Mary, and our eldest is John. They have six and nine years, and Joan will have three come next March."

Thomas handed Joan to her father, who took her without hesitation, confirming what Thomas knew of

Edward Brickenden. He was a good man. He made a noise against Joan's belly, and she squirmed and squealed in laughter.

"We should talk outside," Edward said when he had finished. He passed his daughter to Maggie as Bel also rose.

"What have you found out so far?" asked Bel once they were outside. She wrapped her shawl more closely around herself, her icy breath pluming.

"You heard who was killed?"

"Arthur Wodall, yes. He won't be missed, even by those of his family who remain behind."

"Only his sister, I understand," Thomas said.

"And she is entirely different to her brother," said Edward. "Are you going to catch whoever killed him, Tom?"

"I don't know enough yet, but I will if I can. Was he really as disliked as you both say?"

"No," said Edward. "He was more disliked. I have never come across a man more spiteful or loathsome than Arthur Wodall. Was his father the same?"

"He was not. At least not until he believed I murdered his son. I was promised to his daughter, Susan, but that was called off, of course." Thomas glanced at Bel. "Have you told Edward what happened all those years ago?"

"Why would I? It's old history, and I never expected to see you again. Besides, it doesn't matter anymore. Like I said, old history. Old, old history." She smiled. "But I'm glad Susan Wodall broke things off with you, otherwise we would never have—" Bel glanced at her son, then shrugged, "—done what we did." Her hand came out and briefly squeezed his.

"Are there things I know nothing about?" asked Edward.

"There are many things you know nothing about, my sweet, but this is not one you need worry about. Now, Tom, shall I take you to someone who can help?"

"You can, whoever that is. What about you, Ed?"

"I need to get back to the brickworks. There is another pile of bricks for you that must be fired before nightfall so they can stand overnight. I want to push your masons so you can move into the house before Christmas Day — the Eve would be better." Edward slapped Thomas on the shoulder, kissed his mother's cheek, and went into the house.

"I like his family," Thomas said.

"So do I. Maggie has been good for him. Settled him down. All the boys were wild when they were younger, but have turned into fine young men. I am a fortunate woman." Bel smiled and reached for Thomas's hand again. "Even more fortunate now you have returned." She laughed at his expression. "Oh, don't worry, Tom, I have no designs on you other than friendship. We are both a little too old in the tooth for anything else."

"Are we?"

Bel stared up at his face, hers showing no expression. "We should go into town, then you can take me home on that big horse of yours before it gets dark."

"Bernard told me I would be safe in Lemster with you at my side."

"He's right. Nobody messes with Bel Brickenden."

They walked east to pass through Welsh Gate into the town. Bel led Thomas north along the inner town wall until they came to a wide street with fine houses rising to three stories. The windows on the top two floors would offer fine views west towards the Welsh mountains.

"Where are you taking me?"

"To someone who was once a friend of mine but who married a man who was once an enemy of yours."

"And this helps me how? Is this friend of yours who I think it is?"

"That depends on who you think it is, Tom."

"Lizzie Martin."

"She is Lizzie Dawbney now. It is one reason we drifted apart. Most of it was her doing. I was happy to remain close, but she had ambitions."

"I remember her as rather a meek girl," Thomas said. "I also recall the time when Symon and those other two lads tried to assault her. She fell into a bramble bush and you drove them away and rescued her. You have always been brave, Bel. It's one of the things I admire about you."

"That and my fine figure."

"Yes, that too. What will Lizzie have to tell us? Anything or nothing?"

"We will find out soon enough because her house is the one at the far end, set hard against the Kenwater. Symon has his office at the back. He practices law these days, and word is he is good at it and relatively honest. Not completely honest, of course, because he is a lawyer."

"Do they have children?"

Bel shook her head. "Not between them. Lizzie has a son from a previous marriage. He lives in Gloster. Has an important job according to Lizzie. She and Symon tried for more children when they married, but she lost them all. Half a dozen, so it was not meant to be. These days Symon takes his pleasures elsewhere, and I think Lizzie is grateful for it. Though she, like me, is past an age where getting with child is an issue. Unlike you men. You can seed a girl when you are one hundred. Come on, let's go and reintroduce you to her. I wonder if she will recognise you?"

"*You* did."

"But we were far closer, were we not?"

CHAPTER SEVENTEEN

Had Bel not told Thomas who they were visiting he would not have recognised the woman who rose to greet them when a butler showed them into a finely appointed room. Tall windows looked across a lawn which ran down to the fast-flowing Kenwater.

Lizzie Martin had not aged as well as Bel. She was painfully thin, as though she ate too little, and what she ate did her little good. Her clothes were of good quality but hung loose on her frame. Her hair, once a vibrant red, was now mostly white and thinning, though curled atop her head to disguise the fact. She came across and embraced Bel.

"It is too long since you visited, Bel. I miss our talks."

"As do I."

Once Bel had kissed her cheek Lizzie turned to Thomas. "And who is your tall frien…" Her voice trailed off as a frown drew her brows together. She glanced at Bel. "Is it him? It cannot be. Symon told me Tom had returned, but in my mind he is still the boy I knew all those years ago. It is you, is it not?" She took a step closer, then stopped. A gulf of time existed between them, one she seemed unable to cross. Thomas thought about how it had been when he first saw Bel after all the years spent apart. There had been no gulf between them; none at all.

"Hello, Lizzie. Bel tells me you might be able to help me."

"If I can. In what matter do you need help? Symon tells me you are a Justice of the Peace now." She shook her head at the strangeness of it. "If it is a matter of law, you will do better talking to him."

"It concerns Arthur Wodall. He was murdered last night, and I am investigating his death."

"Word is all over town, but surely it is the responsibility of the sheriff or coroner to look into it, not a mere Justice?"

"I was asked by Prior Bernard to investigate. He trusts me as an honest man who will deal with Wodall's death in the correct manner." His implication that sheriff and coroner might not deal honestly with matters was petty but matched the subtle dismissal Lizzie had made of his own position.

"You hear most news that circulates in town, Lizzie," said Bel. "Have threats been made against Arthur recently?"

"I expect you hear the same gossip I do."

"I come into Lemster less these days, so would welcome you telling us anything you know."

"We should sit, and I am a poor host not to offer you refreshment. Would you prefer ale or wine, Thomas?"

"Neither. I am here for information, not social pleasantries. What have you heard, Lizzie?" He wondered for a moment if she would prefer to be called Elizabeth these days.

Lizzie's eyes returned to Bel. "You know how it is. Arthur was not liked. He was mean-spirited as a boy and grew only meaner the older he got. I blame his father. He turned the lad's mind against Tom, even after we all thought him dead. I can think of nobody who liked him and nobody he liked either. Other than that whore on the Hereford Road, and she only liked his coin. Charged him more than anyone else is what I heard. Even then I doubt it was enough. The man never washed. He stank."

Thomas thought of the body he had seen lying on the slab in the Priory. Its skin had been recently washed, most likely by Prior Bernard or one of the brothers. He tried to recall when they had faced each other on the edge of the town square. Arthur Wodall's clothes were patched, but clean. He wondered if Lizzie's description was coloured by her hatred of the man. And if so, what had sparked that hate?

"His brother used to be sweet on you at one time," he said.

Lizzie waved a hand in dismissal. "Years ago, and I was never sweet on him in return. We were all of us little more than children. You were sweet on Bel, but you still went away and abandoned her. Everyone thought you dead, yet here you stand."

"Can you think of anyone who hated Arthur Wodall enough to kill him? To risk their own life to see him dead?"

"That would have to be some big hate, Tom, and my

answer is no. Not enough to risk their own life, for the gallows it would be if they were caught. Are you going to catch whoever did it?"

"If I can. I have done the same before and believe I am still good enough it to do it again. It is why King Henry made me Justice."

"The last Justice was not good at his job. Symon told me he had never met such an inept individual. Was it you who killed Hugh Clement?"

Thomas shook his head. "Someone else did that. I would have had him live to stand trial before a jury of good men and then hanged." Thomas thought of Philippa Gale, who had not killed Hugh Clement with her own hands but had sent someone else do it. He more than half-believed she might be behind the death of Arthur Wodall too, but could find no reason for it. Unless his musings to Prior Bernard were closer to the truth than he thought. He had made no effort to conceal himself in Hereford. Had Philippa heard he still lived and followed him north?

What he could not understand was why, if he was right, she had not tried a direct attack on him. Not personally, but it was clear she had men willing to kill at her command. Were they a rump of bonemen happy to serve her?

Thomas knew he might have forgotten about Philippa in time, but it seemed she had not forgotten about him. She blamed him for all the ills that had befallen her and wanted retribution. He understood why she killed John Miller, because the lad could link the hand bones with her. Miller would not have known their significance, but he was a witness who had to be removed. Arthur Wodall had been almost an accident, too good an opportunity not to take. Which showed Philippa was willing to do anything, kill anyone, to get to Thomas. The bones had been an invitation to seek her out. And when he did, in Hereford, she was ready for him. Philippa wanted him dead.

The thought made him realise he needed to ride to Ludlow to warn his family. He would not put it past Philippa to take her anger out on them as well as him. She had done it once before when she fired a flintlock at Amal, resulting in the loss of her own hand. Next time, she might not be so unfortunate.

"I thank you for your time, Lizzie." Thomas glanced at Bel. "I will take you home, then I need to ride north."

Bel hugged Lizzie, but the embrace was barely returned.

As they started for the door it opened and a tall man running to fat entered. At first Thomas failed to recognise him, then the shadow of the boy he used to be showed in his features, also in the way he walked — almost a strut, as though the world had best watch out for Symon Dawbney.

He glanced at Bel, nodded, then switched his attention to his wife. "Who is this man, Lizzie? What business has he here?" There was thinly disguised anger beneath his words.

"Do you not recognise me, Symon?"

The man looked at him and shook his head. "Should I?"

"Perhaps not, but I recognise you, even after all the years that have passed since we fought each other."

The man's expression changed. Colour rose in his cheeks and his fists clenched, as if he was expecting to be attacked.

"Tom Berrington? Everyone thought you dead."

"I hear you are a skilled lawyer, and a skilled lawyer practicing his business in Lemster must have heard of my return. Lizzie told me you know I am the Justice of the Peace now."

"I take no heed of gossip. What are you doing here troubling my wife?" He turned his veiled anger on Bel. "Why did you bring him here? He has no business with us."

"I take it you heard what happened to Arthur Wodall?" Thomas asked.

"Assaulted. Killed. By you, according to most accounts."

"I argued with him last night in The Star, and afterwards. I admit to that, but I was back in Ludlow by the time he was attacked."

"Which is what you would say."

"I intend to uncover who killed him and bring them to justice. I was hoping as a respected man in the town I might receive your help, but I see I am mistaken. Good day, lawyer." Thomas took Bel's arm and brushed past Symon on the way out. He could see the man wanted to step aside but pride prevented him from doing so.

Outside, Bel kept her arm linked through his as they walked to the Priory to retrieve Ferrant. A brother had fed and groomed him, so Thomas left some coin in the poor box beside the gate. He mounted Ferrant, then offered a hand to Bel and pulled her up behind him. She wrapped her arms around his waist and leaned her head close to his as he turned Ferrant to the west and urged him into a walk.

"Symon knew full well who you were, Tom. He knows of your return and your elevation. I expect he is put out because you came back after all these years and, by some miracle, became an important man in the district. He has tried to do the same, but it is not in his nature to be liked."

"Another unlikeable man."

Bel laughed. "Oh, Lemster has more than a few of those. Unlikeable women, too."

"Lizzie looked unwell — or afraid."

"Afraid, I think. Symon is difficult to live with, though she tells me he is less demanding than once he was. He is a brutal man, always has been, and has not softened since you knew him. I would visit with Lizzie more often, would ask her to visit me at home where we could talk without being overheard, but he has made her turn her back on our friendship."

"I find it difficult to fathom why she would marry a man like Symon. She must have known what he was like. What happened to Osmund Gifforde? He and Lizzie were close before I left Lemster."

"His father broke them apart. He considered Lizzie's family beneath his and wanted to forge a better connection."

"Did that work out?"

"Osmund married a girl from away. Hereford, I think, but she died giving birth to their first child. A girl that was sent back to her family. Osmund defied his father and

192

came back to Lizzie pleading for forgiveness, but she was already promised to Symon by then."

Thomas considered the small tale, its sorrow and lessons of the world. He glanced to the left as they passed Edmund's house. The washing had been taken in, the scene peaceful. Ahead, a band of blue sky promised a return to better weather, but also of cold. It felt good to have Bel pressed against him, her warmth passing to him. They had grown close again, and he wondered if she felt the same as he did, that there might be unfinished business between them.

At her house, she slid down from behind him and stood looking up.

"You don't have to leave yet, Tom. Come inside and I will make us something to eat. You can stay the night if you want."

"I would like that, but something came to me when we were in Lizzie's house. I believe the death of Arthur Wodall is connected to an earlier death in Ludlow. That of a John Miller."

"I know the Millers," said Bel. "An excellent family. Tell them I am sorry about their son. Do you think the same person killed them both?"

"I believe it likely, and that person was once close to me until I realised what she was. Pure evil. This is all about me and her, Bel."

"Do you speak of the tall, dark-haired beauty you once had a relationship with?"

"I should never have been seduced by her, but I was. I'm sorry, Bel."

"For what? I am neither tall nor dark haired, and no beauty anymore."

"To my eyes you are."

Bel suppressed a smile and waved a hand at him. "You could always sweet talk me, yet you refuse to eat with me or stay under my roof."

"Come with me to Ludlow, then." The idea came to Thomas all at once. "There is room in our accommodation in the castle, and tomorrow or the day after I will find a space for you in the new house your sons have helped to build."

"It's too late, Tom. For both of us, perhaps. Take care on the road, and I may see you at Christmas. Edward tells me he might visit, and if he does I will ride with him."

Thomas turned Ferrant and rode north, following a track he knew would take him to the better road without having to return to Lemster. When, on the brow of a low rise he turned back, there was no sign of Bel. As he rode his mind stilled. By the time he approached Ludlow he knew the death of Arthur Wodall was a distraction. He needed to go back to the fate of John Miller. That was where everything had started.

CHAPTER EIGHTEEN

Thomas woke late, and only then because Will came into his room with a bowl of hot, spiced pottage. He set it on the table beside Thomas's pallet and sat on the corner of it, the bed creaking in protest.

"I thought I had best wake you before the day is all gone. Amal said you told her you wanted to go back to investigating the death of John Miller. I agree it's a good idea. You have been distracted these last few days."

Thomas wondered when the balance of the relationship between himself and his two children had changed. When had he become the child and they the adults? He reached for the bowl of pottage and spooned some into his mouth. It was excellent.

"Did Belia make this?"

Will shook his head. "Amal, but it's Belia's recipe. She asked if there was room in your new workshop at Burway for her to use part of it."

"I have instructed the masons to build a separate

workshop for her and Amal. They are building a reputation and need their own space."

"They are. As are you." Will smiled. "Agnes told me there is much talk about the honest Justice of the Peace."

"I expect there is, but I have been neglecting my duties of late."

"With good reason. Besides, Amal and I have been taking care of the day-to-day work. She keeps a record of payments made or contracts exchanged after the Quarter Session. I stand beside her when they call and look mean if people claim they can't meet their obligations."

"Does that work, or do you have to hit anyone?"

"It has worked so far, but I have a reputation most of them fear. Agnes also told me to remind you who your sister is. She has not seen you in a while."

"I admit to having neglected her. I will go see her today once I have spoken with everyone. How are her daughters? Well?"

"They are, and I have told them to stop swooning over me, that there can be nothing between us." Will's expression of attempted innocence failed. "I have my sight set on someone else. Or rather, she has her sight set on me, and she is a pleasant enough companion, for the moment."

"Someone I know?"

"Grace Miller."

Thomas put his bowl down and swung his feet to the floor. "Is that wise while we are investigating the death of her brother?"

"I'm not stupid, Pa. We don't talk about that."

Thomas found a shirt and hose and pulled them on. He knew he should wash, but bathing could wait until later. The thought made him wonder if he was turning into a real Englishman, who did not need to wash more than once a year.

"What do you talk about, then?"

"Ludlow. This area. Wales. She has family beyond the border, as well as in the counties of Worcester and Hereford. They are Millers too. Next time you decide to go seeking information on Philippa Gale, take me with you. I don't want to see you end up in a river for a third time."

Thomas smiled and retrieved his boots from beneath the bed.

Downstairs, he sent messages to Jorge and Amal to join them.

"What about Usaden?" asked Will, as he took a seat at the big table.

"There is no need for fighting yet, perhaps not for some time. Let him enjoy his new domesticity."

Will shook his head. "I still find it hard to believe Usaden has a woman and lives apart from us, but I agree he is a changed man."

Amal entered the room and sat opposite Will. She drew some journals towards her and opened them, her finger running over the figures entered there.

"What is this woman of Usaden's like?" Thomas asked Will. "Have I ever met her?"

"She is a local girl, so you may have. Her name is Emma. She is young and pretty and good for Usaden."

"How young?"

Will laughed. "Don't worry, Pa, she is old enough. She has seventeen years."

"Not so young, then. How did they meet?"

"According to Usaden, he was drinking in one of the local taverns, of which there is a surfeit, as you know. She was a pot girl, and some rogue tried to drag her into an alley as she went to fetch more ale. Usaden was passing."

"And the man who assaulted her?"

"Usaden let him live, but only after Emma pleaded with him. Had she not, the man would be buried somewhere in the woods. He walked her back inside and within a week they were living together."

"Is Usaden not too old for her?"

"Do you even know how many years he has, Pa?"

Thomas smiled. "Does Usaden know himself?"

"He has thirty-one years," said Amal. "I asked him once, many years ago, and he said he could not be sure, but told me thirty is close enough."

Thomas frowned. "Which would have made him what age when he walked off the galley in Malaga during the siege?" He started to work it out, but again Amal was the quickest.

"He had sixteen years when he came to Malaga. It is easy for me to calculate because that was when I was born."

"It was." A sharp moment of loss passed through Thomas as he thought of his daughter's birth. A birth he could not bear to assist with because to do so would end the life of her mother, Lubna. Even though she was dying anyway. It had been Belia who had brought Amal into the world, while Thomas took retribution on those who had killed his wife.

Amal reached out and covered his hand with hers. "I never knew her, Pa, but she lives within me." She touched her chest with her other hand. "You tell me so all the time."

"Then I must stop. You are yourself. Your own woman. Did you know about Will's sweetheart?"

Amal smiled. "Not sweetheart, but perhaps a little more than a friend."

"Is there anyone for you?" Thomas asked.

"Not yet, but one day there will be. I want children of my own. Lots of them."

Thomas laughed. "Perhaps I should tell the masons to make our house even bigger."

"I expect when I find a man we will want a house of our own. The same for Will. There is no need to build a palace, or even a manor house. What is there will be big enough until then."

Thomas stared at his daughter, seeing her mother, seeing Amal as her own woman with her own desires, wants and needs. He had always known this time would come, but he did not want it to come yet. When it did, he would offer his blessing with good grace.

Amal raised her hand to wipe a tear from Thomas's cheek, then one from her own. "Not yet, Pa. Perhaps not for years." She smiled. "By then, you might have got used to the idea. Now, where is Jorge?"

"I am here, my sweet." Jorge entered at the side of Belia. "What is this all about, Thomas, and is there anything to eat or drink? Ale will do. I never thought I would say these words, but I am getting a taste for it."

"Sit down and I will find something for you, but you need to stop eating so much." Belia patted Jorge's belly, which Thomas noticed was a little rounder than it had been. His friend had been plump when he was a eunuch in the palace of Alhambra, but their friendship, and what it entailed, had slimmed him. Everyone, it seemed, was settling into life in Ludlow.

Thomas took a deep breath and tried to gather his thoughts.

"First, I need to apologise to you all."

"Accepted," said Jorge. "Even if it is long overdue. Dragging us all the way to—"

"Not for that," Thomas said. "For being a fool these last few days. For riding off to Hereford without you or Will and almost getting myself killed. I was obsessed with the idea of Philippa Gale being behind everything and chased after her."

"I don't think you are a fool," said Amal. "I think you are right."

Will offered a nod of agreement. "So do I. Grace has spoken to me some more about her brother. I think she was the only one in their family John felt he could talk to. Grace doesn't judge."

"Then you are fortunate in your choice," said Jorge, who accepted a plate of bread and hard cheese from Belia.

"She told me about a woman who professed love for John, and from the description it could be none other than Philippa. John was pleased to talk about her and no doubt revealed more than he intended, but Grace is like that. She draws things out from people."

"Did she know when Pip first approached him?" Thomas asked Will.

"While he worked for Sir Thomas Cornwell. I expect she recognised John's weakness and took advantage of it.

She needed someone who had access to you, and he was ripe for the plucking."

"But John wasn't working at the castle then."

"He wasn't, but Philippa no doubt still has friends there. Arthur, for one, but there will be others among the servants. She would have had enough influence to find him a position. A lowly one, but he would only need it long enough to leave her gift for you."

"Do you think leaving the hand was his one and only task? Was she always going to kill him once it was done?" Thomas looked at each of them, but it was clear they had no answer to the question, just as he had none. "I still can't see the significance of the bones," he said, "other than the obvious one that it was a message from her. A message to let me know she is still close. Still watching me."

"It was a first approach, that is all, but she showed her hand too soon." Will laughed when he realised what he had said. "I didn't mean it that way, Pa."

Thomas smiled, as did the others. "She would have asked him to provide her with information, hoping perhaps something might reach her she could use. But if that was the case, why kill John Miller so soon?"

"The bones were left because she knew you would recognise their significance," said Jorge. "They were not only to tell you she was close but that she had not forgotten what you did. Killed the man she loved. Killed her father. I think you're right that leaving the bones was all she wanted John Miller to do. Once he had done that his purpose was at an end, but he knew too much for her to let him live."

"So why not kill me instead of leaving some stupid bones? The lad could have used poison. It's not as if I have been hiding myself away."

"She wants you to know who sent them because she expects you to be afraid of what they mean. Yes, she wants to kill you, but she wants you to know that she does. She wants to inflict fear on you first."

"Then she learned little of my nature when we shared a bed."

"I'm not so sure you're right," said Jorge. "Perhaps she knows you too well. Knows you can't turn away from a threat. Knows you will hunt her down, as you did. And when you found her she set a trap. Any other man would lie dead on the bed of the Wye feeding the fish."

"But not you," said Will.

"No. Not me. Perhaps the next time."

"I will be at your side the next time. I think between us we can take care of one woman, even if it is Philippa Gale."

"I keep thinking of her out there somewhere, plotting against me. Watching me. I feared as I rode from Lemster last night that she might try hurting one of you. I want you all to take care. To keep your wits about you."

"We always do, Pa," said Will. "There are enough bad people in the world without her, but I admit she is one of the worst. Tell us what you found out yesterday. Tell us about this recent death. Is it connected to her?"

"I don't know. I want to think it is, but there is nothing to link her to Arthur Wodall other than one brief encounter she had with him when we rode together to look at my old house. He was there that day, though I didn't know then who he was. I might have recognised his father, but not him. He hadn't been born when I left Lemster. I can see no reason for Philippa to kill him."

"Except you argued with him on your return from Hereford. You told us you fought in the market square and there were witnesses."

"Half of Lemster — no, most likely all of Lemster — believes I went back and killed Wodall. But I didn't."

"There is no need to tell us you didn't, Pa," said Amal.

"I expect not. What I found out is whoever killed him must have been more than one person. He was carried to where he was found, but killed elsewhere. I know not where, but there would have been a great deal of blood, and there was none where he lay. If someone saw the blood they would know what it meant and report it to the Priory. I suspect he was killed outside the town walls, close to one of the rivers, which would have carried the evidence away."

"Rivers seem to be a common thread," said Will.

"A coincidence, I suspect, and a convenient one."

"So, what do you intend to do next? I can talk to Grace again. Better I do it rather than you. She will answer more openly to me."

"I intend to go back to the start. To John Miller, so yes, the more you can find out about him the better. We won't know what is significant until we have everything. Will she tell you everything?"

"She will tell me what she knows. Whether that is everything is another matter. What will you be doing, Pa?"

"I have a mind to visit Burford again tomorrow. John

Miller worked there, and it is where Philippa seduced him to her ends. The thread begins there. It makes sense to tease it out more. The steward there seemed a reasonable man, even if his master is not."

"Perhaps not so reasonable. Sir Thomas Cornwell sent James Marshall here again, demanding you change your ruling," said Amal. "He threatened you with all manner of dire consequences if you did not."

"I suspect that was the message he was told to give. Did he threaten you?"

Amal smiled. "You know I would take no notice if he did, but no. Sometimes being a young woman has benefits. It civilises some men while it makes animals of others."

Thomas knew she referred to the attack on her by the last Justice of the Peace, Hugh Clement. Fortunately, there were few lasting effects of her violation, either physical or mental.

"I should ask for an audience with Sir Thomas Cornwell and see what he says to my face."

"I doubt he will see you," said Amal. "I doubt he will see any of us. He prefers to do his bullying at second hand. Take me with you this time, Pa. You know I'm sharp enough to tease out things you might miss."

Thomas started to object, then brought himself up short. Amal was right. She was clever, and he knew there were things he had missed.

"If you come, I want you to talk to the kitchen staff and others. The staff of a big house see much and speak little. They will not tell me of what they have seen, but they might to you." Thomas turned to Jorge. "You will come with me again?"

"As long as you promise not to abandon me like the last time. I feared I might never find my way home, but my horse knew the way and I let it have its head."

"Amal could get you safe home, but no, I will not abandon you."

Thomas hoped he could keep his promise, but did not expect any trouble.

CHAPTER NINETEEN

Thomas spent the late morning and early afternoon making amends for his dereliction of duty. He visited Agnes and her daughters, spending more time than he should in conversation. He learned little, but the normalcy of the encounter soothed his mind. Then he took fresh rolls and a pie with him to the house Usaden now lived in. When he knocked on the door he was almost bowled over by Kin, who twined around his legs, his tail drawing circles in the air.

"He still remembers who you are then," said Usaden. He spoke heavily accented English rather than the Arabic they had once exclusively conversed in. His grasp of the new language had improved a great deal. No doubt his new female companion had something to do with that.

"I brought you a small gift in apology." Thomas held out the hessian sack.

When Usaden took it and peered inside he almost smiled. Thomas dropped his hand to scratch behind Kin's ears. He missed the dog, but knew he was now more loyal to Usaden than to him. It made him think again if he should get a hound of his own. They made good guards, and Kin could fight as well as any man.

"Come in," said Usaden, "and I will introduce you to my friend. Her name is Emma. You missed her last time you called for Kin."

"Will told me you are turning into a contented man."

"I am not sure I want to do that. He visits most days and we talk of old battles and our hope for more in the future."

"Does Emma have anything to say about that?"

"She seems to have much to say on all manner of subjects." This time Usaden's smile reached the surface.

Thomas followed him inside and through to the kitchen at the rear of the house. It was small but more than adequate for the two of them, even if Kin took up a quarter of the floor when he threw himself down in front of the fire.

A short girl rose to greet Thomas. She had deep-red hair and pale skin, but he saw the paleness was natural and owed nothing to illness. Her figure was slight, giving evidence to her youth. Seventeen years, Amal had said, but many women were married and mothers at a much younger age. Her prettiness was marred by a scar that ran down the right side of her face and caused her smile of welcome to lift more on one side than the other.

Thomas held his hand out, but she slid past it and kissed his cheek.

"Excuse my familiarity, but Usaden has told me so much about you I feel you are already a friend."

"Don't apologise. I hope we can become friends. Good friends, like Usaden and I are."

She smiled. "You are more than that to him. Sit, I will bring ale and we can eat these sweet treats you have brought. They are from your sister's shop, no doubt."

"They are." As he sat, Thomas knew he should have questioned Agnes about Emma. No doubt she would know the girl and her family. He wondered how she had acquired the scar but felt it was not his business to ask.

"Have you come to take me away on some new quest?" asked Usaden.

"Not today. I'm sorry to disappoint you. Perhaps soon."

"I doubt there will be another attack on Ludlow. That was interesting, was it not?"

Thomas did not think interesting was the right word, but then he was not someone raised from birth to fight, as Usaden had been.

"If you say so. I might have a task for you, though. Do you see much of Jack Pook these days?"

"I do. We go after birds and rabbits in the woods. He is the better stalker, but I am a better archer. He stays with us often. I like him."

"So do I. Next time you see him, ask what he knows about a man called Arthur Wodall. He was killed in Lemster and I would know who by, and why."

"I will ask. If there is anything to know then Jack will know it. He tells me you have seen a little more of his sister Bel of late."

"A little, yes. We are old friends."

"He told me that as well. Good friends, he said."

"Yes."

Thomas was saved from more explanation when Emma returned with two flagons of fresh ale. Usaden drained half his in a swallow. Thomas had meant to stay only a short time, but two hours passed before he left their small, comfortable home.

He was almost back at the castle when Will appeared.

"Ah, good, you are back. Amal received a message from someone who heard you were looking for furniture for the new house. They have a fine set of beds, tables and chairs from a place near Stretton and want to know if we can collect them today, otherwise they have another buyer who will take it all."

"Is the house ready?"

"Enough to be furnished. I went there earlier while you were still in bed. The masons are starting on the third wing, but waiting for more bricks."

"Edmund said he would bring them today. He might have already done so. Where is this man with the furniture?"

"Ami knows. She can take you there. We will need carts and horses to pull them. I can arrange that."

It took over an hour, by which time the short December day was fading. With dark approaching, Thomas paid the dealer and between them they loaded the carts with the first half of the furniture — which comprised of tables, chairs and beds. Thomas hoped he might sleep beneath his own roof that night, so sent Amal off with Belia to see if they could purchase bedding. There were, he realised as they started off, a great deal of sundry items needed when setting up a home.

They descended the steep, curving road to Dinham

Gate. Usually, they took the Linney Gate but it was too narrow for the carts to pass through. Once at the foot of the slope they headed north along a narrow track above the river. By the time they approached the house the light was fading fast, and the masons greeted them as they returned from work, having to stand aside for the carts to pass.

At the house, Thomas lit what candles and lamps he could find, then took a moment to gaze at the pile of furniture stacked on the carts.

"Where do we start?" he said, half to himself, but Will answered anyway.

"With the first one, piece by piece, until we have everything off and in the house."

Thomas glanced at the sky. It was clear, with sharp stars starting to show, the brightest of all hovering above Dinham Wood.

"That will mean moving everything twice, because I suspect only Amal and Belia know where half of this should go. Take it off the carts, yes, but set it on the ground between the three sides of the building. It doesn't look like rain tonight, but when the others arrive we should start moving what we need. We can set torches outside so we can see what we are doing."

Will nodded his agreement, then lifted down a wide bed without help. Thomas went to the second cart, Jorge to the third, where Usaden helped him unload the contents. By the time Amal and Belia arrived with another cart stacked with linens, cottons and wools, three children perched atop it all, half the carts were empty and torches burned from sconces in the courtyard walls.

"Where do you want to start?" Thomas asked Belia.

"The bedrooms," she said without hesitation. "Are both these wings of the house complete now?" She nodded to the two closest, which had slate roofs finished only the day before.

"They are. At least enough to put furniture in."

"Then if we have enough beds we should put them in there. Leave the ground floor until we have done that, then we will not have to work our way around the rest of the furniture. Once the upper rooms are done I want the kitchen set up. I will light a fire and see if there is anything to make a meal with."

Thomas passed the instructions on and the men started to haul the heavy bed frames up the stairs. Will's strength made the difference, but Jorge was also more useful than Thomas expected. Perhaps his recently gained bulk had as much to do with muscle rather than fat.

It was full dark and cold before they finished. By then, four bedrooms were furnished and Amal directed Will and Jorge towards what was needed for the kitchen. Satisfied they understood, she asked Thomas to help her carry the bedding upstairs so she could ensure everyone had somewhere to sleep. By the time three beds were made up to Amal's satisfaction, smells of cooking rose to greet them as they descended the staircase. The house was still as cold as the ice room in Lemster Priory, but it felt more like a home.

Thomas slept that night beneath a pile of five blankets but woke shivering to the sound of metal on stone. He rose and looked through the newly glazed window to where the masons chipped away at large slabs of slate to fashion smaller tiles. Ladders were set against the fourth side of the building and the finished slates were being tossed up to a lad standing between bare rafters.

Thomas dressed and went outside to discover Will interrogating the foreman about some matter.

"Have you seen Amal?" Thomas asked. "I need to know which of the contracts have been completed from the Quarter Session."

"She went off with some lad."

"Romance?"

"I doubt it. When you find them you will see what I mean. I have been trying to find out if your workshop is finished, but I don't think the masons understand what the building is for. You might have to supervise if you want them to get it right."

"Once I've spoken with Amal. Which direction did she go in?"

"Over there." Will pointed to the unfinished fourth side of the building.

Thomas crossed the muddy central area. One day it would be tiled and a rill would run through it, but today the ground sucked at his boots and made them heavy.

"Ami!" He called out as he entered the building. Inside, the noise of the masons was subdued. Bare walls only half built rose to mark where rooms would stand. The joists to support the upper floor were laid but had no floorboards yet. Similarly, the staircase was also built but lacked a banister and one in four treads.

"Up here, Pa."

Thomas looked up to where Amal stood with her feet planted on separate beams. He hoped she would be careful. He could not see the lad Will had spoken of, so climbed the stairs and picked his own way across the beams. Only then did he see why Will had said romance was unlikely. The lad was barely sixteen, dark haired and pale faced, with a squint that twitched his eye every few moments. He held a mallet in one hand and had a hemp sac around his neck holding nails. A stack of floorboards leaned against the far wall.

"What are you doing here?" Thomas asked Amal.

"Not what am I doing. What is he doing?"

Thomas frowned. "I don't understand. He's laying floorboards. Why are you here with him?"

"Because of this." Amal held out her hand, which was curled into a fist. When she opened it Thomas saw a hank of hair.

Amal moved her hand to indicate he should take it. When he did, he found the hair was extremely fine. He raised it to his nose and sniffed.

"This isn't your hair."

"No. But who else do you know who has hair as dark and fine as mine?"

"Pip."

Amal said nothing. Thomas looked at the lad, who stared at him with open fear on his face.

"'Twas not me, sir. It was forced on me."

"What was forced on you?" Thomas went to take a step closer and almost fell between two of the rafters. "Let's take this downstairs where we will all be safer." He turned and made for the stairs. Half way there, Amal called out.

"Pa, help me!"

Thomas turned to see the youth moving backwards,

213

away from Amal, his mallet raised to stop her following. His agile feet trod a single rafter. When he reached the space where a window would be fitted he turned and climbed out. A moment later, he leapt to the ground.

By the time Thomas reached the window Amal was already looking down and the lad was limping away. Thomas thought he was lucky he hadn't broken a leg or cracked his skull.

"What's going on, Ami?" Even as he spoke, he saw Will run across the ground and bring the lad down.

"Witchcraft," Amal said. "I come down here most days to check on the work and each time I do this boy acts suspiciously. At first I thought it was because I'm a girl and I know how men look at me, but there is more than that. So this morning I followed him up here and found that hair." She leaned out and shouted down to Will. "Have you got him?"

"Of course I have. What do you want done with him?"

"Keep him safe somewhere," Thomas said. "We need to talk to him."

Will grabbed the youth by the scruff of the neck and dragged him off to the finished wing of the building.

Thomas secured his hand around Amal's wrist and they stepped back the way they had come. She tugged him away from the head of the stairs to where a chimney breast was half-constructed.

"You need to see this as well." She knelt and pointed into the deep opening where a fire would one day burn.

Thomas went to his knees and peered in. Had the chimney been finished he would have needed a lamp, but light spilled in through the half-completed roof.

"What am I meant to be looking at?"

"There." Amal climbed in beside him and pointed to a place that looked only a little different from any other. Bricks had been laid only that morning, by the look of the lime plaster. Amal reached in and worked one of them loose. "Can you see now, Pa?"

Thomas could.

"Is that what it looks like?"

"Of course it is." Amal worked the small object loose and held it out to him.

Thomas took it, cleaned the residue of mortar from it to reveal a small bone. He turned it until sure.

"It's from a toe, but a small toe. It would have belonged to a young boy or girl, more likely an infant. What is it doing here?"

"I told you, Pa. Witchcraft. He's been putting hexes in our house."

"Except I don't believe in witchcraft, and I hope neither do you."

"We don't need to, Pa. Whoever put these here believes in it, and that's all that matters to them. Question the boy, but try not to hurt him. This was not his idea. He is only the agent for someone else. And we both know who that is."

CHAPTER TWENTY

By the time Thomas and Amal emerged from the unfinished wing of the building, a cart piled with bricks had pulled up. Edward stood talking to Jorge, while Bel stood apart from her son, looking down the slope to the Teme.

"Go see what Will has done with that lad," Thomas said to Amal. "Tell him I'll be there in a moment."

Bel did not turn until Thomas reached her, then she looked up at him and smiled.

"You have a wonderful position here, Tom." She turned and examined the half-finished building. "And a mighty strange house. Why do you need something so big?"

"Vanity, no doubt. I'm trying to copy a building in Spain that carried great meaning for me. If you think this is big, you should see the Alhambra. It puts Lemster Priory to shame, as well as the Tower of London."

"I only know of the Priory. Perhaps one day you can show me this palace you miss so much."

"I doubt I will ever see it again. Come inside, there is

something I must do, but there will be a fire in the kitchen and Belia will have food on the stove if you have hunger."

"We ate on our way, but a fire would be welcome."

She fell into step beside him as they made their way to the house, skirting around the edge of the quadrangle where the terrace had been roofed on one side so the ground was drier.

"Who was that lad I saw Will dragging away? Has he done something wrong?"

"That's what I mean to find out. He has been setting objects inside the house. Hexes, Amal called them." Thomas reached inside his jacket and pulled out the small bone to show Bel.

She took a single glance at it and stepped away, crossing herself multiple times.

"Where was it, Tom?" Her eyes stayed on the bone.

"In an unfinished hearth."

Bel crossed herself again and muttered a prayer in Latin, then again in English. When Thomas went to return the bone to his pocket she said, "No. Don't place it about your person." She looked around as if searching for something. "You have no holy ground here, do you?"

"I don't know. This land belonged to Wigmore Abbey at one time, so it's possible."

"That is good. That is very good. Was there a building here before you started?"

Thomas frowned, not sure what Bel meant. "There was."

"And was some of it at least fashioned of stone?"

"The chimneys and hearths. Also the surround for a fine entrance door, which I intend to make use of."

"Did you use some of the stone in this new building?"

"Most of it, yes. There are a few scraps and boulders in a pile down there, but most of it was reused."

"Show me these scraps. And then go fetch Will."

Thomas shook his head in confusion but turned and led Bel over to a small depression in the ground where the masons had thrown the waste material. When the building was finished it would be topped with soil and grass.

Bel went into the dip and started working her way through it. She looked back at Thomas. "Why are you still here? Fetch Will. Now."

Thomas turned and ran up to the house.

When he returned a few minutes later with both Will and Amal, Bel sat on a large boulder with her skirt pulled up to keep it clean. Thomas stared at her ankles, then looked away, but not before she caught him doing so.

"Will, come down here and see if you can lift any of the larger pieces. You will need enough to build a small box-like structure, and best if it has a top and sides."

"I should fetch the masons, then."

"No. Someone wants to curse your house, and you don't know which of them might be part of the plan. Besides, it must be built by family. By you, Tom and Amal. Jorge and Belia too. Anyone you consider family."

"I don't believe in curses," Thomas said. "Neither do Will nor Amal, or Jorge or Belia."

"I think Belia might," said Amal. "Even Jorge has a superstitious side to him."

"It doesn't matter what you say you believe, Tom,

magic doesn't care what you believe to carry out its mischief. Now, Will, can you lift that biggest rock or not?"

Will squatted beside the stone Bel pointed at. It measured a foot wide, a little more in length. Will worked his fingers beneath it, then strained. Slowly the rock came up, grasped in his hands.

"Where do you want it?" He grunted at the effort of holding the rock, and Thomas knew no one else among them could have done what Will had.

"I don't know that yet until we fetch one of the cunning-folk. I know one who lives between here and Lemster, but not one here in Ludlow." Bel glanced at Thomas. "Would your sister Agnes know?"

"If *I* knew what you are talking about I might be able to answer. What are cunning-folk?"

Bel looked at Will. "Oh, you can put that down again, on the side of the pit is best. We might be a while yet." She turned back to Thomas. "They can sniff out witchcraft, spells and symbols. We need someone who can go through your entire house and find out if there are more hexes hidden. We must uncover them all. I have a little of the talent, but not enough, though I only had to see that bone to know what it was. I could feel the evil in it."

Thomas held no belief in what Bel spoke of, but he realised she did. She believed deeply in things she could not see, only sense. Was that so different from what he could sometimes do when he touched someone and knew what ailed them?

"Ami, take Bel up to Agnes's house and see what you can find out. If she knows of one of these cunning-folk bring them back down. Offer them whatever payment it takes."

"They will not take coin, Tom," said Bel. "You need to offer a favour, or a promise."

"What kind of favour?"

"That will become clear to you as things go on." Bel reached for Amal's hand. "Come, let us go. The sooner we find someone, the sooner I will know you are all safe."

Thomas and Will watched them walk away until they disappeared from sight.

"Do you believe any of that nonsense, Pa?" asked Will.

"None of it. Do you?"

"I think the same as you, but Belia believes in things that can't be seen. I think she talks with Ami about such ideas as well. A little, at least. They are both rational and scientific, so it's not mere superstition. What are we going to do until they get back?"

"We have a lad to question. Who did you leave him with?"

"Jorge, of course, so we had best go now before he tells the boy his entire history and stunts him for life."

Jorge was indeed talking when they entered a small storeroom. Will had put the boy there because it had no window and only a single door, against which Jorge sat on a stool, so he had to stand to let Thomas and Will enter.

"I hope you don't want me to stay," said Jorge.

"I might need your skill to know if the boy is telling the truth, but I have no intention of torturing him if that is what you fear." Thomas looked around. With four people, the space was cramped. "We should take him to the kitchen. It will be warmer, and I am sure between us we can stop him running." Thomas turned back to the boy. "What is your name?"

All fight had left him. Thomas saw how he might be influenced by flattery, money, or threats. Still, he had to know who had put him up to what he did, so took a step closer, looming over the boy.

"Walter, sir. Walter Mason. My father is the foreman, and I would be grateful if you can send for him. He will sort this misunderstanding out."

Thomas glanced at Jorge, who gave a brief shake of the head. Will caught the movement, and grabbed the boy by his arm and dragged him into the hallway.

The kitchen was warm, the scent of the meal Belia and Amal were cooking filling the air as the three of them entered the room. Will sat Walter Mason down at one end of the table, then went and stood in the doorway, his shoulders almost filling its width.

Thomas sat next to the boy and leaned close.

"It was not your idea to bury these hexes in my house, was it?"

A shake of the head.

"Then whose idea was it?"

"Do not tell my father, sir. He brought me here to help. Told me if I did a good job he would find more work for me. I am not clever. I am not skilled. But I am willing to learn."

Thomas suspected that Walter Mason's squint and less than handsome features caused people to judge him poorly in both intelligence and skill.

"I will send for your father once you tell me who asked you to do this. Did they also supply the objects?"

"She said I would be punished if I was caught."

"And now you are caught. Look over there at my son. He is the tall one with blond hair. Does he scare you more than..." Only now did Thomas hear what the boy had said. "Than this woman? Shall I describe her to you, Walter? For I know who she is. I know her names, but not which one she offered you. What else did she offer you? Herself?"

The boy's face flushed, and he looked away.

"She did, didn't she? I know she is beautiful enough to turn any head. She turned mine once. I want you to tell me her name."

"You already know it, sir."

"I still want you to tell me."

"She told me her name was Philippa. She never told me her family name, only her first; and that I should call her Pip, but..." His voice trailed off.

Thomas could understand the awe he must have felt in her presence. The raw excitement at what she had promised him.

"Where did you get the items you seeded my walls with?"

"She gave them to me, sir. A sack full of them. Stones, carvings, hair, even a wooden comb and a piece of linen. Dark blue it was, but only a small square."

"When did this happen?"

"Father was working for Sir Thomas Cornwell on his house at Burford. A storm had brought a tree down on the roof and we had to repair it. I am only light, so was sent up to tie the rushes on the roof. I did a good job, father said. He paid me a penny."

"How did you meet Philippa Gale?"

"Is that her family name, sir? She told me only the first part."

"She goes by another but will have used that one."

"She never mentioned her name at first, only later. There was some minor damage to a window in the cottage beside the entrance to the estate. Father and myself stayed on to repair it after the other workers left. We removed the damaged glass and put wood over the frame. Father sent me back the following day to fit new glass."

"You went alone?"

"Father said it was a simple repair, so yes."

"And was this is when she seduced you? She did seduce you, didn't she?"

Once again the boy's face flared bright red.

"There is nothing to be ashamed of. She seduced me as well. I understand why a lad like you would be drawn to her."

"I saw her when I was fitting the glass. She came down the stairs only half dressed. Her—" he covered his chest with his hands but could not say the word, "— her things were on display. When she saw me, she drew her robe across herself but I had already seen by then. She invited me inside to thank me. Later, she asked a favour of me, and I could not refuse her. Did not want to refuse her."

Thomas expected more than words had passed between them. Philippa would have wanted to cement the deal with the lad.

"Were you already working on my house?" Thomas asked.

"We were. I told her some rooms were finished, but she wanted me to put a charm in every single one. I had to find an excuse. Some small repair. Ed Brickenden supervised the work, but he said it was for an important man. Is that you, sir?"

"It is. I am Justice of the Peace, and work for Prince Arthur."

The boy nodded in resignation, no doubt expecting punishment. The stocks at least, possibly worse.

"I am sorry, sir. She made me do it. She made me do it all."

"We will talk about your punishment later, but what you do and say next will be considered." Thomas leaned closer. "Tell me, do you remember everywhere you placed an object?"

The lad could not meet his eyes. "Some. I had to..." He took a harsh breath, as if unable to get enough air into himself. "I had to place some in a hurry. In any moment I was alone." He looked around the room they were in. "I know where I placed them in this room. Do you want me to show you?"

Thomas glanced at Will, who offered a nod and went to block the door.

"Yes, show me," Thomas said.

The boy rose and went to the fireplace but could not approach close because of the heat.

"There is one set behind the fire basket, sir. A small figure carved of bone. A second, a length of hair from a boar, is set over here." He crossed to the sill of a window that looked north. He patted the stone. "I put it beneath this. I pushed it into the lime plaster before the stone was set. You will have to scrape the mortar out if you want to remove it."

"Do you believe in what you have done?" Thomas asked.

"I believe there are things in this world we cannot see. Things that can aid us and things that can harm us. She gave me this as protection, and so far it has worked." He reached beneath his shirt and drew out a small pebble, drilled to allow a leather thong to pass through it. "Until now."

Thomas looked at the stone, but it was unimpressive. A river pebble washed by the Teme, most like. As with all such things, he suspected the object less important than the belief of the person who wore it.

Thomas turned to Jorge. "Take Will and go with the boy. Get him to show you what he can remember. Mark each place with this." Thomas picked a length of burned wood from the edge of the fireplace.

"What do we do with him once he is done?" asked Jorge.

"I will think about that while he shows you what he remembers."

Thomas went outside and watched the workmen for a while. He waited to see if anyone else was acting suspiciously, but saw nothing. He tried to think what he could tell the boy's father, who was foreman. Or if he would tell him anything at all, because the germ of an idea had been planted in his mind. An idea that might be dangerous, but one that could also bear fruit. And that fruit would be Philippa Gale. Plucked from her place of safety.

CHAPTER TWENTY-ONE

The day was fading towards its early December end before Amal and Bel returned in the company of a young and beautiful woman with long, red-brown hair tied in an ornate plait that hung to one side. She was tall, her clothing unusual, loose and flowing. It reminded Thomas of the Moorish dress he had once been used to, but hers was more colourful. Thomas had expected someone older, more crone-like. This woman was far from that.

She smiled as she approached. "I have seen you around Ludlow, Thomas Berrington, and heard excellent reports of you from those who live at Croft Manor. My name is Silva Taylor. Bel has known me since I was a babe."

"I am pleased you agreed to help us," Thomas said. "Have they told you what has happened here?"

"Some of it, but I would hear it from you." She looked around. "It will be full dark soon, which is good. I take it you have torches?"

"We do. What do you need from us, Silva?"

"Light my way when I ask. Be quiet when I demand it.

Believe in what I do." She met Thomas's gaze. "If you can. Bel told me you believe only in what you can see and measure."

"Does that matter?"

Silva Taylor laughed. "No, but I always try to persuade unbelievers. She also tells me you do not believe in God either, but I can sympathise more with you on that. Not the God of the Church, but there are other gods. Older gods. So, where is this lad who set the charms?"

Thomas took her into the third, unfinished side of the building. He found Will and Jorge watching over Walter Mason, who sat on his haunches staring at a newly plastered wall. He turned at the sound of their footsteps. When he saw Silva his face paled.

"Ah, it's you is it, Walter? Why does that not surprise me?" She turned to Thomas. "Walter has a minor talent himself. He comes to me now and again, asking for advice, which I willingly give. I like to encourage the curious."

"As do I," Thomas said.

"You can stand aside, Walter," said Silva. "I assume the wall you are staring so hard at has a charm embedded in it?"

"Somewhere, yes, but I have forgotten where I placed it."

"No matter. He can leave if he wants, Thomas. We don't need him anymore."

"I want to talk to him later." Thomas turned to Will. "Can you keep him safe?"

Will did not appear to hear him. His gaze was locked on Silva, who ignored the obvious attention.

"Will?"

Finally, he turned. "Yes, Pa?"

"Take Walter and put him in the small room again."

"Jorge can do that," said Will.

"And you know you are the better man for it. Do as I ask." Thomas waited, holding Will's gaze until he nodded, grasped Walter Mason by the shoulder and dragged him out. After a moment, Jorge followed.

Thomas was aware of a new stubbornness in Will the last few months but seemed unable to find a way to negotiate a way around it. He had thought of talking to Jorge about it, but kept putting the conversation off. Perhaps soon the time would have to come.

"Do you need more light?" Thomas asked Silva. Alone with her now, he was made uneasy by her beauty. More so because she appeared entirely unaware of the effect she had on men.

"Not yet. Sometimes darkness is better. But go to the corner of the room so as not to distract me."

Thomas did as she asked, then crouched to watch her. She circled the room, ignoring for now the wall Walter had been staring at. She held her arms out from her sides, but there were no ornate movements. It was more as if her fingers scented currents in the air. Minutes passed, then she reached into her jacket, pulled out a piece of charcoal and made three quick crosses on two separate walls.

"There are items where I have marked," she said. "The plaster will have to be cut away to find them. I recommend you ask that tall son of yours to do it. He will be faster than anyone else. When I came in I saw the masons had left their tools beside the entrance. They will have to effect repairs when he is finished, but they should not have allowed one of their own to put charms in your walls." She smiled, and Thomas felt the pull of her attraction, even as he knew it to be false. She had no interest in him.

"How do you know there is something where you have marked?"

"Is this more scepticism?"

"No, curiosity. I accept you can do what you claim and am sure I will see the proof of it as soon as Will returns. I would like to know how you can do it. Knowledge is never wasted, however arcane."

"Your son is handsome."

"His mother was a beauty."

"But a different woman from the mother of your daughter."

Thomas laughed. "It hardly needs one of the cunning-folk to see that."

Silva smiled. "I agree. And to answer your question, I am not sure how I do it. My father taught me some when I was small, but he said he only did so because he had already recognised the ability in me. He didn't know the answer to your question either. He is dead now, but not gone." She touched her head, her chest, kissed her finger-tips. It was almost as if she made the sign of the cross but left it incomplete. "He is part of me and always will be. As you are part of your children."

"How do Agnes and Bel know you?"

"Everyone in Ludlow knows me, but in Agnes's instance I consider her a friend. And she bakes the best bread in the whole of Shropshire and Herefordshire. As for Bel, well, everyone in Lemster and around knows Bel. She is the heart of the town. Now, shall we look at some of the other rooms? This is likely to take most of the night, so I will eat with you if you will permit it."

"Of course. You are welcome."

"Yes, I believe I am. As are you, Thomas Berrington."

"Bel told me you would not accept payment, but can I offer you something else?"

"When I know what it is, I will ask it, and you will be pleased to provide it. Most likely a favour, but it might be something else."

When Thomas followed her into the next room she laughed. "Go send your son to me. He will be more useful. Tell him to bring a mallet and a bolster, also a basket to put the charms in. I will say words over each to make them safe once he uncovers them. Then come and find us when the food is ready. We will continue afterwards until the task is finished, however long it takes. Oh, and there is another man. Walter placed some charms, yes, but there is another man. Though I cannot see his face and am unsure of his purpose. Perhaps the boy will know who else is involved. And there is also a woman involved in some way, but she is less clear to me."

She stared at Thomas until he nodded. "Yes, there is a woman."

"Do you have somewhere I can sleep?"

"We can find you somewhere."

"Good. Now go do as I ask."

Thomas passed Silva's orders on to Will, then helped him find a basket and the tools he would need. After Will went to find Silva, Thomas sat beside Bel in the warm kitchen, watching Amal and Belia prepare a meal of rabbit stew flavoured with wild garlic and thyme. There was fresh bread already on the table, which Amal had brought back from Agnes's shop.

"Do you now believe in things you can't see?" asked Bel.

"I believe Silva does, and I believe she has talent. But charms, hexes, spirits, ghosts, the unknown? No, I don't believe in those. I believe in knowledge and the actions of men and women, both for good and evil."

"Then you disappoint me. I always thought you more open-minded."

"Not to superstition."

Bel rose to her feet, but even standing she was barely taller than Thomas sitting.

"I saw Ed and the others preparing to leave when we came back. I had thought to ask if I could stay, but I think it best I return home with them. Goodbye, Tom."

He received no kiss, and knew he had disappointed her. For a moment he considered following her, but he would not change his mind, and better they did not argue. He wondered if her offer to stay had included staying with him. He believed that might have been her intention, and if it was, he had a mind to say yes. They shared a past. A long-distant past, but he had never forgotten her. He supposed people did not forget their first love, even when it was not perfect. Though his memory of Bel Brickenden was close to perfect.

After a moment he rose to his feet, an ache in his legs and back, and went to make a proposal to Walter Mason that might see him escape punishment. He also asked him who the other man was.

"There is no other man," said Walter. "She asked only me. She told me I was the only one."

They stood together, only the two of them in the storeroom. Thomas did not expect trouble.

"Then she lied to you. She does that. She lied to me as well."

"She told me she hates you."

"She does."

"Are you not afraid of her?"

"Why would I be?"

"Because of the charms. She says they have power. She has given them power."

"As I said, she lies. I have something I want you to do. If you agree, you will not be punished for what you did here."

Walter stared at Thomas, and he could almost read the thoughts going through his mind. Agree and walk free. Do as asked and risk the wrath of Philippa Gale.

"Did she tell you I killed her father?" Thomas asked, as much to let Walter know he was a man who also carried wrath. "I have punished men. Killed men who crossed me and never gave them another thought. Do as I ask, and Philippa Gale will also be punished. You need never fear her again. You love her, I know, but you also fear her."

Walter nodded but kept his silence.

"I will tell you what I want, and you can do it or not. I will not ask you to agree here and now, but do it and know you have my protection. Ask anyone in Ludlow what that means." Thomas hoped he spoke the truth.

"When Silva Taylor comes to eat with us I would like you to sit at our table as well. To show we are all friends."

"What is it you want me to do?" asked Walter, and Thomas knew he had scared him enough to at least ask.

So he told him, then led Walter back to the kitchen and sat him next to Amal, who leaned close and chatted to him, even though he would not meet her eyes. They were still there when Silva came into the room.

"Where's Will?"

"Working." Silva was distracted. Until now she had been serene, but no longer. "He told me about the bones."

"The bones in the walls?"

"The bones of a hand left for you in the castle. Do you still have them?"

"I don't know." Thomas turned to his daughter. "Did we throw them away, Ami?"

"You mean did *I* throw them away, don't you? And no, I didn't. They are still in the velvet bag where I placed them." She glanced at Silva. "Do you want me to fetch them?"

"Yes. No. Take me to them. Better you don't handle them more than you need to. I sense a little power in you, but it needs training before you can touch something so evil."

Silva turned away, impatient, waiting for Amal who rose and took her hand as they left the room.

Thomas sat where he was, wondering about the conversation he had witnessed. Wondering if he was losing his wits. He heard them coming back down the stairs a short time later but they did not enter the room, so he rose and went outside.

Silva stood in the centre of the courtyard, the velvet pouch held in both hands. She saw Thomas and called him over.

"Is it the same person sent you these as is putting charms in your house?"

"I believe so."

"Do you know who it is?"

"I do."

"What is her name?"

"Philippa Gale, but she also goes by Gala Uziel."

"Which is her true name?"

"Gala Uziel."

"Then that is what I will use. But you need to know it is not she who created the charms but someone else. Someone I cannot see clearly. A man, I think, but even that is not certain." Her eyes widened in realisation. "I see it now. There is no one else setting charms in your house, Thomas. There is someone out there creating them for the lad to use. Now I hold these bones what I do see clearly is a tall woman, beautiful, with dark hair. It is her who is using this other man, the one I cannot see." Silva shook her head, her hair shimmering in the light. "I need to look for him, but not now. It is the woman who hates you."

"Yes, she does," Thomas said.

"You can both go now. I don't need you, and I need to remove my clothes." She looked around. "It is a pity it is so cold, but that cannot be helped." She ushered Thomas and Amal away.

Inside the house, Amal said, "I hope Will doesn't wander out and catch sight of her."

"I am struggling to accept what is happening here."

"It's not logical, Pa, but Bel believes in it. Aunt Agnes believes in it. Silva clearly believes in it."

"And you?"

"I am your daughter, so more rational. We need proof, Pa. Evidence. But there may be evidence. When Silva took the bones from me I felt something. It might only be in my head, and I believe a lot of what she does is that, but it was as if a weight was lifted from me. She makes people believe the unbelievable and it helps them. I thought myself immune to such, but I think she is skilled at her job. Like you are. Both different, both skilled."

"I have upset Bel," Thomas said, staring at his daughter. "My disbelief sent her away." He reached out and took Amal's hand, comforted by the touch. He considered how a touch could do that — bring comfort, or discomfort.

"She will come back to you because you share something too strong to be broken by a tiny disagreement."

Thomas shook his head. "You are too clever for your years, Ami. Far too clever."

"I am your daughter, Pa, and I have Jorge to thank for some of it. Belia too." Amal's gaze moved away from his and she rose.

When Thomas turned Silva stood in the doorway. Her dress clung to her damp body. Her long hair was wet and dripped water onto the floor. She hugged her arms about herself, shivering.

"Come by the fire." Amal took her arm and led her across the room.

"It is done," said Silva. "The bones have been taken by the river, which will wash the evil from them. And they were evil." She met Thomas's eyes. "You are fortunate Will told me about them." She looked around. "Where is he?"

"I assume he hasn't finished yet."

"Then I need to go to him. We have not found everything yet." She stood, but Thomas put a hand on her wet shoulder, which was ice cold.

"I will fetch him. You need to get warm, and you need hot food inside you. We will all come with you after to find the rest. And then in the morning I will pursue the woman who put them there."

Silva nodded. "Yes, you must find her. The hatred she feels for you is immense. She will not stop until either she or you are dead."

CHAPTER TWENTY-TWO

Silva found Will in one of the upper rooms. He was grimy with plaster dust, which stuck in his hair and against his face. Even looking as he did Silva found him attractive. No ... more than attractive. Thomas had wanted them to eat with the others but she had persuaded him there was still work to do. It was almost not a lie.

"Is this the last room?" she asked.

"I do hope so. I need to bathe, and then I need to sleep."

Silva cocked her head, staring at him, losing herself in him for a moment.

"If you intend to bathe in the Teme you will freeze. I can attest to that."

Will laughed. "Hasn't Pa told you about the arrangements here? He usually tells everyone. He's proud of what he has created."

"I have only just met him, so no, he has not told me." Silva smiled. "Not yet. Do you want to show me?"

"If you want. I need to go there in any case." Will

pointed to a rush basket in one corner. "I put all the items I found in there."

For a moment Will stood unmoving, his chest slowly rising and falling. A broad chest. A flat stomach. Long legs that stood square, solid. Silva knew barely anything about him but wanted to know more.

"Show me, then," she said. "I could do with washing myself as well."

A tiny thrill ran through her at the idea they might wash each other. She had no idea where the thought came from. It arrived complete, as if they had already done the deed and she heard it as a memory. Silva was used to such thoughts. She knew she saw the world differently to other people. Saw the essence beneath the surface. Staring at Will she failed to find his essence. Perhaps he was too new to her; or perhaps he had some power of his own and could cloak himself. Silva knew Bel Brickenden had a little. She was also interested in Amal. In fact all the Berringtons. But at that moment, in particular, Will.

"Do you need to do anything with the objects in the basket?" asked Will, and Silva realised she had been staring at him for too long.

She gave a shake of her head. "They can wait until morning, but we should place them outside the house."

She started across to the basket but Will was faster. They collided with each other, and Will reached out an arm to steady her in case she might fall. Not that Silva would ever fall, but she sensed the power as his arm pulled her against himself. She looked up to discover him staring down at her. His pupils were wide, as she suspected hers also were. She felt him breathing, the rise and fall of his chest, his belly against her side. Then he released her, picked up the basket and walked away. Silva took a deep breath, wondering what was happening to her. There was something about Will she had never experienced before, as if what might happen between them carried an inevitability. She watched his back, his strength, and then he was gone and she followed.

Will walked down to the banks of the river and placed the basket on the slab of rock that Silva had used before. When he turned he smiled to find her behind him.

"Do you want to see this bathing place now?"

Silva nodded, unsure she trusted herself to speak. Why Will? Why now?

Will held out his hand to her, waiting. After a moment, without realising a decision had been made, Silva placed her hand inside his. When he closed his palm around hers a sense of deep safety flooded through her. Safety and arousal.

Did he want her the same way she wanted him? Silva could not be sure, and the lack of certainty unsettled her. She could always read people. Know what thoughts wound through their heads. But not Will. Was it him or her? Or the combination of the two of them? She realised she continued to stand with her hand in his and that he was waiting for her.

He smiled, and she tried to return the smile but saw him frown and knew she had done something wrong.

"This way," he said, and led her away.

Silva could sense the water before she smelled it or felt the warmth emanating from the stone walls. Will led her into a moist chamber. A stone pipe projected from one wall, water dripping from it onto the floor. A deep bath lay to one side, water filling it. The light from the torches reflected from the surface to shimmer against the walls.

"How does it work?" she asked, her voice catching with the wanting of him.

Will released her hand and went to where a metal lever projected from the stone. He pulled it and water gushed from the pipe to splash against the tiles, which were laid so the excess ran into a drain. Will stepped back, leaving the water to run, and turned to face her.

"Are you going to stand there and watch me?"

"Would it upset you if I said yes?"

Will shook his head. Took a step closer until mere inches separated them.

"You are very beautiful," he said.

Silva shrugged. "You are not the first man to tell me that. Nor the first woman. You are also..." She hesitated, searching for the right words. "You are also handsome. And strong. And you give me a sense of safety, of being protected." She gave a nervous laugh. "But you must know you are handsome. Other women will have told you that, I am sure."

"A few." Will closed the gap between them until their bodies touched. Her legs against his. Her breasts against his belly.

Silva put her hands on his waist, feeling the hard strength of him beneath the softness. She knew he could lift her in one hand and hold her aloft if he chose, and the idea he could do so sent a thrill through her because she knew he would never do it. Not unless she asked. Knew he would never harm her. Would always protect her. She tilted her head up in invitation and Will leaned down to press his lips against hers. Silva put a hand behind his head, pulling him harder against herself. She parted her lips in invitation and Will took advantage of it.

The kiss seemed to last an age, and when it was done Silva felt as if all the breath had been stolen from her.

"I want you to wash me," she said.

Will smiled. "Only wash you?"

Silva shook her head. "I want you inside me. I want *you*."

Will pulled at her clothes until she was naked, then stood and admired her. She was slim but fulsome. Curved. Smooth. Beautiful. Her hair hung long to her waist, but her breasts lay revealed and he kissed each one before standing to wait.

Silva pulled at his clothes, impatient until he too stood naked and she studied the wonder of him. His body was pale except where the sun had darkened his arms and face. His manhood stood erect and she reached for it before hesitating. It was all too fast. She had never been this fast before and it scared her. This need for him. This wanting of him. All of him.

Will turned away and stepped beneath the falling water. He soaped himself, facing her, and she went to him and took the soap and used it to clean him. Then she handed it to him and he washed her until her body quaked with a sudden rush of arousal and she cried out.

Will held her, their wet bodies pressed tight.

"I want to sleep beside you tonight," Silva whispered against his chest. "If I am allowed to?"

"You are allowed," said Will.

He reached out and shut off the water, then picked her up and carried her through the sleeping house to his room and lay her on his bed. He stood beside it until she reached out for him.

* * *

It was done. The deed. The act. Pale dawn light woke Silva and she turned on her side to examine Will, still barely able to believe how he could be so beautiful yet so strong. He had been gentle at first, then less so when she demanded more. They had made love until exhaustion took them both. Silva had lain asleep against Will's chest, comforted, sated.

"I know you're looking at me," said Will, and Silva reached out and slapped him.

She sat across his belly and kissed him, then rolled away.

"Is that it?" he asked, lying on his side so he could study her, his fingers tracing her body. "One wonderful moment and then today we get on with our lives?"

"You scare me," said Silva.

"Why? Don't you know I would never hurt you?"

"That is why you scare me." She gave a sigh. "You are not the first man I have lain with—"

"I noticed."

Silva slapped him again. They tussled, which led to something more. When it was done Silva continued with her thought.

"Not the first man, but you scare me because you are the first man I believe I want to spend more time with than anyone else."

"Good," said Will.

"Really? Good?"

He nodded. "I want you to live with me here. I want you to share my bed every single night."

"I … Yes, I want that too, but I also have my own place. I want you to come there, to see where I live."

"Not today, Pa has something for me to do."

"Then soon. I like this house he has built, but it does not have the same power mine does. You will feel it when I take you there."

"Does it worry you that Pa doesn't believe in what you do?"

Silva shook her head. "I don't need him to believe, only to accept I can do things he does not understand." She stared into Will's eyes. "What about you? Do you believe in what I do?"

"I have witnessed it. And…" Will's voice tailed off.

"And what?" Silva lay across him again. "What, Will?"

"I have lain with other women, just as you have lain with other men, but none of them ever touched my heart in the way you do. When we were joined as one I felt something. I don't understand it, but I felt it. The two of us together. More than either of us alone."

"Then there is hope for us, I think. If we want it."

"I want it," said Will. "And I'll work on Pa. So will Ami. Pa doesn't hold with things he can't measure, things he can't see, weigh and judge. But if you demonstrate results he will begin to accept."

"I spoke last night with him about a woman that hates him. I could taste the hatred on him even if he could not."

"Philippa Gale," said Will.

"Why the hatred?"

243

"It is a long story and I will tell it all to you later, once we have returned from Burford. But they were once lovers until she betrayed him. She tried to kill Ami. She tried to kill Pa only the other day."

"In water," said Silva. "That is what I smelled on him. River water. But not the water of the Teme. Each river has its own essence."

"She tried to have him drowned in the Wye, but Pa is harder to kill than most men."

"I sense that in him as well," said Silva. "There is a strength he does not always appreciate, just as there is strength in you. I like it." She smiled. "Like it more in you than him, of course."

"Of course," said Will.

"What time do you need to leave?"

Will glanced at the window, judging the daylight.

"Not for an hour yet."

"Good."

CHAPTER TWENTY-THREE

"Are you sure it was a good idea to ask him to write a letter?" Will rode on one side of Thomas, Jorge on the other. They headed southeast towards Burford Manor, the route now familiar.

"He will not have to see her, and I don't believe the request will raise any suspicion. If it does, she will try to punish me, not Walter."

"So he sends a note to ask for more charms?"

Thomas patted his jacket. "I have the note on my person." The idea had come to him as he watched Silva work. The note told Philippa that some of the charms had been discovered, but Walter's part in the plan had not. He offered to place more if she could provide them.

"Does Walter Mason even know how to write?"

"He doesn't, which is why I had Amal write the note for him, though she disguised her script so it looked more masculine."

"Do men and women write differently?" asked Jorge. "I wouldn't know because I can barely read, let alone write."

"They do," Thomas said.

"And if someone sees you deliver the note? What if Philippa is in residence and has men with her?"

"If she is in residence, then subterfuge won't be required. There are three of us, and I am sure we can take care of any men she might have. We arrest her, and this time we make sure she can't escape punishment. She will hang for John Miller's murder. Hang for Arthur Wodall's as well, even if it was not her who cut his throat — though I believe it may have been. I suspect she likes to take her revenge in person."

"What revenge was there in killing Wodall?" asked Will.

"To throw suspicion on me, of course. Her mind is a thing of wonder, even if it is out of kilter. She is both clever and crazed."

"Perhaps too clever if she thinks you will get the blame for the murder."

"I think perhaps in her own mind I did kill him. I am starting to wonder about her sanity."

"It is because she hates you so much," said Will. "You banished her from Prince Arthur's circle. You killed her father. You destroyed the bonemen. She wants you dead."

"Which confuses me as to why she hasn't tried a more direct approach," said Jorge.

"I think throwing me in the Wye was fairly direct."

"Yet still she failed. Do you think Philippa believes these charms can bring harm to you, or any of us?" Jorge gave a mock shiver which made Thomas laugh.

"I have given that some consideration and believe she must, though Silva said it wasn't Pip creating the charms but someone else, at her request. When I knew her, she gave no sign she believed in such things, but it's unlikely she would confess such beliefs to me. Even more so when I look back at her deceit. She had no feelings for me. It was all a ruse and I fell for it."

"She was beautiful," said Jorge.

"Yes, she was."

"And wanton?"

Thomas said nothing.

"Silva is beautiful, and she believes in magic," said Will.

"Are those things meant to go together?"

They were descending the low rise from Bleathwood Common when Burford Manor appeared ahead between the trees. The small cottage stood alongside the road to Tenbury and Bewdley.

"I doubt it." Thomas reined in Ferrant and slipped from the saddle, holding the reins for Will to take. "I will walk from here. Both of you make some noise when you ride past the cottage. I will approach from the other side. I want to see if she has returned, but doubt it. I will leave the note on the table there."

"No, Pa, give it to me," said Will. "If she's not there, and I agree with you it's unlikely, the note will stay there until it rots. Better I ask someone at the house if they can pass it on to her. It offers me the chance to ask if anyone knows where she is. They might even reveal her location."

Thomas shook his head, not because he disagreed with his son, but because he should have thought of the idea himself.

"All right, do it." He handed the note to Will. "But

everything else stays the same. I approach the cottage and watch in case she is there."

"In that case, have your horse back," said Will. "If she is and sees me leading it she will know you are around somewhere. Tie him to a tree and approach as silently as you can. We will make as much noise as possible." Will looked at Jorge. "I suggest you tell me a coarse joke and we both laugh a great deal."

"Can I provide gestures as well?" Jorge made a motion to demonstrate.

Thomas watched them ride away, then walked into the woods until he was two hundred paces from the rear of the cottage. He tied Ferrant to a branch and returned the way he had come. Forty paces away he crouched to watch.

There was no smoke rising from the chimney. No sign of any candles or lamps. The morning was bright, sharp with frost, so anyone inside might not need candles, but they would need a fire. Thomas believed the cottage abandoned.

Some sixth sense, perhaps? Which made him smile because it was something he believed in but could not prove. It lacked any means of measurement. Perhaps Silva Taylor and he might have a conversation on the subject, except he knew she would rather converse with Will. She had made it more than clear when she sat at their table in the kitchen that she was attracted to him.

Smiles. Glances. An occasional touch of her fingers against the back of his hand. Thomas wondered what had happened with Grace Miller but made no mention of her to Will. He was a grown man. He could break as many hearts as he wanted, which he might well do because Silva was right when she had said he was handsome. He possessed the beauty of his mother, but had learned how to beguile women from Jorge, who was a master of the art. It also helped he was tall and strong — an excellent protector.

Thomas watched Jorge and Will pass the cottage, their laughter coarse and loud. As it faded he rose and approached the small rear door, but when he lifted the latch it remained firm. He cupped his hands and peered through the narrow window but saw nothing. A small room used for washing.

He walked as softly as he could along the side to peer through another window, the fresh glass telling him it was the one Walter Mason had replaced.

Still nothing.

When he tried the front door, he discovered it was also locked. Thomas put his shoulder to it but all he got was a bruise. Still, the idea was sound, so he made his way back to the rear and tried the same method on the smaller door, which gave under pressure.

He entered the washing room and passed through to the main room. He recalled searching the cottage on his previous visit and finding nothing. Philippa might have returned since, so he repeated the process as diligently as his first search. The result was the same until he entered the bedroom. This time he drew his knife, turned the horsehair mattress over and cut the stitches along one side, enough for him to push his hand through. Thomas tried not to think of the lice that might inhabit it as he reached as far as he could. He was about to give up when his fingertips brushed against something other than coarse horsehair. He reached again, his face pressed against the mattress, and grasped the object.

Thomas drew it out then sat on the wooden floor and looked at it.

A stained hessian sack, tied at the neck with a cord. When he opened it he saw a jumble of items. Hanks of hair. Two dead birds. Stones and bones. And a small leather-bound journal, which he opened. This, he hoped, might lead to something. Except, as he looked at the script, he discovered he could not read it. It was not Arabic, nor Spanish or English. The letters were unfamiliar and he wondered if it was some manner of code. Thomas slipped both the sack and journal beneath his jacket. If Philippa Gale returned, and if she received his note and came here to do what it asked her, she would discover them missing. She would know who the thief was. The thought did not trouble him, but he hoped it might trouble her.

Would it ruin his plans or not? Thomas did not know. All he could do was throw the dice and see where they landed. If they were not in his favour, he would have to come up with another idea. A better plan. He might even ask Will's advice.

Thomas knew he should consult his son more. Should consult Amal, too. Even Jorge, for he knew many things Thomas did not. He had already fallen out with Bel when he should have lied to avoid hurting her feelings. He knew such deception was not in his nature but wondered if he should make more of an effort to learn diplomacy.

Thomas wedged the narrow back door shut as best he could, but if or when Philippa returned, she would know someone had been here whether or not it stood open. He stood outside, staring towards the manor house, the roof just visible above the treetops. Dark clouds gathered in the east to augur more snow before dark. He considered fetching Ferrant and riding to join Will and Jorge, but knew there was no need. Will made friends easily, and Jorge won people over without trying. They would deliver Thomas's note and, with good fortune, return soon with information on Philippa's whereabouts. If not, there was the coded journal now in his possession and the papers he had retrieved from Peter Gifforde's house after he died. Thomas had read some, but was sure Amal would have read them all. And perhaps she could decipher the journal.

When, after a half hour there was no sign of the others, Thomas walked into the woods and sat against an oak while Ferrant grazed on frosted grass. His eyes grew heavy, and he was on the point of falling asleep when a sound startled him. It was the snap of a twig, and he came to his feet to look around. The woods were not dense, but a hundred paces away anyone might be hidden. He wondered if the sound had been in his dreams, but could not be sure.

"Who is there?" He thought of the three men in Hereford. Big men. Hard men. Could he fight all three?

He walked to Ferrant and drew his sword from the scabbard tied to the saddle. Another sound came, laughter, but still no sign of whoever was making it. Thomas knew he had been sleeping badly. Had lain awake the night before wondering if he could ever reconcile himself with Bel after what had happened. Knowing he wanted to but not knowing how. Being himself, it seemed, was not enough.

He also thought about Silva Taylor and Will. They had spent until the small hours searching the house, both finished and unfinished sections. The sounds of hammer on metal, metal on plaster, came often enough to keep Thomas only just below the surface of sleep. And then it had grown quiet and he sank into a deeper slumber without dreams. In the morning when he came down, Silva sat at the kitchen table, she and Will with their heads almost touching as they spoke too softly to be overheard.

Another sound brought him back to the present. Horses coming along the road he could glimpse between the trees. Thomas mounted Ferrant and turned him in the sound's direction. Only when he saw Will's blond hair did he encourage Ferrant into a trot to intercept them.

"What did they say about the note?" Thomas asked.

Will and Jorge reined their mounts in and all three sat facing each other.

"Half the staff have gone with their master to his house in Derbyshire," said Will. "They professed to know nothing of any Philippa Gale but took the note in any case. They told us perhaps someone else would know of her when they returned."

"Which will be when?"

"They said February, most like."

"So it does us no good."

Will shook his head and urged his horse into a walk. They had started along the bank of the Ledwych brook when more hoofbeats sounded and all three reined in their mounts to look back. Six men approached at speed, coming from the direction of Burford Manor.

"Do you know them?" Thomas asked.

"Didn't see them when we were there. Most of the staff were women and boys. Perhaps they're not from the house."

Thomas narrowed his eyes, a foreboding of danger coming to him. "Two of those men helped put me in the river in Hereford. They serve Philippa."

Will nodded as though he expected something like this, or more likely hoped for it.

"I'll take the three shortest, you the middle ones. Jorge can deal with the last," said Will.

"I would rather deal with the shortest if it's all the same to you," said Jorge.

"Usaden is short," said Will. "Would you rather fight him or a man of more regular size?"

"None of those men is Usaden."

"We do as Will says," Thomas said. "Perhaps they're not coming to fight, in which case you can talk them into submission."

CHAPTER TWENTY-FOUR

Thomas watched the men approach. Not slowing, riding hard. They were not coming to talk. He set his hand on the hilt of his sword and drew it. The approaching men did the same. Two hundred paces separated them now. No distance at all with the speed they were travelling.

"Jorge, behind me and Will. Move. Now."

Jorge urged his horse to the rear, though he too had drawn his sword. Will had not brought his axe but was skilled with all weapons.

At last, the riders began to slow. They stopped, their horse's breath pluming in the cold air.

"What right have you to be here?" The man who spoke was one Thomas recognised. He had been giving the orders in Hereford, though they had been Philippa's orders.

"This is common land; we need no reason to ride it. What business have you with us?"

The man reached into his jacket and withdrew a sheet of

paper. Thomas recognised it as the note Amal had written asking for more charms. Whoever Will had given it to must have passed it on to these men. It did not come as a surprise but was a disappointment. He had hoped Philippa might have less influence than the presence of the letter suggested.

"This business. Why do you write to my mistress? What is she to you? If your last lesson was not enough then we will have to repeat it, on all three of you."

"If you serve Philippa then you know what I am to her. You will also know why she wants me dead. Are you here to kill me again? You did a poor job of it the last time. And I should warn you my son — he is the big one — is a fearsome warrior."

Will smiled, but there was nothing of welcome in it.

"Big he may be, but we outnumber you two to one, and we are also fearsome warriors."

"Have you come to talk or fight, because I see only one of those at the moment?" Thomas wanted to anger them, but these men were too experienced for that. "I see you have opened my letter to Pip. It was sealed and not addressed to you, unless you are also a woman?"

Thomas deliberately used the short form of Philippa's name. He did not know how close these men were to her but wanted to make it clear he had been.

"My mistress trusts me in all matters. And no, we are not here to fight you. We are here to kill you. Even the big one I am meant to be afraid of."

The man spat on the ground and urged his horse forward. As he did so an arrow hummed past Thomas's shoulder and thunked into the pommel of the man's saddle between his legs. An inch higher and it would have unmanned him.

Thomas recognised the fletch on the arrow and twisted around. Usaden stood on the edge of the treeline, a short Moorish bow already notched with a second arrow. Jack Pook stood beside him, an English bow in his hands.

Thomas turned back to the men. "My friend on the hillside is an excellent archer. Do not mistake what he did for an error. He meant to hit your pommel rather than you. The next arrow will seek a different target if you fail to see sense."

The man cursed and came forward again.

Usaden's second arrow caught the man in the shoulder, spinning him around and spilling him to the ground. Jack Pook's shaft spun harmlessly through the space where the man's chest had been when it was released. The man's companions kept coming.

"Try not to kill anyone," Thomas shouted, hoping Will would hear him above the rush of blood through his veins. Hoping Usaden might also hear, for he was the one the men should truly fear.

He loosened his right leg, and when a rider came at him he deflected the blow of his sword and kicked out. A second man tumbled to the cold, hard ground. He landed awkwardly and Thomas heard the snap of his collarbone. The man would not be wielding a sword for some time, maybe never if he received the wrong treatment.

Will had downed two more. The remaining pair turned and rode hard back towards the manor house.

"Do we go after them, Pa?" Will was not even breathing hard, unlike Thomas.

"Let them go. It will send a message just as well as my note."

Thomas dismounted. He checked on two of the fallen men. One was unconscious, the other attempting to rise. When Will came to stand beside him, Thomas held his hand out to prevent him knocking the man down again.

"Go check on their leader. See if he is going to live or needs my attention for his wound."

Thomas gripped the shoulder of the man getting to his feet and dug his fingers into a knot of nerves — only lightly, but enough to be felt.

"You work for Philippa Gale, yes?"

The man shook his head and nodded at their leader. "I work for Gilbert."

"But he works for Philippa?"

"He does."

"The same thing. Were you in Hereford when your master and two others tried to kill me?"

"I was not."

"But you heard of it?"

"Perhaps I did. Your companion could do with a good wetting, too. It might shrink him down some."

"I will send him back and you can tell him that yourself. Are you a brave enough man, I wonder?" Thomas knew he would get nothing more from the man, so released him and turned his back. He had no fear of attack because both Usaden and Jack Pook had descended the low slope, together with Kin, and stood waiting for instructions.

"Who are they?" asked Usaden.

"They work for Philippa. I sent her a note, but it seems she's not here. Did you follow us?"

Usaden shook his head. "Me and Jack were after rabbits for the pot. We come this way now and again. It's good country for coneys."

Thomas laughed at how Usaden had picked up the local word for rabbits. He wondered how much time he and Jack spent together, then decided he might as well ask.

"He stays with me and Emma now and again," said Usaden. "More now than again these days. I think he likes to toast his feet before our fire, and Emma is a good cook. Her sister is also fine pretty, older than Emma and a widow, but still far too young for Jack. He tells me he is older even than you, Thomas, but it is hard to tell with him."

Thomas found it difficult to believe the change he saw in Usaden. He wondered if finding Emma had softened him. Though there had been little sign of it with the attackers. Kin came to him and snuffled his hand and Thomas stroked the dog's ears. Kin twisted his head in pleasure at the attention.

"We were fortunate you were passing."

"You would have managed fine without us," said Usaden, "but it felt good to fight again, even though I miss it less than I thought I would. We saw you asleep under that oak. Kin wanted to come to you then but I stopped him." He smiled. "Jack broke a twig to see if you heard it, and you did. It is good to see you are finally learning a little fieldcraft."

Thomas glanced to where Will still stood over the man called Gilbert.

"Come with me. I want you to frighten the man your arrow hit."

Usaden continued to smile, but there was a coldness in it now.

When they reached Gilbert, Thomas sent Will away. Usaden squatted and stared at the man, his face a complete blank, his eyes dark and unreadable. He was the Usaden of old. A killer without heart or soul, and the injured man saw it.

"Where is Philippa Gale?" Thomas asked, crouching beside Usaden.

Gilbert tried to sit up, but winced and lay on his back again.

"I am bleeding to death. Fetch me a surgeon."

"I am a surgeon." Thomas leaned close, touched the wound. The arrow was lodged deep but had missed any major blood vessels. "Do you want me to fix you? I can. I always carry the tools of my trade in my saddlebag. There will be some pain, but less than if you let the wound fester."

"You will try to kill me. My mistress told me about you, Thomas Berrington."

Thomas jerked the shaft of the embedded arrow and the man cried out.

"Then no doubt she also told you I am a healer. I can leave you here to bleed to death or for your wound to become infected and poison your blood, or I can remove the arrow and stitch your wound. I wager it won't be the first time you have had such done."

"Why would you do such a thing?"

"Because I want a message sent to your mistress, and I want you to pass another on from me. A personal message. Do we have an understanding?"

"I tossed you in the river not three nights since."

"And you failed to kill me. That was a mistake." Thomas held his hands out to show he was still in the world. "Yes or no? Otherwise, I have business to attend to."

The man glared at Thomas, his eyes avoiding Usaden. Finally, he nodded.

"Do your worst, then."

When Thomas returned he had a sharp blade, some herbs, a needle and a length of gut.

"This is going to hurt," he said. There was a little hashish and poppy mixture in his saddlebag, but he did not want to waste any on this man.

"Life is pain."

Thomas nodded at Usaden, who sat across the man and held him down, while Thomas grasped the shaft of the arrow and snapped the top from it. Then he used all his weight to drive the arrow down and out through Gilbert's back. He ignored his screams, rolled him over and pulled the shaft all the way through. The wound bled, but not enough to kill him. Thomas packed it with herbs before roughly stitching it front and back, then tied a lint dressing over it.

"When you see your mistress, remember to tell her Thomas Berrington did this for you. Tell her also I will not come after her if she sends me a promise this is finished between us. I have a life here. A family. I don't want to be looking over my shoulder every moment of every day. You will tell her?"

"For what good it will do, aye, I will tell her."

"Make sure she knows this can end. And if it doesn't, tell her I will come for her. My patience grows thin."

CHAPTER TWENTY-FIVE

The Yule log brought by Edward Brickenden continued to smoulder in the fireplace on the first day of January when Thomas mounted Ferrant and rode south in the company of Will and Amal. Father and children on a chilly, snow-dusted day with a sky so pale the world seemed turned upside down.

After his encounter with Philippa's men near Burford, Thomas had waited for word but heard nothing. He was trying to work out whether the lack of any response meant she had given up or was planning a new assault. Either way he was content and looking forward to the day.

As they reached Ludford Bridge Grace Miller appeared and waved to Will. Will waved back but did not slow.

"Have you told her about Silva?" Thomas asked once they were over the bridge. He glanced at the row of cottages and noted the one rented by John Miller had smoke rising from the chimney to show it had a new tenant.

"Told her what?"

"I notice Silva has been sleeping in your room this last week or more."

"I would never marry Grace, and she knows it. I am too…" Will had to search for the words. "I have too many hard edges to make a husband for her. And a husband is what she seeks."

"I hope you were careful with her."

"If you mean have I put her with child, then yes, I was careful. Do you take me for a fool, Pa?"

"I would never do that."

"It sounded as if you were."

Thomas rode on for a while. He noticed Amal smiling at his discomfort. When he scowled at her she laughed, the sound sweet in the chill air.

"These hard edges … does Silva not mind them?" Thomas asked Will.

Will smiled. "She tells me she can live with them until she smooths them away."

"You and she have grown close quickly."

"She likes me, and I like her."

"She is older than you."

"And…?"

"Nothing. I was only pointing the fact out. Why has she reached her age without marrying?"

"She says she has never met the right man."

Beyond Will, Thomas saw Amal hug herself and purse her lips in a kissing gesture. He had to stop himself from laughing.

"Do you think you might be the right man?"

"It's not what I think, Pa. It's what she thinks."

"Of course. But you may be?"

Will only shrugged. He urged his horse into a trot and rode ahead. Amal came closer to her father.

"He likes her a lot," she said. "So do I, but not in the same way, of course."

"I like her too."

"But not her profession. The cunning-folk are well-respected, Pa. She and Belia have spoken a great deal about herbs and plants. They share much of the same knowledge. Both examined the contents of that sack you brought back from Philippa's cottage. She told me she believes that the hexes and charms there were not produced by Philippa. She continues to claim there is someone else, employed by Philippa. Another of the cunning-folk perhaps, but if so, one turned to the dark, not the light."

"No one told me any of this."

"We didn't want to worry you. You have been exhausted, Pa. We all want you to recover."

"I have not been exhausted; I have been busy."

Amal smiled. "If you say so."

"Silva has no idea who this other person, this man, is?"

"It worries her she can't see him, but no. She senses him but not all of the time. She told me if you deal with Philippa, most likely this man will fade away like a bad smell. It is not him who hates you."

"Did you have time to look at the journal I brought from her cottage?"

"I did, and you are right. It's some kind of code, but not one I have broken yet."

"Do you think you can?"

"I don't know until I do. If I find the key it will unlock everything, but I may never find the key. Why are we going to Lemster?"

"I told you, to see Bel and her boys."

"I thought you and she had fallen out."

"I want to apologise. Perhaps you are right, and I have not been myself."

"Might I be getting a new Ma?" asked Amal, her face so innocent that Thomas laughed, loud enough to cause Will to turn to look back at them.

"I doubt it will come to that, but I would like Bel and me to be friends again."

"She was your first love, wasn't she?"

Thomas nodded, but said nothing.

"I like her, too," said Amal.

"That's good."

"I expect it is."

Ahead, Silva Taylor came walking down from Overton Wood. Will slowed and offered his hand to pull her up behind him. She settled herself on the saddle and placed her arms around his waist as he urged his horse into a walk.

"Did you know she was coming with us?" Thomas asked Amal.

"She wants to see Bel, too. They are friends."

"Is that where she lives, in the direction she came from?"

"I think so."

"Sir Richard Croft's house lies that way."

"I know, but you don't have to draw connections

between everything and everyone in the world, Pa. Sometimes a coincidence is nothing more than a coincidence."

"I think it might soon be time for me to ride south to Spain, Ami. You and Will are too clever for me these days."

"Don't do that, Pa. Not unless we all go. I would come with you in a heartbeat, but Will may not." She inclined her head towards where her brother and Silva were talking.

"He likes her that much?"

"I think so. She is exquisite, strange, and clever. Will has never been with a woman who is all three, and he likes it. She is a challenge to him. Was my mother a challenge for you, Pa? I know Helena was, but in a different way."

"Lubna challenged me in the same way you do. She was clever. She was beautiful. But she wasn't strange. She would question me, correct me, and I took her advice less than I should have." Staring at Amal, it almost seemed to Thomas that his dead wife sat astride the horse rather than his daughter. There were subtle differences, but more similarities, and he looked away before she saw the tears in his eyes.

"You can't bring her back, Pa, but you don't have to live the rest of your life alone."

"I have you and Will, Jorge and Belia and their children. I'm not alone."

"You know that's not what I meant. If Bel is who you want to be with then tell her. I think she wants to be with you too. You have both lived your lives, had wives, husbands, and children of your own, but now you are both alone. You can close the circle if you want to."

"Bel isn't alone."

"Don't be stupid, Pa, you know what I mean. Don't do what you always do and analyse everything to death. Go with your heart for once instead of your head."

"I'm not so sure my head is what it used to be."

Amal laughed. "Still good enough, I expect. And you have us to help you now."

Thomas smiled at her. "Do you know that is exactly what your mother would say to me? So perhaps you are right. We shall see."

"Yes. We shall see."

After a while, as they approached Brimfield, Thomas said, "What about you, Ami? Is there anyone in your life?"

"I have fourteen years, Pa. I don't want anyone. Not yet, and not in the way Will wants Silva."

"Is it because of what happened at Hugh Clement's manor house?"

"No. I was raped but am healed now. If I want sex I can, but I don't want it, not yet. One day I will, but with someone I love. I have put what he did behind me. If you hear nothing more from Philippa you should do the same with her."

Thomas tried to work through everything Amal had said. He stumbled a little on her saying 'if I want sex' but knew she was of an age. Girls of thirteen, twelve even, were married to older men and expected to bear child after child even if they lost half at birth.

"Prior Bernard offered me the manor house and I

turned him down," Thomas said. "Perhaps I should have said yes so you could set fire to it. Burn it to the ground."

"I would feel no better or worse. I told you, it's in the past. Have you not been hurt in the past and had to learn to forget it?"

Thomas thought of putting a knife into his father's heart, to prevent hours of slow agony, and nodded. He thought of Helena rejecting him after Will was born. Of other betrayals, too many over the years, aware most of them involved women. Which no doubt said something about him, some lesson he had yet to learn.

"Yes, I have," he said. "Many times."

They rode in silence, each nursing their own thoughts, until Amal said, "Did you bring it?"

Thomas patted his jacket.

"Is it the one I helped you choose?"

Thomas thought of the two of them on their knees, holding open a chest between them which contained some of his wealth. The contents had glittered in the lamplight as he tried to make a decision. An important decision.

"It is."

"Then tell her what it means."

They reached Bel's house and the brickworks by mid-morning. One of James's children saw them coming and ran inside to warn of the visitors. Bel came out as Thomas and the others dismounted, unstrapped their saddles and led the horses into a paddock.

Will shook James's hand, kissed his wife on the cheek, then tossed two of the youngest children high into the air to loud squeals. Silva hugged Bel, then Amal did the same.

Thomas stood watching but made no move. In the end it was Bel who came to him. She apologised first before he had the chance.

"I'm sorry, Tom. About what I said to you. I know you're a rational man and don't understand things which are not." She touched his arm.

"I came to tell you I was sorry. Can we put it behind us and start again?"

Bel smiled. "Are we not too old and set in our ways to start over, Tom?"

"No." He looked into her eyes. "I hope not. Oh, and I have something for you." He reached into his jacket, but she put a hand out to stop him.

"I have something for you as well. We can reveal our gifts together." She took his hand and tugged him to go with her.

Thomas looked at Amal as if for permission and she laughed, already turning away to talk with the others. Then Thomas was at the side of the house, but not inside yet because Bel led him to the stairs he recalled from many years before. She took him up into the room above the house. It was as he remembered it. A fire, table, chairs and a bed. He had a recollection of Edward telling him it was used to store hay now. Bel must have deliberately restored it to how it had been when they were young. Had she also thought of what they had done in the room? Thomas suspected she had, because he thought of it too. Their first time together. Not something ever forgotten.

On the table lay something wrapped in blue linen.

Thomas reached into his jacket again and withdrew

his own gift, also wrapped in linen, except his was white. He set it down beside Bel's.

"What is it, Tom?"

"Unwrap it and you will see. What is mine?"

Bel smiled. "Isn't it obvious?"

Thomas waited for her to make the first move. He was nervous. The emotion sat strange with him because he had forgotten how it felt.

"Take it, Tom," she said, and he heard the same nervousness in the tremble of her voice.

He knew this might go on all day and neither of them would know what the other had offered, so he lifted the linen. As he did so, he realised it was not a wrapping but the gift itself. He let the material unfurl to the floor.

"Put it on," said Bel. There was a glistening in her eyes, and he knew this meant a great deal to her. As it did to him. "What is the name of it? Amal didn't tell me, only how to make one. I hope I have done it right."

"It's a tagelmust, and yes, you have done it right. I lost my last one."

"Amal told me that as well. She told me someone stole it, so I thought you might need a new one. She says it means a lot to you. How do you wear it?"

"It can be worn in several ways," Thomas said.

"Show me them all."

"I will show you one, and then you must open your own gift." Thomas wrapped the tagelmust around his head so it formed a loose covering, then he twisted the rest around his neck, tossing the last length over his shoulder.

Bel stared at him, no expression on her face.

"Is that how you looked when you lived in Spain?"

"Without the jacket and hose. I wore a long robe most of the time."

"People must dress differently there than they do here."

"Not these days, but for most of the time I lived in Moorish al-Andalus I dressed as they did. The people, the manner of dress, the food — all of it was different. It was an alien land, and I loved it."

"I love this land, Tom."

"I know." There were things between them both said and unsaid. This was the time to say them, but Thomas did not, and neither did Bel.

Instead, she reached for her gift and unwrapped it. A small brooch fell into her hand. It was finely crafted in gold, with bright red rubies and agate set into the filigree. A gold pin allowed it to be attached to a coat, a shirt or jacket.

"It's beautiful, Tom. What is it?"

"A pomegranate. It is the symbol of Granada, the city I lived in. It is also a symbol of long life and beauty. Which is why I thought of you when I chose it."

Bel laughed. "Do you mean I am old?"

"No. I mean you are beautiful."

Bel shook her head. "I was once. The prettiest girl in Lemster, everyone said. Not that it is much of a claim. I know I am that no longer."

"You are still beautiful to me." Thomas felt a twining of fear in his chest. It was now things would change between them or not. He wished he had spoken with Jorge about what to say, but it was too late now. Better it came from him. His heart and his mind.

"I can't take this, Tom. It must be worth a fortune."

"Ten fortunes, but it is yours."

"When would I ever wear it?"

"It doesn't matter. It's still yours."

"Did you buy it?"

"I acquired it from a man who no longer had a need for it, along with much else, but that is what I chose for you."

Bel was close enough to kiss. Thomas thought it was about time he did so. But as he leaned close the door opened and Edward stepped into the room. He hesitated, then came forward.

"We are about to put food on the table, Ma." He looked between the two of them. "Or shall I send some up here for you?" He tried to look innocent but failed.

"We will come down, Ed. Give us a moment."

Edward nodded and stepped out, shutting the door as he left.

"Kiss me now," said Bel, "for I know that is what you were about to do." She put her hands on his shoulders. "And kiss me like you used to, when we were little more than children, but old enough not to act like children."

So Thomas did. And by the time they went down to the table piled with food, everyone laughed and some of them even clapped.

"Tell me, Silva," said Bel as she sat beside her, while Thomas had to sit three places farther along the table, "what did you find in Tom's house, and is it safe now if I want to visit?"

CHAPTER TWENTY-SIX

It was several days before Thomas went to Usaden's house to ask if he knew where Jack Pook was, but as Emma let him in he saw the man in front of the fire with his feet up on a stool.

"You will regret that when you go out in the cold," Thomas said.

"Then I will just have to stay here. Emma's sister is coming later so she can rub them for me."

Thomas looked at the woman Usaden lived with. "I take it your sister is both older and far less pretty than you?"

"She is older, yes. As for pretty, it is not my place to say. She has taken a shine to Jack for some reason. Are you here for Usaden? If so he is out, but will be home soon."

"No, it's Jack I want."

"Then I will get on with preparing supper."

Jack put his feet on the floor and looked around for his boots. He found one and pulled it on. The other was under the table and Thomas tossed it to him. Outside, they walked uphill to Market Square. A few stalls sold vegetables, cheeses and live chickens; on another were rolls of cloth, but the weather kept most people indoors.

"I assume you wanted to have our talk in private," said Jack. "Does this concern my sister? If so, you have my blessing."

"It's not about Bel, and is she not old enough not to need your blessing?"

"It would do no harm."

"No, you are right. I wanted to ask how well you know the woods above Burford."

"Well enough. Not as well as I know those between here and Lemster, but better than any other man, I would say."

"Have you ever seen a place to leave something you didn't want found other than by the person it was meant for?"

"A secret place? There are many of those, Tom. Why do you want to know?"

"I assume you heard about Walter Mason and what he did?"

"Amal came to ask Emma about cunning-folk. She didn't know any, so it was fortunate I was there. I told her about Silva Taylor and where she lives. There are others, but Silva is the best."

"It was you, was it? Have you heard my son has set his sights on her?"

"Silva will put him straight. Oh, she takes a man now and again, but never lets it get serious. You might be wise to tell him that before he gets his heart broke. He might be big and strong, but women can hurt a man more than swords or arrows. Do you want me to go out that way and look, now I know what it is I'm looking for?"

"I will make it worth your while."

"I need no payment from you, Tom."

"I might find you a position working for me."

Jack laughed. "Me work? No offence, but I would be a poor excuse for a worker, and soon enough the woods would call again."

As he turned away Thomas stopped him.

"I have another question before you go."

Jack smiled. "If you want to know whether Bel talks about you, then she does. If you want to know what she says about you, then you will wait a long time before you hear anything from me."

"It's not that, but now I know she talks to you of me it answers something for me. But it's Emma I want to ask you about. She seems sweet, but does she not find your presence under her roof vexatious?"

The humour drained from Jack's face. "I have not forced myself on them. I went there once with Usaden and Emma told me they have a spare room if I wanted to use it now and again." Jack shrugged one shoulder. "Now and again seems to have turned into most of the time, I admit, but I spoke with her about it and she enjoys having us both there. And … well, at this time of year I feel the cold more than I used to. Come spring and I will sleep under the stars again."

"I meant nothing by the question," Thomas said.

"Yes, you did, but I forgive you. It's your job to ask

awkward questions, Tom. And I know you love Usaden like another son. As he loves you."

With that, Jack strode away. Not back to the house he now shared with Usaden and Emma, but down Broad Street, which would allow him to cross the river and make his way towards Burford.

Thomas watched him go. He had not meant for Jack to begin the search this soon but knew that was his nature. Jack, like Usaden, was instinctive. It was no surprise they had become firm friends.

It was the second week of January before Prince Arthur and his bride returned from their Christmas sojourn at Tickenhill House in Bewdley. They had been there almost four weeks. Catherine had told Thomas before leaving that the house there was smaller, warmer, and would be a good place to spend time together while the world carried on elsewhere. There had been a fragility to her when they spoke, but two days after their return her mood had changed when she came to the house at Burway with a small guard. She was both relaxed and open. Thomas showed her the works on his house, which had progressed since the discovery and removal of the charms in the walls, which he did not mention. The damage done in their removal had been repaired. From the now flag-tiled courtyard he pointed to his workshop, which was almost complete, and a second half constructed where Belia and Amal would work from.

"This is a fine house, Thomas," said Catherine as she

stood beside him, wrapped in a thick fur cloak. The weather had been cold throughout the month and showed little sign of improvement. "Apart from the snow on the ground, it reminds me of Spain."

"Which is my intention, Your Grace."

Catherine scowled. "Call me by name. You of all men can call me by name. As can your children." She smiled. "And Jorge, I suppose."

"I suspect you couldn't stop him. Have you heard from your mother?"

"A letter came four days after Christmas. She says she is well. So is father, though he is in Naples attempting to quell another uprising."

"Then no doubt he is content."

"He does so like to fight. I wrote back and told her of my life in England, of my new husband and his nature, and a little of your new position." Catherine looked away as a faint flush coloured her cheeks. "I came here because I have not seen you or the others since before Christmas, but I have another reason. A delicate reason."

"Are you...?"

Catherine looked at him wide-eyed as she worked out what he had not quite asked, before laughing.

"No, not that. Not yet. Which is what the delicate reason concerns."

"Then best talk to Amal about it."

"No, I intend to ask you." Except she did not ask. "Show me the inside of your workshop. Is it like the one in Granada?"

"Larger," Thomas said, "and better organised."

"That would not be difficult."

Thomas offered his arm as they passed through the gate, and Catherine placed her hand on it as he led her across the frost-hard ground. He was aware of the guards' eyes on them as they crossed to the workshop.

The building was single storey, but the roof was high. The door was not yet hung but stood beside the opening for it. Inside, benches and shelves lined three of the walls, with a large table in the centre. All were new. All fashioned of elm that shone from the oiling of the wood. Some shelves already held herbs, roots, leaves, flowers, poppy heads, and three long hanks of hemp. More would have to be grown, but Thomas suspected he might have to send to Spain or elsewhere. He did not expect England would be warm enough to allow the sticky white resin to form.

"It is wonderful," said Catherine. "Mother would approve. As she would approve of the place you have created here, and your position. Do you miss Spain?"

"Answer me first. Do you?"

"Of course, but my place is here now in England, at the side of Arthur." She took a pace away and turned to face him. Her next words came in a rush before she could bite them back. "I need to give him a son, Thomas. We slept apart during Lent of course, as we had to, but at Bewdley we shared the same bed. Yet still I bleed every month. I came to ask you for help. You know about children. You have so many."

"A few, yes." Thomas was aware Catherine knew Jorge's children were also his. "But I am the wrong man to ask. I heal people, but any advice I might offer on affairs of the heart and other places would be suspect. You should speak to Jorge, or better yet Belia, for she is more familiar with the ways of women and knows remedies I do not. But I will say you should not be concerned. Sometimes these things take time, and soon enough you will be with child. I assume … you are doing what is expected?"

Catherine laughed, the sound seeming to release some of her tension. "We are. Sometimes several times a day." She tried for a look of innocence but failed. "There was little else to do at Tickenhill."

"It will happen, I promise. But talk to Belia. She is better able to help than me."

"Except you have always looked out for me. I have grown used to it. You are closer to me than anyone else in this land."

"That will change. You have not been married three months yet. In another year, you will go to Arthur with your worries, a babe at your hip."

"I will always come to you. You are my last connection to my homeland."

"You have your ladies about you."

"Less so now than I once did. They do not speak English, and Arthur likes those around me to do so. There are times I am lonely, but I know that will ease with time. Send Amal to visit, I would like that."

"Ask her yourself. She is inside the house."

"And Will?"

"Yes, him too. As are Jorge and Belia. It will be just like old times in Spain. Look, I have even used Moorish bricks around the doors and windows."

"I noticed. You will get even more of a reputation for being strange."

"I have a reputation for being strange?"

"You know you do, both here and in Spain, but it is the kind of strange I like, as does my mother. And I have one more favour to ask."

"Then ask it." Thomas offered his arm again and led her out of the workshop towards the house.

"Make some excuse to see Arthur, on business perhaps. I have this, which is reason enough to visit." Catherine handed him a sealed letter. "He gave it to me to pass on to you. Use it as an excuse."

"I need no excuse to ask for a meeting with your husband, Cat. I like the lad." Thomas turned the letter over, examining the Prince's seal. "What is it about?"

"Read it and you will find out. And when you visit, I want you to look at him carefully. I worry Arthur sickens for something. He is pale and complains of being tired all the time. I know John Argentine will never allow you to examine him, but I know you can tell much from sitting with him."

"Are you sure it is not you who tires him?"

Catherine laughed again, covering her mouth. "Perhaps, but he always seems able to rise to the occasion." Her eyes sparked at the wickedness of their talk.

"I will come today. Perhaps I can accompany you when you return to the castle."

"After noon, then. I want to see all of your marvellous house and talk with my friends here. I feel safer with you, Will and Jorge than anywhere else, so I can send my guards away."

"I expect they have their orders and can't leave without you. Will is down by the river building some kind of structure from old stone. Perhaps your guards can help."

"Should I go to say hello?"

"He would like that." Thomas hesitated a moment, then spoke. It was only fair that Catherine should know. "He has a new friend. A woman by the name of Silva Taylor. They have grown close."

"Then I am pleased for him. You know how I felt about your son, however such feelings were naught but dreams in the mind of a young princess. I am happy with my lot and wish him every happiness as well."

When Thomas returned to the castle with Catherine, Prince Arthur was in the great chamber, together with Gruffydd ap Rhys and Sir Richard Pole.

"I see Catherine gave you my note," said Arthur. "She told me she would be all morning with you, so we waited until now for you to arrive. I assumed you would accompany her back. Did you read the note?"

"I did, Your Grace, and understood it without fully understanding why it was sent to me. Surely murder is a matter for the sheriff, or you three here."

"I would agree, but the sheriff is not yet returned from his holdings in Northamptonshire and this matter is of less importance than we can be seen to deal with. You can turn my request down if you feel it is beneath you. The man will have to wait in his cell for the sheriff's return."

"I will speak with him and any witnesses, and decide

once I have done so. I am uneasy at sentencing a man to hang."

"As are we all. But if he is guilty, then hang he will. Have you ever seen a man hang, Thomas?"

"I have, but took no pleasure from it."

"Good. The mob howls and screams, but it can be a painful way to die unless the hangman knows his job. Now, I hear you have been investigating other deaths while I have been away."

"I have, Your Grace." Thomas considered it wise not to mention his suspicion of Philippa Gale's involvement, aware the Prince still liked her. Left to his own devices, he was likely to pardon all her crimes.

"And?" asked Sir Richard Pole.

"I am making little progress. Have you heard about the other killing in Lemster?"

"I have not, but we returned only a few days ago. Besides, we trust you. Do we need to be concerned?"

Thomas knew that Sir Richard and Gruffydd had taken the opportunity of Prince Arthur's absence to visit their own holdings. One to London, the other to south-west Wales.

"Not if you trust me to deal with it." Thomas thought matters would be best managed without having to report to the castle for confirmation of every decision. "But I will report my findings regularly."

"Not too regularly," said Gruffydd. "There is much to do. Easter is not far off and the Prince wants to make it a spectacle to celebrate his new wife. You will be part of it, won't you?"

"If you can find a role for me." Easter was over two

months away and he hoped they might forget. "Is the man accused of murder housed in Ludlow?"

"In a cell hard by the gatehouse. You would know that if you still lived in the rooms assigned to you." Gruffydd waved a hand when he saw Thomas's expression. "It's not a criticism, Tom. I know you need your own place to show you are not a servant of the castle. I hear your house is a thing of wonder."

"I wouldn't say that, but it will be comfortable. You are welcome to visit any time you want. All of you." Thomas suspected Prince Arthur might, but not Sir Richard. "If we are done, I will go speak with this man."

Gruffydd glanced at Sir Richard and Prince Arthur. "Are we done?"

"For now," said Sir Richard.

The cell was colder than the outside air, dark, and stank. A wooden bucket in one corner was already full of ordure which slopped over to the stone floor. There was no pallet, no chair, no stool. A short man crouched in the opposite corner to the bucket, but he would have no way of escaping the stink.

"When was the last time they emptied your bucket?" Thomas asked as soon as the cell door slammed behind him.

"They have not. I try to hold it in now."

Thomas turned and hammered on the door, but it was long minutes before a small panel opened.

"What?"

"Send someone to empty the bucket in here."

"Why?"

"Because it's full."

"Then tell him to stop shitting." The panel started to close, but Thomas pushed a hand into the space.

"Do you know who I am?" He heard the privilege in his words and hated it, but knew no other way.

"Don't know, don't care."

"Then I suggest you go to Sir Richard Croft and ask him who Thomas Berrington is and what business he has being here."

"Why should I do that?"

"Because if you don't I will make it my business to have you dismissed, and for the whole of Ludlow to know the reason."

"He killed someone."

"He is accused of murder, which is why I am here, to discover whether he is guilty or not. Now do as I ask or walk out through the gate, and as you go send me someone who will listen to reason." Thomas removed his hand.

"It will do you no good, sir," said the crouching man.

"Then I will make the same demand until it does do some good." Thomas squatted in front of the man. He could smell him, but tried to ignore it. "Now tell me, are you guilty of what you are accused?"

"I killed my wife, true enough, but it was kill her or have her kill me, sir. She came at me with a carving knife."

"Why?"

"I told her the food she gave me was not fit for our pigs."

"And she came at you with a knife for that?"

The man nodded, the movement barely visible in the gloom. "It may not have been the first time I said it. I took the knife from her, but she grabbed another. We tussled. I did not mean to kill her, sir. She was a good wife. Apart from the food."

"You stuck her by accident?"

"I did, sir."

The cell door opened and a young lad came in with a cloth held over his nose and mouth. He walked to the bucket and looked down at it but made no move to lift it.

"Empty it and there's a ha'penny in it for you," Thomas said.

The lad looked at him, back at the bucket.

"A penny, then,' Thomas added. 'And make sure you wash it out before you bring it back."

Once the lad had taken the bucket out, Thomas turned back to the prisoner to see him smiling. The expression closed down at once, but too late. Thomas knew the man's words of innocence were a lie. He rose to his feet.

"I will call an inquest and you will tell your tale to a jury of your peers. They will decide your fate."

"People in Ludlow dislike me, sir."

"Then you will be out of luck."

Thomas turned and left the cell. He passed the lad on his way out and handed him a penny. The bucket was empty, but the washing perfunctory. Not that it mattered. The man in the cell would not live long enough to fill it again.

CHAPTER TWENTY-SEVEN

The prisoner was hanged on the last day of February. Thomas presided over the inquest, and the jury of fifteen men all found him guilty. Thomas had no choice in the punishment, but it sat heavily with him all the same. He made himself attend, but ensured the hangman was well-paid and came recommended. The drop was long and the man's neck snapped clean, though his legs kicked for some time after life had fled. Thomas remained until after the body was cut down and the crowd dispersed. Many had nodded to him as they passed. A few stopped to exchange words. Nobody blamed him for sentencing the man to be hanged. Many told him he had made the right decision. So why, Thomas wondered, did it not feel right to him? He knew if he remained as Justice of the Peace such decisions would come his way again. It was the nature of the job.

So lost was he in his own thoughts, he did not hear Will approach until his son spoke.

"He deserved his punishment, Pa. He killed his wife."

"Did you speak with him?"

"I did. He told me the same story he did you, but when I pushed the truth came out. He had planned on killing her for some time."

"I know. I asked others. He was seeing another woman, a far younger woman, and wanted his freedom."

"There was no need to kill her. He could have walked away."

"Not without consequences. There are laws against such things, and I expect I am meant to apply them. I also expect I am supposed to know what they all are."

"Ami is doing that," said Will. "She reads more books than I thought there were in England. She will steer you right. You have us both, Pa. One the brain, the other the brawn."

"And which is which?"

Will punched his father softly on the shoulder, as if afraid he might do some damage.

"What I can't understand," Thomas said, "is why he thought killing her was the sensible choice and how he believed he could get away with it."

"Self-defence, he claimed. We have done the same often enough, have we not?"

"Yes, I expect we have. But never in cold blood, and never without good reason."

Thomas turned away, and Will fell in step at his side. It felt right, the two of them striding through the town they were making their home.

"Amal has a message for you, by the way."

"What does it say? Is it anything to do with John Miller or Arthur Wodall?" Thomas was aware the trail had gone cold in both cases. If there ever had been a trail to follow. It felt like it once, but no more. At least Philippa's threats had ceased. Perhaps his message had been heeded and this was the end of it.

"It's addressed to you, Pa, so I don't know what it says."

They stopped at Agnes's bakery to buy bread and rolls, then continued out through Linney Gate to descend the slope to the banks of the Teme. When they arrived at the almost complete house the rolls were still warm, and Jack Pook sat at the wide kitchen table with his bare feet stretched out in front of the fire.

"I have already warned you about that," Thomas said, working his own boots off. He wanted to bathe and change out of the formal clothes expected of him but knew both would have to wait.

"You have, and I will ignore your sound advice yet again. Bel sends her regards, by the way. She wants to know when you intend to call on her again. And I think I have found that place you asked me to search for all those weeks ago."

"Is it close to Burford?"

"Close enough to walk in a half hour, yes."

"Can you show me once I have changed out of these stupid clothes?"

"I almost didn't recognise you, and yes I can."

"Was there any sign of the spot being used?"

"Not recently, but I'm sure it's the place. An old sheep pen on Burford rise. There's a loose stone with a small chamber behind, just the right size to hide something in. You go get changed, Tom, and I'll stay here until you're ready." Jack reached for one of the rolls and bit into it.

Thomas was on his way to his room, thinking he might change his mind and bathe, when he met Amal coming the other way from her own room.

"I have a note for you," she said.

"Will told me. Is it in your room?"

"In your workshop on the table. I thought you more likely to go there first."

"Jack is in the kitchen waiting for me. He thinks he found the place Philippa has been using to send messages to people, but it hasn't been used for a while, he says."

"Since she killed John Miller, and we put a stop to Walter Mason and that other man. She has no one to send her messages for her anymore. Though I think the message you have may be from her. Perhaps it is what we all want. A truce. Peace between you and her."

Thomas stared at Amal, then turned and descended the stairs. He was halfway to his workshop before he remembered he had taken his boots off, but continued anyway.

The single folded sheet sat in the middle of the table, the seal uppermost. Thomas examined it but there was no mark. Just wax pressed down with something solid. He broke it and read the words.

Thomas, I need you. I am dying and have to confess before it is too late. Come to the cottage. I will be waiting.

He ran back to the house, the note in his hand. Inside, he gave it to Amal while he pulled on his boots.

"We will have to look at this hiding place another day, Jack," he said. "I have something I must do."

"I will come too," said Amal. "If Philippa is truly sick, I can help."

"And if it is a ploy to draw me to her and she is waiting with a dozen men? I will take Will and Usaden with me."

"I will come as well," said Jack Pook, as he searched for his own boots. "I know that land like I know myself."

"I am still coming," said Amal. "I will stay back if there is trouble, but I will be there."

The expression on her face brooked no refusal, so Thomas only nodded. He would ask Will to ride close by her, to offer protection if there was trouble. He wondered whether he expected any, but had no answer. He had almost dismissed Philippa from his mind, aware now that had been a mistake.

It was late morning before they crossed Ludford Bridge and headed south and east along now familiar tracks. As February drew to an end the land was slowly waking from its winter slumber. The first buds, as yet uncurled, showed on the many apple, pear, plum and damson trees. It was too soon for hawthorn, but the previous season's red berries still clung to some branches. The ground underfoot was softer than it had been a week before, and a westerly wind carried the promise of a night without frost.

As they approached Burford, Thomas slowed and called the others to a halt. Ahead lay the cottage at the entrance to Sir Thomas Cornwell's estate. A curl of smoke rose from the chimney. Outside stood a single figure, a man dressed in a leather fighting jerkin. Five horses were tied to the railing of a wooden fence.

Thomas dismounted. "Stay here." He glanced at Will. "You know what to do."

Only after he received a nod from his son did Thomas walk towards the cottage. The guard waited until Thomas was a hundred paces away, then came to meet him. Thomas studied his face, but the man was not familiar to him.

"You are Berrington?"

Thomas nodded.

"Who are the others? The message my mistress sent was meant only for you."

"They are my family and would not allow me to come here alone. In case there were six men waiting for me. But I see there are only five, unless you do not have a horse."

"We are not here to attack you. We protect her. She is sick."

"What ails her?"

"Come inside and you will see."

Thomas stared into the man's eyes, searching for some duplicity, but if any lay there he was not skilled enough to discern it. Perhaps he should have asked Jorge to come with them, but it was too late now.

"I will look at her, but I want all of you out of that cottage before I enter."

"No."

Thomas turned and started back to the others.

"Wait!" The man followed him. "We cannot leave her at your mercy. We know what lies between you and her. I do not trust you will not do her more harm. Two of us must remain with her."

"One."

The man shook his head.

"Then two of us as well," Thomas said. He turned and called back to the others. "Amal, come to me. Bring my saddle bag. Will, come closer but wait at a distance."

"You and a girl?" said the man with a smile. "Does she have a knife?"

"I hope so. I make sure of it ever since she was attacked."

The man looked beyond Thomas to where Amal descended the slope, with a heavy saddle bag across her shoulder.

"She is the one?"

"If you refer to events at Hugh Clement's manor house then yes, she is the one."

"My mistress tells me the girl is to blame for all that has befallen her. I am not sure I can let her enter with you."

"Whatever has befallen Philippa is no fault of Amal's. It is all mine. So, do you intend to stop me from entering the cottage?"

"Wait here." The man turned, ran to the cottage and went inside, leaving the door half open.

"Did he say what was wrong with her?" asked Amal when she reached Thomas.

"He didn't, but I suspect I already know." He held up his right hand, pleased when Amal nodded her understanding.

"I hear rumours there is sickness in surrounding districts," said Amal. "Some kind of sweating."

"I have heard of nothing in Ludlow."

"Shrewsbury, I was told. And to the east. Worcester, Bewdley, other towns. Arthur and Catherine have only recently returned from Bewdley." Amal smiled. "Though according to Cat they spent most of their time in bed."

"Has she spoken with you or Belia about that? She asked me why she isn't with child yet and I urged her to patience."

"She has, to both of us. We offered her the same advice you did. Time, and..." Amal's gaze left her father. "That man is coming back."

Thomas turned, his hand resting against the hilt of a knife at his waist, but as the man came closer he saw it would not be needed.

"Me and one other," said the man. "The others will leave."

Even as he spoke men came out from the cottage, pulling on jerkins and coats. They walked to their horses, mounted and rode off. Not towards Burford Manor, which Thomas expected, but west on the road that would lead them eventually to Lemster, or Hereford if they turned south. Except they did not. They rode a quarter mile then stopped, waiting.

Thomas glanced back at Will, who nodded and urged his horse towards where the three men waited.

As soon as Thomas entered the cottage, he knew what ailed Philippa Gale. He wrapped his new tagelmust across his nose and mouth. The stench was faint in the first room, where the two protectors stood, but as he entered the bedroom it grew stronger. Amal appeared to be unaffected, or was better at ignoring it.

Philippa Gale lay half under the covers of the bed. She wore a thin shift stained with vomit, but that was not the cause of the cloying smell. Her right arm was extended over the edge of the bed. It was almost black to the elbow, and green puss gathered around the stump of her wrist.

Thomas stood at the foot of the bed, staring at her. Amal went to the gangrenous arm and touched it.

"She is hot, Pa."

"She will be."

"You came," said Philippa. "I did not think you would."

"I have been seeking you for a long time. Why would I not come when you send for me?"

Philippa looked at Amal. "Am I dying?"

It was Thomas who answered. "Yes, you will die unless we do something." He looked around. "But not here. Ami, go outside and call Will. Send him to the manor house to ask for a cart. We will take her to Burway, to my workshop."

Amal stopped beside her father and whispered. "The arm will have to come off."

"Of course it will."

When his daughter had gone Thomas took her place at the bedside. He pulled up a three-legged stool and reached for Philippa's arm. His fingers probed beneath the armpit, not liking what he found there. More inflammation. He did not know if she could be saved. If it was even worth the trying. Better to finish her now to avoid days or weeks of searing agony.

"Save me, Tom. For old times' sake."

He almost laughed. "There are no old times between us, unless they are all in your head. I will save you if I can, but only so you can hang for the murder of John Miller and Arthur Wodall."

Philippa tried to smile, but the expression was closer to a grimace. "You would not do that to me, not after what we shared."

"Don't expect mercy from me, Pip. I have none in my soul, either for you or your father, who almost killed me before killing himself. I will do what I can for you, but only so I can put the deaths behind me."

Philippa stared at him, a strange expression on her face. As if she had knowledge and secrets Thomas knew nothing about.

"I admit to killing the boy. John was so willing, so eager to please, but his usefulness had come to an end." Her words were matter-of-fact, as if using and killing John Miller, a lad whose bed she had shared, meant nothing to her. But Thomas supposed he should know that already because it is what she had done to him.

"What other name did you give?" she asked. "I killed only one, not two."

"But you sent men to put me in the Wye. Or do you deny that as well?"

"No. You came after me and had to be dealt with. I thought drowning would be a kinder death than a blade, but I should have told them to cut you as well."

"After I saw you in Hereford, did you really leave to the east with your men?"

"They accompanied me as far as Lugwardine to ensure my safety, then I sent them back. I wanted to know your body had been found. If not, I told them to spread word you might be on the bed of the river." Philippa met Thomas's eyes, a surety in her own, a coldness. "I know you can be resourceful, and I needed to be sure you were dead."

"Yet here I am. Not dead. You need to employ a better class of assassin."

"They are hard to find. I once had someone I could trust, but he betrayed me."

"Who is the other man?" Thomas asked as he continued to examine Philippa's arm. He knew what he would have to do, the knowledge distant from him, emotionless.

"What other man?"

"The one you set to make charms to place in my house. I know it wasn't you — so who?"

Philippa shook her head. "Why should I tell you, even if I knew?"

"Because you came to me for help. That indicates a trade. I save your life. You tell me who made the charms."

"If I knew his name I would tell you, but I do not. I asked an old crone to find me the best practitioner in the west. She would not tell me, but offered to act as a go-between. Even when I paid her in gold she refused to give me a name."

"What if I don't believe you?"

"It is no concern of mine whether you do or not. I speak the truth."

"And the crone? What is her name?"

"So you can question her for the other name?" Philippa smiled, but the expression was strained. "I thought you

296

knew me better than that. Why would I leave a trail to follow? The woman had lived many summers, but will not see another." Philippa grimaced as pain lanced through her. "Are you resourceful enough to fix my arm?"

Thomas shook his head. "You should have come to me sooner. It can't be fixed. The corruption has gone too far. The arm will have to come off."

CHAPTER TWENTY-EIGHT

"This is all we have left." Amal held a small cotton sack out to her father. It looked empty.

Thomas took it from her and peered inside. Dust and grains. "It's not enough for what she is about to go through. Have you asked Belia if she has any?"

"That was from her. You no longer have any poppy left, and very little hemp, but if I go through all the drawers I might find something. Is there anything else you can use?"

"Alcohol, but I would rather not in her condition."

"Why are you doing this, Pa? She tried to kill you more than once, and almost succeeded. You know she has killed other men. Let her die."

"That's a possibility, except you know without treatment her death will be long and agonising."

"Opening a vein would be the kindest," said Amal.

Thomas stared at his daughter, wondering when she had become so cold-hearted. Or rational. Yes, he thought, rational. As he should be, because Amal was making sense.

"Is Silva around?"

"She is. Do you want me to fetch her?"

"If you would."

When she was gone Thomas turned back to Philippa Gale. She was barely conscious, and he hoped she had not heard their conversation. She was also naked from the waist up, though he knew he should remove her skirt as well so he could check her body for other lesions. Dark veins twisted along her arm, into her shoulder, across her chest. The sickness would reach her heart soon and it would stutter and stop. He reached out and felt her neck, the pulse there faint and fast.

"You still want to touch me, then," murmured Philippa.

"Only checking you are still alive. It might have saved me some trouble."

"What are you going to do to me?" Her words were slurred.

"That depends how far the infection has spread. Everything below your elbow is dead. Above it, there are signs it may have travelled farther. Your arm will have to come off at the shoulder."

Philippa shook her head. "You have already taken my hand. You can't take my arm as well."

"You took your hand when you tried to kill my daughter."

"She must have done something to the flintlock. I have used them before and that has never happened."

"Well, that time it did. I either remove your entire arm or you die. Choose."

Philippa said nothing.

Amal returned with Silva Taylor. She came to the table and stared down at Philippa before turning to Thomas. There was no disgust on her face.

"Amal tells me you have some herbs to stop pain but not enough. Do you want me to find you something?"

"Do you have anything?"

"I have dried herbs, barks and roots that can help. There will be little fresh at this time of year, but I will fetch what I have." She looked again at Philippa. "Is this the woman Will told me about?"

"It is. Go now. I want to start as soon as I can."

"Will can take me on his horse, it will be faster. I will be as quick as I can."

Thomas and Amal washed Philippa's body, including her diseased arm. Both of them were used to the work, losing themselves in the familiarity of it. Philippa cried out several times but Thomas refused to give her anything for the pain. He would need all the herbs he had for when the cutting started.

It was almost an hour before Silva returned. Will came as far as the door to look in, then turned away.

"I have mushrooms, also mandrake, hemlock and henbane already mixed in a liquor of alcohol. If you add your poppy to it I believe it may be enough. I also brought leeches, which you should put on the putrid arm. They will draw out some of the infection and also help to ease the pain, but they will not be enough on their own. What are you going to do to her?"

"Expose the joint at the shoulder, then cut and cauterise to remove the entire arm. I will know when I do it if the infection has spread into her chest. In which case I will end her life quickly, for there is nothing else can be done."

"You have done this before?"

"I have, but only on the field of battle, and with no pain relief."

"Did the men survive?"

"About half of them."

Silva nodded. "Then you are an excellent surgeon. Do you want me to help?"

"I have Amal, but we may need you to hold Philippa down even with everything we give her."

"Then ask Will to come back. I can help, of course, but Will is the strongest of us all. What about Jorge?"

"He will pass out at what has to be done, but yes, send for Will if he agrees to come. It will not be a pretty sight."

"He tells me he has seen worse. He told me he saw his mother die."

Thomas might have corrected Silva, but she had already gone. Lubna had not been Will's mother, but he called her that, so perhaps what he said was closer to the truth than the truth itself.

Thomas looked at the pot holding the leeches, then picked two out and set them against Philippa's arm. He did not believe in bleeding, but knew in some circumstances it was the right treatment. This was one of those times.

He handed the pot to Amal, who set the remaining leeches to their work while Thomas mixed the liquor Silva had brought together with what remained of his own. He poured powdered willow bark into a cup and added a small amount of wine before sitting Philippa up and making her drink it all. After a short while he repeated the process, this time with the combination he'd made with what Silva had brought.

He stood next to Amal and watched the woman who wanted him dead slip into a doze, then a deeper state of unconsciousness.

Silva returned with Will.

"I want you both to hold her down. She is drugged now, but will writhe like a headless snake once we start."

Will nodded and went to the far side, away from the rotting arm. If the smell bothered him, he gave no sign.

"I asked Belia to build a fire outside," said Silva. "The arm must be burned, the ashes scattered in the clean waters of the Teme to remove all trace of the poison from her."

Thomas had forgotten her strange beliefs, but knew the first was a good idea. He did not have to believe the rest.

Thomas pinched Philippa's good arm, pleased when she failed to respond.

"All right, let's get this done."

He cut into the flesh where the shoulder joint lay. As he did so Amal leaned against him, using an iron rod that had been resting in a brazier to cauterise the blood vessels. Time passed without either of them aware of it. As Thomas exposed more raw flesh he nodded in satisfaction, because he saw no sign the infection had reached Philippa's chest.

Eventually he looked at Will, who continued to hold

Philippa down. "Come here and hold her while I pull her shoulder out."

Will stood close but said, "You hold her, Pa. I can jerk it free faster than you."

Thomas considered only a moment before nodding. He put his arms around Philippa's chest, grasping her tight. Will gripped the arm between elbow and shoulder, set one foot against the side of the table, then with a sudden jerk, almost fell backwards as the arm popped loose, now that no flesh or tendons held it in place.

"Give it to me, I will do it," said Silva. "I need to speak the right words of power if its evil is not to taint this house and you, Thomas."

Will looked at his father, who nodded. He handed the arm to Silva, who took it outside.

"Do you need me for anything else, Pa?" asked Will.

"No, go with her."

When they were gone Thomas started to close the wound, but Amal pushed him aside. "I can do this. You know my needlework is better than yours."

"It will not be pretty whatever we do." But Thomas allowed her to take the needle and gut from him as a sudden weariness ran through him. "Tell me, Ami, how close are Will and Silva?"

Amal's face showed a deep concentration as she drew the damaged flesh of Philippa's shoulder together. "I think they are serious. Both Silva and Will."

"Serious?"

Amal smiled without looking away from her work. "Yes. Serious. I assume even you know what serious means."

Thomas watched his daughter work, pulling the skin together to seal the wound, pleased she was so skilled. He had taught her some of this work, but she was naturally more adept at some tasks than him. It felt right that she was. As if it was the way the world was meant to work, even if often it did not.

"Can you finish without me?"

Amal nodded, the tip of her tongue poking out as she concentrated. Thomas went outside, breathing deep of the cold, clean air. Close to the river, he saw smoke rising from a fire, and Silva and Will standing beside it. He walked down but stood a few paces away, not wanting to interfere, aware that Will had stepped outside of his influence now. Thomas believed he was looking at the new life his son would share with this woman. He was about to turn away when Will saw him and waved him to join them.

Thomas closed the gap and stared down at the embers. Some pieces of bone remained, but the flesh had been consumed.

"Why the river?" he asked, recalling Silva's words, and how she had washed the bones of the hand left for him in the Teme.

"It will remove whatever evil might be present. The bones will sink to the bottom and be distributed. The ash will be scattered far and wide, some eaten by fish, others dissolved away completely. Eventually, some may reach the ocean and be even more diluted. The evil held within her flesh will be destroyed."

"The arm wasn't evil; it was filled with corruption."

Silva looked into Thomas's eyes. "I know you are a

rational man and do not believe in everything I do, but I do not hold that against you. Other people believe and that is enough."

Thomas wanted to ask his son if he believed but could not while Silva was there. More than likely he could never ask, because the new relationship between Silva and Will would make it impossible.

"I believe we agree on more things than we disagree on," he said. "Using herbs. Using rationality. Even your beliefs are genuinely held and rational to you."

"Rationality is whatever works, and I see what works — as do you. Does your beautiful house not feel warmer than it did? Safer?"

Thomas smiled. "Warmer, yes, because it's almost finished, and there are fires burning in all parts, and the heating beneath the floors makes everywhere warm."

"That is rational," said Silva. "Where did you learn how to do it?"

"From the Moors in al-Andalus, which is now part of Spain. I believe they may have learned it from the Romans, or reinvented it themselves."

"You will need more of your herbs, the poppy in particular. I have used it in the past but it is difficult to get in this land, and even more difficult to grow. It needs heat to set the white paste. There are poppies in England, but not the kind you want."

"We have some seeds and I intend to try growing them. I plan on building a place with glass walls and roof. I have read about them but never seen one, but I think it can be done. It will be placed on the south-facing slope to see if the poppy will grow there."

"And the hemp," said Silva. "You can grow that outside in the summer, but it does not produce as well. I would like to see your house of glass when it is finished."

"It's not started yet but will be soon. You know you are welcome to live permanently under our roof if you wish."

"Will has already asked me, but I need to give it thought." Silva reached out and touched Will's hand. He smiled and twined his fingers through hers. "Is that woman going to live?"

"I don't know. She might, she might not."

"More likely not, I would say, yet still you tried. I saw your skill in how you removed her arm and know of nobody else who could have done it as well. Yet it might all come to naught."

"I still had to do it."

"Will tells me you loved her once."

"Philippa?" Thomas shook his head. "What we shared wasn't love. And I have no feelings for her now."

"Not even hate at what she did?"

"Not even hate."

"What will become of her if she lives?"

"I intend to visit the castle later and ask if she can be housed there. Not in the cells, but somewhere secure. The last time she was held there she escaped, but I will ensure more care is taken this time."

"You will save her so she can hang?"

"That will not be my decision."

Silva inclined her head, and Thomas wondered what her true feelings were about his rationality. Will was also rational, but less so. What did they talk about when they lay together? Perhaps nothing. Perhaps everything.

Silva glanced down at the smouldering grey ashes. "They are ready now, Thomas. It must be you who scatters them because of the connection you have with her."

"Had."

"You cannot undo a connection as simply as that. Come, do it, and then you can go to the castle. I will bring more herbs, for she will have much pain when she wakes."

Thomas watched Silva fill a clay pot with the ashes. She handed it to Thomas, and he waded into the icy river to his waist before tipping the contents into the lead-coloured water. It surprised him to discover he felt better for doing so.

CHAPTER TWENTY-NINE

"I want to know what you are doing with Philippa and where she is being kept." Prince Arthur stared at Thomas, no softness in his expression. Beside him stood Sir Richard Pole. The third man who would normally be with them, Gruffydd ap Rhys, was not present, and Thomas thought it best not to ask where he was. Nine days had passed since Thomas removed Philippa's arm, and she was healing. She could walk unassisted, but never alone. Amal and Silva accompanied her most of the time. Silva tried to find out who she had used to create the charms embedded in Thomas's house, but so far failed to glean anything useful.

"She is held captive in my house at Burway."

"Why are you keeping her there?"

"I consider it the safest place after the last time she escaped. I have those I trust around me, and her quarters are not like the cells in the castle. She is comfortable."

"But not free."

Thomas stared at the Prince. He was pale, but winter could do that to a man.

"She killed John Miller, Your Grace."

"So you claim," said Sir Richard. "Where is your proof?"

Thomas held back the sigh that threatened to emerge. "She was seen and heard in the lad's cottage the night he died. She twisted him to her will, then killed him when he was of no more use."

"And your proof is what — hearsay?" asked Sir Richard.

"Bring her to the castle," said Prince Arthur. "Sir Richard and myself will question her. If she is guilty, as you claim, we will be able tell. If so, she will be held here until an inquest can be arranged. But you cannot preside over it, Thomas. You are too close to her. I will ask Sir Thomas Cornwell, as sheriff of Shropshire, to call it."

Thomas opened his mouth to speak then closed it. He inclined his head. "As you wish, Your Grace. I will fetch her."

"No. I will send men to bring her. Your involvement in this matter is at an end. You serve me well as Justice of the Peace. Return to that role, return to your family. Princess Catherine speaks highly of you, otherwise your position might not be so secure. Bear that in mind before you investigate deaths that are beyond your remit."

"Philippa has lost her arm, Your Grace. I would ask that I may attend her to ensure she suffers no more ill effects than necessary."

"Your request is denied. John Argentine will tend to her. You are dismissed."

Thomas backed away, aware how close he was to angering both men. He would need to agree to the Prince's request, at least until the summer. No doubt the Prince would forget all about it once Catherine was with child. If she was not by then something would be very wrong between them.

Thomas stood on the edge of Market Square and watched a dozen soldiers, accompanied by Sir Richard Pole, emerge to take the road to Dinham Gate. It was the longer way to reach Burway, and the track beside the river was heavy with mud, but Thomas had no intention of telling them that. After they disappeared he walked across to his sister Agnes's bakery and went inside. He felt the need to touch his roots, and Agnes was the only original Berrington remaining, other than himself. He was still there an hour later when her daughters Jilly and Rose came in, their cheeks pink from the cold.

"That lady you used to live with has just gone into the castle on the back of a cart, Uncle Thomas," said Rose. "She was wrapped up like a mummer. I saw Will following the men, but he didn't enter with them."

Thomas was unsurprised his son would ensure Philippa arrived at the castle without incident. No doubt, somewhere not too far distant, Philippa's men were seeking ways to free her.

Thomas embraced Agnes, kissed each girl on the cheek, then went out to where Will stood on the far side of the square.

"I should have sent a message they were coming for her," Thomas said when he stood beside Will.

"I knew you came to the castle, and Sir Richard told

me Arthur wanted her held closer." Will glanced at his father. "He is too soft on her. Do you think she and the Prince ever..." He raised an eyebrow.

"I wouldn't put it past her, not with any man or boy. It is her way."

"Was her way," said Will. "She will be less alluring for the lack of an arm. What are we going to do now?"

"We are going to do as told and try not to make trouble."

Will laughed. "You? And me? Not to mention Jorge."

They walked across Market Square towards Linney and the gate that would offer the short route home.

"Or Silva." Thomas glanced at his son. Tall, good looking, strong as an ox. "I notice she spends most nights with you."

"I know you don't agree with her beliefs, Pa, and to be honest I find some of them difficult to believe myself, but she is unlike anyone I have ever known. I love her."

"Does she love you?"

"I think so. She says it often enough."

"Good. It's gone time you found someone, and despite what you say, I both like and admire her."

"What about you and Bel, Pa? Everyone knows you're going to end up together. Well, everyone apart from the two of you."

"At our age there is no need to rush into things. Is Jack Pook still staying with Usaden and Emma?"

"The last I heard, yes. Why?"

"I think we should have someone keep an eye on the castle. Sir Richard and Arthur no doubt mean to hold Philippa until she stands before judgement, but she has escaped before. We need to look out for strangers as well."

Will nodded. "I'll ask them both to keep watch. I can take a turn too. We all can. Perhaps Agnes will allow us to watch from one of her upper rooms." He turned away from his father and left him to descend the slope alone.

When Thomas returned to the house, Amal was cleaning the room where Philippa had been held captive. She had scrubbed the walls and was starting on the stone floor, which was warm from the channels of water running beneath it.

"We should think about employing someone to do these kinds of jobs," Thomas said.

"Why, when I can do them myself?"

"I noticed you and Belia are busier than you were. Better you spend time on healing and advice than scrubbing floors."

Amal sat on her heels and looked up at her father. "You know some people call us witches, don't you?"

"I didn't. Which people?"

"You can't kill everyone, Pa. Besides, it's not as if they mean it in a bad way. Witches around here are well-respected healers. But you are right, we are busy. I think our reputation has spread. People know we can genuinely heal. Most of the others shake a stick at a wound or offer some potion that makes people throw up, or worse."

"Do you consult with Silva?"

"We do. She is as skilled in herbs as Belia. More skilled in those to be found in the woods and glades of the countryside around here. You should spend more time with her. Talk to her. She will be useful to us all."

"You know she and Will are living together?"

Amal smiled. "You are always the last to hear of such things, aren't you? When are you going to invite Bel to live under our roof?"

"Not you as well." But Thomas smiled as he left his daughter to finish what she was doing.

A week had passed, and life appeared to be settling into normality — if their strange extended family could ever be considered normal — when Catherine arrived in the company of half a dozen armed men. She left her guards outside before passing through the arched entrance to the inner courtyard, where she stopped to stare. Thomas was crossing it, intending to go to his workshop, when he saw her.

"Are you coming in to see the others? We are all here."

"Yes, I will come inside, but I am here to tell you something first." She touched his arm. "Do not go rushing off when I tell you. I want to hear your news after. All the news from everyone. My men can stand outside in the cold, which will do them good. They are always grumbling."

Thomas offered his arm to escort her inside, aware word would spread that Princess Catherine visited the strange house, the strange people, in Burway.

"What is this news, then? Is Arthur unwell?"

"He is not well, but he does not need your skills at the moment. John Argentine attends him and he rallies only to fade again. It is the winter, he says. It is not good for his constitution."

"The winter is almost over, and I am sure Arthur will rally once he gets some sun on his face. Sir Richard Pole told me Argentine also attends to Philippa. Does her wound heal?"

"She is the reason I came. She has left the castle."

Thomas stopped, making Catherine do the same.

"For where? Another cell somewhere, I trust."

"No cell. She has not been held captive the entire time she has been at the castle. Instead, she used the fine rooms you and your family lived in until you came here. She had visitors, men from outside, but also my husband, who I think is a little infatuated with her. I forgive him because she is still beautiful, even with only one arm. She disguises its lack well."

"She must still be in pain. It is but thirty days since I removed the arm."

"She does not complain."

"So where has she gone?"

"That I do not know, only that she is gone. I am glad she has. I will have Arthur's attention on me now instead of her."

"He has known her a long time. Since he was a babe in his nurse's arms."

"As he always tells me, but it does not make the role of a wife easier. He has even stopped—" Catherine broke off abruptly as she realised what she had been about to say, and Thomas did not press her. He had no need to. *Arthur is a fool*, he thought.

Thomas wanted to leave to find out more about where

Philippa had gone but knew he could not until Catherine left. He would accompany her to the castle when she did, after she had eaten spiced food with them and warmed her feet at their hearth. In this out-of-place house, an homage to Andalucia, it would feel almost as if that was where they still lived. Until they emerged into the grey, cold England of early March.

The light was fading as Thomas walked beside Catherine's white mare along the eastern bank of the Teme. Half her guard rode ahead, the others behind. Thomas had not bothered with a horse and kept up easily. A princess was not expected to ride above a slow walk.

Once within the castle walls, Thomas searched out Gruffydd ap Rhys, hoping he had returned. He found him, together with Sir Richard Pole, in their usual haunt at the top of Mortimer's Tower. There was wine and ale, as always, and both men looked west to where the sun sank towards the wooded hills leading to Wales.

Thomas helped himself to a flagon of ale and joined them, unsure yet of his welcome, but Gruffydd slapped him on the shoulder in greeting.

"It has been a while since the three of us stood here setting the world to rights, Tom. Did you miss us, or have you come for the reason I suspect?"

"Who freed her?"

"It was not either of us," said Sir Richard. "Philippa spent a great deal of time with the Prince. With Catherine too, but often alone with Arthur. My wife commented on it, but they are old friends so nobody wanted to say anything. Though I think Catherine may have. I take it she came to tell you?"

"She did." Thomas shook his head. "Philippa is accused of murder — a murder she committed with her own hand. She should have been locked away safe. Why was she not?" Thomas knew he had gone too far with his words, but it was done now.

"Because of who she is, Tom," said Gruffydd. "Arthur grew up beside her. She is as close to him as his sisters — perhaps closer. Whatever anyone else might say about her, he believes her innocent. Believes whatever she tells him. And he doesn't know you like he does her, so why would you expect him to believe you over her?"

"Why am I Justice of the Peace in that case?"

"Ah well, most Justices don't go around trying to punish the guilty. You are a hard example to the rest of us."

"So she escapes justice?"

"That depends," said Sir Richard.

Thomas looked at both men. "On what?"

"On whether you choose to follow her and impose your own justice," said Gruffydd.

"And what would Arthur say about that?"

"Prince Arthur, if he ever heard of it, would not approve," said Sir Richard. "But who will tell him? Not me. What about you, Gruff?"

Gruffydd shook his head. "Tell him what?"

"When did she leave?"

"At midday yesterday. She went east, so a visit to Sir Thomas Cornwell might prove enlightening. She was close to him at the end of last year, and he might offer her a haven away from Ludlow while she continues to heal." Sir Richard smiled. "John Argentine examined her and was forced to say you had done a fine job, though it did not come easy for him. He even admitted he could not have done what you did. Go find her, Thomas. There is something wrong with her and she will not stop until she has punished everyone she believes is against her. First among those are you and your family, but I fear the Prince may also be on that list. Do what you must, but if it involves what I think, then do not tell us anything about it. But God speed."

CHAPTER THIRTY

Thomas rode between Will and Jorge. Usaden followed forty paces behind, scanning the surrounding woods and landscape. Kin ran into the woods and back out. Thomas drew Ferrant to a halt outside the cottage Philippa once lived in, but had no need to dismount to see she was no longer using it. The door at the front stood open, and it looked as if someone had tried to burn it. When he leaned closer, he smelled soot and damp, and suspected someone had wanted to destroy any remnant of evidence that might remain there. He turned Ferrant and rode on towards Burford Manor.

James Marshall waited for them in the yard, four sturdy young men behind him for support.

"I did not expect you to come so soon, Thomas Berrington. Do I need to ask what you are here for? Or should I say who?"

Thomas dismounted while the others remained in their saddles.

"I need to talk with your master. Face to face. I take it he has returned from Derbyshire?"

"He has, but I do not bother him with unwelcome callers. State your business and if I think Sir Thomas needs to know of it I will tell it him myself."

"Not good enough. I must stand before him. I need to see his eyes when I ask my questions."

"You are getting above yourself, Justice of the Peace or not. Sir Thomas has been sheriff of Shropshire, Herefordshire and Worcestershire, and will be so again. You might work for Ludlow Castle, but that holds no weight here."

"You know who I am. Stand aside so I can search the house myself. Or do you believe you and your master stand above the law of the land?"

"You will enter only after you come past the five of us. I have heard your reputation—" James Marshall inclined his head, "—and that of your son, but you will not attack us."

Thomas took a pace closer. "Don't be so sure about that. I wish you no harm, nor your men, but there are four of us, and two of the men with me are equal to any six, if not more. I ask again. Stand aside."

"And you know I cannot."

Thomas had run out of bluff, and suspected the man in front of him knew it. Which is when a short, portly figure appeared in the elegant doorway behind them.

"What is going on here, Charles? We send beggars away, do we not?"

Thomas took two paces and pushed James Marshall aside so hard the man fell to one knee. The four behind closed ranks, but Thomas was through them as well in a moment. He did not have to look around to know that Will would be close behind, with Usaden roaming the sides.

Ahead of him, Sir Thomas Cornwell moved backwards so fast his heel caught on the doorstep and he fell on his backside. By the time he recovered himself Thomas stood over him. He offered a hand in assistance but it was refused.

"I know who you are," the man said as he got to his feet, trying to make himself taller and failing. "And I know people who will cut you down to size. You have exceeded your remit in coming here."

"I have no remit, only vengeance in my heart." Thomas could see the man wanted to run, but even the coward that he was knew he must stand his ground. To run would trigger a chase, and he would not want that. "Where is Philippa Gale? Is she here with you?"

"Who?"

Thomas shook his head. "I heard you were a clever man, Sir Thomas. Now I see that is wrong. She is here, and I want her. She must stand trial for murder, likely more. I know she lived in the cottage next to the road." Thomas leaned closer. "I also suspect you will have visited her, or she came to you." He saw from the man's expression he had struck close to the bone.

"She came here because we are friends, and I do not abandon my friends like some men. She is here no more."

"Where then? At your property in Derbyshire? Or do you have her squirrelled away somewhere safe? Though I doubt you will want her now. She is half the woman she was. I take it you saw what I did to her?"

"She told me she was sick and you saved her."

Cornwell's words came as a shock. It sounded as if there was a hint of respect hidden deep within them.

"She speaks the truth now and again. I need to see her. If she is here say so and I will take her and be gone. If not, I will harry you until you tell me where she is."

"London," said Cornwell. "Yes, she came here, but I sent her on her way. She told me she was going to London. She asked for money, and I gave her what little I could."

"How many men were with her?"

"A dozen." Cornwell looked beyond Thomas. "More than the four of you could handle. Trained soldiers. Killers. I saw it in their eyes." He straightened again, as if to show he still possessed some courage.

"When was this?"

"Two days since, early in the morning. She was gone before the dew was burned off the grass. Good riddance to her. Beautiful she might be but there is something dark within her."

"In which case, I would have thought that might draw you even more to her."

"Do not disrespect me, Justice. I am a man of repute in these parts. If it comes to people choosing between us, you will find yourself badly served. Before you leave, dragging your ragtag band with you, tell me how you plan to reverse the decision you made against me at the Quarter Session, which is clearly wrong."

"I spoke with Sir Richard Croft, who was man enough to attend the Session himself, unlike you. I studied both petitions and ruled against you. You had no case. You still have no case. Try bringing another false claim to my table and I will rule the same way again. You might think me another weak Justice like those who came before, but you are wrong. I am not someone to be turned from the path of justice."

"Then you are a fool. Be gone from here before the rest of my men return."

Thomas laughed. "How many men do you have? Not enough, I wager."

When Thomas turned, he saw Will, Usaden and Jorge with their backs to him as they faced off against James Marshall and his four men. Cornwell must have also seen them as he spoke, their presence no doubt influencing his words. Thomas considered the words most likely true. All except the threats. They might work against weaker men, men who owed a living to the man, but Thomas had no need to bend a knee to Cornwell. Not now, not ever. He nodded at James Marshall as he passed, aware the steward might be punished for not stopping him. So be it. Men choose their masters as much as masters choose their men.

"Do we follow her now?" asked Will when they had covered a quarter mile. "If so, we need to turn around."

"Not yet," Thomas said. "Yes, we could chase after her, but she has almost two days head start. If she is wise enough, she will have changed horses and ridden as hard as she can. She will feel the pain of it in her condition, but no doubt she fears the pain less than she fears me. As soon as she reaches London she will disappear among the throng."

"So we give up?"

Thomas heard the disgust in Will's voice.

"No. We try to be clever. I still have the papers we took from Peter Gifforde's cottage in Wigmore. I have some recollection of property contracts. Amal will go through them and redouble her efforts to decipher Philippa's journal. She is better at that manner of work than anyone else I know."

"And if she finds nothing?"

"Then we go to London. The two of us. You and me. And we search until we find her."

"And if we don't find her?"

"We will." Thomas wished he felt more confident than he sounded.

They rode on, the sun lowering through grey cloud. The light was as dull as the sky. It was a nothing kind of day, which had brought nothing of worth.

Thomas avoided passing through Ludlow, instead leading them to the east of the town so they approached Burway from the north. The bulk of the castle rose behind the new buildings that sat above the river. Pale flowers were opening on some of the fruit trees and he wondered if they might be on his land. If so, what to do with them?

He realised there was much he knew as a lad that he had since forgotten. Silva would be a source of knowledge for all things that grew in the district, even if the suddenness of her relationship with Will still came as a shock. Sometimes, being a father could be hard. But then, so could life. Relationships. Friendships. Enmity.

Had he made a mistake in threatening Sir Thomas Cornwell? More than likely, but it was too late to change it now. Perhaps the man had the influence he claimed and could ruin them all. In which case, Thomas knew a land that might welcome his return. Except, even as the thought came to him, he knew he could not abandon Catherine. Not yet. One day she would be Queen of this land and Thomas would not be allowed to approach her again. There would be time then for a few last years amid the beauty of Andalusia, with the sun on his face.

It was late when Amal knocked on the door of his room. He had been studying an old book he had brought from Spain. It was not Spanish. It was not even from the Arabic nations that spanned the east. He believed it might be Greek, even though the text was in Latin. Thomas had taken it from his library because a faint memory had been sparked. The book told of herbs and medicines that could not be explained through any rational means. It reminded him of the work Silva did, and he wanted an understanding of it. He had seen the results she could achieve. Seen how both Amal and Belia listened to her and incorporated some of her ideas into their own work. Thomas was beginning to think in a different way. Sometimes it was not the medicine that cured a man or woman but the idea of the medicine.

"I've found something, Pa," said Amal. She looked pale; her eyes less bright than normal.

"Show me." Thomas made space and his daughter set three sheets of paper on the table, then went to sit on the edge of his bed.

He read the first, the second, the third before turning to her.

"This says that Philippa owns two houses in London

324

we did not know about. You have done well, my sweet. Go to your own bed. You look exhausted."

Amal smiled and kissed his cheek, but as she drew away Thomas grasped her wrist and held her. He placed a hand on her face.

"You are warm. How do you feel?"

"Shivery. A little sick. I'm all right, Pa, just tired."

"Does anyone else feel the same way?"

"Not that they have said, and they would come to me or Belia if they did."

"Not Silva?"

"The children don't know her well enough yet, so they will go to Belia first. I'm all right, Pa. I may have been working too hard." She smiled. "Perhaps you have been working me too hard. I will feel better in the morning."

"Call me if you wake in the night and feel worse. Promise me."

"Of course I will." She kissed his forehead and left.

Thomas stared after her, afraid of losing her, afraid of losing any of them. He was familiar with how sickness could steal through a town. He had lost his brother and mother to the pestilence that came to Lemster — had caught it himself but recovered. He had rarely been sick a day since, and wondered if it offered him some manner of protection. It was another idea he had recorded in his journal, which was heavy with theories and notions, some rational, others less so.

He read the documents again before pushing them away. Lethargy filled him because he knew that come morning he had to leave in pursuit of Philippa Gale. Why did he ever have to meet her? Why did he have to fall under her spell? How did he miss the evil that lurked within her? He usually saw it in others but had not in her. He knew if Jorge had been with him, when he first came to England, he would have recognised her for what she was. Pure evil.

But Jorge had not been with him.

Thomas undressed and got into bed.

He stared at the ceiling where small glass panels cut into the walls allowed moonlight to filter through and form patterns. He had told Will only the two of them would go, but changed his mind. If Jorge agreed, he wanted him to travel with them as well. He thought of Usaden and determined to ask him, if only to give the man the opportunity to refuse, because he would be upset not to be asked. Usaden might have found himself a woman and a place at her hearth, but at his core he was loyal to Thomas, and always would be. So he would ask Usaden. The four of them, five if he included Kin. On the trail of trouble, as they had been so many times before.

Tomorrow...

Except in the morning, Amal's fever was worse, and she was barely conscious. Sweat poured from her, and Thomas mixed willow bark powder in ale and made her drink it. He sent for Belia, and when she arrived Silva was with her. Jorge and Will stood outside the door, reluctant to enter.

It was Silva who made the diagnosis.

"I have seen it before," she said. "They call it the sweating sickness."

"And how do we cure it?"

"You can't. She will live or die. We will know more

within the day, by tomorrow morning at the latest. We need to keep her cool, get her fever down."

"I gave her willow bark."

"Good. I have other remedies. I will tell you each of them and you can say whether to use them or not. You may doubt me, Thomas, but I have treated this before." Silva rose and went to the door. "Will, come lift your sister up and carry her to the river."

"I can do it," Thomas said.

"But you don't have to."

Will lifted Amal as if she weighed nothing, and took her outside. The others followed as he carried his sister to the banks of the Teme, then waded in.

"Dunk her, but keep her head above water," said Silva.

"I'm not stupid." Will held Amal as he slid her entire, slim body beneath the cold water, icy with snowmelt from the hills around its source on the Welsh border. "How long do I need to hold her here?"

"Until her teeth chatter," said Silva, and Will laughed.

"In that case, I believe I am already cured. I should not have waded so deep."

Thomas went into the river after his son. He held Amal's hand, and she briefly curled her fingers around his, which he took as a good sign. He watched her skin pale and take on a blue tint.

"Enough," he said, and Will handed her to him.

He laid her on her bed and looked at Silva. "What now?"

"It sounds wrong, but now we keep her warm. If she sweats too much, draw back the covers, but she needs to sweat a little. Belia can do that while I show you what I intend to give her. My herbs are in the other workshop."

Thomas followed her. He stood as she mixed seeds, flowers, roots and herbs. She explained each, and he nodded for her to proceed, familiar with some but not their uses in medicine.

"When Amal is recovered, you and I must sit down and you can tell me everything you know."

"I know many things, Thomas, not all of which you will listen to. Do you accept me now?"

"If my son accepts you, then so do I. Are you and he serious? It is none of my business, but…"

"I love him," said Silva, "like I have never loved another. And he loves me. Already we are talking of children." She smiled. "You will be a grandfather at last. Better late than never, I expect. And yes, we must talk. I know much but so do you. We know different things, just as Belia knows things neither of us does. We must combine our talents, accept each other's talents so we can become more than each of us alone. If you are willing to accept and learn."

"When Amal is well."

"Yes. When Amal is well."

CHAPTER THIRTY-ONE

Five days passed before Thomas was sure Amal had recovered enough for him to leave the house. She told him to go sooner, but he could not bear to. Could not bear the thought he might have lost his daughter, who looked so much like her mother who he had failed to save.

Now, he rode south towards Lemster. He needed something he could barely define, knowing only that Bel might be part of the cure to what ailed him. It was nothing physical. It was in his head and soul. He had made a place for himself and his family at Burway, but still something was missing.

Bel's kitchen was chaos when he arrived. Children crawled on the floor, yet more played with them, so it was near impossible to work out how many there were.

Bel saw him enter and came across to kiss him on the cheek. "Help me, Tom. I can barely take a step for fear of treading on one of them."

"Whose are they all?"

"They belong to Edmund and James, but I have a

suspicion someone may have sneaked one or two strays into their number. Unless the boys have more children than I know about. They are outside if it's them you are here to see. Edmund says you have one more load of bricks due and then you will be finished."

"For Belia and Amal's workshop. But it is you I came to see."

Bel looked at him, then wiped hair from her face with the back of her hand.

"Well, here I am, Tom. Now help and see if you can amuse some of the older ones. And perhaps have a few of the youngsters on your lap. They like to be jiggled up and down."

"Don't we all," Thomas said, which made Bel laugh and swat at him with the wooden spoon in her hand. He took it as a good sign, so went and did as asked.

He was telling the older children a story about Spain and the beautiful princess who lived there and came to England to marry a prince, when Edward and James came in for their midday meal. The children all squealed and ran to hug their legs or waists, which told Thomas his storytelling might need some work.

James took most of the children with him when he left, saying he would take them to his house before returning to work. Eventually, Thomas found himself almost alone with Bel for the first time since arriving, except for four children, who sat in a circle passing a sewn ball to each other. The game had no apparent start or finish, or even any rules.

Bel reached out and stroked Thomas's face. "You need a shave, Tom." She touched his hair. "And a haircut. If you wait until we get rid of these last four, I will cut your hair for you."

"It has been a while."

"I can tell. Is that a yes?"

"It is."

"Why are you here?"

"Amal almost died. She had the sweating sickness and she almost died." As the words emerged Thomas felt a tightness in his chest and knew he was on the point of breaking down.

Bel saw it as well and reached for his hand. "Tell me later, when we are alone. She is recovered now?"

Thomas nodded.

"Then all is well." She squeezed his hand. "Lizzie called the other day and asked about you. I think on behalf of her husband."

"It is nice you still talk."

"Except we do not often," said Bel. "She will listen to no word of criticism of Symon, even though many in Lemster speak them. She came to tell me to have nothing to do with you. That Symon claims it is you who killed Arthur Wodall and he says he has proof of it."

"So why has a constable not come to arrest me?"

"She didn't tell me that, but most likely because Symon is talking out of his arse as usual. Words come cheap, particularly to one like him."

"What happened between you and Lizzie? It wasn't always this way."

Bel offered a sad smile. "Life happened. She married young. Younger even than me. Had one child, a son, then her husband died."

"Was it anyone I knew?"

Bel shook her head. "Man from Hereford way, but not Hereford. I knew where at one time but have forgotten."

"When did she marry Symon?"

"When she finally gave in to his demands. You know he always wanted her, even when you and he were boys. In the end she gave in and married him. Symon wanted more children, but they never managed it. He always blamed Lizzie."

"Except she had a son by her first marriage, so more than likely it was Symon who couldn't set a spark in her. Where is her son now? He must be full grown."

"He lives in Gloster, works on the docks there."

"Does Lizzie believe Symon's accusations against me?"

"She came to tell me about them, so she must. She is hard now, not like she used to be."

"I always thought her fragile in some way when we were young. Is the hardness a cover, do you think?"

"Perhaps. Whatever it is I dislike it, and don't have to like her. I was surprised when she came here. Less surprised when she told me the reason."

"I should confront Symon."

"And get yourself into trouble again?"

"Again? That was forty-seven years ago, Bel, and what happened was none of my doing."

She squeezed his hand, still grasped in hers. "I know, I am sorry. None of it was your fault. But Symon still accuses you. There are others in Lemster who do as well. Best if you ignore what he says and return to Ludlow. That is your home now. Edmund tells me your house is a

332

wonder now it's finished. I will have to come to see it again."

"Come now, Bel. Come..." Thomas broke off, unable to say the words in case she rejected him.

"What, Tom?" A smile played across her lips, still pretty despite the lines that ran from their corners, and he suspected she knew what he had been about to say.

"Come later," he said. "Once I have confronted Symon Dawbney."

"Don't do it. Nothing good will come of it, and he will only use it to blacken your name further."

"I can't let it pass, Bel. I'm sorry, but I can't." He released her hand and turned away, the unresolved threads of what might have been teasing apart to blow away in the wind. He glanced at the children, who had stopped playing their game and now stared at him. It felt like an accusation, but was likely not, only his own mind drawing conclusions that had no basis.

Outside, he mounted Ferrant and rode east into Lemster. He tied the horse to a post outside the Priory and made his way to the house where Lizzie and Symon lived but did not make it that far. As he crossed the town square, Symon Dawbney was coming towards him and veered to intercept him.

"Berrington, I heard you were in Lemster."

"And I hear you are spinning false accusations against me. I have come for an apology." He looked around. Several people had stopped to watch the confrontation, no doubt hoping a fight was about to start. "In front of these witnesses."

"They can hear your confession." Symon punched him

in the chest. It was a soft punch from a man who had gone soft. Symon had been a big lad who had used his size to bully others, but Thomas had been faster and beaten him one against one.

He glanced around again to judge whether any of the watchers might side with Symon, knowing none would side with him. It looked as if Bel has spoken the truth. Symon Dawbney was not well liked in Lemster.

"I confess to not liking you, Symon. Is that what you mean?"

"You cannot speak to me like that anymore, Tom Berrington. I am an important man now."

"And I am Justice of the Peace, appointed by King Henry himself."

"So you say. I hear you are as crooked as the last one. More so. I also hear Arthur Wodall discovered what you were up to and was on his way to the Prior to tell him when you killed him." It was Symon's turn to look around at the crowd, which had grown as the prospect of the fight grew. He raised his voice. "I raise the hue and cry. Arrest this man for the murder of Arthur Wodall."

A few in the crowd cheered. Most remained silent.

Thomas was well aware that raising the hue and cry had implications, both for him and Symon. To raise it, there was a duty on all in the town to respond, but also a duty on the caller not to do so for any petty reason. And Thomas knew Symon had little reason.

Thomas raised his own voice. "Some of you might know me but most will not. I once lived in Lemster. Now I am Justice of the Peace for the district. Symon Dawbney has hated me ever since we were boys. You need to decide who you prefer to believe. Him or me."

"You can say anything you want," said Symon. "And you are right; nobody here knows who you are."

"I do."

Thomas turned to discover Bel standing on the edge of the circle of onlookers.

"He is Tom Berrington, and no better man ever came from Lemster, nor ever will. Had he stayed I would have married him. You might not know Tom but you know me. Who do you choose to believe — me or Symon Dawbney?"

Thomas saw Bel's eyes widen and turned, but not fast enough. Symon caught him with a hard blow on the side of the head and he went to his knees. Symon came in faster than Thomas thought him capable of, using his feet now. A kick to the belly, a kick to the head, but the last one mostly missed. Then Thomas was on his feet again.

"I will allow you those. Now go home before I hit you back."

"You would not dare, not in front of all these people."

"Yet you attacked me without cause. Everyone saw you strike me when my back was turned, just like the coward you are." The faces Thomas could see did not appear to favour Symon, but they did not favour him either. Bel had made a difference, but was it enough?

A new figure came running through the crowd. Lizzie Dawbney had arrived, and she flung herself at Thomas, her fingers curled like the claws of a wild animal. He was forced to take a step back, then to grasp her tight to stop her scratching his eyes out. She squirmed against him, and he was forced to tighten his grip.

"Look," she cried out, "he has his hands on my breasts and backside. His cock is hard. I swear to you I can feel it. He wants to violate me."

Thomas threw her away, but she came back at him, and this time Symon was at her side, his fists swinging. Thomas ducked the first blow, then punched Lizzie as softly as he could in order to push her away. Symon came at him again, unleashing a flurry of blows which would bruise Thomas's face come nightfall. Thomas had had enough.

He stepped back, then stepped close. He hit out, three strikes. The first caught Symon on the side of the head and snapped it around. The other two were not required, because Symon's knees were already sagging. Thomas hit him twice more to make a point. By the time Symon's head cracked against the cobbles he was already unconscious. Thomas turned away. Only as Bel came past him did he remember Lizzie. When he turned, she had found a knife from somewhere, or more likely brought it with her. Thomas started forward but knew he would be too late. Bel moved faster, her arms out. She embraced Lizzie, ignoring the knife in her hand.

"It is over, my sweet," said Bel, her voice soft. "This was not Tom's doing, you know it was not."

Thomas waited, knowing his presence might spark more tumult. He watched as Bel lowered one hand and took the knife from Lizzie. She held it back behind her and Thomas came close and took it from her. Lizzie's eyes were no longer on him, her face no longer twisted with hatred. She cried against Bel, who stroked her back until she calmed.

"I will take Lizzie home and stay with her a while," said Bel. "Best you take the road on the other side of the Kenwater, Tom. I don't think anyone will blame you for what you did or come after you, but it will be safer. You can stay with me tonight. I can even lock the doors. First time in forty years, but needs must."

Thomas thought about it, then nodded.

"And if I stay, where will I sleep?"

"At my side, of course. Too long have I fought my desire for you since you returned. Unless you have none for me, in which case..." Bel stared into his eyes.

"I loved you before any other, and that means something."

"And now, Tom?"

"And now I want to lie at your side in your house with the door locked. And tomorrow I will ask if you want to live with me at my house."

Bel laughed. "Let's take things easy, Tom. That's a lot to offer an old woman."

"You will always be a girl to me, Bel. You know you will."

"And you will always be my Tom."

As he walked away, Thomas decided it might be in his best interest to avoid Lemster in future. Every time he came, he seemed to get into trouble.

In the morning, someone came knocking at the locked door. When Thomas opened the small window and looked down he found Prior Bernard and half a dozen brothers standing outside.

"What do you want?"

"I heard you might be here," said the Prior. "You need to put some clothes on and come with me. Symon Dawbney is dead, and the town is claiming you did it."

CHAPTER THIRTY-TWO

"Am I under arrest?" Thomas walked beside Prior Bernard. He had left Ferrant at Bel's house, as none of the brothers had arrived on horseback.

"Why would you need to ask, Tom?"

"Because you came with six brothers, not alone."

Prior Bernard smiled. "I expect you could defeat all six without drawing sweat."

"But I might not fare so well against you, Bernard."

"Prior Bernard. One day you will remember your manners, though it is getting a little late for that at your age. Am I meant to call you Sir Thomas, or duke? Do you have any other new honours bestowed on you these days?"

"Tom will do, like always. And you didn't answer me. Am I under arrest?"

"You are Justice of the Peace and a man is dead. That is the reason I came for you."

"Why to Bel's house and not Ludlow?"

"You were seen riding off together yesterday. I consid-

339

ered it worth trying Bel first to save myself the longer journey. Besides, you were there. Are you reconciled now?"

"I don't believe we were ever not. I went away, that is all. Then I came back."

"Forty-seven years is not forty-seven hours, nor forty-seven days or even months."

"Bel knows that. She made a life for herself, but she is a widow now and we have a past. A short one, I grant you, but sometimes the relationships we build when young can last a lifetime."

"Well, yours appear to have done so."

"Do you have Symon's body at the Priory?"

"Of course."

"You have examined him?"

"I have, but want you to do so as well. I used to be more skilled than you, but that has changed, as it should. The pupil must exceed the teacher."

"Only because you taught me so well."

"You were always my best student. It is a shame you did not return sooner. You would have made a better Prior than me."

Thomas laughed, the sound fading as they approached the town walls and a group of men confronted them. Thomas recognised none, but expected Prior Bernard knew each of them.

"What is this, a welcoming party?" asked Prior Bernard.

"We are here for him." A tall, well-dressed man at the front nodded at Thomas. "Let us have him and the rest of you can go your way in peace."

Prior Bernard strode towards the man, his face barely hiding his fury. "Who are you to tell me what to do, Harold Dawbney? Have you been elevated so high?"

The man's eyes did not move from Prior Bernard. Behind the group of two dozen, Thomas saw Lizzie Dawbney with an expression of pure hatred on her face. Thomas assumed Harold Dawbney was the child of her first marriage, but if so he had taken his mother's new family name. Had she brought him to Lemster for this confrontation? Thomas recalled Bel telling him Lizzie's son lived in Gloster, but little else. It made no difference. The men had to be dealt with. The others did not concern him. Men liked to pretend they were hard, but most were not. If it came to a fight more than half would fall back. But not Harold Dawbney, and not his mother.

Thomas watched Prior Bernard, sure the same consideration would be going through his mind. Nobody moved. Prior Bernard stood his ground, as did Harold Dawbney. To tip the balance — believing if trouble was coming better to start it than let it fester —Thomas stepped forward to stand beside the Prior.

Harold Dawbney's gaze locked with his, and Thomas saw the hatred in it. He wondered why. Symon Dawbney was not his father. Neither had he been a man to foster love in his children, particularly if they were not his own. Gloster was too far away to have travelled overnight to Lemster. Which meant Harold had already been here.

If the man attacked, Thomas would protect the Prior, and Harold Dawbney would be the first to hit the cobbled roadway. Except trouble did not come. What came instead was the sound of hooves from behind, and all eyes moved to watch the newcomers. Thomas waited to make sure Harold would not take advantage of the distraction before turning. What he saw were four men on fine horses. He recognised the lead rider, Sir Robert Croft. One of the other riders was his steward, Charles Carter, another Paul Pryce, his stable master. It seemed most of the gathered men, together with Lizzie Dawbney, knew who the newcomers were. Sir Robert Croft was lord and master of much of their holdings, and it would not do to antagonise him.

"What is going on here?" he asked, a firmness in his voice that hinted he had already guessed some of it for himself.

"A man has been killed," said Harold Dawbney.

"My husband Symon, Sir Robert." Lizzie stepped through the crowd to stand beside her son. "He has done work for you in the past, sir. Good work."

Sir Robert Croft made no show of his opinion on that.

"I accuse this man, Thomas Berrington, of my husband's murder." Lizzie pointed a finger at Thomas. "They fought in town yesterday. He came back and stuck my husband. Killed him."

"What say you to this accusation, Thomas Berrington?" Sir Robert's eyes gave nothing away.

"It is false, Sir Robert. Yes, we fought yesterday, but it was not my doing. Symon attacked me. I knew the man as a boy, but that was long ago. What he has against me now is a mystery. These people are preventing me from doing my job as Justice of the Peace."

"I can see they are blocking the King's highway and preventing me entering the town to do business. I have dealings in Lemster this day and do not welcome a mob greeting me." Sir Robert twisted in his saddle. "What say you to this, Prior Bernard? You know the town better than anyone else. Is a man dead?"

"He is, sir. His body lies in the Priory and I came to fetch Thomas to examine him. He is a skilled physician and can tell more about a dead man than when he was alive."

Sir Robert hid a smile. "I have spoken with Thomas Berrington before, also on matters of murder, and he impressed me then. If he has also impressed you, Prior Bernard, then I cannot see how he is guilty of the accusation made against him." He scanned the crowd, which now had less than half the people in it, the others slinking away through the town gate. "Disperse, all of you. If there is a murderer to be caught, then these men need to do their work. Go, all of you."

"But my Symon—"

Sir Robert spoke over Lizzie. "Your Symon will not get justice at the hands of a mob, half of whom are here for the entertainment. I will send someone to talk to you later about your future, Lizzie. Now, return to your homes."

Sir Robert rode close to Thomas and Prior Bernard, and leaned down so his voice would not be overheard. "Sort this out, but come tell me your conclusions. I will be at The Star later taking my midday meal, but will return home afterwards. If it takes longer than that, Thomas can come to me there. He knows the way."

Sir Robert led his small band through the gate, leaving only Thomas, the Prior and the brothers outside.

"Let us follow the walls to the far side," said Prior

Bernard. "Nobody would attack me or my brothers, but I fear for you, Tom."

"I can take care of myself."

"I know, but humour an old man."

They entered Lemster through the Priory gate, which opened directly into the grounds. Thomas sent one brother back to Bel's house with a message to send Ferrant with the man, so Thomas would have him to ride to Sir Richard Croft's manor house. Once that was done, Prior Bernard dismissed the others and took Thomas to the small, cold room set hard against the infirmary.

Symon Dawbney was stretched out on a table, covered with a linen sheet. His face was waxy and pale. *This is getting to be a habit*, Thomas thought, *to stand in this room witness to another death.*

"Where was he found?"

"Three doors down from his own house. Tell me what you see, Tom."

Thomas removed the sheet and draped it across a chair. Someone had already stripped the body, making it easier to make a judgement.

"A single knife wound to the belly." Thomas touched the entrance of the wound. "A long blade, I would say. He might have survived but it sliced his liver and he bled to death." He lifted the body to examine the back, but there was no sign of an exit wound. "Over six inches, but less than twelve, struck hard and fast. Symon would have been in a lot of pain and death would not have come fast enough to spare him that." Thomas looked at the Prior, who nodded.

"Agreed. What else?"

"Should there be anything else? I see no other wound."

"The body, Tom. The skin."

Thomas turned back to the body, unsure of what Prior Bernard wanted of him. Then he realised and went to work. After a time, he asked for help to turn Symon Dawbney's body over.

"He has bad skin. His manhood is inflamed and weeping. There are sores and lesions on his buttocks and legs. I have seen it before in Spain. Have you?"

Prior Bernard shook his head. "I was hoping you might know what it is, and if the town needs warning it might spread."

"It's some time since you were there. This disease first appeared less than ten years ago. There were cases in Sevilla and Cadiz, but I hear it came from Naples. I didn't see my first case until later, when a mariner came to Granada and died. We had to burn his body, but I suspect it was too late by then and he had already passed it on to others. To women."

"Do we need to burn Symon's body?"

"I doubt it. It's not transmittable through the air or even touch, unless someone had sex with him. When he was alive, of course."

Prior Bernard scowled. "I am a brother, Tom. We do not partake of sins of the flesh or even contemplate them."

"You and I know that is not true, but I will accept your word. I believe the disease came to Naples, then Spain, after the journeys to the new worlds. Sailors are the same everywhere, and I heard enough tales about how a handful of glass beads would be payment enough to lie with native women. Many of whom were most exotic and beautiful. The disease can take some time to show, which means Symon may have had it for years. Where he got it from is another matter. It's unusual in England. But someone should warn Lizzie to keep an eye on herself. I will get Bel to tell her. Better from her than you or me."

"I agree. Ask Bel whether they still had relations. That does not always survive in a marriage after the initial lust wears off."

"Did he use whores in town?"

"He was a powerful man, so of course he did."

"Then they will need to be told as well. With luck we can stop the spread, but it might prove difficult. However, the fact his cock is likely to have rotted off before many more years passed has little to do with why he was killed."

"I heard you took a knife from Lizzie yesterday."

"I did, and left it on the stone seat outside the Priory gate. I didn't look for it when we entered, but it may still be there."

"I will send a brother to look once we are done here. I believe you, Tom, but others will not. Particularly if the knife is no longer there. How big was it?"

"Around eight inches. A kitchen knife she brought from home."

"So the right size."

"Yes. The right size."

"I take it Bel can account for what you did last night?"

Thomas suppressed a smile. "She can."

Prior Bernard made no effort to hide his own smile. "She remains a handsome woman."

"She does." Thomas glanced at Symon's body. "You can release him to his wife now, but I suggest a brother wrap him in a shroud first. There is nothing more to be learned. I take it there are no witnesses?"

"There are not. He was discovered a little before dawn, when a neighbour left for work in the fields and almost fell over him. He came directly here to report it."

"Did Symon have enemies?" Thomas asked.

"Too many to count, but none I would say willing to hang for the killing of him. Symon was not an honest lawyer, charging more than he should, making arbitrary rulings to suit himself. But murder? No. Nobody hated him that much. He was an annoyance, nothing more. A scab on the town that people tried not to scratch for fear of making it worse."

"Might this be connected to Arthur Wodall's death?"

"You are the Justice, you tell me."

"How long since the last killing in Lemster — other than these recent ones?"

Prior Bernard stared at Thomas for a long time until his point was made.

"As long as that?"

"As long as that. Which is why the town came to confront you, I suspect. There are people who were here when Raulf Wodall was killed, and there are still people who believe it was you who killed him. Not me, Tom, I never did, but others do. You must see how it appears to them. A boy dies and you are accused. You go away. There are no more deaths other than by accident or sickness. Then you return, and now two men have died within weeks of each other, and both held some manner of grudge against you. You cannot blame people, Tom."

"I can't. But it makes it even more important I find out

who killed each of them. Both died of a knife wound. One to the throat, the other to the liver. I suspect I know who killed Arthur Wodall — Philippa's men — but they will never be found, never be punished for it. I am less sure in Symon's case." Thomas stared into space for a moment, grateful Prior Bernard allowed him the time to think. "I would like to know if Philippa Gale had any dealings with Symon."

"Lizzie might allow someone to examine the records in his office, but it would not be you."

"My daughter, perhaps. Or is she too close to me?"

"I think it would have to be a man. Lizzie does not hold with women having power over anything."

"Then I have someone who can do it. You met Jorge."

"The pretty one?"

"Yes, the pretty one, but he has a brain beneath that beauty. I will send him, along with my daughter once she is fully recovered. Amal will find anything if it is to be found, but she must pretend to be his assistant."

"Your daughter is unwell?"

"The sweating sickness, but she grows better by the day, otherwise I would not have left her. Besides, there are better healers than me looking after her. Do you know a woman by the name of Silva Taylor?"

"I do. She is one of the cunning-folk. I am meant to condemn them but do not. Silva is a highly skilled herbalist. If I ever fell ill and you were not available, I would send for her. If she is helping your daughter then she is in expert hands."

"Silva is with my son at the moment. They are lovers."

Prior Bernard stared at Thomas. "Many men have

wanted to lie with Silva over the years, but I never heard of her taking a lover. I do not doubt your word, only that it comes as a surprise."

"My son is tall and rather handsome in his own way. He is also as strong as an ox and an excellent protector."

"It is still a surprise. What are you going to do about Symon's killing, Tom?"

"I plan on returning to Bel to see if she will talk to Lizzie."

"Do not forget, Sir Richard Croft wants to hear what progress has been made. He will not want the scandal of murder hanging over the town for long. He considers it his fiefdom, which it probably is."

"If Bel agrees to come back to town, I will leave her with Lizzie and call on Sir Richard, tell him what we know. It is still early enough that he will not have taken his dinner yet."

CHAPTER THIRTY-THREE

Bel once more perched on Ferrant behind Thomas. This time her arms around his waist were more active, so he had to keep telling her she was likely to make them both tumble to the ground. She would stop for a moment, only to start up again.

Thomas half expected a second welcoming committee as they approached the town gate, but all that greeted them was a farmer, who tipped his hat as he urged a cow along the roadway. Most likely the gesture was directed at Bel, who he would recognise.

"What do you want me to ask her, Tom?" Bel asked as they approached Lizzie's house.

"Tell her you have come on behalf of the man who is looking into her husband's death, then ask if she knows anyone who might want to see him dead. Ask if the name Philippa Gale is familiar, and if so, whether Symon ever had dealings with her."

"I assume it best not to mention you?"

"That might be best. See what you can find out. Ask

her how their marriage was. And ask when they last had relations."

"Is that not too personal?"

"I have my reasons. Symon had a disease that is caught by lying with a woman infected with it. Lizzie might already know, but if not she deserves to. I will ask Amal and Belia to examine her when they arrive. Prior Bernard sent a monk with a message for them."

"Can anyone catch this disease?"

"Only if they lie together."

"Like we did last night?"

"Yes, like we did last night. But one of us would have to have it, and I know I don't and suspect neither do you. Unless you and Symon had a liaison I know nothing of."

Bel made a sound of disgust and Thomas laughed, until he remembered where they were going and stopped.

Bel slid from behind him when they reached Lizzie's house, but kept her hand against his leg. "Stay close for a while, Tom. She was calm when I brought her home yesterday but I am unsure what manner of reception I might get. Besides, that big son of hers may be with her."

"I will stand at the end of the road. If you need me shout as loud as you can."

Bel smiled. "I will." She offered a quick kiss, then went directly to the door, as if wanting to get this done while she still had the courage.

At the corner, Thomas stood back so Lizzie would not see him, and a moment later Bel entered the substantial house. Thomas moved a little closer, his hand still on Ferrant's reins. He was about to turn away when the door opened again and Bel came running out. Lizzie followed,

351

a knife in her hand as long as the one Thomas had taken from her the day before. He had reached the house next to Lizzie's when she caught up with Bel and the knife came down in a savage blow.

Bel screamed and went to her knees, her hand clutching at a wound.

Thomas punched Lizzie in the face when she slashed out at him, breaking her nose. He hit her a second time, then kicked the blade away as she fell backwards, cracking the back of her skull on the stone step.

Thomas turned to Bel.

"How bad is it, Tom? Has she killed me?"

"Take your hand away, I need to see." He gripped her wrist and drew her hand from the wound. Blood already soaked half her shirt and more pulsed out as he looked.

"I'm going to have to rip your top," he said.

"Do what you must. I can't die now I have found you again."

He tore the linen to reveal the wound. It was deep, but Lizzie had struck at Bel's shoulder, and though the wound bled profusely, no underlying organs had been hit.

"I need to stitch this, but not here. I am going to take you to the Priory. Can you ride Ferrant if I lead him?"

"I'd rather hold on to you."

"I fear you might slip off. You will live, Bel, but only if I close the wound."

He lifted her up and heaved her onto the saddle before gripping the reins and leading Ferrant away. Which is when Harold Dawbney ran out through the door and howled when he saw his mother. He knelt at her side, then turned to look at Thomas and Bel.

352

"You have killed her!"

"Perhaps. But she meant to kill Bel. Me too."

Harold picked up the knife and ran at Thomas.

Thomas slapped Ferrant on the rump, sending him trotting away with Bel clinging to his mane, then turned, stepped to one side and tripped Harold. His own speed did the rest. He fell on his face and skidded along the gravel road. Thomas fell on his back and twisted the knife from his fingers.

"I can hit you here and knock whatever wits you have from your head, or you can stop this now," Thomas said.

"Never."

Thomas hit him. Not enough to kill him, but enough that he would wake in a quarter hour with an aching head. He dragged him back inside the house, then checked on Lizzie. He feared her skull might have cracked when she hit the step, but when he slid his hand beneath there was no blood. He dragged her in after her son and closed the door before looking both ways along the street, grateful this part of Lemster was quiet. Nobody had seen the brief altercation. He walked back to Ferrant, who waited patiently, and led him at a run to the Priory.

"Are you sure of this, Bel?" Prior Bernard had allowed her into the cloisters, much to the consternation of some of the brothers. He had taken them to the infirmary, where Thomas exposed her shoulder. He had cleaned the wound and was now stitching it closed. The Prior tried not to stare at the pale expanse of Bel's exposed skin.

"That's what she shouted at me when she picked up the knife."

"He deserved it? That is what she said? Are you sure she meant Symon?"

"I am."

"He was found only a few doors down from his own house," Thomas said. "It makes sense. He comes home late, drunk perhaps, and Lizzie knows what is coming her way, so she sticks the knife in him before he can do anything to her."

Prior Bernard let his breath go and shook his head. "The stupidity of people should not surprise me after all these years, but it does. Why did she not simply leave him?"

"Wives don't do that," said Bel. "However awful their husband. And Symon was one of the worst. Lizzie made excuses for him all the time. Claimed his temper was her fault."

"She will have to be taken into custody," said Prior Bernard. "Both her and her son. He may well have been part of this. He may even be the one who struck the blow. It is not as if Symon was his father."

"Did you tell me Harold worked on the docks in Gloster?" Thomas asked Bel.

"That's what she told me, yes."

"Then she must have told him to come here days ago. This was all planned. Both of them will hang."

"Let me try talking with Lizzie first and find the truth of what you claim," said Bel.

"If she will talk. I think she might have lost her wits."

Prior Bernard looked at each of them before shaking his head, but it was a shake of sorrow rather than negation. "Talk to her but take Tom with you even if his presence angers her. But let him finish closing your wound first."

After the Prior had gone Bel laughed. "It's lucky you didn't have to remove my shirt entirely, Tom. I think the sight would have been too much for him."

"It was almost too much for me last night. Bernard was a soldier before he became a brother. He has seen women's breasts before. Most likely often."

"But he's never seen mine."

"Then that is his loss." Thomas cut off the ends of the gut and used a sharp blade to trim the loose ends close to Bel's skin. "There, as good as new. Well, not as new. You will have a scar."

"Not as many as you do."

"For which you should be grateful. Now, we had best confront Lizzie, and then I want you to come home with me. I need to keep an eye on how your wound heals over the next week."

"Is that all you want to keep an eye on?"

Thomas only smiled. The smile remained on his face until they reached Lizzie Dawbney's house, where they discovered it would not be possible to speak to her. The front door stood open, and at first Thomas feared the worst, that she had taken her own life out of guilt at what she had done. He peered into the interior and called out, but no answer came.

"Wait out here," he said to Bel before stepping inside.

The house appeared as if Lizzie had gone to the

market for something and forgotten to shut her door. Everything was in place.

Thomas called out again, with the same result as before. When he looked back, he found Bel had followed him in.

"I told you to stay outside."

"She has gone. I spoke with the neighbour. They saw Lizzie and her son leaving only moments before we arrived. If you had sewn a little faster we would have caught them."

"We still could. I can fetch Ferrant and ride after them. Did the neighbour say which way they went?"

"South, to Gloster no doubt, where her son lives. Let them run, Tom. For old times' sake."

"She killed her husband."

"For which the whole of Lemster would make her a saint. Symon will not be missed. Lizzie has some healing to do, but not the same kind as me. Her healing is in her mind. She has been under his influence so long she no longer knows who she truly is."

"I should send a message to the authorities in Gloster."

"Yes, you should. But you will not if I ask it. Or perhaps you will."

Bel stared into his eyes and Thomas knew this was another of those tipping points in life that could change his future. Agree with Bel and he would not be doing his job. Do what he should and Bel would not ride north with him. Their night before would never be repeated. This incident had nothing to do with Philippa Gale. That made the difference, together with the night he had spent in Bel's bed.

"For old times' sake," he said. Bel smiled and came on tiptoe to kiss his cheek.

They returned to the Priory for Ferrant, who was eating from a sack tied at his neck that a brother had brought out for him. Thomas went inside and told Prior Bernard that Lizzie had fled, but not where to.

"Will you try to find her?"

"I won't."

"What if she returns?"

"She won't do that. What will happen to her house? Did Symon own it?"

"It belongs to the Priory. I will send some brothers to pack up their things and find somewhere to store them. If she returns, she will have to be arrested, so the house can be rented out to someone else. It is a fine house and will soon find a new tenant. I will leave the furniture there; it will save someone else refitting it. But their belongings will be stored for a year. After that, if she still stays away it will be sold and the money distributed to the poor of the district."

"Can you ask the brothers to pack up all Symon's papers and store them as well? They no doubt contain information on his dealings and might be of use to someone."

"Or more evidence of his dishonesty," said Prior Bernard. "But I will do as you ask. I will even set one of the cleverer brothers to go through them to see if anything of interest lies in their pages. If I can find a clever brother, that is. I would do it myself but have not the time. And neither do you, Tom, so do not ask for them."

357

"I wasn't going to. I can think of nothing duller than reading the details of legal business, but I have a daughter who will do it for me."

As he turned away Prior Bernard said, "Do not forget to report to Sir Richard Croft. He asked you to and will not have forgotten. Tell him what you told me rather than the truth."

Bel was waiting outside, patting Ferrant's neck when Thomas emerged, and they made their way to the town square, but the goodwife of The Star told them Sir Richard Croft had finished eating and left an hour since.

"Do you need anything from your house?" Thomas asked.

"A few clothes, perhaps, and I need to tell Edmund I am coming home with you. I don't suppose it will come as a surprise."

"We do that first, then ride to Croft Manor. It's only a little out of our way. We can call there on our way and tell Sir Richard the matter is closed."

"Don't tell him where Lizzie has gone."

"I will say she has run off but we don't know where." Thomas was aware of the lies he had told that day. They sat uneasily with him, and he hoped none would come back to punish him later.

CHAPTER THIRTY-FOUR

"Bel has been here almost two weeks now," said Amal. "Is she staying?"

She and Thomas stood in the now finished workshop created for her and Belia, set forty paces from his own. This one stood on an outcrop of rock above the river because Silva had chosen the spot. She said it held power. Despite his scepticism, Thomas agreed it was a good place to build on. Bel had been sharing his room in the main house, and so far they had not yet fallen out.

"You had best ask her, not me."

"Do you want her to?"

"Yes."

"I know she was your first love, which is why I think she will stay. I wonder who my first love will be?"

"There is no rush, my sweet."

"I have almost fourteen years, Pa. I know girls younger than me that are married and have children."

"Not much younger than you."

"No, not much younger, but even so."

Thomas touched his daughter's cheek. "You will find someone soon enough. Boys like you. They would be fools not to, but you must not be a fool either."

"Have you never been foolish, Pa?"

Thomas knew he had slipped up. "Yes, I have, and regret my foolishness. Everyone makes mistakes. You will make mistakes, even as clever as you are. If you are clever enough you will learn from them, which means they are not really mistakes, only an education."

Amal laughed. "Do you think Silva is an education for Will?"

"They make a fine couple, don't they?"

"They do, but I know you don't believe everything she claims. I think the house feels safer after she and Will removed all those charms Philippa had buried in the walls. Don't you think so too?"

"It feels warmer for the coming in of April."

Amal shook her head, and Thomas knew she considered him a lost cause as far as Silva's arts were concerned.

"She is a fine herbalist, though." He made some slight effort to recover the situation.

"She is. As good as Belia, but different. This is an unfamiliar land, so I suppose that is only to be expected." Amal picked up the small clay pot of herbs she had come to the workshop for. Silva was cooking their midday meal and had asked for them. Thomas had accompanied his daughter to judge how her recovery was progressing. There was no sign of her illness. Like Bel's shoulder, she was fully healed.

As they walked back towards the house, the sound of a horse reached them and Thomas saw a rider appear. As he approached, Thomas moved between the man and Amal without even realising he was doing so. The rider pulled up and dropped to the ground.

"You are Thomas Berrington?"

"I am."

"Sir Richard Pole says you are to come at once to the castle."

"On what matter?"

"He did not tell me, only you are to come. And bring the woman who lives here with you."

"Bel?"

"Yes, Belia was the name he gave. Bring her," he said. The man mounted his horse again. "Shall I tell him you are coming?"

"Yes, tell him. As soon as I can."

"No," said the man. "At once."

When he was gone, Amal said, "You had best do as he asks, Pa. They wouldn't send for you without reason. Perhaps they have captured Philippa."

"Then why ask for Belia? I want you to come as well."

"And Silva?"

"She isn't known in the castle like you are, but yes."

"You know what they want, don't you?"

"I hope I'm wrong, but yes, I think I do. Which is why I want you with me."

It took longer than Thomas liked, but in the end they all went. Jorge and Will took the children to Agnes's house while Thomas, Belia, Silva and Amal entered the castle.

"They are both sick," said Sir Richard Pole. His wife, Margaret, stood behind him.

"When did it start?" Thomas asked.

"Last night. Arthur complained of a headache and feeling cold. John Argentine bled him and put him to bed. Catherine said she felt fine, but when her maid woke her this morning her bedclothes were soaked with sweat."

"Why have you sent for me? You know Argentine won't allow me to treat Prince Arthur."

"I do, but the boy asked for you specifically. I expect Catherine has been singing your praises to him so he believes you can cure him. Can you, Thomas?"

"I don't know."

Sir Richard glanced at the three women before his gaze settled on Amal. "I heard your daughter caught it and she looks hale now."

"She did, and she is."

"So you can cure Arthur. And Catherine."

Thomas wondered if Catherine had been added as an afterthought. Save the future King of England. Another wife could be found if the first died.

"Where is John Argentine now?"

"Praying in St Clement's Church. I think it might be all he has left to try. Which is why I sent for you."

"I will see Arthur now then, before the man returns. Amal and Silva must attend to Catherine. Belia will come with me. Is that acceptable to you, Sir Richard?"

"Save the Prince and anything is acceptable to me. Maggie will take you to him. Princess Catherine's rooms are in the same corridor, so the others can go to her." Sir Richard took a few steps until he was almost touching Thomas. "Do everything you can. The Prince must not die. Understand?"

"Yes, I understand." Thomas knew he had to speak the words, but also that they were not enough on their own. As he followed Lady Margaret Pole through the inner corridors and chambers of the castle, he cursed John Argentine for bleeding the Prince. It would only weaken the boy.

Lady Margaret pointed along the corridor to where Amal and Silva would find Catherine, then opened a door which led into an outer chamber. She strode across it to the far door.

"The guards and servants have been sent away because we trust you, Thomas. There will be only the two of you with him. We do not want the sickness to spread."

"It is already in the town," Thomas said. "You cannot stop it, only fight it."

"Save him like you did your daughter." With that, Lady Margaret turned away and Thomas and Belia entered the room.

Prince Arthur was propped half-upright on a pile of pillows, his long, slim body almost crushed beneath a heap of blankets, a thick sheepskin lying atop them. Thomas's first action was to pull most of them off. As he did so, the Prince's eyes opened and he attempted a smile.

"I see you have come. My thanks, Thomas." His eyes tracked to Belia. "Send her into the outer room for a moment. I need to talk to you, man to man."

Thomas nodded at Belia, who backed out, newly versed in the protocol of power.

Thomas touched Arthur's shoulder. His skin was hot, wet with sweat. He looked around until he found what he knew would be there. A bowl of water and a towel. He brought it across, wetted the towel and wiped the Prince's body.

"Is someone with Catherine?"

"Amal and Silva."

"I know Amal, but not this Silva you speak of. Is she skilled?"

"She is. Would I send anyone who is not skilled to Catherine?"

"She speaks of you often, and most fondly. Almost as if you were her father."

"I probably saw more of her than her own father, who was away a great deal fighting one skirmish or another. She grew up as much in my house as in her palaces."

"She talks of your daughter as well. And your son."

"Like I said, we were all close."

"Save us both and you can be close again. All of us can be close. My court will not be like those of the past, peopled by men of influence and power. I want my rule to be one of knowledge and discovery. There is a new world to explore and I would have Englishmen join the Spaniards in spreading the word of God to the heathens in those lands."

Thomas made no reply. He found the marks where John Argentine had bled the Prince and inwardly cursed.

"I am cold, Thomas. Put the blankets on me again."

"Not yet. I need you to be cold. The fever must break if you are to recover. I dipped my daughter in the Teme when she was sick and I think it helped. You have an ice room in the castle, don't you?"

Arthur shook his head as if unsure. "I suppose we must. The cooks make us frozen delights. Why?"

"I will send Belia for ice. It may help."

"I am already so cold. I need no ice."

"I am your physician now, Prince. Which means you do as I say, at least until you are recovered. Then you can take my head if you wish."

Thomas was pleased when Arthur smiled.

"I think not. I may need you again in the future. But…"

Thomas waited, continuing to wipe down the Prince's body.

"If I should weaken and die, I want you to do something for me."

"I would rather save you than have that happen."

"As would I. But we both know this wicked sickness takes people who do not deserve to die. Rich or poor. Paupers and princes alike. If I should die, I want my heart buried here in Ludlow. My father will have other plans for the rest of me, but my heart must stay here. If I…" A great shiver ran through the Prince, and when Thomas touched his cheek, it was almost burning. "If I die, I want you to do that for me. Place it in St Clement's." Arthur summoned enough energy to grip Thomas's hand. "Promise me, Thomas. Promise me now."

"I promise, my Prince. But it will not happen."

"I pray for that too. I pray for that for both of us."

The conversation appeared to have exhausted the last of Arthur's strength and he sank back against the pillows. Thomas went to the door and called Belia in. She had brought herbs, and Thomas mixed a strong liquor with mead and willow bark. Between them, they sat the half-conscious Arthur upright and fed the mixture to him.

"Do Amal and Silva have the same for Catherine?" Thomas asked.

"We all have the same herbs, yes."

"Is there anything else we can give him for his fever?"

"Only what you are doing now. Keep him cool, but not too cold."

"There is an ice chamber somewhere in the castle. Go see if you can find it. Ask for Lady Margaret Pole, she will know where it is. And …" Thomas hesitated, then said what he had to. "Ask Lady Margaret to send for a priest. If Arthur comes close to death he must have the last rites."

Belia looked into Thomas's eyes, then turned and left the room.

When Thomas turned back Arthur's eyes were open again.

"Argentine will be upset when he returns to find you here, Tom." The Prince's words were slurred, and when Thomas touched him he felt hotter than ever.

"I will challenge him to a sword fight if he tries to have me expelled."

"That would not be much of a contest, would it? And I hope the priest has a wasted journey." His voice was softer again, and Thomas could almost see the life-force ebbing from him.

"As do I, Your Grace."

Thomas looked around as if there might be something he could use, but he had only what Belia had brought and didn't know enough of her potions to choose something at random. He wished now he had not sent her away.

He sat on the edge of the bed, reached for Arthur's hand and held it between both of his. Arthur briefly squeezed his fingers, but the strength was leaching from him.

"Do not forget, Tom. My heart. The church. Save ... save Catherine..."

When Belia returned Thomas still held the Prince's hand, but it was already cooling. His unseeing eyes continued to stare at the thick canopy over the bed, and eventually Thomas reached out and closed them before standing. As he did so the door opened and a priest entered, breathing hard.

"He has gone," Thomas said.

The priest stared at him for a long time before coming forward. "Then I will say the words for him." The man crossed himself. "God rest the eternal soul of Arthur, Prince of Wales." He began to unpack incense, a cross, a rosary and bottle of holy water.

Thomas left him to it.

Outside, he said, "You and I have work to do, and I need to speak with Sir Richard before we do it. Go to Amal and Silva and do what you can there. Take the ice with you; it might help Catherine. It is too late for her husband. Don't tell her he is dead yet, not until she is recovered." Thomas looked around, a sense of panic flooding him. Prince Arthur was dead. Everything had changed with his last heartbeat. Catherine was a widow. A single woman again, yet barely more than a girl.

Thomas did not know what her future might hold, but feared for her.

When he found Sir Richard Pole and told him, he was sure Arthur's last request would not be honoured.

"He told me the same thing," said Sir Richard. "In fact,

he had it written down so there would be no dispute. Will you do it?"

"He asked me to, and I believe I can do it while honouring his body. If I may, I will have Amal and Belia prepare herbs and lotions to keep his body sweet until it can be carried to London for burial."

"Worcester," said Sir Richard. "That too is written. He is to be laid to rest in the cathedral there, but yes, his heart will lie in St Clement's Church. I will arrange a place, but it must be our secret. Arthur is a Tudor, and there are still those who do not accept a Tudor as their sovereign." Sir Richard wiped a hand across his face, which was damp with sweat, but in his case the cause was from shock and worry. "Damn it, but this is going to cause trouble. Harry is still too young, but he will have to step up. He is no Arthur, though, far from it."

"He will have to be," Thomas said.

"Of course, I forget you know the lad. He is too high-spirited to make a good king, unlike his brother. Arthur would have been a great king. He would have changed the face of England forever. Two nations united. New worlds to explore. All gone now. All gone." Sir Richard turned away, then stopped. "How is Princess Catherine?"

"I came straight to you with the news, Sir Richard, but intend to go to her now. What will become of her?"

Sir Richard looked surprised, as if the thought had not occurred to him. "I do not know. She will be found a place somewhere I expect, but she will never be Queen."

"Perhaps she can return to Spain."

"No. That would mean repaying her dowry, and Henry will never countenance that. A nunnery most like, or marriage to a duke, if one can be found in need of a wife." Sir Richard's eyes met Thomas's. "Perhaps it would be better for her if she dies as well. She can lie alongside Arthur, both in a state of grace."

As Thomas ran up the stairs to Catherine's room he made a decision. If she did die, he would do the same for her as he had promised Arthur. Except he would return Catherine's heart to Spain himself, so that it might lie in the great Cathedral of Sevilla.

CHAPTER THIRTY-FIVE

Thomas stood next to Amal and Belia in a cellar beneath Ludlow Castle. It was cold, with blocks of ice set on the stone platform in the centre. The room was used in more normal times for the butchery of game. Deer, most likely, judging by the size of the platform. Channels were cut in the floor to carry away the blood and gore, and buckets of water were set along shelves for when needed. The body of Arthur, Prince of Wales, lay naked on a slab, only a linen cloth protecting his modesty. Not that he was likely to care anymore, but there were women present.

"You are sure Catherine is improving?" Thomas asked Belia, but it was Amal who replied.

"Yes, she is. There is danger yet, but this sweating sickness takes people fast if it takes them at all. Her fever has broken and now she is merely cold. Shivering. Silva is with her and knows to send a message at once if there is any change." Amal looked at the long, pale body of the Prince. "What do you want us to do, Pa?" There was no hesitation in her voice.

They had done this work before but, Thomas had to admit, it had been mostly Belia who had prepared corpses for burial a score of times, likely more. For Amal, this would be a learning experience. It was women's work. Always had been, and that was unlikely to change soon. The preparation of the body was Belia and Amal's responsibility, but the removal of the bodily organs was Thomas's.

"You don't need to stay, Amal, if you would prefer not to witness this. It's different with someone you know. I can open the body, remove his heart and organs, then Belia can pack herbs and liquors into him before we sew him back up." Thomas glanced at Belia. "Do you have everything you need?"

"I thought I had not, but Silva has enough of what I require and has sent for it. How long until he is interred?"

"I don't know. I asked Sir Richard Pole and he said at least two weeks, perhaps three. Can you make sure he stays sweet that long?"

Belia nodded. "I can. A month if needs be." She met Thomas's eyes. "It is not like it used to be, is it? When we lived in al-Andalus, a body had to be buried before sunset."

"No, it's not the same." They all knew that England was not Spain. And now Spain was no longer the home of the Moors, whose customs were different.

"I will stay if I can," said Amal. "I want to see how you work."

"If you're sure. It won't be pretty."

Amal smiled. "I did not expect it would be, but I still want to stay. I want to learn."

"I doubt you will ever be allowed to cut anyone. That is a man's work. Just as birthing is a woman's work."

"It might not always be so, Pa, and perhaps one day I will save someone's life with my knowledge, just as you do."

"Then stay." Thomas glanced at Belia.

"I will go to Silva," Belia said. "Better two with Catherine than one, and the herbs she has sent for will be taken to her. I have seen the inside of bodies before, and it is not a pleasant sight."

When he and Amal were alone, Thomas took a sharp blade and sliced into Arthur's chest, then reached for a short saw. Amal stood close beside him, one hand on his back, as she took in everything he did. When the heart was cut free, she brought the cedar box over so Thomas could place it inside. The other organs within the cavity would not receive such treatment. Buckets waited for them and they would be taken away to be burned in secret. As he worked, Thomas explained what everything was before he removed it, pleased that Amal wanted to learn. This was not work for the fainthearted, but despite her sex, he knew Amal was not that. She had a core of iron and a sharp intelligence, as well as a drive to learn everything she could.

"Why is Arthur's physician not doing this, Pa?" Amal held a bucket out for him to place the liver in.

"He was asked and refused. He said it was work for a butcher, not a physician." Thomas smiled. "Do you know they used to call me butcher in al-Andalus?"

"Everyone knows that, Pa. Do you think you could have saved Arthur if you were sent for sooner?"

"I don't know. This sweating is a new sickness and nobody knows how it affects people. You recovered, and Catherine will as well, but why it takes some and spares others is a mystery to me."

"If it is a mystery to you, Pa, then it is a mystery to everyone. Silva said she wanted to look in Arthur's room if she is allowed."

"Why?"

"For the same reason she showed Will where all the charms were in our house. She thinks there may be some in his room. No doubt John Miller had access to make up his fires and may have left a gift, just as he left one for you. I know you don't believe in everything Silva does, but she has skill. You have seen what she can do. It's not magic, but it appears to others as if it is."

"There must be a rational explanation, but if so, it's beyond me. And yes, I admit I doubted her, but she has proven herself to us all. And her knowledge of herbs is prodigious."

"It is."

Thomas worked on until Arthur's body cavity was empty and clean. He straightened, aware of an ache in his back from leaning over.

"I must go to see Catherine now. I will send Belia down so you can embalm the body. Can you close him up?"

"Or course I can." Amal stared at Arthur. "I have never seen someone I know dead, Pa. It's strange, isn't it? He doesn't seem to be the same person. Something has left him. The spark of life is gone."

"Yes, it's strange. I hope you never have to see it again."

"If I follow in your footsteps I am sure I will, but it does not touch me too much. I liked him."

"So did I."

When Thomas entered Catherine's room she was sitting up in bed. She was pale, but offered a smile. "How is Arthur, Thomas?"

He stopped where he was. Had nobody told her? He glanced at Belia, who would not meet his eyes. When he looked back at Catherine, he saw she knew the truth from the small exchange that had taken place. She was a clever girl.

"When did he die?" she asked.

"Two hours ago. I have been with him until now otherwise I would have come to you sooner." He offered a nod to Belia, who returned it before leaving the room.

"Did he suffer?"

"He felt no pain. Arthur slipped away peacefully, and spoke of you at the end." Thomas lied, but it was a small lie meant to offer comfort.

"I should have gone to him. I should have died instead of him." She met Thomas's gaze. "What will happen now? He was to be King after his father. What will happen to me?"

"I don't know, Cat. I wish I did, but I don't." Thomas moved closer to the bed, aware of the etiquette he broke. "Silva has something she needs to do, so we have to leave you for a moment, but I will return as soon as I can."

"I thank you for your help," Catherine said stiffly, falling back on protocol.

Thomas admired her for doing so. Her emotions must roil inside but she gave no appearance of it. She was a

Princess. She would have made a fine Queen, but no longer.

Thomas led Silva along the corridor to Arthur's room. It remained as it had when he left, the bedclothes on the floor, falling after Thomas had lifted Arthur's body and carried it out. Word had been sent that the rooms were to be untouched until their work was finished.

"Do what you need to," he said to Silva. "I have to return to Catherine."

"She talked of you, Tom. And Will and Amal. She loves you all."

"Perhaps."

Thomas drew up a chair close to Catherine's bed and sat. He reached out and felt her neck. The pulse there was rapid but steady. She felt warm, but was no longer burning up.

"You need to sleep now."

"I cannot. I am consumed by grief to know I will never see Arthur's sweet face again."

"You can see him, but you may not want to."

"Does he ... will I be shocked? I have never seen a dead body, let alone one so close to me."

"I think it would be good for you to say goodbye. I can arrange it if you ask, but the decision is yours."

Catherine looked away, and Thomas allowed her time, saying nothing. He studied her profile, aware of how well he knew her features. She shared some with her mother, but she was also different. A little taller. A little slimmer — but age accounted for most of that. He knew inside she was strong like her mother. She would not buckle beneath the grief she felt. In this world death was never far away, its causes myriad.

"Yes, I want to see him." Tears overspilled her eyes and tracked down her cheeks.

"Then I will arrange it. Stay here and I will bring Silva back to sit with you."

"I need no one, Thomas. I prefer to mourn my husband alone."

"Very well. But I will post someone outside the door. If you need anything, call out."

Catherine offered a nod of agreement and Thomas returned to Arthur's room, where Silva sat on the side of the bed.

"This is a most comfortable mattress. Do you think we can get one like it?"

"I expect so. Did you find anything?"

Silva reached for a small, velvet bag and held it out. "Look for yourself."

Thomas opened the neck and peered inside, but it was too dark to make out what lay there. He took it to the window where there was more light.

"A dead mouse?" He shook his head. "There are dead mice everywhere in the castle."

"I agree, but none I wager with a woman's dark hair wrapped around its neck. Take it out, Tom, and you will see."

He tipped the tiny body onto his palm. Silva was right. Fine, dark hair was wrapped around the throat of the mouse. The hair was long and reminded him of a noose.

"Where was it?"

"Under his pillow, stuffed inside the mattress."

"Does it…" He hesitated, almost unable to ask, because it went against every belief he held. Except Silva's skill was not in doubt. He had seen what she could do. "Does it have power?"

"Of course it does. The mouse represents Arthur. The hair a hangman's noose. It is powerful indeed."

"Would it have affected him?"

Silva rose and came to stand in front of Thomas. He noticed how tall she was, her eyes almost level with his. The thought reminded him of Philippa, who was also tall. That thought sparked another, and he stroked the black hair with his fingers. The movement filled him with a certainty. This was Philippa's hair, just as fine as the hank of it she'd had set in the walls of his own house.

"Yes, it would have affected him," said Silva. "That is my belief. You can feel it, can't you, when you stroke her hair? Even you can sense the power of what she has done."

"Her hair is familiar to me, that is all."

"But you know it to be hers."

Thomas stroked the hair again, uneasy at the dark emotions that rose through him, because of the memories of what he and Philippa had shared. With a jerk, he threw the dead mouse across the room.

"Yes, I can see you feel it."

"John Miller will have placed it in the bed. He would have had access to this room as he did mine. Arthur would not have known it was there."

"He would not, but it would still have power."

"Arthur was someone who'd stood up for Philippa through everything. Why would she want to harm him? It makes no sense. She would want him to live in case she needed his mercy again in the future."

"Things have changed, have they not? Will talks to me, tells me much. Of his past. Your past. Of Catherine." Silva smiled. "And yes, he has told me how they used to feel about each other. How, underneath, they still might. But he is mine now, heart and soul. What if Philippa wanted to hurt both Arthur and Catherine? I need to check her bed-chamber as well. But Arthur's death will hurt her sorely."

"Philippa is not rational. Perhaps she never has been, but if so, she hid it well from me, from everyone, for a long time."

"Will also told me what happened to her father. That you killed him. Is that not enough to send a daughter mad?" Silva touched his arm. "You have little faith, Tom, I know. You are a rational man, but sometimes rationality does not explain everything." She smiled. "Don't worry, I have no wish to convert you. Only to educate you that there is more in this world than in your science. Now, how is Catherine?"

"She wants to see Arthur."

"Is that wise?"

"I intend to find that out now. Will you sit with her while I do?"

"Of course. I like her, and if there are charms in her room I will sense them."

When Thomas returned to Amal and Belia they had completed their work. If not for the livid scar that ran from navel to neck, Arthur looked almost alive.

When Thomas told them what Catherine wanted Belia

said, "Not here. Return him to his room, and you should dress him in a high-necked shirt. I will ask Catherine's ladies for some rouge and will colour his cheeks. Only then can you take her to see her husband."

Thomas was glad Belia and Amal were there. Pleased they had done such an excellent job. He wrapped Arthur's body in the sheet he had carried him down in and sent them ahead, to ensure he was not seen as he took him back to the room in which he had died. Within a quarter hour, he led Catherine along the corridor. She leaned heavily against him, Amal on her other side.

At the doorway Thomas stopped.

"You should enter on your own, Cat."

"No. Come with me, Thomas. And you, Amal. I need friends around me when I see him."

Thomas opened the door and led her inside. The air was sweetened with herbs Belia had spread beneath the bed. The lamps were dim, and a filigreed screen had been placed before the window. Catherine stopped halfway to the bed and Thomas moved back.

Time passed, but it did not matter. They would stay all day and into the next if that was what Catherine wanted. She moved closer, then closer still.

She sat on the side of the bed and reached for her husband's hand, clutching it to her breast. He looked alive, but the coldness of his hand would tell her differently.

"Goodnight, my sweet." The words barely reached Thomas and Amal. "Sleep well in heaven." She leaned across and kissed his forehead.

They remained there for a full half hour. Only when

the bells of St Laurence's Church rang out the hour did Catherine stir herself and rise.

She said nothing when she reached Thomas, but held out her hand so he could support her back to her room. Which is where they left her after sending two of her Spanish ladies to watch over her, with firm instructions to send a message if she showed any sign of a relapse.

Thomas sent Belia, Silva and Amal home to Burway, but his own work was not yet done. He went in search of Sir Richard Pole. The man would be busy, because there was much to arrange, but he needed to know that Prince Arthur had been prepared, and that his heart lay in the cedar box in the cellar.

It was growing dark by the time Thomas passed through Linney Gate and descended towards his house. His mind was fixed on the future. With Arthur dead, Ludlow Castle would no longer have a purpose. And Thomas wondered if he would, either.

CHAPTER THIRTY-SIX

A hand on his shoulder brought Thomas awake from some place too deep for dreams. He rolled onto his back, grateful for their lack.

He dreamed often of Prince Arthur's death two months before, spent more waking hours wondering what he might have done to save him. He knew most likely nothing. Sometimes people were taken. The sweating sickness took without rhyme or reason. Particularly the young. Particularly the underserving. Now Arthur's heart lay buried in St Laurence Church, his body in Worcester Cathedral. All of England knew of his passing and wondered what the future might bring. Change was unwelcome. Thomas tried to forget what promise Arthur had offered. A promise now dead. Ludlow Castle lacked a purpose now the Prince of Wales was dead. Thomas had started to wonder if he, too, lacked a purpose. Even Philippa Gale's threats had ceased, and he wondered if his saving her life had changed her. Had she forgotten him? Forgiven him? Though what forgiveness was due he did not know. So the absence of dreams was welcome, as was the hand on his shoulder.

"What is it?"

Bel was a dark shape against darkness, no light beyond the windows, only a faint illumination from a candle burning in the corridor beyond their room.

"I heard something."

Thomas sighed. "The wind. A fox. Go back to sleep."

"There is no wind, and I know what a fox sounds like. I think someone is outside."

Thomas sat up and cocked his head to one side, but all he heard was the soft whisper of the Teme as it ran across a band of rock beyond Belia's workshop. And then he heard what Bel had.

A scratching.

Soft, almost silent, but there.

Thomas threw back the covers and stood. He walked naked to the small window, which stood a quarter way open because the June night was warm. He peered out as far as he could but saw nothing. The sound of the river was louder, and then the scratching came again and he leaned farther out but still saw nothing.

He turned back and pulled on a shirt and hose, then went barefoot into the corridor and along its length, through a door into the next wing of the house where Will and Silva lived. The door to their bedroom was ajar and Thomas knocked on it. When he received no reply he pushed it open to discover the bed unslept in.

"Where's Will?" Thomas asked Bel when he returned to their room. She had risen too and wore a long robe that almost touched the floor. The window was closed, the shutters drawn to stop the light of a candle showing.

"He and Silva have gone to her cottage in the woods above Croft. He told you, but you never listen, do you? Or you listen then forget."

"I forgot." Thomas heard the noise again, less circumspect now as if whoever made it was losing patience. "Stay here. Throw the bolt across the door until I return. I will knock three times, then another twice."

Downstairs in the wide kitchen, Thomas found Amal standing in the faint glow from the fireplace. She, like Bel, wore a long linen robe, her dark hair cascading down her back.

"There's someone outside, Pa," she said.

"I know. Go back upstairs and bar your door. I'm going out to see who it is."

"No, you're not."

"Do you expect me to wait here for them to break in?"

"This house is built strong; they will have difficulty doing that."

"All it takes is a loose catch, and I didn't check them before we went to bed. Did you?"

Amal shook her head. "Will usually does it. I'll come with you."

"Not in a white robe you won't."

"What, shall I take it off then?" She started to lift it. "My skin is dark enough they probably won't see me."

"Go put something else on while I fetch a weapon."

"Two weapons," said Amal. "One for me."

"Go and wake Jorge. I will fetch a knife for him."

"And another for me." Amal stared at him; even in the faint glow her expression set firm.

"One for you as well, then. Go. Now."

She went, bare feet soft on the floor — short, exotic, perfect. Brave. Just as her mother had been. Thomas went to the small room they used as an armoury and selected five knives. Two for himself, two for Jorge, one for Amal if she insisted. But he would make her stay inside. He considered leaving Jorge inside as well, knowing he would come if asked, also knowing his skills as a fighter were not as honed as Thomas's. But he had a strong heart.

Thomas took one of the knives and walked through darkness, along the corridor that ran from wing to wing, until the noises that had woken Bel grew louder. On a corner, between one wing and the next, men stood outside. Thomas could make them out even in the dark, pale faces set against the night. One of them had something in his hand and was trying to force the window open.

The knife slipped and the man cursed. Another came forward and said something too soft for Thomas to hear, but it was clear from his actions what it had been. "Let me try."

Thomas moved to the side, trying to see how many there were. Eight, he thought, but there could be more trying to gain entry elsewhere. A frontal assault would be difficult. The building rose to thirty feet on all sides, and the only entrance was barred by heavy, oak doors. If someone brought a ladder tall enough they might reach the roof, but then would need another to descend into the courtyard. Once there, if they managed to gain entry, they

384

would find the doors to each of the wings also barred from within. Thomas had not intended his house to be a fortress but it seemed that is what he had created. It was meant to emulate, in some small way, the palace of Alhambra in Granada. In doing so, it served the same purpose as the palace. A place of beauty, but also a place of protection.

The new man was having no more success than the first at opening the window and Thomas made a mental note to thank the masons for their work. He also decided to go outside and confront them, but not yet. He went back to the kitchen to find Jorge there with Amal.

"How many?" asked Jorge, his expression set. He was afraid, but ready to do what was asked of him.

"I saw eight, but there may be more. I'm going out after them. Once I go through the gate I need you to bar it from inside and come back here. Make sure all the doors to the courtyard are barred."

"And how will you get back in?"

"I will knock at a window, of course, and you can come and let me in."

"Oh my, you have a plan," said Jorge.

Thomas shook his head. "Amal, go to Belia and tell her to wake the children. I want her to take them into Ludlow. Tell her to go to Usaden and send him here. You will also go with them."

Amal turned and left. Thomas knew when the time came he would have trouble making her go, but he did not want her in the house if the men managed to gain entrance.

He also turned away, knowing Jorge, despite his fear,

would follow. He unbarred the door to the courtyard and stepped out. In the confines of the space, the sound of running water from the rill along its centre was louder here than the river was. Between them, they raised the heavy bar from the high gate and Thomas opened it wide enough to slip out. He waited until he heard Jorge replace the bar, then started away.

The night air carried a chill, and a low mist rose above the river, to wash like a tide across the grass. At the corner, Thomas stopped and peered around it. He saw the men, but could still not count their number accurately. There was no moon and the only illumination came from the faint stars. Ludlow perched on the hill, the now abandoned castle dark. A few lights showed in some of the windows of houses but not enough to help down here by the banks of the Teme.

Eight men, perhaps. No more than ten, he was sure.

Could he take ten? At one time he would not have hesitated. Now, he had sixty years, and on some days his leg ached where many years before he had taken a sword thrust. He did not feel old but knew he was. He had fought not so long since, and in the heat of battle all his aches and pains fell away. His skill remained. He was not as fast as he had once been, but fast enough. Years of conflict had honed his skill, and he still possessed enough of it.

But ten men? In the dark? Without knowing who they were?

Thomas pulled back and made his way along the way he had come. Instead of trying to attract Jorge's attention at the gate he went on. He stopped and looked around the corner on the north side of the building but saw nobody there. He ran along its length and did the same on the eastern side. Again nothing. Which meant all the attackers were on the southern side. It told Thomas only the direction they had most likely come from, but not from where. He was still standing watching their fruitless attempt to break into his house when a tap at the window beside him made him jump and his heart race.

Amal peered out at him as she opened the window.

"Belia and the children are ready, and Jorge has a plan of sorts. Are you coming in or staying out there?"

"What's this plan?"

"You cause a diversion of some kind. Maybe fetch Ferrant and ride at them. Something, anyway. While you do that, Belia and the children will leave through the gate and Jorge will go with them. He says he needs to protect them. Bel says she will stay here. So will I."

"No. You and Bel both go with Belia. Jorge stays here with me."

Amal shut the window and walked away.

Thomas tapped on it and she returned.

"All right then, but if you stay Jorge will have to go with them as protection."

Amal stifled a laugh with her palm. "And you thought I would be able to protect them as well as Jorge can?" She shook her head in disbelief. "So, are you staying out there or coming in?"

"Coming in. Stand back."

Thomas grasped the sill of the window and drew himself up. He went in head first, which was a mistake, and landed awkwardly.

When he straightened up, Amal said, "Well, that is a sight I can never unsee, Pa."

In the kitchen, Belia stood with the children. Each of them held a knife, even young Leila. The sight of the blade in her hand dismayed Thomas, and he knew he had let them all down.

"I will come out with you through the gate," he said. "Then I will make a lot of noise. And when you hear it, run to the trees by the river and make your way to Ludlow. You know where to go?"

"To Emma's house, and tell Usaden to come here as quickly as he can."

Thomas nodded. "Are you ready?" He glanced at Bel. "I can't persuade you to go with them?"

"I stay with you, whatever happens."

Thomas knew any attempt to argue would only delay matters so said nothing. For the second time that night, he and Jorge removed the heavy bar closing the gate and they all slipped outside. As they did so Thomas heard a loud crash, the breaking of glass, and knew the intruders had grown tired of attempting to gain entry silently.

"Go!" he hissed. "Run for the trees."

As soon as he saw they had reached cover Thomas went back inside. He hesitated at the heavy doors then decided to leave them open. The intruders were already inside, and it might make an escape easier if he, Amal and Bel needed to do so.

He wondered where the two of them were. Had they retreated upstairs? He hoped so, and that they had bolted their doors.

Thomas slipped off his boots as soon as he entered the

house and trod barefoot across the stone floor. Men were inside the house. But where? He stood in the dark, listening. Nothing. And then, distantly, the scrape of a boot heel against the floor. Upstairs. Where Amal and Bel were.

Thomas moved to the stairs, his head moving so he could pick up any sound. He heard voices, too muffled by distance to work out what was being said. Then more movement, this time from several places. The men had split up to conduct their search.

Thomas did not have to consider why they had come. He had been too lax in assuming Philippa Gale had given up her feud against him. He knew now it would never end while one or other of them remained alive.

He heard a sudden noise at the head of the stairs, a cry, and then a figure came tumbling down, its limbs crashing against the steps. A man landed at Thomas's feet and lay unmoving. Blood spread in a pool, and when he knelt Thomas saw the man had been stabbed. An expert strike, which had cut into the major artery in his neck. Only Bel and Amal remained in the house, and of the two only Amal would know the exact place to strike.

Thomas rose and ascended the stairs two at a time. At the top he looked along the corridor but saw no sign of Amal, nor of the intruders. He started forward, his hand reaching out for the latch on his and Bel's bedroom, relieved to find it locked. As he moved on a figure came at him from where it had been hiding in a doorway and Thomas raised a hand to deflect a wicked blow from above. All around was darkness, so all he saw was a pale face. He struck out, missed, struck again and this time his aim was true. The man grunted and went to his knees.

Thomas pulled his blade free and used it to end the man's life. When he looked past him it was to discover Amal crouched in a corner.

She came across to him.

"How many?" Thomas whispered.

"Ten in total. Eight now."

"Bel?"

"Did as you told her. She's locked in your room."

"Unlike you."

Amal made no reply.

"Where are the others? I saw none downstairs."

"They opened the door into Jorge's accommodation and went through there. They are looking for you, Pa. I overheard them say your name. Are we going to follow them?"

"I am going to follow them. You are to stay here."

There was just enough light to show the stubborn expression on Amal's face.

"I am no safer here than with you. Less, most likely. They will discover soon enough they can move from one wing of the house to the next. Better we are together, Pa."

Thomas opened his mouth to object, but realised Amal was right. If she came with him he could at least offer some protection.

He nodded. "Stay behind me, then."

"Of couse … like a good daughter always should." She grinned, then pulled him down to kiss his cheek.

It took longer to move through the next wing of the house because the door to all the rooms were unlocked. At the first Thomas glanced inside but saw nothing. The next room was where Jorge and Belia slept, the door shut.

Thomas pressed his ear to it, then held up two fingers so Amal could see, and she nodded and stood against the far wall.

Thomas eased the latch, then pushed the door wide in a sudden rush. The intruders had lit lamps and the light almost blinded him. He saw a shape approach, jerked to one side and thrust out. A third man fell. Then the other was on him and they fought, too close for blades. The man was strong, and skilled. He pushed Thomas back until his head cracked against the wall. Thomas tried to push him away only the discover he could not. Neither could he use his knife. He tried to stamp down on the man's feet but they were leather shod and his own bare feet had no effect.

The man laughed.

Then the sound stopped and he fell away sideways.

Amal stood facing him, her knife red.

"I got him in the long blood vessel along his spine, Pa. He won't get up again."

Thomas stared at his daughter, wondering quite what he had raised; but also grateful to her.

"I need to keep one of them alive if you can manage to do that."

Amal grinned. "I'll see what I can do. Six now, Pa. Good odds, I think."

Even better odds as a figure appeared in the doorway. Usaden stood there, barely breathing.

"I came as fast as I could. Where are they?"

Thomas pointed. "Along that way."

Usaden glanced at Amal. "What is she doing here?"

"Saving her father's life."

Usaden turned away.

"Now will you go back to Bel?"

Amal stared at him, her expression stubborn.

"Then stay here, but come no farther." Thomas turned away before she could argue.

By the time he reached the next wing three bodies lay on the floor and he moved faster before Usaden killed them all.

He was almost too late.

When Thomas found him Usaden was a snake preparing to strike.

"No," Thomas said, not raising his voice. "I need one to question, and he is the only man left."

Usaden stepped back and Thomas stepped forward.

"Now, tell me where Philippa Gale is, and why she sent you to kill me."

"Why should I?"

"Because if you don't I will let my friend here do what he wants with you. It will be painful, and it will be long."

"You will kill me anyway."

"I may not, so you have to decide. Certain death, screaming in agony, or the possibility of life."

Thomas waited until he saw acceptance on the man's face.

"Tell me what you want to know, Thomas Berrington."

CHAPTER THIRTY-SEVEN

Six days had passed since the attack on Thomas's house and his questioning of the final attacker. The man had confirmed Philippa Gale sent them. Also confirmed she had not forgotten what Thomas had done to her and her father. She wanted an end to him.

Thomas had been tempted to kill the man, but in the end allowed him to live, sending him back with a message to give Philippa.

He was coming for her.

An easterly wind brought a sharp stench, then through the gloom of low clouds the spire of St Paul's Cathedral emerged. Gradually, Thomas made out the city walls and knew they could rest for the night at Bel Savage. They had made good time, completing the journey in just over four days without the need to change horses, though Ferrant had been limping for the last hour and Thomas would need to ask a farrier to look at his front leg. He suspected a thrown shoe, hoped for nothing more serious. He had purchased Ferrant the day he stepped on English soil for the first time in over forty years, and had grown fond of the horse. He was placid and slow, but could keep going all day. Alongside him, Will rode a tall charger bought from a soldier who considered it too old, but it was still a fine horse and big enough that Will did not look as though he rode a donkey. Jorge rode a horse Thomas had purchased in Ludlow, a kindly mare who tried not to throw him at every opportunity. Jorge had complained his backside hurt on their journey, but both Thomas and Will had ignored him. Ahead of them, Usaden and Kin roamed.

The road grew busier as they approached Ludgate, the stench of the city growing with the population. Thomas knew they would get used to it, but it did not mean it would be welcome.

Peggy Spicer, goodwife of the Bel Savage, greeted Thomas like an old friend. She kissed him on the side of his mouth, then shook the hands of Will and Jorge. She was less sure of Usaden, and ignored Kin, who was not the only hound in the big room. Yes, she had a room with four beds, so it should suit as long as the dog slept on the floor. And yes, she would ask the farrier to check on Thomas's horse.

A half hour later, Thomas descended the narrow stairs, and asked for food and a bottle of good wine for the three of them. The bells of the myriad churches and St Paul's Cathedral struck the hour, though which of them struck it correctly could not be determined. Thomas went to check on Ferrant, pleased when the farrier told him he had already re-shod the front hoof. He asked if Thomas wanted him to do the other three, as the shoes were showing signs of wear. He told him to do all the horses and paid him enough to ensure it would be done come morning. Then he returned to the inn.

Peggy Spicer brought the wine and set it on the table, together with three flagons, before taking the seat beside Thomas.

"I can find a private room for the two of us if you like, Tom." She made a point of reminding him of their liaison of a few months before.

"My thanks, and tempting as it is, I have other business tonight."

"Your companion is handsome too, is he not? Would he be interested? Or the tall one?"

Thomas smiled. "The tall one is my son and has a woman at home. The pretty one is a eunuch, and the third also has a woman. Do you not recall they stayed here with you some months ago?"

"I have many clients. Am I expected to remember every one of them?"

"You remembered me."

"But we shared time together, did we not?" Peggy Spicer frowned. "The pretty one doesn't look like a eunuch."

"How many eunuchs do you know, Peggy?"

She thought for a moment. "None. But from what I hear, they don't look like him."

"Jorge is one of a kind." Thomas leaned a little closer to her and lowered his voice. "What news of the bonemen?"

"Gone," said Peggy. "None seen these last six months, not since that night we frolicked together in your room."

"Have you heard if they bother anyone else?"

"Not around here, but they might still work south of the river or to the east. Whatever happened to that princess you had coming over from Spain, Tom?"

"She came. You know she did. She married Prince Arthur in the cathedral not two hundred paces from here. She lives in Ludlow now." Thomas wondered what King Henry's plans were now for the crown of England. He was still young enough for his younger son to come of age.

"Where is this Ludlow? Is it nice?"

"It's in the west, hard against the border of Wales, and yes, it is nice enough. It smells sweeter than London."

"You get used to that," said Peggy. "You hardly need to —" She broke off and stood when Will and Jorge came towards the table. Her eyes were on Jorge as he approached, and Thomas knew she was doubting his word about him being a eunuch.

"I need to talk to you later if I can," Thomas said to her before the others reached them.

"I will be here all night. I will get your food if you are ready. We have a fine mutton pottage made fresh this morning."

Jorge caught Peggy's wrist as she passed and kissed the back of her hand, causing her face to flush bright red.

"She's a pretty one," he said, taking one of the comfortable, curved-back chairs. "And as buxom as they come."

"And you have an even prettier one at home, though not as buxom, I admit. You all do, so behave yourselves. We are not here for amusement."

"Of which I wager she could provide all a man might want," said Jorge.

"She is still off limits." There were times Thomas wondered about Jorge's claims of infidelity because he had never witnessed him being unfaithful. But it was true almost all women were fascinated by him, and thanks to Thomas, he could satisfy a woman without fear of setting a child in her.

Will leaned to one side when a young woman set trenchers in front of them, steam rising from the pottage set in each. "Do we start our search for Philippa tomorrow?"

"Once I have seen the King. I want to find out what Cornwell might have told him. Also, I was there when Arthur breathed his last. I can tell him it was peaceful. I hear he still grieves for his son."

"Which is understandable, but he also needs to rule a country. And he must know what Cornwell is like."

"Of course, but the man has a great deal of influence in the Marches, and Henry will want to keep him on side. It wouldn't surprise me if after they spoke he tells me to reverse my judgement."

"Does Croft not have influence as well?"

"He is a different manner of man to Cornwell. He is also not the reason we are here. Once I have seen King Henry we start our search for Philippa."

"She should not be difficult to find if she's in London," said Will. "There can be few women who look like her lacking an entire right arm. She will find it difficult to bend men to her will now."

"What some men want would surprise you," said Jorge. "There is nothing they might not find attractive."

Will stared at Jorge for a moment, then returned to his

food. Usaden ignored them, offering pieces torn from his gravy-soaked trencher to Kin, who lay at his feet.

"What are we doing here, Pa? Did you ask about the bonemen?"

"Of course. Peggy tells me they are no more, but we also need to satisfy ourselves of that in the morning."

"Do we take prisoners like last time and question them?"

"Not if there are no bonemen. If we come across some, then perhaps. I go to see Henry early, but once I return we will visit their old headquarters on London Bridge and watch. If any bonemen are left, that is where they will be. So you may drink as much as you want tonight because you can sleep until noon if you wish."

Jorge's smile was so blissful it made Thomas laugh.

Peggy Spicer had been right. As Thomas followed Cheapside east, he barely noticed the stink from the piles of ordure in the alleys or the miasma that rose from the Thames. At the Tower, the easterly wind brought cleaner air from the farmland and marsh beyond. Thomas stated his business and was told to wait. He sat on the same stone bench where Philippa Gale had first come to take him to the King all those months before. He contemplated whether he could have done anything different, before concluding most likely not. She had been persuasive, beautiful, and seductive. Thomas had been a stranger in a changed England, and in need of companionship. She must have seen something to make her choose him. Had it been his connection to Catherine, he wondered, or something else? Philippa was already at home with the English royals. Had she wanted influence amongst the Spanish as well? Thomas thought he should ask Jorge, for if anyone knew the mind of a woman it would be him. He had left him sleeping in their room beneath the eaves. Will and Usaden rose with Thomas, but struck off at St Paul's in search of information on the bonemen.

Thomas was almost dozing when someone kicked his foot. He opened his eyes, expecting to see a page. Instead, a boy stood there, red-haired, fair of limb, with a pink face.

"I thought father sent you to Ludlow, Tom. Do you know my brother is dead?"

"I was with Arthur when he died, Harry." Thomas wondered if he could still call the young Duke of York Harry now he was heir to the throne of England. But the lad appeared not to mind. In a few years he might, but not yet.

"Did he suffer?" The question was at odds with Harry's benign expression. Perhaps he had not been close enough to his brother to feel his death deeply.

"He was at peace."

"Why could you not save him?"

"Sometimes people can't be saved. A sickness came to the town and took half who caught it, often in less than a day."

Harry took a step away. "Did you catch it, Tom?"

He shook his head. "I did not. I believe some people are spared it."

"Catherine lived."

"She did."

"How is she now?"

"Well."

"Perhaps I should marry her. It will save father having to return her dowry."

"I don't think Spain will ask for it back, not unless Catherine returns as well. She is a few years older than you, mind."

"Experience counts. That's what father always says. What are you doing here?"

"I have asked for an audience with your father the King."

"He is not in a good mood, I warn you, but come with me and I will take you to him. You can tell him Arthur died without pain, and you were with him at the end. Did you pray?"

"I did." Thomas thought the lie a wise choice. "And a priest did the same."

"Good. He sits in heaven now, which will make him even more elevated than the throne of England would." Harry turned away and Thomas fell into step beside him. The lad had grown in the months since he had last seen him, in both confidence and stature.

Without Harry at his side, Thomas was unsure he would have gained access to the King. Apart from the young duke, there was an air of melancholy hanging over the palace. The servants avoided eye contact, as if to do so might cause anger or grief.

Two men moved together in front of a half-open door, allowing only Harry to enter. Thomas stayed where he was, waiting, knowing he might get no farther. If he was now banished he would not blame the King, but would prefer to plead his case face to face. One positive, if he was refused, was that Cornwell had no doubt suffered the same fate. But it did not happen. Harry appeared at the door and motioned Thomas inside, and the guards moved aside to admit him.

King Henry sat on a wooden chair large enough to be a throne had it been gilded. His Queen was nowhere to be seen.

"I wondered how long it would take before you dragged yourself here to face me. I will not welcome you, Thomas Berrington, not yet. Sir Thomas Cornwell has already told me what you have been doing. He claims my son would have lived had it not been for you."

So, Cornwell beat me to it, Thomas thought. He bowed, avoiding the King's gaze, aware the next few moments would spin the dice one way or the other. He thought of the King's love of gambling and wondered if they could in fact throw dice to judge his fate.

"What have you to say to me?" The King spoke more harshly than the last time they had met.

"First, Your Grace, that no one could have saved your son. This sweating sickness is new. Nobody knows how to treat it. But I can tell you that your son died peacefully, and without pain."

"You know this how? John Argentine has been to see me and did not say such."

"John Argentine was not present with Prince Arthur at the end, Your Grace. He was in St Laurence's Church, praying for his soul. I was with your son when he died. I held his hand as his last breath left him. As for Sir Thomas Cornwell, the man is a liar. He knows nothing of what went on in the castle. He throws false accusations at me because I was foolish enough to rule against him at a Quarter Session."

When Henry said nothing for a long time Thomas risked a quick glance up at him. The man had tears tracking his cheeks. Thomas looked away quickly before he saw his grief had been witnessed. Still grief unmanned the King; Thomas had heard the mutterings of those at court. They considered it time Henry put his pain aside and took more care of his country.

"Who attended Princess Catherine?" Henry asked at last, his voice still unsteady.

"My daughter Amal and two others I have trained. It was not appropriate for me to attend her. I thought it better I stay with your son."

"Might that have been a mistake if Catherine lived and Arthur died?"

Thomas considered whether to mention the charms Silva had found beneath Arthur's bed, then decided the King did not need to know. Either he would dismiss them as trivial superstition or consider they had some relevance and may have hastened Arthur's death. Neither opinion would alleviate his grief.

"I did all I could, Your Grace, but it was God who took him in the end, to sit at his right hand."

"I don't suppose Catherine is with child, is she?"

"Not as far as I know, Your Grace, and if she was I believe I would."

"Yes, I expect you would. I am unsure if you are not

too close to that girl. As I hear rumours you were too close to her mother."

"There are always rumours, Your Grace. Men of intelligence ignore them."

"At least there is no child. It would make matters difficult if she bore a boy. He would step over Harry for the crown, but would take longer to reach his majority."

"There is no child, Your Grace."

"Hmm."

Thomas waited.

Somewhere a clavichord played and a girl sang high and clear. Thomas wondered if it was one of the princesses. If so, she sang well.

"Cornwell told me your house was attacked. He made a point of saying it was nothing to do with him."

"I made no claim it was, Your Grace. But yes, men attacked me and my household, which comprised of several women and children. They would have killed us all had they succeeded."

"I hear you have only recently completed this house, and it is strange."

"For England, yes, Your Grace."

"Cornwell is not a man who likes to be bested, and I believe you have crossed him."

"I made a judgement on the merits of a case brought before me, Your Grace. I judged Sir Thomas was in the wrong."

"He often is, but still expects to get his own way. Croft is another matter. He has been here whining about injustice. He gets on with the job of managing his estates and looking out for my interests.

"If you wish to appoint a new Justice of the Peace I will stand aside, Your Grace."

"Why in God's name would I want to do that? It is rare enough to find an honest Justice, and I intend to make the most of you. Sir Richard Pole came to offer his condolences and gave an excellent report of you, as did Lady Margaret to my wife. Now stand up, Thomas, and look me in the eye. I will not take your head this day so you can behave like a normal man and not a sycophant. I will not have them around me, damn it. Now come tell Elizabeth what you told me. She wakes in the night with a scream on her tongue at the thought of Arthur dying in paroxysms."

It was some time later, after the Queen had joined them, that Thomas found the courage to ask after Catherine's fate.

"She is recovered now, Your Grace, but remains unsure of her future."

"As she should be. I cannot allow her to return to Spain or I will have to give up half her dowry, and that I cannot afford."

Thomas took it as a sign of King Henry's acceptance of him that he spoke so freely on the matter.

"She is fond of England now and has no wish to return to her native land." It was a lie, but perhaps what Henry wanted to hear.

"She cannot return to Ludlow, not without Arthur. She lives now at Durham House. She can keep her

Spanish ladies with her, but I need to know where she is."

"Would I be allowed to visit, Your Grace?"

Henry looked at Thomas. "Do you want to?"

"My family knows her well, and she might welcome familiar faces."

"She will have her ladies, I told you that."

"Very well, Your Grace." Thomas knew he could not press his case further, but the Queen made an intervention.

She reached out and touched her husband's hand. "The friends of youth remain with us always, do they not? Your uncle Jasper was closer than a father to you. Would it be so wrong to allow Thomas and his children to visit occasionally?"

Henry's face darkened, but he made no comment one way or the other.

His wife removed her hand. "What do you plan on doing with the rest of your time in London, Thomas? The weather is fine now. A trip along the river can be most beneficial, and if you go as far as Richmond you will see our new palace, which is almost finished. We hope to live there before the summer is out. At least we will be away from the fetid air of the city."

Thomas suppressed a smile that the stink affected commoner and royalty alike. Perhaps royalty more than the commoner, the latter being more used to it.

"I will see if I can find a wherry willing to take me that far, otherwise I may ride west to see this wonder."

"You can see it firsthand next time you visit, Thomas," said the King. "Do you have a wife?"

"I believe I do." And when Henry frowned. "At least I may have come summer."

"Do not be hasty," said the Queen. "It is different for such as us, but ordinary folk should choose carefully rather than have a partner chosen for them."

Thomas considered her words close to treason, was it not for the look of love she offered the King.

"I believe I have chosen well, Your Grace."

CHAPTER THIRTY-EIGHT

The afternoon was half gone before Thomas and the others walked east along Cheapside, weaving between stalls erected by traders selling a surfeit of wares. The street was busy with men and women making their way to and from work, gentlemen on horseback, and delivery carts half-blocking the roadway.

London Bridge was also thick with crowds, most coming into the city from the south. A stall selling fresh bread and meat provided something for Jorge, Will and Usaden to dine on. Thomas was replete with the food he had eaten at the Tower. They idled while looking at a three-storey house on the far side of the bridge. It was familiar to all three who had fought there. Where two had almost lost their lives and Galib Uziel, Philippa Gale's father, had lost his.

"Either the men you seek are gone or they are rebuilding their headquarters," said Jorge.

Thomas nodded in agreement, his gaze following the

comings and goings of workmen who carried planks of recently sawn wood through the wide, front door.

"More likely the new owners are making the place their own. It was hardly fit for a family to live in as it was."

"Would a family want to live here above the river?" asked Jorge.

"They would. The bridge is considered a fashionable location. I expect such houses don't come cheap."

"Is it big inside?"

"It is, and mostly empty. I would like to see inside again." Thomas glanced at Will, who gave a nod of agreement. Jorge seemed less sure when Thomas met his eyes.

"We can ask," said Will. "Or rather, I suggest Jorge ask. He can work with men as well as women when he puts his mind to it."

Jorge patted Will's cheek. "You know me so well, young man."

He strode across the road while Thomas, Will, and Usaden stayed where they were. Kin wandered off after another hound. Jorge made his way to a man who was organising the carrying of wood from two carts into the building and spoke to him. The man frowned at first but, as Jorge worked his magic, the frown faded. Eventually he looked across at Thomas, Will and Usaden, and nodded.

"What did you tell him?" asked Thomas when they joined him.

"That despite how you dress, you are a man of much wealth who already owns several houses in London and would like them updated to the latest style. He asked how many houses and I told him eight. Is that too many?"

"Eight appears to have been a good number if he is letting us in."

Thomas entered once the door was clear of men and wood. The last time he had been in the building the ground floor had been a single space, with wide, wooden stairs leading to the upper floors. Now it was being divided into rooms. Chalk marks on the floor indicated where walls were to be erected. Several carpenters worked at nailing heavy beams to the walls so planks could be attached to them.

"May we look upstairs?" Thomas asked a passing man.

"Go where you like, sir, but take care of your footing. Some boards up there have been removed."

Thomas ascended the stairs with the others following behind. The middle floor had been where Galib Uziel lived, but now it was torn apart. As promised, much of the floor was ripped up. However, where a ladder once led to the upper floor a new staircase had been fitted, leading to an almost completed gallery.

Once they had ascended, Thomas walked to the opening that still remained, looking down onto the Thames. Will and Usaden came to stand beside him, but Jorge hung back, once again talking with some of the men.

Will gripped the side of the open door and looked down. The tide was on the turn and the water between the stone buttresses was growing troubled. There had been a full ebb when Thomas and Galib Uziel had plummeted together through this space. Only one of them had survived that night.

"She has nothing to do with this place anymore, nor do the bonemen," said Will. "We are wasting our time."

"I wanted to see it once more."

"I understand, but we should go. The bonemen are finished, and we have the properties Amal identified to look at yet. If Philippa has returned to one of them — what will you do then, Pa?"

"Arrest her. I would take her to the Tower and have her locked away, but she always manages to sweet talk her way out of captivity. She was close to the King and Queen for a long time, but they will change their opinion of her when I tell them how she acted against Arthur."

"The woman is pure evil, but men are drawn to her. Just like you were."

"Yes," Thomas said. "Just like I was."

He turned away from the door. Will was right. This was a distraction, but he was glad they had come, glad they had gained entrance. Standing here at the place that might have been his last on earth brought a sense of closure.

Outside, Usaden gave a single whistle and Kin appeared, winding his way through the legs of the crowd, and they made their way back into the city. It was still early evening and would stay light a while yet, so Thomas consulted the note Amal had made for him, then asked someone for direction to both locations. Once he heard where each house lay they headed to the nearest, which was close to the Tower but inside the city wall.

A maze of narrow alleys cut between the thorough-fares of Fanchurchestrete and Algatestrete. They were cramped, but perhaps because of being closer to the

Tower, not as fetid as those further west. Gardens lay behind walls where apple and pear trees grew, their fruit starting to set. The house lay on a corner of three alleys. It rose two storeys and had windows on either side of the door, which showed it was larger than most houses in these parts. Space within the city wall was at a premium, houses close to the Tower even more so. Thomas suspected before long the fruit trees in the gardens would be grubbed up and the land used for more houses.

Across the street lay the Northumberland Inn. A few men stood outside watching the strangers, no doubt wondering what they wanted. Or who they sought.

"Go buy some ale and draw them into conversation," Thomas said to Jorge, "before they call the watch on us."

"Can I buy wine instead?"

"Here? No, get ale. Take Usaden with you. Pretend he is your servant from the east."

Jorge glanced at Usaden, who showed no reaction.

Thomas crossed the street and hammered on the heavy door of the house Amal had listed. He wondered what he would do if Philippa opened it herself. Push her inside and arrest her? Could they get her to the Tower without people coming to her aid?

A woman bundled between four men? He thought not.

It was not Philippa who opened the door but a young woman with red hair and a pink face.

"What do you want?"

"I am looking for a friend of mine by the name of Philippa Gale."

"Not here, sir. We rent this house. Me and my

husband, his father, my mother, and our children. Eight of them. It's why we need somewhere the size of this."

"Who do you pay rent to?"

"My husband knows, but he won't be back until dark. He works at the docks. A fine trade, he says, and sometimes he brings home a little something that fell off a cart." She smiled for the first time.

"Dark, you say?"

She nodded.

"And your husband's father would not know who you pay rent to?"

"He's not as sharp as he used to be, sir. Deaf, and talks little these days unless he wants feeding. Come back later, but not too late. My Jack likes to be abed early for he rises early too."

Thomas thanked the woman and turned away, then thought of something else. The door was half-closed, but he prevented it from closing all the way with his foot.

"Does the name Gala Uziel mean anything to you?"

Her face changed as if a light had been played on to it. "Oh yes, sir, we all know Gala. She used to live nearby and called often, but I haven't seen her in close to a year. I heard she works for someone important now and moved away."

"Where did she live?"

"She has a house in Hart Home Alley, sir, but she hasn't lived there for some time."

"Where might I find this alley?"

"That's easy, sir. Go past Northumberland Inn and cross almost straight over Fanchurchestrete and you will find it. Not as nice as here, but there is a pleasant square halfway along, which is where she has her house."

Thomas thanked her again and handed across a small coin for her time, which she slipped into a pocket of her dress.

"The men over there know her," said Jorge, as he joined Thomas and Will. "I described her and the conversation became rather bawdy, which I did nothing to discourage."

"They haven't seen her in almost a year?" Thomas said.

"How did you know?"

"The woman I spoke to said Gala Uziel hasn't been seen in that long. I believe it is to her they pay rent, and Gala Uziel is Philippa Gale."

"It is the former name those men used as well. Where are we going now?"

"To the house she used to live in."

"The other address Amal gave you?"

"No. That house is in Mynchen Lane, which is west of where we are. This house we have no record of, which makes me wonder how many others she owns in the city. She could fashion a good living from the rents paid on them."

"More than she could as leader of the bonemen?" said Will.

"No, I suppose not, but it would be a safer income."

"Would you expect her to choose the safer option, Pa?"

"Of course not." They came to the wider thoroughfare of Fanchurchestrete and saw the entrance to a narrow alley almost opposite.

The small square sat a hundred paces along the alley,

where taller houses rose on both sides and a stone cross sat at its centre. The square was all the woman had said, so Thomas knocked on the first door to his left. When there was no response he moved to the next, then the next. It was early evening and either the people who lived here had not returned home or were still working. Only when he reached the second door on the other side of the square did he get a response.

The door was opened by a girl of little more than twelve years. She wore a cook's apron and had flour on her face.

"I'm busy. Bring it through and leave it in the kitchen."

Thomas smiled, wishing he had asked Jorge to do the knocking, but it was too late now. Though he saw the girl's eyes move to look behind him.

"You have us confused. We are not delivery men. I am looking for a woman by the name of Gala Uziel, who is meant to live in this square. Or she may go by the name of Philippa Gale."

"The first name," said the girl. She spoke to Thomas, but her eyes had been captured by Jorge.

Thomas stepped aside to let him continue the questioning while he went back to Will and Usaden, who had remained beside the stone cross.

Usaden patted it with his hand. "These things are everywhere in this city. Are the English truly so religious?"

"You are asking the wrong man, but I believe they are. Their lives are not always easy and it offers comfort to believe it is someone's fault other than their own. They believe some magical influence might improve their lot."

"Then they are fools."

"Not for seeking comfort," Thomas said, and Usaden shrugged.

"She doesn't live here anymore," said Jorge as he returned, "but I learned something that will surprise you."

Thomas waited, then said, "Which is?"

Jorge smiled. "She used to live here, it is true, but she also owns every single house in the square. According to the girl, who is rather pretty beneath the flour, she owns houses all over London but lives in none of them."

"Did she say where she does live?"

"She did not."

"So we are no further forward." Thomas kicked the stone cross with his boot. When no bolt of lightning came from the heavens he kicked it again and cursed.

"We start again in the morning," said Will. "If we come early there will be more people about, and one of them may know more than the girl. There is little else we can do tonight."

Thomas wanted to object, but knew Will was right. He would have to find some residue of patience, but found it hard.

As they walked north along the alley, on the assumption it might provide an easier return to the Bel Savage, six men appeared at the head of it, blocking their way.

Thomas slowed, judging them. None spoke. None asked his name. Most likely because they already knew it.

"Jorge, when you spoke to the men at the inn did any of them slip away?"

"Two. They said they had to leave for work."

"Kin, to me," Thomas whispered. The dog padded to his side and waited for more instruction.

"You are Gala's men, I take it?" he asked the men. He used her born name because so had those he had spoken to. Philippa Gale was a construct, but a long-lived one. He wondered how long before she went to work for the King and Queen she had created it.

"You should have taken more care with your questions here in London," one man said. "We know who you are and why you are here."

"What do you want?"

"We want you dead." The man looked the others over. "We have no instructions regarding your friends, but it will be safer to kill you all." He drew a sword. A moment later, his companions did the same.

"Six more behind us," said Will softly. "I'll take them, with Jorge. You, Usaden and Kin attack those in front."

"I will stand with Thomas," said Jorge.

"Yes, do that," said Usaden. He turned away and ran at the men behind them, which Thomas did not even look at.

Instead, he drew his own sword and advanced on the attackers. The leading man grinned and came at him fast.

"Kin, attack." There was no need for him to raise his voice. The dog was a dark blur in the evening shadows. He leapt and tore the throat from one man before dropping behind him. Which caused three of the others to turn as Kin came back at them.

Thomas killed the man to the leader's left, then disarmed the man himself.

"Kin, enough."

The remaining men ran along the alley, all courage lost. Thomas had seen it before. Kin was not a creature anyone wanted to face. He padded back to Thomas's side and lay down, panting, his head on his foot.

Thomas risked a glance behind. Two men lay on the ground. The others had also fled. Usaden and Will also did that to their men, unmanning them with their skill. Nobody who witnessed it wanted to face them.

"Run me through, then," the man said, when Thomas turned back to him.

"You will live to see the dawn. Return to your mistress and tell her you failed. Tell her I am coming for her tomorrow, and this time I offer no mercy."

"Who do I say you are?"

Thomas smiled. "You told me you know who I am."

He waited.

The man glanced behind him, but his companions had gone.

"No doubt they will wait for you," Thomas said. "We will go now. Bring your companions back and take your dead with you."

"And if I raise the hue and cry and say you fell on us without warning?"

"I came only today from conversing with King Henry. Raise it if you wish, but know whose word carries most weight if you do."

When the man had gone, Thomas turned in the other direction and started walking. "Usaden, wait out of sight and follow them when they go." He did not need to tell him not to be seen.

Usaden slipped away, Kin at his side, and took the first

alley he came to. He would wait until the men came to carry their dead away, then follow. Their leader might go to report to Philippa or not, but if not, even that information would be useful.

"Do you feel even a moment of guilt at taking their lives?" asked Jorge, but there was no judgement in his voice.

"It was they who attacked us. I feel less guilt than I would regret at losing my own life." He put an arm around Jorge's shoulder. "Even more at losing a friend."

Jorge made a show of looking around. "Who would that be?"

Thomas patted his cheek.

"We are getting closer to her," said Will.

"Yes, I think we are. Tonight we eat well and get drunk, but only a little. Tomorrow we end this thing so we can sleep easy in our beds in Burway."

Except, when they reached the Bel Savage, someone was waiting for them.

"Two women," said Peggy Spicer. "I showed them to your room. I take it that was all right?"

Thomas wondered who the women were and why Peggy was unconcerned. Perhaps she thought them bawds. He ran up the stairs intending to throw them out, but when he opened the door, he found Amal lying on one cot and Silva on another. Both appeared to have only woken from sleep at the sound of his approach.

"What are you doing here?"

"I found something, Pa." Amal sat up, brushing her hair back through her fingers. "Belia told me I couldn't make the journey alone so Silva offered to accompany me. But I could have done it."

"What have you found?" Thomas held a hand up. "Wait, you can't stay in this room. There are already four of us. Come down and I will get you another."

"Two more rooms," said Silva. "So I may sleep next to Will. I will pay."

Thomas shook his head in frustration. "I can afford two more rooms. I can afford the entire inn. Now tell me what you have found."

"The place where Philippa Gale lives. Where she has always lived." Amal reached into her shirt and drew out a small sheet of paper. She held it out to her father. "I finally deciphered her journal. It was in code, of course, but also in Spanish, which is why it took me so long. It contains everything, Pa. A record of all she has done. You are not the first man she has taken against, but the only one who has fought back. She killed the others. All of them. She is evil. Pure evil."

CHAPTER THIRTY-NINE

Usaden returned while three of them remained in the main room of the Bel Savage. It was warm from burning fires and the bodies of patrons. Peggy Spicer had found two more rooms. One was small, with a single cot for Amal, the other a little larger for Will and Silva, who had gone upstairs early.

Thomas wore a stern expression to discourage the gazes of men who appeared fascinated by Amal, but Jorge told him he should stop. She needed to get used to men staring at her. It was only natural because she was a beautiful young woman. And besides, she had already proven she could take care of herself if need be.

Amal rose and embraced Usaden, kissing both cheeks. Thomas suspected, other than Emma, she was the only one who would be allowed to do so. Thomas called the puller over for more ale and asked him to send food for one. As Usaden sat, Kin wriggled under the table and lay down, knowing he would be passed titbits. Thomas drew out the note Amal had brought him but turned it face down for the moment.

"What did you find out?"

"You were right. Once they disposed of the bodies — thrown into the river without hesitation — their leader took two men with him. I almost followed the others to see where they would lead, but I knew you wanted Philippa, and it was more likely he would report to her. We passed out through a Bishop's Gate, then travelled north. They were on foot, so it was simple enough to follow at first, but beyond an extensive Friary they mounted horses from a stable. Fortunately, they did not ride hard and Kin and me were more than fast enough to keep up."

"I take it they went to Philippa?"

"They did. It took near an hour and was almost full dark by the time they got there, but she came out with a lamp, and I saw her face and lack of an arm. It was her, Thomas."

"Tell me where." Thomas laid his finger on the note.

"Two leagues northeast of the city wall, close to a place I was told was a royal hunting ground by the name of Epping Forest. She lives in a mill house set on a river called the Lea. Whether it grinds flour I do not know, but the wheel still turns."

"Did you see anyone else?"

"Only the three men who came to her, but I did not enter. I knew you would want to do that tomorrow."

"You did well." Thomas turned the note over as a trencher was placed in front of Usaden, then fresh flagons of ale for them all. "Amal brought me this today. And that should be your last flagon of ale, my sweet."

She made a face, but only sipped at the ale.

"The description matches exactly what you have told me. Ami found it in the coded journal I took from Cornwell's cottage where Philippa stayed."

"I took me weeks to decipher it, but once I found the key everything fell into place," said Amal. "And then we had to ride hard to reach you."

Thomas reached out and touched her hand. "You did well."

"When do we attack her?" asked Usaden.

"How long to get there if we take horses?"

"Two hours, I would say. We can leave through the gate beside this inn and follow the wall around, then go across country. I can lead you directly there."

Thomas did not doubt it. Usaden always knew exactly where he was.

"I won't disturb Will and Silva yet, but I need to tell him we have to rise early. Before dawn. Which is very early at this time of year."

"Then you should go to your beds now," said Amal. "I will stay here and tell them when I go up. They should be finished by then. Besides, I can hear them at home, so it's no secret what they are up to." She offered a smile that almost broke Thomas's heart, because it told him she was growing up fast. She would be the next to find someone. So be it. He was younger when he and Bel had first shared the pleasures of each other.

"I won't let you stay down here without a chaperone," Thomas said.

"I need to finish my food," said Usaden. "And I can enter our room without waking either of you, so I will stay with Amal. If you think she is safe with me."

"Safer with you than any man I know." Thomas rose and stretched, then waved Jorge to follow him. The night was almost half gone, and dawn came early at this time of year so they would not get much sleep. But enough, he was sure.

They rode out through Ludgate and turned north along Old Bailey. After passing Newgate, the small group bore east across Finsbury Field. The sun was rising to promise a fine day. As they moved away from London's walls the air grew sweeter. Ferrant's limp appeared to be healed by new shoes and all the horses were frisky for being out after two days in stables. Amal had wanted to come but Thomas refused. There would be fighting, he was sure, and as well as she had acquitted herself during the attack on Burway, he would not have her face those he expected to meet.

As they crested a low rise, they saw the first of Philippa's men gathered on the edge of a vast swathe of forest which ran away into the distance. The silver glitter of a river wound across the flat land. Other streams joined it in succession, each making it a little wider. There were several mills along its length, as well as houses scattered across the low land, but Usaden pointed to one mill set apart from the others.

It confirmed what Thomas suspected. Philippa did not

want anyone close enough to see the comings and goings of her men. Did they still call themselves bonemen, he wondered? If so, they no longer troubled the west of London. Perhaps they had chosen new territories, or were infiltrating the smaller towns that lay around London. They would make easier pickings for men such as themselves, as they had believed Ludlow and Lemster would.

They had crossed half the flat land when a group of riders detached themselves from those flanking the forest of Epping and forged the river to approach them.

"How many?" Thomas leaned across to Usaden, who had the better eyes.

"Forty. Too many for us."

"I will not turn and run."

"I tell you, Thomas, they are too many. We retreat and try again. Tomorrow or the day after."

"These men will still be here a week from now. A month from now. Philippa won't rest until I am dead."

"Turn away and I will come back tonight and seek them out. I will kill those I can, then do the same the night after until their numbers are enough for us to fight."

"And if they catch you?"

Usaden considered no comment necessary.

Thomas drew Ferrant to a halt and stared forward as the men approached. They were in no hurry, and for a moment he considered they might not be coming for them. Best not to assume that, he thought.

Four hundred paces away most of them halted. Six men rode forward until they were yards from Thomas's group. Jorge was tense. Will and Usaden were relaxed. Thomas somewhere in between.

"Which of you pale-skinned men is Thomas Berrington?"

"That would be me." Thomas urged Ferrant forward, closing the distance by half.

"I have a message for you. Come with me, discuss the grievance between you and my mistress face to face, and the rest of your family will be spared. Refuse and everyone dies." The man's eyes flickered to one side for a moment. "And tell your man to stay where he is."

"Usaden," Thomas said, knowing he would be obeyed. Then to the man, "Her men failed last time they invaded my home. They will fail again the next time, and the time after that. I will meet Gala Uziel, but on my terms. The two of us, face to face yes, but everyone else at least a quarter mile away. We talk. I find out what hatred she still bears me."

"You will kill her."

"I give her my word I will not do that, nor arrest her. She might well hate me, but she knows my word is good. I want this ended as much as she does."

The man shook his head. "She will not agree."

"It is not your decision. It is hers. Give her my terms and see what she says. We are not going anywhere. Unless you wish to attack us now? I am sure she has told you that is an option as well. So be it, as long as you know at least half of you will die."

"But all of you."

Thomas shrugged.

He waited.

A hawk hovering on a rising wind hung motionless in

the air until, in the interval between two blinks, it plummeted into the long grass.

"Stay here." The man turned his horse and rode away without looking back. The bulk of his men made space for him to pass through and he continued on to the watermill.

Thomas narrowed his eyes to stare at the mill house, but nobody came out to meet him. Instead, the man dismounted and went inside. He was not there long before emerging and remounting his horse.

"So?" Thomas asked when he reached him.

"She says she will meet with you, but your men must stay here. Or they may return to London if they wish. We will not stop them."

"Where is the meeting?"

"There is a cottage in the forest. She is already on her way there."

"I saw nobody leave the mill."

"There is an entrance directly to the river. She has a small boat and took that."

"How do I know I can trust you?"

The man raised a shoulder. "You cannot, but it was you who agreed to the meeting. She told me it is past time things were settled between the two of you."

Thomas knew it was no genuine answer. He suspected he already knew there was only one manner of settling things between them which would satisfy Philippa. But it was true he had agreed to meet with her. Was it one more risk he was willing to take?

"Let me talk to my companions. Return to your men.

If I approach, then I agree. If we ride away together, I do not."

"I have been told if you refuse now, after asking, I am free to attack you."

Thomas turned away and rode back to the others.

"Well?" asked Will.

When Thomas explained Will shook his head.

"It's a trap. She will capture you, or kill you there and then."

"I agree, it may well be, but I have to stop this thing. Philippa will not let go of it."

"And if she kills you? Will that be enough for her?"

"I don't know."

"I suspect not," said Will. "She will send men like the last time, and if we kill them all she will send more, until a time comes when we are defeated."

"Which is why I am going to talk to her." Thomas's voice was sharper than he intended, but it was too late to apologise. "You are all to ride back to London."

Will shook his head. "Do you really expect us to do that?"

"Of course not, but make sure you are not seen. Usaden, you can sneak through any men they set. Will and Jorge, stay back until Usaden returns to tell you I am safe."

"And then?"

"If she plays fair, we capture her and take her out before her men can catch us."

Will laughed and shook his head. "God's teeth, Pa, Jorge could come up with a better plan than that."

"Then tell it to me. Any of you."

"I like it," said Usaden. "It carries risk, which I also like, but has a great return if it works."

"Don't look at me," said Jorge. "My plans carry no weight here. Tell him what to do, Will."

"We all of us ride hard. They will not catch us before we reach the city if we go directly south. Then you go to the King and ask him for men."

"He won't send any," said Thomas. "Philippa lived among them for sixteen years. Henry still wants to believe what she has done is out of character."

"Then we recruit an army," said Will. "You can afford a hundred men, two hundred. We return with us at their head and take her men, then you can have your face-to-face talk with her. Once you are safe."

"It will take too long, and we would have to train any men we recruit." Thomas let his breath go. "If I die then I die. I have lived longer than most."

Before Will could object again, he turned Ferrant and rode away. He knew he was being stubborn, but was tired of always looking over his shoulder. His life had changed, and he had gained much. He had found Bel again, built a fine house, set himself as a man of stature in Ludlow. Was he willing to give it all up? His new life was built on sand if Philippa did not stop her feud.

He reached the men. "Tell me how to find this cottage."

The man smiled and told him how to reach it.

As he rode on Thomas grew convinced it had to be a trap, but still he continued. Why had the forty men not attacked him when he was alone with them? Did that offer the promise of Philippa wanting to talk as much as he did? Perhaps saving her life, even at the expense of an arm, had changed her opinion of him. Or perhaps not.

It was not too late to turn south and ride hard, but he did not. Instead, he forded the river Lea and rode into the scattered forest, in search of an abandoned cottage in a clearing.

CHAPTER FORTY

Had Thomas not been riding to almost certain death the journey would have proven pleasant. The trees were set apart, their branches in full leaf to cast dappled shade over the thick loam. Rabbits ran through the undergrowth. Squirrels leapt from branch to branch, small and lithe, their tawny coats catching the rays of sunlight. The chatter of birds filled the air with sweet music, and darting swallows and swifts reminded him of Spain.

A hint of a path allowed Thomas to ride with little thought, and his mind grew still because he knew there was nothing more he could do. The coming meeting would decide everything. When he looked around he saw no men or horses, only Ferrant's slow plod, and that was almost silent. A tributary of the Lea appeared, narrow and shallow, and they splashed through it. On the far side the ground rose a little, and before long, Thomas saw a building appear.

The man who had told him how to find it had said it was almost derelict, but that was not the case. Someone had been making repairs. New areas of thatch showed among the old. Windows had been glazed, and the lime plaster on the walls renewed so it showed as a patchwork of bright against faded. Twine hung from around the roofline and small objects twisted and turned in the light breeze. Feathers, the bodies of mice, the tails of squirrels and rabbits. Thomas knew their purpose. They were protective charms, which made him wonder if they were Philippa's doing, and if so how she had managed to hide such a talent from him.

Two horses were tied to the branch of a tree that had come down in a storm but was still connected to the trunk with stretched tendons which kept it alive. Thomas dismounted and tied Ferrant beside the other horses, wondering who the second person was. As he walked to the open door, he saw tracks through the grass, as if something had been dragged to leave two lines a few feet apart. They reminded him of the tracks he had seen in Lemster after Arthur Wodall had been murdered, and he wondered if someone had been dragged along here.

"Is that you at last, Tom? Come inside." Philippa's voice was unmistakable.

"I would rather we speak out here in the fresh air."

He expected her to refuse, so was surprised when she appeared in the doorway. As she came into the sunshine he finally discovered what had happened to the tagelmust taken from his room all those months before. Philippa had wrapped it around her hair, but lacked the skill to wear it properly so the ends hung long at her sides. She saw him recognise it and smiled. It was his, it defined him, and she had wanted it. Why, Thomas did not know.

Her face was as beautiful as ever, even after knowing everything she had done. She wore a long robe that both clung to her curves and hid the lack of a right arm.

"Are you thirsty after your ride? I have ale but no wine."

"Nothing for me."

"Very well. Wait there. I will only be a moment."

Philippa turned back into the house, disappearing almost at once into its gloom. Thomas watched the door, wondering if she was about to bring one of her men back. There had to be another person, unless she had brought a riderless horse as some kind of ruse. Thomas had long ago stopped trying to work out what strange thoughts passed through her mind. When she appeared again, her back was to him and she was straining to drag something, a heavy rope wrapped across her shoulder, the effort made harder by the lack of a second arm.

As Philippa came fully through the door Thomas caught sight of what she was dragging, and his heart stuttered a beat in shock. Now he saw what had made the two lines across the ground. Philippa dragged a platform on which a chair was strapped. Two runners allowed the entire device to be dragged, but it was hard work for one woman on her own.

Philippa stopped and turned to face Thomas, her breath coming hard.

"You can come and help if you like, Tom. He won't bite. Not unless you get too close, then I make no promises. He hates you even more than I do, and I didn't believe that was possible until he found me again."

Thomas stared at Galib Uziel, who stared back, his

dark eyes aflame with hatred. Thomas unwound the rope from Philippa and wrapped it across his own shoulders, then dragged the carriage into the sunlight before freeing himself. He stretched, turning all the way around to look into the shade between the trees. He saw nothing, but that did not mean they were not being watched.

"I thought you dead," Thomas said, crouching in front of Galib Uziel.

"And I you, until my daughter told me different." The man's voice was coarser than the last time they had spoken, no doubt a result of his injuries. "We should both have died. That would have been for the best."

"Except you can't walk and I was barely harmed, other than almost drowning. How did you survive?"

"I clung to the cage, but my body was broken. Had a wherryman not dragged me out I would have died."

"You searched for your daughter?"

Galib Uziel shook his head. The movement was hard, sharp, and Thomas imagined broken bones and damaged tendons. The man slumped to one side in the chair. It was clear he was incapable of supporting himself.

"Gala had already gone north to plot your destruction. I did not see her for near a month before she returned to the city. I had a few men with me and they told me she was back, so I sent them to her, unsure how she would react to me being alive. But she is a loving daughter and took me in. All the records relating to me show me as being dead. I am a wraith — all the better to destroy you."

"It was you who tried to destroy me. You have only yourself to blame for your fate."

"No. You came after me. After my men. You destroyed

Gala's hand, took her arm, and ruined our plans for expansion. This is all your doing, Thomas Berrington."

Thomas stood and looked at Philippa, for he could not think of her as Gala.

"So what now? Do we discuss matters like civilised people, or do we fight to the death?"

"You would like that, wouldn't you? Though I admit I never thought of you as a bully, and only a bully would fight a woman with only one arm."

"Why not stop this now?" Thomas said. "I saved you once, then again when you came to me a second time. Is that not enough? Let us put the past aside and get on with our lives." He glanced at Galib Uziel. "Though I suspect your father has little of mercy left in him. I also suspect he has little life left to him."

He watched Philippa attempt to suppress her emotions.

"I have a deal to propose," she said.

Thomas waited. A movement behind the cottage drew his attention and he said, in order to cover it, "This is an idyllic spot. You should live here rather than that old mill."

"It is more convenient to reach London from. This is royal land. The cottage belongs to the King and was a hunting lodge at one time. I once pleasured a knight of the realm within its walls." Philippa smiled. "In fact, a second time out here on the grass as well."

"What do you want from me?"

"Examine my father. I want to know if there is anything you can do for him. Despite my hatred, I admit only you could have saved my life when you took my arm. I want you to do the same for him."

"Here?"

"No, at the mill. There is more space, and clearly a plentiful supply of clean water. I recall you have an excessive fondness for clean water. I am surprised all that bathing has not unmanned you."

"You will never find out. And if I agree to your request?"

"It is over between us. I will stop pursuing you."

"And if I can do nothing for your father?"

"It will still be over. You are right, he has little time left, and I would spend it making his last days easier. I will take him south, perhaps back to Spain where he was born. The warmth might help."

"It might." Thomas turned to Galib Uziel and knelt in front of him. "And what do you say to these terms your daughter has set before me?"

"I also agree to them. Even if you can do nothing for me, it is over."

Thomas stood and looked around. He glimpsed Usaden again, but unless someone knew he was there they would never see him.

"In that case I also agree. I will examine you. There may be some pain, but I will try to inflict no more than necessary. I can promise nothing, but I will do whatever I can. If you return to Spain, take a carrack to the south. It will be kinder on you."

Thomas did not know why, but he held out his hand to Philippa, a sealing of the deal. Instead of taking it, she came close and kissed his mouth. Thomas expected the sting of a blade in his back, but none came. The kiss reminded him of what they had once shared. It also

435

brought a sense of disgust, both at himself and against her.

Thomas dragged Galib Uziel's contrivance to the horses, then lifted the man onto the saddle where straps hung ready to hold him in place. The man weighed hardly anything. They left the sledge on the edge of the clearing and rode back through the forest.

At the mill, Thomas lifted Galib Uziel down from his horse and carried him inside like a child in his arms. All the way the man's eyes continued to burn. The degradation of being carried like a babe made matters worse. The knowledge he had no alternative only added to his humiliation.

"Upstairs," said Philippa. "There is a bed for him there, or a bench if you need a firm surface."

"I will have to strip him."

"As I have done many times to wash him. He can do nothing for himself, and it is my duty as a loving daughter. I will help you."

The room filled the entire space at the top of the mill, a hatch in the floor which opened to a ladder. Despite being completely unlike the house of the bonemen on London Bridge, it reminded Thomas of it in some ways. Not its size, for it was only a tenth as large. Perhaps it was the opening to one side where the moving waterwheel could be seen. Its creaking filled the air so they had to speak louder to be heard.

Between them they stripped Galib Uziel, and Thomas laid him on his front on the bench. The flesh along his back was wasted, and every bone showed. At least it made seeing the damage done to him easier. A quick check on his legs told Thomas there was no hope of restoring their use. Too many bones had been broken and badly healed.

"Who did you go to after your fall?" Thomas asked.

"A physician I have used before. A Moor. Do they not make the best physicians?"

"Not the one you visited. I might have been able to save your legs, but it is too late now even if I re-broke them. You will never walk again."

Galib Uziel said nothing.

Thomas raised the man's arms, one after the other.

"Try to press back down when I draw them up." It felt strange to work on a man who wanted him dead, but it would not be the first time he had done so. "Good. Now the other way," he said, as Galib Uziel resisted. "You still have some strength in them. I am going to examine your spine. It will hurt."

"Do your worst. My life is constant pain." Galib Uziel cackled a humourless laugh. "Of course, you have already done your worst to me."

Thomas knew there was no point objecting. The man believed what he would.

He found nodes in the spine which he manipulated, easing their tension a little. When he was done, he turned the man over. All of his ribs had been broken but were now fully healed, though misshapen. Thomas gripped his chin and moved his head one way then the other. Galib Uziel grimaced.

"That hurts?"

"A great deal."

"It's probably one reason your legs don't work, apart from the damage done to them. There is trauma in your neck that is pinching the long nerves that run within the spine. A good doctor could help by manipulating your arms, but that is all I can offer. If you return to Spain, there are still many excellent physicians in Malaga. I will provide you with some names if you ask."

"No need. You will never leave this place alive. Dress me, daughter, for I do not want to be naked when your men kill him."

Thomas looked around. "What men?"

Philippa walked to a small window. "The men out here."

Thomas pushed her aside. Forty men stood at a small distance from the mill, all of them heavily armed. In the distance, on a low rise, two men sat on horseback. Jorge and Will. There was no sign of Usaden, and Thomas wondered if he had gone to London in search of help.

"I have treated your father to the best of my ability. No one could have done more. I thought we had struck a deal."

Philippa raised a shoulder, the one lacking an arm. It made the gesture strange.

"You were always too gullible. Did you really think after all you have done to me, to my father, we can allow you to walk away?"

Thomas's mind searched for a solution but failed to find one. Not one that would allow him to escape. He scanned the room in search of a weapon but there was nothing. The heavy, creaking waterwheel continued to turn, its noise almost driving the wits from his head. From below, the sound of voices rose as Philippa's men entered the mill, coming for him.

Thomas's gaze fell on the only possibility.

Three lamps burned in the upper room, each set on shelves in two of the walls. Their wicks burned yellow, a curl of smoke rising from each. Thomas moved fast. He grabbed one and ran to the stairwell, where he dropped the lamp, relieved his aim was true. It fell between the crossing spars of the staircase and burst against the ground floor, spraying burning oil everywhere. Two men screamed in agony as the fire caught them. Within moments the stairs began to burn, as well as the floorboards.

"If I die," Thomas said, "we all die."

CHAPTER FORTY-ONE

From below, Thomas heard shouts as the men outside tried to reach the stairs, but they were well alight now and the ground floor room burned hard, beating them back. He looked through the window and saw them milling about with no purpose. Their plan had been to storm the building and come for him. No doubt he would be held down and his throat cut so Philippa and her father could watch him die. Now they still might, but their own bodies would burn as well. He wondered what had made him toss the burning lamp down the stairs. He did not know what he would do after, and still did not. Looking through the window again, he saw Philippa's men still confused.

Then, beyond them, two riders and a dog came hard. Will took the lead, his axe swinging loose from his wrist on a leather thong. His horse came with head down, hooves a blur. Jorge followed, a sword in his hand. He would be afraid, but would do whatever he could, even if only to act as a distraction for Will's work. Kin came in the lead, a black streak, with lips curled back to show long teeth. He darted in, snapping, biting, too fast to be countered before he moved on. Will reached the edge of the men, who had only just seen the attack, and brought down three before any could respond. Then he too was gone, to draw back and sit a hundred paces from them. Of Usaden, there was still no sign.

"You fool. You have killed us all." Philippa slapped Thomas's face, but he barely felt the sting of it.

She went to the hatch and looked through, then lifted her skirts and started down. Smoke billowed up past her. Already it writhed like a tide against the ceiling to spill out through the opening onto the river. More tendrils rose through gaps in the floorboards.

Galib Uziel was on his front, using his arms to drag himself towards the opening, beyond which lay the turning waterwheel. Thomas ignored him while he tried to think of what he could do. The smoke befuddled him, and already his head spun. Too little clean air. Too much heat. It rose from the floor, which he imagined was glowing. Philippa had to be dead. No one could live through the heat rising from below.

Except, as he turned and passed Galib Uziel she reappeared through the hatch, her hair smoking. It was not aflame, but her entire body was wreathed in grey smoke. The hem of her skirts had burned and her legs were bare to the thigh, mottled with angry red welts and blisters. The charred ends of the stolen tagelmust she still wore also smoked.

She turned and slammed the hatch shut, then dragged

the table across and set it on it. A pointless gesture, but what else could she do? Only then did she turn to find Thomas standing next to the turning wheel. She screamed and came at him with her fingers curled, nails like talons. Thomas easily stepped aside, and she almost fell out into the relentlessly turning padels. She recovered, but it gave Thomas an idea.

There was a risk, of course, but not to take it meant they would all die an agonising death within minutes. The only thing stopping him was whether to take the risk alone or help the others to escape the flames that now licked through gaps in the floorboards. And then, because he was Thomas Berrington, and despite all these two had done to him, he knew he had only one choice.

He turned and lifted Galib Uziel, who was still a yard from the opening. He carried him and when the wheel offered a chance, set him between two of the padels and let him go. The man stared back at him with hate in his eyes, then he was gone.

Thomas turned and grabbed Philippa's remaining arm and dragged her to the opening. She resisted, and he almost left her to the fire. The heat was growing unbearable, and he knew if he hesitated the floor would soon give way and they would both plunge to their deaths in the flames.

Leave her, he thought, *go alone*. As he turned to step out a slim figure appeared. Usaden stood with a foot either side of a padel and as he rose, he stepped from the wheel into the smoke-filled room, as if stepping across a firm, stone floor. He had a knife in each hand and passed one to

Thomas. As he did so, a wild scream came from behind and Usaden moved fast.

Thomas turned to see Philippa, the tagelmust now alight, her hair and dress as well. She came like a wraith from hell, her one hand held high to grasp a dagger of her own. Her eyes were only on Thomas, her intention clear.

Thomas raised his own blade, but it was not needed. Usaden darted in and slammed his knife into Philippa. Once. Twice. Three times. The blows as fast as the strike of a snake.

Philippa staggered back, blood pouring down her chest. The remains of the burning tagelmust hung down to the floor and her heel caught in it, tumbling her over. When she hit the floor, it collapsed beneath her and she fell through, greedy flames rising to accept her body.

"It might be an idea to follow me down, Thomas," said Usaden, as if this was only a walk through the woods.

Thomas nodded. He watched how Usaden waited, then stepped out onto the wheel. As he descended Thomas followed, but as he was about to take the step, he saw Galib Uziel rise from his left. He was lodged between two of the padels, his useless legs tangled. His body was soaked, steaming as it rose alongside the burning mill. His eyes were open but sightless. He rose then moved on, and as he did so Thomas stepped out. He almost lost his footing, one leg sliding beneath a padel, and he dragged it out, fearful of ending up like Galib Uziel. Then the wheel took him down. He judged the distance, the danger of the flames now spearing through the side of the mill, then leapt. The water accepted him, a blessed coolness covering him as a reminder of how close he had come to being burned alive. He stayed below the surface, letting the water carry him. When his lungs ached he surfaced. Usaden was there and offered a hand, which Thomas took.

He lay on the grass bank and watched as the mill disappeared in a column of flames. From somewhere within came a great groan and the waterwheel tilted away, tilted back, then fell to break into pieces. The fire consumed it, together with the body of Galib Uziel and his daughter. It was done. Over at last, and Thomas could barely believe it.

"Well, Thomas, what do we do now?" said Usaden. "I have weapons. We can help Will and Jorge, or lie here until you are ready to make a decision."

Thomas stared up into the dark eyes of the man he called a good friend. He reached up and slapped him on the shoulder.

"Best help, I suppose."

"If they need any."

"There were over forty men the last time I looked."

"When was that?"

"A while ago, I admit."

"There were only thirty when I came to get you. I thought you might need my help more than Will and Jorge."

"I had a plan."

"I saw it." Usaden gave no sign whether he approved, but hardly needed to.

Thomas knew he had been a fool.

By the time they waded the Lea and emerged around the blazing ruins of the mill, it was all over.

Thirty men stood with their weapons on the ground and arms above their heads.

Will dismounted and stood with his axe in his hand, but had no need of it. He was blood-spattered and grinning. Jorge remained on horseback, his expression set, as if to do so might make him look dangerous. It almost worked.

"What do we do with them, Pa?" asked Will, when Thomas reached him. His eyes scanned his father, taking in the damage, the patches of hair burned away, his eyebrows gone, as well as the beard on one side of his face.

"Go talk to them. I'm in no state to do so. Tell them they can go. Leave their weapons. Toss the bodies of their dead into the flames. Tell them never to come after us again. I doubt it needs saying because we have defeated them once more, but there is no harm in reminding them."

Will nodded, and as Thomas walked away, swaying a little, he went to the man he considered the last remaining leader and gave their terms. By the time Thomas pulled himself into the saddle atop Ferrant the men had turned away and were leaving, going south towards London.

Kin came to Ferrant and lifted his front legs up. Upright, he was almost as tall as the horse. Thomas reached down and stroked his head. Kin opened his mouth in what looked like a grin but was probably not. He was a dog, and Thomas laughed as he remembered Kin was due a treat on their return to Ludlow. Richard Croft had a bitch about to go into heat and he wanted Kin to mount her.

"Go for it, lad," Thomas said, his voice low, and Kin wagged his long, curved tail in delight, not because he had any idea what Thomas was talking about but because he liked the way he said it. Then Kin dropped to the ground and ran at full tilt in a wide circle around the horses as they turned and started back for the Bel Savage.

CHAPTER FORTY-TWO

A messenger came. When Amal brought the note to his room Thomas was asleep, alone in bed. She shook her father, and laughed when he grumbled as he came awake.

"They want you at the castle, Pa." She held out the note.

Thomas washed his hands across his face. "Do I even need to read it?"

"Sir Richard and Gruffydd are waiting for you, so no, I expect you don't. I will leave you to get dressed. Bel says she will come into town with you, and I think I might too. It is weeks since I saw Aunt Agnes and her girls. Apart from which we need bread."

"I thought you baked your own now." Thomas swung his legs out.

"I do, but Aunt Agnes's is so much better even though I use the mix she gave me. She has tried to show me how but I can never make it like her. Besides, we can afford to buy our bread from her, can't we?"

"Yes, I suppose we can. Tell the messenger I will be down as soon as I have washed."

Amal looked at him, her head cocked to the side, as he pulled on trousers and a linen shirt. "You should wear a hat, Pa. There is still a bald patch here." She touched her head.

"It will grow out. Bel cut it short so it looks less odd, but you may be right. Now go, so I can wash myself."

Amal ran to the door but left it open when she exited. Thomas poured water and studied his face in the glazed mirror, then soaped his face and ran a sharp blade across it. He had vowed he would never shave again, but today he would make an exception. Already he suspected he knew what the two men he had grown to call friends wanted. Change was coming, and often times change was bad. Particularly here in an out-of-the-way town in an out-of-the-way region of England, set hard against the border of Wales. Change came slowly to Ludlow unless it was forced on it, and the death of Prince Arthur had proven to be just such a force.

Amal, Bel and Will walked with him, ascending the steep slope to pass through Linney Gate into town. Thomas left them at Agnes's bakery and went on alone. There were no guards at the gatehouse and no sign of any in the wide outer bailey. He found Sir Richard Pole and Gruffydd ap Rhys in the Armoury.

"Tom, well met, my friend." Gruffydd embraced him before Sir Richard offered his hand.

"I hear the argument between you and that woman is finally resolved," said Sir Richard.

"She will trouble me no more, nor anyone else."

"Dead or banished?"

Thomas raised a shoulder, unwilling to offer anything more, and both men appeared satisfied with that. Sometimes it was better not to know some things, otherwise hard decisions might have to be made.

"Will anyone be left here after today?" Thomas asked. "I assume that is what you are here for, though there was no need to send for me as I already expected it."

"We will set a small guard to protect the buildings and contents, but most of the staff will be let go. You can make use of any rooms you see fit. I doubt another prince will ever come here." Sir Richard looked around at the finely appointed room. "You could even move your entire family in if you want."

"I have a fine house, built with my own hands." Thomas laughed. "Well, not my hands, but I did my bit."

Sir Richard smiled. "I have still not seen this wonder of yours. Perhaps we can find time to visit before we leave."

"Where do you go to?"

"I shall return to my estates in Bedfordshire once I have reported to the King."

"And you to Pembrokeshire?" Thomas asked Gruffydd.

He nodded. "Tenby, which has a fine harbour and an even finer castle. I am at home there. Come visit, Tom. The air is the cleanest in the whole land."

"Perhaps I will, but I am busy enough here."

"I hear Henry wants you to continue as Justice of the Peace," said Sir Richard. "Work this year out and then carry on for another. I know it is unusual, but so is an honest Justice. I also hear he may make you coroner. The current one grows old."

Thomas laughed. "So do I. What should I do about Sir Thomas Cornwell when he causes trouble again, as he no doubt will?"

"He has been warned off. You should have no major trouble with him. Besides, he spends most of his time in Derbyshire now. He has more land there, and the locals are more willing to obey him than they are here. Do you accept the post?"

Thomas nodded. "I do."

"And try not to get into any more trouble," said Sir Richard. "If you can manage it, which I doubt."

"Tom isn't a man to turn away from trouble," said Gruffydd. "He is the kind of man this bandit country needs."

"Can I appoint my own staff?" Thomas asked.

"As long as you pay for them you can appoint whoever you want. If you mean that big son of yours then I think it a capital idea. But do not start getting any clever ideas. You are still here at the will of King Henry, and he can soon have you dismissed. I believe he is not entirely sure what to do with you. But young Harry likes you well enough, so bide your time until he is King."

"How is Catherine settling in?"

"Her movements are restricted, but she has her Spanish ladies around her. Maria de Rojas shares her rooms with her. I hear that when she tries to speak their native tongue Catherine chastises her and the others. She says she is English now."

Thomas shook his head. "She will never return to Spain, will she?"

"No, she will not."

As Thomas crossed Market Square to visit with his sister, his mind was troubled. There was little to keep him in Ludlow, or England. He had always thought when the day came that he was no longer needed to protect Catherine he would return to Granada. Now, she was protected by her ladies in London and by the King of England. Except Thomas could not turn his back on her, even if he might never see her again. He had promised her mother he would protect her daughter. Whether Catherine was close or not, he would do what he could.

The smell of baking filled his senses as he entered Agnes's house. Jilly and Rose ran to embrace their Uncle Thomas, kissing him on both cheeks before running off again — no doubt to stare with unrequited longing at Will.

"So," said Amal, as she greeted him. "Are we staying or going?"

"Staying. They offered me the free run of the castle if I want it, which I don't. It will be closed up, a skeleton guard left."

"So we remain in Burway?"

"We do."

"Good. I like it there."

Thomas smiled. "So do I. When we return, I want to talk with everyone. We need to bring my ancestors to lie in ground I own. With summer upon us it is the right time. I will need you all to help, if you are willing. It means digging—" he smiled, "—and bones. But at least it will only be bones after all this time, and friendly ones."

"When have I ever been bothered by bones, Pa?" Amal embraced her father, hugging him tight, and Thomas kissed the top of her head, so she would not look up to see the tears in his eyes.

Everything changes, he thought, and nothing changes — not in the hearts of those who strive to do better.

HISTORICAL NOTE

For *A Death of Promise*, I carried out extensive research on Ludlow, Lemster, and the role of Justice of the Peace, as well as finding out even more about Prince Arthur and Catherine of Aragon's brief marriage and life in Ludlow. Sir Richard Croft and Sir Thomas Cornwell are based on real characters, but their actions are pure fiction. A little earlier than the time of this book, they went to war against each other, with over two hundred men attacking Lemster. I used this, with some changes, in the attack on Ludlow at the end of *Men of Bone*.

All dates use the Julian Calendar, which was still in use in 1501/2. It was not replaced by the Gregorian calendar until September 1752, when people complained vociferously that the government had stolen twelve days from them. Because of this, the date of Arthur's death I use is April 2nd, but some sources use a later day in April because of the discrepancy between calendars.

The role of the coroner was different in the 15th and 16th centuries than it is today. The role of coroner was created in 1149 for the collection of taxes under Norman rule. Over the centuries, it evolved to include the investigation of sudden, violent or unnatural death through the medium of an inquest. The coroner also had several other responsibilities, including wrecks of the sea, fires, both fatal and non-fatal, and any discovery of buried treasure in the community.

Following the death of Arthur, Catherine of Aragon either chose not to attend his funeral in Worcester, or more likely was prevented from doing so. However, sources show she attended a small ceremony in St Laurence's Church when Arthur's heart was buried there.

Over the years, the question of whether Catherine was still a virgin or not when Arthur died has been much debated, as has also the manner of his death. I chose not to inflict poison on the poor lad, though the sweating sickness — the most likely cause of his death — would have been bad enough. For the purpose of my book, I chose for them to behave as most young couples of fifteen and sixteen years of age would given free rein, and have normal marital relations. Records show that Arthur and Catherine spent the Christmas period following Lent, when such relations between them would have been forbidden, at Tickenhill House in Bewdley. Some indications say they spent the time in close familiarity, perhaps the last happy time Catherine was to experience for several years.

Following Arthur's death, Catherine was made a semi-prisoner in Durham House in London, where King Henry could keep a close eye on her. The King was concerned that, with the death of Arthur, Spain might ask for all or a portion of her dowry to be returned and refuse the second payment due. Because of this, he needed to find another suitable husband for her, and even considering marrying her himself after the death of his wife following childbirth in 1503. Fortunately or not, he chose not to, and we all know who Catherine's second husband was. But all of this is for future adventures with Thomas, Will, Amal and Jorge, together with their growing band of friends and family.

Finally, I need to end with an apology. In *A Death of Promise*, one of the early victims is a man called Arthur Wodall, who Thomas met in *Men of Bone* at his old house. In that earlier book, I confused the characters and called him Walter Gifforde, but that was my mistake. I have since updated *Men of Bone* with the correct characters, but if mention of Arthur Wodall gave you some pause, I apologise.

13th March 2022

ABOUT THE AUTHOR

David Penny published 4 novels in the 1970's before being seduced by a steady salary. He has now returned to his true love of writing with a series of historical mysteries set in Moorish Spain at the end of the 15th Century. He is currently working on the next book in the series.

Find out more about David Penny
www.davidpenny.com

Made in the USA
Las Vegas, NV
25 October 2022